To Sallye
You will enjoy your
sisters' editing

Dream great dreams
Do great deeds

Jim O'Bell
7-30-13

VAMPIRE DEFENSE

VAMPIRE DEFENSE

James D. Bell

SARTORIS
LITERARY
GROUP

"A traditional publisher with a non-traditional approach to publishing."

Sartoris Literary Group, Inc.
Jackson, Mississippi
www.sartorisliterary.com

THIS BOOK IS DEDICATED TO MY WIFE AND BEST

FRIEND, JOANNE,

A BEAUTIFUL IRISH REDHEAD. I COULD NEVER

HAVE COMPLETED THIS WORK WITHOUT HER

ENCOURAGEMENT AND INSPIRATION

1

The spring storm had been brewing all day.

The atmosphere was humid and warm as the wind shook the old oaks. Towering dark clouds rolled in from the southwest as the sun descended over the horizon. Light reflected from the clouds to give everything a peach-colored glow as day turned into dusk.

Two boys on bicycles raced through the old Belhaven neighborhood under a canopy of swaying limbs. Jack and Patrick imagined they were flying into the eye of a hurricane as leaves swirled about them and lightning burned yellow in the heart of the approaching thunderhead. They could not have realized that they were about to be part of a storm far more devastating than the one above. A storm of hate, love, fear and courage was only a few blocks away and racing toward them.

"You won't go near that house," sneered Patrick.

"You won't either."

"Oh yeah, I've been there."

"When?"

"My dad and I went over when the new owner moved in. The owner wasn't there, but the guy who lives with him was there telling the movers where to put the boxes."

"What was he like?"

"I liked him. He had a funny accent. His name was 'Got Fried' or something. Dad said he acted sort a funny and he wouldn't let us in the house—too big of a mess he said."

"The place still looks haunted," said Jack. "You hardly ever see any lights on, and my sister said she heard weird snarls and sounds coming from there one night."

The eleven year olds heard the first murmurings of distant thunder as they stopped their bikes across the street from the house. The ninety-year-old Victorian house was one of the biggest in the neighborhood, but after years of desertion it had fallen into disrepair. The neighbors had hoped that the new owner would fix up the once majestic home, but he had done little in the two months since he moved in. The house was dark and looked devoid of life, as usual. It was a two-story mansion with a gabled attic on the third level. A tower stretched three stories high on the northeast corner, and an elaborate porch wrapped around the house on two sides.

"Well, Patrick, are you ready to go knock on the door?"

"I will if you will."

They parked their bikes on the sidewalk and started to cross the street. Somehow it just didn't seem right to park their bikes on the same side of the street as the old house. The thunderhead loomed above the roof. The cloud was suddenly lit from within by lightning and glowed bright yellow, outlining the spire and gables. The boys were still in the middle of the street when Patrick stopped.

"Jack! I saw something in the window!"

Just then there was a rush of wind and a crackling sound above as a limb snapped and crashed into the yard ahead of them.

"No way, Jack," said Patrick as he began backtracking. "I'm not going up there, no, uh-uh."

Jack turned to look at Patrick, then at the house, then at Patrick again.

With their nerves already on edge, both boys jumped at the sound of screeching tires! They looked down the street in time to see first one car, and then another slide around the corner half a block away and race up the street towards them.

"Run!" yelled Jack as both boys dashed back onto the sidewalk and dove into a holly bush.

They started complaining about their choice of hiding places, but in an instant their eyes were riveted across the street, their mouths agape.

The first car slid to a stop in front of the house. The driver's door opened even before the car stopped. The second car swerved to the left, jumped the curb, scraped along the left side of the first car, smacked the open door and sent it bouncing down the sidewalk.

"Wow!" said both boys under their breaths simultaneously.

As the second car stopped, it blocked the now empty space where the driver's door of the first car had been. The first driver climbed out of the passenger door. The boys could see that he was an average sized man with blond hair wet with perspiration, but what they remembered most was the look of sheer terror on his face.

A short, dark-haired man jumped out of the second car.

"That's 'Got Fried'!" exclaimed Patrick, pointing at the second driver.

People ran into their front lawns to see what was going on in their usually quiet neighborhood. Mrs. Adams left her porch and ran to the street in time to see the first driver reach into his car, grab a duffle bag and run around the front of both cars. "Got Fried" growled like a wild animal, leaped with amazing agility over the hood of his car and tackled the first man. Jack left the bush to get a closer look. Patrick remained motionless, his eyes glued on the struggle. "Got Fried" had a gun in his hand, and the men were struggling over it.

"God help me!" screamed the blond man.

Just then, in a flash of lightning, Patrick saw the gun in the blond man's hand. Two shots rang out and thunder shook the neighborhood, drowning the sound of Mrs. Adams' screams. She ran back into her house to call the police while other neighbors stood and stared in disbelief.

The blond man paused over the motionless body of "Got Fried" for a brief moment before he scooped the duffle bag off the ground and ran to the door of the house. With a swift kick the door burst open, and he disappeared into the dark foyer.

Three neighbors, Mr. Richards and the Bakers, ran to the aid of the fallen man, but they found a lifeless body.

It was a matter of minutes before Patrolman Ayers arrived. Black smoke billowed from the eaves of the old house, so Ayers promptly called the fire department. An ambulance and a second patrol car reached the scene as Patrolman Ayers knelt beside the fallen man.

"Where is the perpetrator?" Ayers asked Mr. Richards.

"He went in the house."

"Who is he?"

"I don't know. He is medium height, kind of thin, blond hair. He's carrying a bag and a gun. He kicked the door open and rushed in."

"Is there anyone else in the house?"

"I think so. There have been some strange sounds coming from the house since he went in. We heard the sounds of a struggle and gunshots. There were flashing lights, and something else, something strange."

Then a sudden shriek occurred so loud and so shrill that everyone instinctively threw their hands over their ears. The sound subsided to a rumbling groan as flames broke through the roof and enveloped the tower.

Mr. Richards gasped at the sound and said, "What the..."

"It must be the house collapsing," said Ayers as he turned and began waving people away from the blazing building. "We'd better get these people back."

"That's him—That's the murderer!" shouted Becky Baker, pointing at the doorway.

Everyone saw the silhouette of a man against a background of flames, stumbling through the foyer. Ayers raced towards him and met him at the doorway. The exhausted man leaned on the patrolman as the two of them made their way off the porch and into the yard. The man was sooty and red from the heat. His shirt was torn, exposing deep scratch marks across his chest and blood dripped from his cheek. Blood was spattered on his clothes. He clutched a mallet in his right hand. His eyes were glazed with a distant look.

"Is anyone else in the house?" demanded Ayers.

The blond man turned slowly towards Ayers and said, "No, there's no one left alive."

"What do you mean?

"I killed him."

"Who did you kill?" asked Officer Ayers knowing that this was a critical moment that might reveal the truth. The suspect was still in the emotion of the moment and had not had time to consider his legal plight, invent excuses or talk to a lawyer.

"Who did you kill?"

"The vampire!"

Ayers stared at him in stunned silence.

"It's finally over."

"No, buddy, I think this is just the beginning."

That night, Ayers' superiors determined that it would be better not to publicly mention the "vampire" statement, at least not yet.

The fire department was unable to control the flames, and the old house was utterly razed. Three skeletal remains were found in the rubble the next day.

2

A heavy iron bar door slammed closed behind the young lawyer. He was 6'1", medium build and dressed in a conservative dark suit that chafed against the large strawberry on his left hip that he earned in a weekend rugby game. In his left hand he clutched a manila folder, a yellow legal pad and the morning newspaper. He made an effort to ignore the pain on his hip, strode confidently toward the uniformed officer standing behind a desk and said, "Can I see Travis Thomas please?"

The officer said, "Are you his lawyer?"

"Yes, that's right."

The officer chuckled and said, "Oh yeah, Travis T again."

The young lawyer said, "Oh, you've seen him before have you?"

The officer just nodded his head and laughed as he flipped through a file. After finding Travis's name he picked up the phone and said, "Is this the fourth floor? Send Thomas on down to see his lawyer." The young lawyer eased himself into a plastic chair, careful not to put too much weight on his left hip, and waited for his client to be brought down. He knew from plenty of experience that the minor scrapes and bruises he gained from his favorite sport would be hardly noticeable in a day or two.

He opened his newspaper to banner headlines. FOUR MURDERED IN BELHAVEN. A smaller headline read: THREE DIE IN BLAZE, ONE SHOT IN FRONT YARD. There was a color picture of a flaming house. In the foreground was a handcuffed man in tattered clothes. The caption said: "Halbert Boyd charged with four counts of murder. D. A. says death penalty will be sought." The young lawyer studied the picture and read the story with interest.

Wow! What a case, thought John Brooks as he read, "a neighborhood full of witnesses and a spontaneous confession." *I'm glad I don't have that case.* Even as he thought those words, he knew they weren't true. He had been practicing law for almost four years and had developed a good reputation among those who knew him and his work. He was already trying twenty percent of the worst criminal trials in the county, and he had half of all of the not guilty verdicts in the county; but he was still not generally known. His cases did not tend to make the news. He secretly wished for a high profile case, believing that the public would then know who he was and would think of him when they needed an

13

attorney.

After three or four minutes an elevator door opened and out stepped a young police officer with a young black man dressed in drab green fatigues. John walked towards the man in fatigues and said, "Are you Travis Thomas?"

"No sir. My name is William Thomas."

Brooks turned slowly towards the officer at the desk. "I need to see Travis Thomas. This is William Thomas."

"Oh, did they send you the wrong inmate? Hey, Patterson, take him back up, and bring us Travis T, Travis Thomas."

As the elevator doors slid closed, John slumped back into his seat and looked impatiently at his watch. The room was a drab blue with a badly worn tile floor. John opened his newspaper again and finished reading about the Belhaven murders. The D. A., Buddy Tellers, was already calling Boyd the "Butcher of Belhaven." Tellers had a way with words and was never shy when talking to the press. He was, after all, a politician, and always had at least one eye focused on the next election.

"I wonder who his press agent is," mumbled John.

After another five or six minutes, the elevator door slid open. Out stepped another black man in green fatigues. Without leaving his seat, John said, "Are you Travis Thomas?"

"That's right. But everybody calls me Travis T."

"I'm not sure I would advertise that."

"Huh?"

"Follow me."

The lawyer led Travis T through a door into a short hall that opened into two large drunk tanks and a small room with a sign on the door that said, "Attorney Conference Room". The attorney conference room was occupied, so John looked into the adjoining drunk tank and saw that the room was empty.

"Let's go in here," he said, and closed the door behind them.

John knew that the door would not lock without the key. The room was about 20 feet square with a tile bench around the perimeter. There was a drain in the middle of the tile floor, which completed the room's furnishings. The two men moved to a corner of the room and sat on the bench.

"My name is Brooks, John Brooks," said the young lawyer as he handed his client a business card.

"You said that like 'Bond, James Bond,'" laughed Travis.

"I just got a call from the court. I have been appointed to represent you."

"Appointed huh? You one of the State's lawyers?"

14

"No, I am a private lawyer, but I was appointed in this case to represent you. The only thing I know about this case right now is that you are here in the City Jail charged with armed robbery. If you want help, you are going to have to tell me why you are here and what you know about this charge."

"I don't know nothin'."

"How long have you been in jail?"

"Three days."

"How'd you get here?"

"I don't know."

"Oh, come on. You know how you got in jail. You were arrested by the police, right?"

"Yes sir, I was ... ah ... at my girlfriend's house and they came up and say I been robbin' some store and my girlfriend, she know I been with her all that night long. She tell you."

"What night was that?"

"What night?"

"Let's start over. What store did they say that you robbed?"

"Well, I don't know."

"When do they say you robbed the store?"

"Well, I don't know, but my girlfriend, she'll tell you I was with her all the night long."

"How would your girlfriend know you were with her when the place was robbed if you don't know when the place was robbed?"

"What? What you mean? Are you tryin' to ask me some trick question? I thought you was supposed to be my lawyer."

"Never mind. Well, what's your girlfriend's name?"

"Ah, Ah, it's Ruby."

"Where does Ruby live?"

"Oh, she lives uh, uh off of Highway 80."

"Where on Highway 80?"

"I don't know. It ain't on Highway 80. It's off Highway 80."

"What's the name of the street?"

"Uh, I don't know."

"Have you talked to the police about this charge?"

"No, I ain't said nothin' to nobody. I know my rights. No sir, I ain't made no statement. I didn't do it. You gotta help me. I'm an innocent man."

"Have you ever been in trouble before?"

"No sir."

"I think you've been in this jail before."

"Well, you know, for drinking. That sort of thing."

"What sort of thing besides drinking?"

"Oh, just fightin', that's all. And I just got out of the pen for something I didn't do."

"All right, Travis, I got it. I'll go see what I can find out about this charge. Don't talk to anybody about your case except me. Okay?"

"Don't worry, I'm not sayin' nothin' to nobody."

As John was leaving, Travis T decided that this might be an opportunity to make a little money and make his new lawyer beholden to him. "Hey, look, you're trying to help me, and maybe I can help you. Look, are you interested in any suits? I know some guys from the pen who have some good suits."

John stopped and considered the comment. *Maybe this guy knows someone who has a good lawsuit.* So, John said, "Sure, have these guys call me."

"Great! What size do you wear?"

John paused for a moment, then laughed. "Travis, I thought you were talking about lawsuits. No, I am not interested in any suits that some guys from the pen have, and, considering that you just got out of the pen, you shouldn't have anything to do with them either."

"Are you some kind of Boy Scout or something?" asked Travis T. "Okay, suit yourself." Then he laughed. "Get it? Suit yourself? Ha, ha, ha."

3

The young man was dressed in black. Black T-shirt, black pants, heavy black boots, and a black trench coat. His skin was pale white, in stark contrast to his dark hair and eyebrows. He was staring intently with dark, angry eyes at the morning newspaper headline:

FOUR MURDERED IN BELHAVEN

He dropped the paper on the street. Pages began to flutter in the breeze. A puff of wind scattered the pages and one section tumbled away. He looked up from the ground, first at the police precinct in front of him, and then at the line of nearby police cars.

"Boyd must die," he said to no one in particular, repeating the instructions that he had received from "the Bishop." He set his jaw with determination, reached into his trench coat, produced a crowbar, and began smashing the windows on the nearest police cruiser.

Seconds later police officers erupted from the precinct like hornets from a disturbed nest, guns drawn, shouting:

"Freeze!"

"Don't move!"

"Are you crazy?"

By then, the young man's arms were full of articles taken from the cruiser, including a radio, handcuffs, a nightstick, a shotgun, and other items. He dropped his load and slowly raised his hands over his head. He was thrown against the cruiser. In seconds, the officers had ripped his trench coat off, handcuffed him, and searched him.

"This guy has no I.D. What's your name?"

"John Smith."

"Where do you live?"

"Wherever I lay my head."

"Where are you from, kid?"

"Hell."

The officer paused for a moment and looked into a pair of empty eyes. For a moment, the officer believed him. He felt a shiver run up his spine.

"Wherever you're from, you're going to jail, buddy."

4

When John Brooks stepped into the offices of the Robbery Homicide Division, a plain-clothes police officer, Captain Rico Townsend, was alone in a room packed wall-to-wall with ancient metal desks. Phones rang on two of the desks, unanswered.

Townsend had curly hair, a mustache, and looked like he had been there and done that. He was looking down at a file as John walked in. Without looking up, he said, "What can we do for you today, Lawyer Brooks?"

Not wanting to show Rico that he was impressed that he knew he was there without looking up, John went straight to the point. "Well, Rico, you can drop the charges against my client."

"That's what I like about you Brooks. You always go straight to the point. No beating around the bush."

"Kind of like you, Rico. Straight to the point."

"Yeah, well, once in a while the bush needs a little beating. It tends to flush out whatever is in it. Who's your innocent client today?"

"Travis Thomas."

"Oh ho! Travis T! His mama named him right. Why don't you join us for the line-up, and then we will talk about your request to drop charges."

"Line-up?"

"Isn't that why you're here? We're about to start right now."

"Whoa, slow down. Can I see the other participants?"

"Sure, you can see them now."

Detective Rico led the way into a small, darkened theater. Several rows of seats faced a large one-way, mirrored glass.

"The victim will be here in a few minutes. You can see the participants before she gets here."

A moment later six men walked into the adjoining room and lined up against a measured, white wall. The second one was Travis Thomas. They were told to face left, then forward and then right. John thought to himself that Rico had done a good job selecting participants. They were all about the same height and had similar hair and skin tone.

"Not bad, Rico. This is a lot better than the last line-up I attended."

"I'm not worried about the line-up. I've had to deal with Travis T before. You could put anybody you want in the line-up, because Travis will always stand out in a crowd."

18

"Really? What has he done before?"

Rico handed John a five-page rap sheet.

"Wow!" said John as he read from the list, "business burglary, house burglary, strong armed robbery, grand theft, counterfeiting!"

"Yeah, you name it, he's done it. He was on probation for a string of larcenies by trick when we picked him up for this. He has always been a wise guy. A real smart one, too. The counterfeit charge was one of my favorites. He taped the ends of twenty dollar bills onto one dollar bills to turn ones into twenties."

"I can tell from this rap sheet that he is one of your favorites, but that doesn't mean he pulled this one off."

"We'll see."

Just then, two more officers entered the room with a nervous fortyish-year-old lady. She was ushered to a seat. Rico spoke into an intercom and commanded each man, one at a time, to step forward, then turn left and right.

"Do you recognize anyone?"

"Number two looks familiar, but they all look so much alike. I'm not really sure."

Rico grimaced and glanced at John, who could not suppress his smile. An uncertain identification would not meet the "beyond a reasonable doubt" standard, and Travis would walk.

"Just a minute, Brooks," said Rico. "Don't start smiling cause we're not through yet." He turned to the intercom and said, "number one, repeat the following words, 'I gotta gun and I know how to use it. Give me all the money.'"

Before the first man could respond, Travis T burst out with laughter, saying, "that ain't even what I said, man. Y'all ain't got nothin' on me." He looked to his left and right sharing a knowing smile with the others around him, nodding his head vigorously and swinging his arms slightly. "That's right. Y'all gotta let me go." He pointed at the one-way window with both hands, with emphasis on "let" and on "me" and on "go".

The victim exclaimed, "That's him! I would know that voice anywhere. That's him! I would know that smirky expression anywhere."

The other men in the line-up were stunned for a moment; then they all started laughing and shaking their heads.

"What? What are you laughing at," shouted Travis.

"What happened to that smile on your face Lawyer Brooks? I told you Travis T would stand out in any crowd."

Brooks could only shake his head.

As Rico started to leave the room, he said, "By the way, your request

19

for voluntary dismissal is denied."

John said, "Rico, is it all right if I ask the victim a few questions?"

"You never give up, do you? Well, no harm can come of it now. This case is a lock. Go ahead. Ms. Sturgent, this is John Brooks. He is the lawyer for the man that robbed you. He's going to ask you a few questions."

"Well, okay," said Ms. Sturgent, as she looked timidly at John.

John smiled and said, "I am so sorry for what you have gone through. It must have been terrible."

"It was the most terrible thing I have ever experienced. It was terrifying to find out that he had a gun and was going to use it if he had to."

"You just said something interesting. You said you found out he had a gun. How did you find that out?"

"Well, I just heard it in the line-up. Up until then, I had no idea. Once I realized he was armed, why, I began shaking all over. I've only just now gotten control of myself. You can understand how terrifying that would be, to realize that this animal could have shot me to death for practically nothing!"

"Practically nothing? What did he take?"

"He tricked me out of $20 is what he did. Oh, my, if I had known he had a gun, why, I don't know what I would have done. I probably would have fainted."

"How did he trick you out of $20?"

"He bought a pack of cigarettes and paid with a $50 dollar bill. When he got his change back, he decided he wanted the 50 back, and he got me confused by swapping bills back and forth, until the next thing I knew, he was out the door, and I was $20 short in my register. So I called the police and told them that I had been robbed."

Robbery is a term that has a specific meaning to a police officer or lawyer. Robbery is the taking of something of value from a person or presence of another by force or by threat. To the general public, robbery can mean any crime of theft. John considered this a moment and said, "The man who took this money, he didn't say the words that were used in the line-up, did he?"

"Why, no. Otherwise I would have known he had a gun. But once I heard him speak, I knew that was him. I am certain of it. I would know that voice anywhere." She looked at Rico and said, "When will I get my twenty dollars back?"

*   *   *

John followed Rico back to Robbery Homicide.

"Yeah, yeah, so, somebody overcharged Thomas. Whoever took the

20

initial complaint didn't ask enough questions. But that doesn't mean I'm going to just let him go."

"You can charge him with a misdemeanor, Rico, but not with robbery."

"Yeah, I heard her. But, you might not have heard me. He's on probation. What he did was a violation of probation and I plan to let the judge decide if it needs to be revoked. Jail is the best place for Travis T."

5

While John was talking with Rico, Court Administrator Sandra Voner and Senior Circuit Judge Robert Richards were reviewing the list of persons who needed a court-appointed lawyer. Sometimes the public defender has a conflict or is otherwise not available. On those occasions, the Court appoints a lawyer from a list of those who volunteer for the task. They are paid a small flat fee when the case is complete.

For the past month the public defender had been complaining that his workload was too great and that he could not handle any more high-profile cases until the County agreed to provide him with more staff. Ordinarily, the Judge would not be interested in who the Court Administrator appointed from the list of lawyers; but today, Hal Boyd, the Butcher of Belhaven, needed a lawyer.

"Who is the next lawyer on the list?"

"Johnson," said the Administrator.

"Hmm. Brooks is my preference for a case like this. This is going to be intense and I don't want any claim of ineffective assistance of counsel to cause a reversal of any conviction. That claim would never succeed with Brooks. I only want to try Boyd once."

"Brooks would be the best choice, but I just appointed him to another case this morning," Sandra said.

"Has he already taken it?"

"Yes sir."

Judge Richards sighed and scratched his chin.

"Give him Boyd. Skip him the next time he comes up."

"As good as done," said Sandra as she picked up the phone to call Brooks' office. She was not surprised to learn from Karen, his secretary, that John was already at work on the case assigned to him this morning. "I've got another one for you, Karen."

"That's unusual. Two in one day!"

"Well, it's not a usual case. It's the Butcher of Belhaven!"

"No way!"

"That's right. I don't know if we are doing you a favor, but Judge Richards specifically wanted John on this case because he said he wanted to make sure that Boyd had the best representation possible. He said he didn't want any claim of ineffective assistance of counsel to make him try the case again if there was a conviction."

22

"Nobody will do it better than John."

"We know. Good luck."

As soon as Karen hung up the phone, she called out for John's partner, "Jackson! Come quick! Go find John. We've just been appointed to the Butcher of Belhaven case!"

* * *

Brooks walked quickly away from the police department towards his office with long brisk strides. The wind muffed his brown hair, and his brow was furrowed.

"Why so glum, chum?"

It was the familiar voice of Jackson Bradley, John's partner. Jackson had cut across the street when he saw John and could see that he looked troubled. John stopped to let Jackson catch up, watching the tall, thin lawyer approach. Jackson had a Groucho Marx mustache. He always wore a nice suit during the workday, but, because he was so thin, his coat looked like it was still on the hanger. At the sight of Jackson, John's mood began to change for the better.

"You should have been there Jackson. Our new client confessed at the line-up, and he doesn't realize it yet."

"I want to hear about this! What happened?"

"When asked to repeat the robber's words, Travis T, that's our client's name, believe it or not, says, "That ain't even what I said, man. Y'all ain't got nothin' on me.""

Jackson leaned back and directed a hardy belly laugh toward the sky, howling, "He's a regular Einstein!"

John couldn't help but laugh with him.

"Travis T! We've got to keep up with all these characters and put them in our book one day," said Jackson.

"Jackson, that's just it. We keep laboring in the fields, but we aren't getting the cases that anyone cares about. Nobody is ever going to be interested in the kind of cases we get. Nobody wants to hear about Travis Thomas, aka Travis T."

"Cheer up John. You're the best trial lawyer in town. I've known that since the first time I saw you in court. Everybody else is catching on. The big cases are just around the corner, I just know it."

Because Jackson was grinning without apparent reason, John took a closer look at the eyes behind his thick glasses, looking for a clue for his behavior. Jackson was smart, at times brilliant, with a quick wit; but, he had a tendency to say the wrong thing at the right time.

"What are you smiling about, Jackson?"

"Oh, nothing. Let's head back to the office and see what's going on."

John told him that he thought he could get the charges against Travis

23

reduced to larceny by trick instead of armed robbery. The difference would be huge, since armed robbery had a minimum three-year sentence, and no parole was available for the first ten years of an armed robbery sentence.

"By the way, speaking of Einsteins like Travis T, Skip made an appointment to see us."

"Oh no, what is it this time?"

"The Attorney General is suing him for his new slogan, claiming that it is false advertising."

"What's the slogan?"

"The Middleman."

John paused and turned toward Jackson, an incredulous look on his face. "Skip, the middleman?"

"Yeah, he's a middleman, who just happens to be named Skip."

"What does he do as a middleman?"

"He makes deals for anything and everything, for a fee, so he printed up some business cards with his new slogan, 'Skip the Middleman.' The first place he called on was the Consumers Union, where he sold them office supplies. When they figured out that he sold them half the stuff at twice the price, they complained to the AG."

"Go figure. He started with the Consumers Union? You're right. He is another Einstein. But, surely, that's not why you are smiling. You're trying to change the subject, aren't you?"

"It's that killer instinct that makes you so good at cross examination," said Jackson with a wink. "What do you know? We're back at the office. Let's see if we have any messages."

As they were about to go up the stairs, a tall, lean, professional-looking young lady stepped out of the stairway door.

"Jennifer, what brings you here?" asked John.

"Karen called and said your calendars were not syncing correctly," explained Jennifer Wolfe. "A default setting needed to be reset, and everything is humming now."

"You are the best," said John. "We never could get anyone to fix our computers before we found you."

"That's right," agreed Jackson, thankful for the change of subject. "We hardly ever have computer problems anymore. By the way, did you hear about the kleptomaniac who, when charged with shoplifting, used her doctor's prescription as a defense?"

"No. Why don't you tell us about her, Jackson?" asked Jennifer as she put her hands on her hips, waiting for his corny response.

"She explained that her doctor told her that if she felt that certain urge coming on, she should take something for it."

"And, so, she did," responded John with a smile.

"That's right, just following doctor's orders," laughed Jennifer. "Jackson, you are like the guy who told his friends ten puns to see if he could get them to laugh."

"The problem was, no pun in ten did," finished Jackson in his best Groucho imitation.

"You two tell really bad old jokes," said John.

"Karen is looking for you," said Jennifer. "She seems pretty excited about something. I think you better get up there."

"That's what I was thinking," said Jackson with a laugh, obviously enjoying the banter.

They parted from Jennifer and trotted up the stairs.

6

Jackson and John were still laughing when they walked into the office. Their extraordinarily efficient secretary Karen Wilkes, who just happened to be one of the best looking women in town, met them. Today her red hair was in a ponytail. Her blue eyes sparkled with excitement as she handed two pink slips to John.

"Seriously, this is no laughing matter. Here are your messages."

"This is a message from Mitch reminding me that I haven't been to rugby practice in a while, and we are going to be playing Mobile in a couple of weeks. Is that what all the mystery is about between you two?"

"No, the second message is from the Court Administrator," said Karen. "You have been appointed to another case."

"Another! I just got one this morning. We usually just get one every month or two."

"This case is not like the one this morning," said Karen. "This is Hal Boyd."

John froze in mid step, half way to his office. He looked quickly at his note, then at Karen, then at Jackson. "You're kidding."

"It's true—you represent Boyd, the Butcher of Belhaven," said Jackson.

A flood of emotion swept through John as the gravity of this news sunk in. His heart and his mind were racing.

"When did this call come in?"

"About fifteen minutes ago," replied Karen. "I sent Jackson out to find you."

"Is he in the city jail?"

"Yes."

"I've got to go there now. Jackson, you had better come with me. Karen, please call Mitch for me and let him know that I want to be there, but I have been snowed lately. Please remind me to call him back as soon as we can come up for air."

"Let me grab my things," said Jackson as he stepped into his office and swept a legal pad off his desk. They left their second floor office, hurried past the elevator and down the stairs. They crossed the street at mid-block in front of City Hall, a beautiful and imposing antebellum building with giant white columns. They walked quickly past the County Courthouse towards the Police Department, located in the next block.

"You sure you want to represent this s.o.b.?" asked Jackson. "I know you've been wanting a high profile case, but this one is a sure loser. I am not so sure this one will enhance your reputation. But it will generate the attention you have been secretly craving."

"It's not a matter of whether I want to; I don't know if I'm qualified. Four murders and the death penalty! This is heavy stuff, Jackson."

"I'm not concerned about whether or not you can do it. I know nobody can handle this case better than you will. I just don't know whether you ought to take it, because I know how much you'll put into it, and this guy hasn't got a chance. Your perfect record will be ruined. Besides, anybody who would burn three people to death and shoot another guy in cold blood probably ought to get gassed, or injected, or hung or whatever it is they will be doing in twenty years when they finally execute him. Heck, in twenty years, they will probably tickle them to death."

"No, that would be cruel and unusual punishment."

Jackson and John shared another laugh, and John thought about how lucky he was to share his practice and his life with such a loyal and funny friend. Even so, Jackson's comments condemning their new client troubled him.

As they arrived at the police department, John reached for the door, grabbed the handle and stopped. "Jackson, first, we don't know that he killed anybody; second, if he did, we don't know if he has legal justification or excuse; third, if he did, and if he doesn't, we don't know whether there are mitigating factors that should reduce his penalty; and fourth, we don't know if he is a s.o.b."

"You just proved my point," said Jackson as he slowly shook his head and slapped John on the shoulder.

When John and Jackson arrived in the receiving area of the jail, the shift had changed and an overly robust 300-pound sergeant was in charge. He was booking a new prisoner, an extremely pale young man with dark hair and black eyes.

"Brooks and Bradley together!" boomed the sergeant. "What gives us this rare privilege? Must be an important case."

"Just routine, Sergeant Wilson," replied Jackson nonchalantly as he sauntered over to the counter where the sergeant stood. "We need to see Halbert Boyd."

"Boyd!" said Sergeant Wilson. "You've got your work cut out for you this time. It looks like your lucky streak is about to be broken, Brooks. How many criminal trials have you won in a row? Four?"

"Seven," said Jackson as he blew on his knuckles and rubbed them against his chest. "He's seven for seven, but who's counting. Besides me."

"It's just another case," responded John, as he noticed the pale young man staring at him with a burning intensity.

"Yeah, sure," said Sergeant Wilson as he typed on his keyboard. "Smith, have a seat in the corner until I can get back to you."

The young man shuffled in leg irons to a nearby seat.

John noticed that Travis T was sitting behind the counter near Smith, apparently still waiting to be taken back to his cell. He walked over to him and said, "Travis, the line-up did not go very well."

"Yeah, I know. I thought about it later. Me and my big mouth! I don't know when to shut up."

"I'll see what I can do for you, but it's going to be an uphill battle. I think that we can get the charge reduced to larceny by trick, but, they want to revoke your probation, and that will be tough to defend."

"Man, that would be great, getting the armed robbery off of me. Armed robbery is hard time. They stuck me with that charge because they are tired of foolin' around with me, and they really want to put me away. I heard what the sergeant said about you. I didn't know you were such a big wheel lawyer. Why would you be interested in helping me with my case? There's nothin' in it for you."

"Travis, you're a human being, created in the image of God, and you're my client. I'll give you my best effort, but I can't promise anything. We'll talk later, in private. I feel sure that we will at least get the robbery charge reduced."

"To say he's created in the image of God is stretching the concept a bit, don't you think?" said Smith.

"We all are, my friend," said John.

"Not me!" shouted Smith.

"Oh, sounds like you hit a nerve, John," said Jackson.

"We reflect His image imperfectly, but we are all made in His image," said Brooks to John Smith. "Even you, my young friend."

"I'm no friend of yours," said Smith as he spat at Brooks. The spittle sprayed along the floor, missing its mark. "Anyone who wants to help Boyd is no friend of mine."

"Hold on, partner," said Wilson. "Another outburst like that and I'll make your stay with us even more unpleasant."

Travis T eyed Smith uneasily and then turned to John and said, "I don't know, Mr. Brooks. I done confessed to a crime I didn't even commit, and I didn't even realize I was confessing. Man, I am in trouble this time for sure. I could take the time for larceny, but armed robbery carries serious time. I'm nothing but a worthless loser."

"You got that right," said Smith.

28

"Things may not be as bad as they seem. I'm pretty sure we can get the charge reduced. Just hang in there."

Travis T said, "No, man, nobody cares what happens to me. Once you walk out that door, you'll forget about me, unless there is a pay check in it for you." After saying this he looked John in the eyes and saw sincerity, something he was not used to seeing. John reached into his coat pocket and pulled out a pocket sized New Testament and handed it to Travis.

Jackson, an avid agnostic, rolled his eyes and said, "Here we go again."

Sergeant Wilson interrupted him and said, "Give your partner a break, Bradley. That's one of the reasons Brooks stands out. He stands for something. And because he stands for something, sometimes doors open for him when they don't open for anybody else."

John smiled at the two of them and sat next to Travis. "Let me show you something. Did you realize that God created you for a purpose?"

"Ha! Yeah, he was created to live in squalor and be a dead-beat criminal," laughed Smith.

Travis furrowed his brow as he first looked at Smith, then he turned back to John.

"What you mean?"

"Before God created the world, He knew you would be here now, in this place, and He assigned a great and essential task for you to perform."

Smith laughed derisively.

Travis looked at Smith again, then back at John. "You done lost your mind. No. I'm not worthy. God wouldn't waste His time with me."

"None of us are worthy, but He appointed you, Travis, to be holy and blameless in His sight."

"Now I know you've lost your mind," laughed Smith.

Jackson and Sergeant Wilson watched with amusement.

"That can't be," said Travis as he shook his head. "I don't believe you."

"You don't have to believe me. You believe God's Word don't you?"

"Sure," said Travis over Smith's laughter.

John turned the pocket New Testament to Ephesians, pointed to a passage in the first chapter and read out loud, "He chose us in Him before the foundation of the world, that we would be holy and blameless before Him." He paused a moment, collecting his thoughts. "That means that He knew you would be here, right now, before He created the world."

"Huh. It really says that about me?"

"And look here in chapter two, 'For we are His workmanship, created in Christ Jesus...' "

"STOP IT! SHUT UP!" shouted Smith as he covered his ears. He recoiled as though he was in pain.

John continued: "'. . . for good works, which God prepared beforehand so that we would walk in them.' Beforehand, that is before you realized it, before you were ready, indeed, before you were born, He prepared a good work for you to do. You are meant to do something good, for God. That's why you are here."

"Let me see that." Travis took the Bible and read for himself. "Yeah, it says that. About me! Huh. Who would a thought?"

Sergeant Wilson was impressed with the conversation. He knew from experience that it would take more than jail time to ever change the Travis Ts of the world. When Wilson found Boyd's information on the computer, he paused. His mood suddenly changed. He cleared his throat, and shifted his weight. His hand covered his mouth, then slid down his face in a chin stroking gesture. He looked at John, then at Jackson and sighed. "I have a note that Boyd is not available to see anyone until . . ."

"Until what?" demanded John. He handed the pocket New Testament to Travis and said, "This is yours. I have to check on this now."

He turned away from Travis Thomas and walked back to the counter. Travis noticed that Smith followed every move that Brooks made. *That kid gives me the willies*, thought Travis. Then he looked at the Bible in his hands. *Nobody ever gave me one of these before*, he thought as he thumbed through the pages.

John placed his hands on the counter and peered into the monitor.

Sergeant Wilson stepped back from the computer with this hands open. "See for yourself. Hey, I'm not going to try to keep you away from a client. It ain't right."

"Thanks Sarge—I owe you one," said John earnestly as he reached over the counter and entered the print command.

Sergeant Wilson turned his back and pretended not to notice as John pulled the sheet from the printer and headed for the steel door. He pushed the button that remotely released the lock. A buzzing sound indicated that the door would open just as John and Jackson reached it and pulled it open.

Travis T watched them pass through the door. Then he noticed that Smith was staring a hole through him. "Don't look at me. I hardly know him. The Court appointed him to me today. I didn't have nothing to do with it. If you don't like him, then I don't like him neither. Just don't be looking at me with that evil eye."

7

"That's enough, Thomas," said Sergeant Wilson. "Let's get back to booking you in, Smith."

As the heavy door clanged shut behind them, Jackson took the note from John, saying, "I've got to see this." He looked it over and then read it aloud: "Boyd is not available to see anyone until after we finish taking his statement. This includes any attorney."

Jackson waved the note in the air. "That's dumb. That could cause any statement he makes to be suppressed. They could lose their case with a stupid mistake like that. Do you suppose these guys ever heard of Miranda?"

"They know what they're doing, Jackson. They are taking a chance, and interpreting Miranda the way they want to. Maybe Boyd hasn't asked for a lawyer so they don't feel obligated to volunteer one for him. But they know that someone might hire a lawyer for him, or the Court might appoint one for him. If they can claim that they didn't know about his lawyer, and can delay us long enough to get a statement from him, then they don't have to worry about some lawyer throwing a monkey wrench in their investigation by telling Boyd not to talk."

"You wouldn't think they would want to go to that much trouble with this case. It's a cinch. Open and shut. Why risk losing on a technicality?"

Together they stepped into an elevator.

"Good question. Maybe they don't think it's open and shut after all. Or, maybe they're not worried about losing. Maybe they think the case is a cinch, too. They figure that even if some of the evidence they receive now is excluded at a trial, they will still have enough to convict him. The chance that we would find out about this was small, so they figure the risk is worth it."

"So what are they after?" asked Jackson as they waited for the elevator to get to their floor.

"This is a high profile case. They are trying to foreclose defenses now by looking for motives, elements of aggravation that they can use against him. They hope to use Boyd's own words to defeat any plea of mitigation or mercy that he might make later. In other words, they are trying to make their case for the big D. The death penalty."

Jackson felt a chill on his spine as the thought of being on the losing end of a death penalty case sank in.

"Either that, or they think that there are other perpetrators involved, or maybe other potential victims. That may be it. Maybe there are other possible victims."

"Great, a serial killer."

"Maybe they will claim exigent circumstances—that is, they think that other potential victims are at risk, and they have to get information fast to save them," continued John. "Who knows? All we can do is speculate.

"Yeah, that and crash the party," added Jackson

"Exactly."

As soon as the elevator doors began sliding open, John and Jackson squeezed out and hurried down the hall to a door marked "Interrogation Rooms". The door was locked. John knocked, waited a moment and knocked louder.

"Jackson, see if you can find someone in authority who will let us in. I'll keep trying here."

Jackson trotted down the hall toward the office of the Robbery Homicide Division. *If I don't have luck there, I'll go to the police chief's office,* thought Jackson as he approached the door.

As Jackson ran down the hall, John banged on the door and hollered, "I need in. This is urgent. Let me in."

After two minutes of non-stop shouting and beating on the door, he began to feel conspicuously ignored. Finally, the door cracked and an officer stood in the opening.

"Who are you?" asked the plain-clothes officer.

"I'm John Brooks. I'm here to see my client, Hal Boyd."

"Nobody here by that name."

"I have a message that he is here," replied John as he pushed his way through the doorway.

The plain-clothes officer stuck a hand on John's chest and said, "Hold it buddy, you can't come in here."

"Let him in, Chadwick. We're not getting anywhere anyway," said someone from behind the door. Chadwick moved aside, and John stepped into a short hallway with small rooms to the left and right. "In here, Brooks."

John stepped into a small interrogation room that contained three plastic chairs, a small table and two men. The tile floor was scuffed and littered with ground-in cigarette butts. The air was thick with smoke.

"How'd you know it was me, Red?" John asked the red-haired man seated across from Boyd.

"I'd know your knock anywhere," said Red.

At that moment Jackson arrived with Rico.

"What seems to be the problem here gentlemen?" asked Rico.

"No problem, Captain," replied Red. "Mr. Brooks here was just about to start talking to his client. Chadwick and I were just leaving."

Red slid his chair out from under the table, rose and brushed past John. "We'll be outside if you need us. Don't loan him any matches."

"This room isn't bugged is it?" John asked Rico.

"It's clean," replied Rico.

"You know us well enough that you don't have to ask that question," retorted Red as he feigned a hurt look.

"That's very reassuring," countered Jackson. "Hey, Red, Sergeant Wilson told me to tell you he needs you to help him find an escapee. He's a midget fortune-teller. Wilson says he needs you to put out an APB for a small medium at large."

"Very funny, Bradley."

John sat in the chair Red had just vacated. Jackson closed the door and took the remaining chair. Boyd was across the table from them staring at a spot on the floor. His shoulders sagged and his arms hung limp in his lap. His back was slightly arched. He had not registered any recognition that anyone else was in the room.

"My name is John Brooks. I'm your lawyer. This is my partner, Jackson Bradley."

John held his business card out, but after several seconds, Boyd had not taken the card and had not looked up. John and Jackson looked at each other. Jackson circled his ear with his index finger and shrugged. John reached out and placed the card in Boyd's shirt pocket.

"Look, you've been charged with four murders and it's a sure bet that they will be going after the death penalty. I'm here to help you, but I can't help if you won't talk to me."

"I don't want your help. I don't want a lawyer. I don't care what they do to me. I am ready to die. I did what I had to do. My reason for living is finished."

"At least he's talking," said Jackson.

"Why don't you care, Hal?" asked John.

Boyd raised his head slowly and fixed his eyes on John. The eyes were empty, devoid of emotion. John suppressed a shudder as he looked into those empty eyes and thought about the charges against Boyd. In spite of himself, the thought crept into his mind that he was looking into the eyes of a cold blooded, heartless killer. John blinked and looked down at his notepad.

Boyd seemed to sense John's thoughts. He let out a short, sarcastic chuckle and said, "See, you think they ought to execute me, too. You don't care. I don't care. Just let them do what they will."

"Hal, I care. Tell me what happened."

"Haven't the police told you?"

"I want you to tell me."

"I did what I had to do."

John felt a shudder go through him again.

"What did you do?"

John paused. There was no response.

"Why did you have to do it?" probed John.

"I'm through talking. Nobody could understand."

"Try me." John cajoled and pleaded with Boyd for another twenty minutes, but Boyd said nothing. Finally, he said, "Why don't you care what they do to you?"

"Because Sally is gone. There's no point in living. Because of what he did to Sally."

"Sally?"

"The woman I love. She was the sweetest angel who ever lived."

Motive, thought John. "Was Sally your girlfriend?"

"She was my fiancée; before he came along."

"What did he do to her?"

"He killed her."

Now we're getting somewhere. "He? Who is he?"

"You wouldn't believe me. You wouldn't understand. Nobody will believe me. Nobody will understand. I did what I had to do. They can do whatever they want to me. I don't care."

"When did he kill her? Was it that night?"

"No. It was three years ago. I did what I had to do. I'm ready to accept the consequences."

"If you don't tell me what happened and let me help you, they might blame you for Sally's death. Let me help you, Hal."

Hal looked at John in the eyes, studying him, trying to see if he was sincere. John held his gaze.

"Okay," said Boyd, "but I warn you, it is going to be hard to accept. I had to kill him because he was a vampire."

34

8

An hour later Rico knocked on the door and cut the interview short.

"You will have to continue this in the jail. I can't let you stay indefinitely in our interrogation room. I will have your client returned to the jail. In the meantime, why don't you step into my office?"

John and Jackson said goodbye to Hal, and promised to see him in the jail soon to continue their discussion. They left the interrogation room and stood in the hallway for a moment.

"This reminds me of the kleptomaniac joke you told me this morning," John whispered to Jackson. "She had to take something. He had to kill someone. We are going to need some really good mental health witnesses."

"John, that guy is absolutely nuts. He completely believes his story."

"Yeah, but his story is internally consistent," said John as they entered the homicide office. "He doesn't exhibit the usual disjointed ramblings of a crazy guy. He really believed that this man was a vampire and that he had to kill this vampire."

Rico and Red were already there. As soon as they entered the office, Red looked up and said, "You're going down this time, Brooks. You've got a bad, bad boy."

"Tell me how bad he is."

"He's a serial killer. Your boy's been traveling all over the country, and wherever he goes dead bodies turn up."

"Red, people die everywhere all the time," said Jackson. "It's a fact of life. I bet people died in every city you visited on each of your vacations. Maybe we should investigate you as a serial killer."

"Well, you never know."

Rico nodded and said, "It appears Red is right."

Rico slid a file across the table.

John began turning the pages. There was a summary of an ongoing investigation into a series of murders in Seattle, San Francisco, Tucson, El Paso, San Antonio, Houston, and New Orleans.

"Eighteen murders in all," said Rico. "We entered his name in the data base, and this is what we got. The phone's been ringing off the wall from departments everywhere. What you have there is the report of an ongoing investigation into a series of murders over a period of six years. There are a few common threads. One, they involve victims with peculiar neck injuries; two, the murders seem to have been moving from

35

West to East; and three, your man was seen near the murder scene around the time of the murders in four of the cities. He has been a 'person of interest' that the FBI has wanted to talk to for the last three years, but he's been on the lamb ever since his fiancée was murdered. He is a suspect in her homicide as well."

Jackson and John stared at each other in stunned silence.

"And now he turns up here, with four more dead bodies," said Red. "I got my first serial killer, and you're about to lose your first case, hot shot."

John eased into a chair. "Wow! This is some heavy stuff. I'm telling you the truth, I am stunned."

"Remember the way he looked at you?" asked Jackson.

John felt chilled to the bone. He shivered visibly.

Red laughed, and said, "We finally got to you, didn't we?"

"Mind if I have a copy of this?"

"You got to waive your preliminary first."

A preliminary hearing is conducted in some cases. It requires the prosecution to produce enough evidence to convince the judge that the defendant probably committed the crime for which he is charged. This is much less than the burden to be used at trial, where the jury must be convinced of guilt beyond a reasonable doubt. Discovery rules, which require the prosecutor to share the evidence he has obtained with the defense, generally begin after the preliminary hearing is either held or waived. Sometimes the hearing is waived in order to get information by way of discovery quicker. Sometimes the hearing is waived in order to reduce the impact of negative pre-trial publicity.

"Come on Red, you've beat me down already. You've got a lock cinch on a career case, and you want to nit pick me. Besides, you will want to be in that courtroom at the preliminary hearing. Every network in the country will be there. They will be begging you for your book rights. Who is going to play you in the movie? Bruce Willis or Vin Diesel?"

Red smiled and looked at Rico, who shrugged. "Yeah, you're right. No harm in letting you get it now. You're going to get it soon enough anyway. Besides, I kind of want to see how you plan to squirm out of this one."

9

An hour later, Jackson, John and Karen were back at the office, reading, marking and studying the police report. Karen made work copies that they could mark and highlight. She kept the original copy in a separate folder.

"It looks mighty bad, John," said Jackson.

"It gives me the creeps," said Karen with a shiver.

"Yeah, I agree, it looks bad. We need to go see Mr. Hal Boyd again."

"You've got another appointment in a half hour. Skip the Middleman is coming in."

With the two new cases in the office today, John didn't think he had time to see Skip 'The Middleman' Schaffer and hear about another one of Skip's brushes with the law. Skip was maybe two inches over five feet tall, but it was hard to tell because he always wore elevator shoes. He talked fast and thought of himself as a snappy dresser. Skip would be the only one who thought so. In fact, his wardrobe was, in a word, remarkable.

He had come up with dozens of get rich schemes in his 36 years on earth. Some were so wild and out of this world that Jackson joked that Skip was from another planet. Sometimes John thought that Jackson might be right. John successfully defended Skip on a charge of false pretense when Skip tried to open a dehydrated bottled water company. Skip explained to potential investors that dehydrated water cost a lot less to ship, and they would save a lot on product costs if the purchaser would just add water to the bottle, water that Skip and his investors wouldn't have to buy.

Skip was delighted almost to delirium when he finally obtained a check from an investor for fifty grand. Delight turned into dismay when he learned that the investment was part of a sting operation instituted by the Mississippi Attorney General's office. Skip was arrested but never indicted. Skip hired John, who convinced the AG that Skip was just using a little creativity to sell a supply of plastic bottles he obtained through the bankruptcy of a local cleaning product company.

"Nobody could possibly be fooled if they bought an empty bottle of dehydrated water," explained John. "It's sort of like the Pet Rock fad. Nobody believed the rock was really a pet. The only difference was, this never became a fad."

John pointed out that there were no investors, other than the AG's own sting operation. "It looks like the only one taken in by this supposed fraud was your office," asserted John.

The AG reluctantly dropped the charges, but said, "Skip is on my radar. We'll get him one of these days."

Skip was so delighted with the result that he gave John a whole case of dehydrated water as a way of saying thanks. He also sent clients to John from time to time and often sought John's advice, but always after he had already gotten too deep into another scheme.

Now he was in trouble for his moniker, Skip 'the Middleman.' The AG thought that this was an open and shut case of false pretense, since Skip was a middleman; but a potential customer might be misled into thinking that they were skipping the middleman, and thus getting a better deal. Instead, they would be paying Skip a premium for arranging the delivery of whatever product or service they desired. Whatever the customer wanted, Skip would always say, "We can do that!"

"Let's reschedule Skip," says John.

"He says it's urgent," said Karen. "And, you need a fee."

"Good grief. I guess I'll see him."

"Get paid this time." scolded Karen. "You're broke, and you can't afford to keep giving your time away."

Karen kept up with her time and skimped on her hours reporting only a fraction of the time she actually worked because she knew that there was seldom enough money in the account to pay her.

"Okay, why don't you collect the money before I see him this time?"

"Glad to. I just don't know how much to charge."

"You decide. In fact, why don't you set and collect the fees on all of our cases. I hate to deal with the money part. Just make sure we charge and collect enough to get all of our business and personal bills paid. Don't forget to get enough to pay yourself."

"Okay, but with all these new responsibilities, I'm giving myself a raise."

"Are we paying you?" asked Jackson. "I thought you did this for fun, like the rest of us."

10

Sandra Storcovsky couldn't believe that once again she was assigned to some back woods story, this time in Podunk, Mississippi. She felt that she had paid her dues on small assignments, working for CTN, the world's largest cable television news network. Most of her stories did not amount to much, and too often her camera appearance was edited out.

"You would think that with a 24/7 need for breaking news, I could get my break with a big story," she said to no one in particular as she drove to the airport.

Her first big job in front of a camera was in Cleveland. Her extraordinary good looks and rich feminine voice made her an instant hit. She was destined for the big time, she was told, and she hired an agent. Major networks, maybe even movies, were in her future. But, the name had to change, said her agent, who added, "Storcovsky just doesn't do anything for me."

"But I'm proud of my name."

"You don't have to change your name sweetheart. We just want an AKA you can operate under. We need something catchy, memorable, so that you will stand out in the crowd. Let's face it. There are a lot of pretty faces out there and even more who have a lot of talent. But, most of them don't make it. If you get your one big shot, you need to be remembered."

"I don't know. Maybe you're right."

"Of course I'm right. I'm always right. The sooner you realize that, the sooner I can get you to the big time."

And so, Storcovsky became Storm, and Sandy Storm was born. She landed a coveted job at CTN, but the big story hadn't come her way, until now. She did not know yet that she had been handed the case of the century.

"Well, Bret," she said to her cameraman as they boarded the plane to Mississippi, "We'll just make the best of this assignment. We may have to get a little creative to find something interesting in Mississippi."

"Actually, there are plenty of interesting things in Mississippi. There is great music, original musicians, prize winning writers, fantastic food, friendly people; it's really an interesting place."

"How do you know anything about it?"

"I was in Oxford, Mississippi, for the Presidential Debate at Ole Miss. The world press was there by the thousands. Everyone was blown away,

39

because we all had a negative image of Mississippi based on all of the bad press and redneck jokes we have heard all of our lives. Instead, we found Oxford to be a really beautiful, cosmopolitan, yet Mayberry like town, with intelligent, interesting and friendly people. It was a lot of fun."

"In other words, you met a girl."

"Yeah, how did you know? Those southern girls are really something. But don't worry about the assignment. You will make something happen. If anybody can make a mountain out of mundane, you can. In the meantime, I plan to call an old friend and see if she can meet us."

She stared at Bret for a moment, wondering if he had complimented her, or insulted her. Bret just smiled. In the meantime, back at CTN headquarters in Atlanta, word arrived that the murders in Jackson might be tied to murders in several cities. While Sandy Storm was in flight, arrangements were being made for a satellite truck to meet her for on-the-scene reports. By the time Sandy arrived in front of the courthouse on Pascagoula Street in Jackson, her mood had changed dramatically because she received a report that Boyd was a "person of interest" in multiple murders around the country.

"A serial killer, and we are the first national reporters on the scene! Bret, can you believe our luck that we have this story!"

She climbed out of the van onto the sidewalk. She couldn't help noticing an outlandishly dressed really short man walking in her direction along the sidewalk.

"Bret, get a look at this."

Bret stepped out of the van in time to see a man clad in a purple satin shirt, leather pants, an oversized yellow cowboy hat and a pair of red cowboy boots sauntering toward them.

Skip 'the Middleman' couldn't help but notice that the most gorgeous woman he had ever laid eyes on could not take her eyes off of him. He had been hurrying down the sidewalk because he was a few minutes late for his appointment with John Brooks. But, once he saw how she was looking at him, he slowed down so that she could get a better look.

Who knows, he said to himself, *maybe there is a little chemistry here*.

Skip found that girls were always looking at him, but, apparently, finding just the right chemistry was hard to come by. He saw she was with a guy, who didn't seem too bright. He had a sort of uncomprehending look about him, and his mouth hung open.

You can do a lot better, babe, thought Skip. Then he noticed the satellite truck, and his mind leaped to the conclusion that this spectacularly beautiful woman was with a news organization.

Possibilities and speculations about endless opportunities flooded the space beneath his cowboy hat and, quick as a flash, he delivered his card to Sandy and Bret and introduced himself.

"Welcome to our fair city. I'm Skip the Middleman, at your service."

Bret continued to stare with his mouth open.

Sandy chuckled and said, "So, you're a one-man welcoming committee. What a . . . ah . . . pleasant surprise."

"That's right! If there is anything you need, any information you might require, anyone you would like to know, just let Skip know, and I'll make it happen, fast."

"Is that so?"

"You bet. Test me. Name it. Anything you want, I'll get it now."

"Okay. I'll do that. I'm interested in the Butcher of Belhaven case."

"You've come to the right place. I know everything about that case. Maybe you should get your camera ready. I can tell you all about it. I will be your first interview."

"Maybe later. Right now, I want to find the lawyers involved. Do you know the prosecutor and the defense lawyer? My text message says the defense lawyer is a guy named Brooks."

Skip's face lit up for a moment. He could not believe his luck, but he had to play this right. Fast, but not too fast. "Oh, John Brooks. Excellent lawyer. Best we've ever had. World renowned lawyer!"

"That's funny, I've never heard of him before now."

"Trust me, Brooks would be a good interview for you indeed, but nobody interviews him. He's too busy, too important. He always wins his criminal cases, and he recently won one of those big intimate domain cases."

"Intimate domain?" said Sandy with a slight giggle.

"I think he means eminent domain," whispered Bret.

"Yeah, I think so," said Sandy under her breath while she smiled at Skip.

"Yep. If a reporter were to get to him, why, that in itself would be a coup to be proud of," continued Skip.

"You must know how to get in touch with this Brooks guy, or, you wouldn't build him up so much."

Oops, must have overplayed my hand, thought Skip. *Better recoup fast.*

"Well, you have come to the right place. As a matter of fact, John owes me a favor or two. If you want to see him, I could probably get you in right now. You would be the first interview about this case. Follow me. We're just a block away."

Sandy looked at Bret, who shrugged, picked up his camera and said,

41

"Let's see where he takes us."

"I thought you said he was a busy lawyer. Is he going to see us with no notice at all?"

"Don't worry. I told you we are good friends and he owes me. He will be so glad to see me that he will drop whatever he is doing and bring us right into the inner-sanctum. Trust me."

While they walked down the street, Skip never stopped talking. Sandy and Bret were pleasantly surprised when, after walking less than a block, they were at the law office of Brooks and Bradley. The sign indicated the office was upstairs at a two-story building. They looked at each other, smiled, shrugged, and followed Skip up the stairs and through the door into the office.

"At least he knows where the office is," whispered Bret.

Karen looked up from her computer as Skip entered. Just before the others followed him into the room, she said, "Skip. I'll let John know you are here. I'm certain he can see you now."

She buzzed John's office.

Skip looked over his shoulder and, with a big grin, said, "See, I told ya."

"Skip, you can go right in. Are these people with you?"

She noticed the remarkably good looking woman, and felt a little uneasy. She didn't even notice the man with the camera until everyone started moving through John's door. Realizing that something wasn't right, she rose from her chair and quickly moved around the desk while she called out, "Jackson. Come here now!"

Jackson was so startled by Karen's urgent tone that he launched himself from behind his desk into the lobby, banging his knee on his desk in route. As Jackson limped into the lobby, Skip entered John's office and John rose to greet him. As always, he was astounded at Skip's attire, but this time, something even more remarkable occurred. Skip brought with him the most beautiful woman John had ever laid eyes on. Sandy hair. High cheek bones. An elegant nose. Striking blue eyes. A full complement of feminine curves. And legs that seemed to reach to the first floor.

"John, let me introduce you to my new friend . . . uh . . . Ms. . . . uh."

"Storm—Sandy Storm," said Sandy as she stretched out a long, tan, thin, yet muscular arm and gave John a firm handshake.

"Peas, have a sleet," said John in a slightly squeaky voice. He coughed self-consciously, cleared his throat and sat, almost missing his chair. He was off balance as he fell rather heavily into the chair, causing it to roll backwards. Embarrassed that his voice had squeaked at an

42

inopportune moment, he tried to make up for it by deepening his voice slightly.

"What can I . . . ah . . . . why are you . . .ah . . .?"

His mind had failed him. He was momentarily under a spell. His surging male hormones interrupted his thoughts, and all he could think to do was to stare at her. She settled into what had always been a plain wooden chair. But now, somehow that chair looked as though it had been made to accept her form. It was as though it had been made for her, and the chair knew it. The air around her was electric. Fresher. The room seemed more elegant. Her eyes peered into his. He became lost in her eyes.

Karen rushed to John's side and whispered in his ear. At first, John paid no attention to Karen. Indeed, he didn't realize she was there. He became aware of a familiar voice whispering his name, "John! John! What are these people doing here? Why is this cameraman here? Who are they? Close your mouth. You're gawking."

Sandy Storm absorbed the scene and thought John was an attractive young man, but, like many men, saw only her good looks. *Men never see me for who I am,* she thought as she watched with interest the interchange between Karen and John.

John finally realized that Karen was speaking to him, and the spell cast by Sandy Storm was broken. Karen took a defense position between John and the intruders as though she was ready to fight them off. Her brow was furrowed and her hands were on her hips. She looked angry. Then John noticed the cameraman filming everything and his brain seemed to return to his body.

"Thank you, Karen," he said. "I can take it from here."

Bret captured everything with his camera. In his viewfinder he saw Karen look down at John, then look at Sandy with squinty eyes. Then Karen slowly walked out of the camera view.

"Skip—why is this cameraman filming our interview?" asked John.

"Well, John, that's what famous national reporters for CTN do, they film their interviews."

"Why would CTN be interested in our interview?"

"We are not here to film your interview with Skip, though I am certain that our viewers would find it to be most interesting," said Sandy. "We are here to interview you."

"Pardon?"

"I understand you are representing the Butcher of Belhaven, and I wanted to know what the theory of your defense will be."

In every life there are pivotal moments, points in time when multiple possible futures intersect. Sometimes we realize the moment is upon us

43

and we recognize a Rubicon before us. We cross and risk all, or we stay on the safe side of the river; however, most of the time we have no idea how our decision will impact our future. John knew that he was taking a risk with his response, but he had no idea that his response would change his life. From this moment, nothing would be the same. He considered the enormous amount of bad publicity Hal Boyd had already received. The police and prosecution were already tainting the potential jury pool with strategic press releases. He thought that this might be an opportunity to change the tone for the better. He was right about changing the tone, but nothing could prepare him for what was about to happen.

"I don't accept the moniker you used. His name is Hal. As for the man in the front yard, self-defense applies. Hal was assaulted and the other man pulled a gun on Hal. After a struggle, Hal was able to wrestle the gun from him and defend himself. Two of the people in the house were killed by the third person in the house, not by Hal."

"Really, and what is the defense that you will use for the last victim, the one that you just admitted that your client killed?"

Sandy was proud that she had caught this neophyte in a possible error.

"Insanity."

Jackson's eyes opened wide as he wondered whether this interview was going too far.

"Well, that's not very original."

"Well, actually, it is a very rare defense."

"And it is rarely successful, wouldn't you say?"

"Yes."

"Juries don't like the insanity defense do they?"

"That is true."

This guy gives direct answers, thought Sandy. *I think I can corner him and put him away.* She asked, "Why do you think your insanity defense will be successful when so many have failed?"

"Hal Boyd honestly believed that the homicide he committed was necessary, justified and excusable."

"What do you mean by that?"

"He believed that he was killing a vampire."

Storm sat in stunned silence for several seconds. "Bret, did you get that?"

"I got it and we're still hot."

Sandy cleared her throat. "Surely, you jest?"

"No."

"Are you saying that the victim, or one of them, was a vampire?"

"No, I am saying that Hal Boyd was suffering from such a powerful

44

delusion that he honestly believed that his intended victim was a vampire who had to be stopped in order to save other people."

"Perhaps you could explain to our viewers how you think this insanity defense will operate to your client's advantage."

"Mississippi has one of the most conservative and difficult to prove insanity defenses in the common law world."

"So, it is harder to prove insanity as a defense here than in many other places?"

"That's right."

"And has a Vampire Defense succeeded anywhere else?"

"Not to my knowledge."

"So how will this outlandish, no, I'm sorry, unusual defense succeed here, when it has never succeeded anywhere else?"

"Well, I am not prepared to say that the defense has never succeeded. What I am prepared to say is that Mississippi recognizes the very strict McNaughten Rule of insanity. Our criminal laws are designed to punish criminal intent. That is why most accidental homicides are not considered crimes. The McNaughten Rule focuses on the Defendant's ability to form the intent to commit a crime. It operates in two instances to excuse criminal behavior because of a lack of criminal intent. The first instance can be simply stated as follows: if a person is so crazy that they don't know what they are doing, they have not formed the intent to commit a crime, and they are therefore not criminally responsible for their actions. The person would be placed in a proper institution for treatment, but that person would not be considered a criminal."

"That would not be the case here since Boyd apparently knew he was trying to kill a vampire," observed Storm.

"Exactly right. He does not fit the first instance."

"What is the second instance, the one that you say makes Boyd's homicides excusable?"

"The second instance under the McNaughten Rule is that a person is suffering from such a powerful disease, mental illness or delusion that he does not know that what he is doing is wrong."

"Really? So, you are saying that Boyd did not know that it was wrong to kill those people?"

"We are talking about two homicides right now. The first was in self-defense. As for the second, Boyd did not know that it was wrong to kill a vampire. Indeed, he believed that it was not only right, but necessary to kill what he honestly believed was a vampire."

"Well, that about wraps it up for now," said Storm, almost gleefully. She could hardly wait to send her story upstream. She knew that her ticket to the big time had just been punched. "If I have some follow-up questions is it alright if I give you a call?"

"Certainly."

Sandy Storm and Bret said their goodbyes and excused themselves.

11

Karen, Jackson, and Skip were too stunned to move or to speak for several moments. Karen was the first to respond. She shook her head, and said, "John, you have really opened Pandora's box. I don't know if you should have done that."

"That was great!" shouted Skip. "I think we're going to be rich and famous!"

"We?" queried Karen. "How did you become part of this?"

"I brought us the publicity. Let's face it. With publicity like this, there is no telling how far we can go. John, all you need is a skilled advisor like me, and the sky is the limit. Karen, if y'all stick with me, I'll have you wearing diamonds in no time."

"Skip, I am dealing with Hal's life," said John. "His life is not a get-rich-quick scheme."

"That's exactly why we will go far, because you are sincere and you've got the skills and the talent to give the vampire slayer the best possible defense. While you, Jackson and Karen are busy working the case, I can work the publicity angles; we will all become household names."

"Sorry, Skip, but I am not interested."

"Interested or not," said Jackson, "I think that your life just changed. This is going to be big. But, Skip, I just don't see this working out between us. John is just not your kind of guy."

"Yeah, well, not everyone can be as stylish and as flashy as me. But, John, I could teach you."

"That's okay, Skip. I appreciate your offer, but I believe that I will pass for now. If I need your help, I will call you. Now, as for your case, do you think this is something that we could talk about next week? I really have a lot on my plate this week."

"Yeah, sure." Skip looked dejected. Then with a pleading look, he said, "John, hear me out. I have always been a wannabe. I've always been on the outside looking in. I always wanted to be part of something big, but I can never get there. This is big. I want to be part of it. Let me help. I'll take any role. I'll get the coffee. I'll be your runner. I will look for witnesses. This excites me. What if we could prove that this guy was McDonalds insane? You said that was rare, right? If we win, we will be the best-known law firm in the country. No, in the world!"

"It's McNaughten, not McDonalds," said Jackson.

"Yeah, whatever. Same difference. It's not my job to know the law. I just want to help any way that I can. Let me be a part of this. I will be doing something useful for the first time in my life. I have missed out on everything. Every time that I should have turned right I turned left. I have always just missed the big one. Now, finally, I stumbled into the beginning of the next really big one, and for once I can see which way to turn. Please, don't let me miss out on this. I won't let you down. I promise."

There was a long pause, while John looked squarely into Skip's eyes trying to measure him. The fact that John did not immediately tell Skip no indicated to Jackson that John just might give in.

"We have to keep secrets here," said Jackson. "We don't reveal what we have learned to anyone, unless the client and John authorize it. I don't think that you can keep a secret."

"My mouth is like a steel trap. Nothing gets out without prior approval. Nobody can keep a secret like me."

"By the way, John, did Hal authorize you to make the statement you just made?" asked Karen.

"Yes, although he didn't like the idea of an insanity plea, he accepted my advice and agreed that I could go that route if I felt it was appropriate. I didn't think the opportunity would happen so quickly, but with all of the negative publicity released by the police and the prosecutor, I thought getting our view out was necessary."

"Do you think you went too far?" asked Jackson.

"We can assert our client's position on the allegations and the basis of the defense. I hope I didn't go beyond that. Now we've got work to do. Jackson, will you gather all of the case law you can find on the McNaughten defense? Give me a skinny on it as soon as you can. Tomorrow morning wouldn't be too soon. While you're at it, take a look at the publicity rules. We have never had to deal with publicity before this bomb was dropped on us. We have two cases to win. Two dragons to slay, if you will. We have to overcome the legal charge. That is the big dragon to slay; but, we must also overcome the negative publicity. That is the other dragon. If we don't slay that dragon or at least neutralize it, we won't be able to handle the big one. Negative publicity can poison the potential jury base and make it next to impossible to win this case. I want you to research the various ways we can get our position out to the public so that the public doesn't pre-judge Boyd without violating the rules and the law."

"That's where I come in," said Skip with evident excitement.

"No, Skip. That is first and foremost a legal question. Jackson will figure that out for us."

48

"Karen, I need for you to identify each potential witness or information source identified in the documents produced today by the police. We will need to create a 'Cast of Characters' like we've done in other cases and compile everything we can find on each potential witness. I like the way you used three ring binders for witness notebooks in the Evans matter. We will need that here. Jackson, we need the same for the law. We want indexed and tabbed notebooks on legal issues so that we can quickly find the law."

"What about me?" asked Skip.

Karen looked at John and shook her head no. John glanced at Jackson, who mouthed the word no.

"Skip, do you know how to research news stories?"

"Sure," lied Skip.

"Karen, please make a list of the dates and places where each homicide occurred along with the victims' names. Give a copy of that to Skip."

"Oookaaay," said Karen, reluctantly.

"Skip, go to the library and find every article you can on any of the previous homicides. If there are any witnesses or persons with information, get their identities. Find out how to get in touch with them. Don't contact them. Bring that information to Jackson, along with all of the newspaper articles."

"And what will you be doing while the rest of us do your bidding, Mr. Hot Shot—storm chasing?" asked Karen.

"Ooooh," said Jackson and Skip.

"I have no interest in Ms. Storm."

"That's the first time that I have ever heard you lie," said Karen. "This crush you have for her must be more serious than I thought."

There was tremendous tension in the air. John was perplexed by the sudden change in the atmosphere.

"I plan to contact Doctor Webster to arrange psychological and psychiatric evaluations, interviews and treatment, re-read the police report, study Jackson's summary of the law, and continue with the interviews of our client. Ms. Storm will not cross my mind."

Posed with her hand on her hip and using an affected, overly feminine voice, Karen asked, "If I have any follow up questions can I give you a call?"

"Certainly."

John picked up the phone to call Dr. Webster. Everyone else remained in the room avoiding Karen's eyes. "Well. Don't ya'll have something to be doing?"

When Jackson, Skip, and Karen stepped into the lobby, Karen

49

grabbed Skip by the arm and whirled him around. She looked down at him, with her face just inches from his.

"Skip, I hope you realize that a really good man has just placed a lot of trust in you. If you do anything to let him down, and I mean anything, I want you to know that I will personally make you about six inches shorter than you already are; and when I'm done, your voice will be several octaves higher. Do you understand me?"

Skip gulped and said, "Ah, yes, ma'am."

Karen stormed away, her red hair flouncing, leaving Jackson and Skip staring after her.

"Wow! She sure is sexy when she gets mad," said Skip.

"There may be more to her expression of anger than meets the eye, Skip. My advice to you is to do what she says, because I believe she will do you harm if you harm John. And by the way, so will I."

*   *   *

Ms. Storm's next stop was at the office of the District Attorney. Buddy Tellers was comfortable in front of a camera. It was clear that he was experienced in dealing with the press, and he relished the idea that his interview would be televised nationwide and maybe worldwide. He used strong, expressive words that Storm knew would make good headlines.

Within hours all of the networks were broadcasting portions of Sandy's interviews, and headlines appeared around the country: "Defense Theory Ridiculous!" "No Hope of Success With Vampire Defense." "Defense Attorney Looking for Headlines at Expense of Client." "Brooks Trying to Play the Court and Public for a Fool, Says District Attorney."

Tellers gave her the name of her next interviewee, Dr. Curtis Bishop, Professor of Psychology and Philosophy at the recently opened branch of Tulane University in Madison, Mississippi. Professor Bishop greeted Sandy and Bret warmly and led them into his cluttered office. Professor Bishop was dressed in a tweed jacket, blue shirt and yellow tie. His wire rim glasses set off eyes that were wide apart. Sandy had heard that his classes were very popular because of the wide range of unusual subjects he was willing to discuss.

"Well, Ms. Storm, you have taken this town by storm," laughed Professor Bishop. "I have already seen your interviews with Mr. Tellers and with Mr. Brooks. Boyd certainly has a colorful defense team, with Mr. Brooks' interesting theory and his clownishly dressed assistant. The only worthy member of the defense team seemed to be that attractive red-headed assistant, what was her name? It looked as though she was ready to stand by her man and fight. At least she was loyal, however

50

misplaced that loyalty might be."

"Karen Wilkes, I believe." She eyed his bookshelves. "I see you have a number of books on para-psychology, the occult, religious cults and even flying saucers."

"Yes, I find that those subjects are great discussion starters in class. They lubricate young minds and expand the thought processes so that my students can begin thinking creatively. We sometimes take field trips to supposedly haunted places. It keeps the class interested and provokes discussion on the psychological process that may be involved in such legends."

"So, are you a believer in those phenomenon?"

"I am glad you used the word phenomenon. I think that the real phenomenon is the degree to which some of these legends take hold and are believed by members of the public. I think that it would make an interesting study to determine why some legends persist through the ages in spite of the advancement of modern science."

Sandy noted that he had not answered her question. "I understand you study some of these phenomenon?"

"Why, yes, I find it to be a stimulating avocation. I enjoy debunking ghost stories, magic tricks, and UFO stories. I have published a few articles on the subject and I am working on a book even as we speak. I have been offering a $25,000 reward for any supposed paranormal activity or phenomenon that I am unable to debunk."

"Have you ever had to pay the reward?"

"Not as yet. I also enjoy debating religious zealots. I like to study them to see what makes them think the way they do. I believe that religious zealotry can sometimes be associated with mental illness."

"I take it that you are not a believer?"

"Oh, I am a believer, just not in the way most people believe, especially here in the Bible belt. I don't believe in traditional religion. I believe in the advancement of science and mankind instead. It has been said that religion is the opiate of the masses and the last refuge of scoundrels."

"Why do you think that vampire stories are so fascinating to people, even today?"

"We are fascinated by the possibility that one day a new creature will evolve out of the human race that will be a sort of super-human. We believe that we are at the top of the food chain. One day something will evolve that will surpass us. It may look entirely different from us, or it may evolve from us and look like us. When that happens, the new creature will be a sort of super-man of extraordinary intelligence and strength against whom we will have no defense. The vampire story that

51

has been passed on to us is the story of such a man, evolved somehow from us. He bears our likeness, yet has powers against which we are helpless. He feeds upon us like we feed upon cattle. Thus, in our psyche, we have a love-hate, fear-awe relationship with the concept of the vampire. In some respects, we worship him as a god, yet we want to destroy him because we want to halt evolution before evolution destroys us."

Professor Bishop paused. To Sandy, his eyes seemed to be focused on some far away point. Then, he turned to her, looked into her eyes, smiled and said, "At least, that is how some theorists explain our fascination with vampires."

"That's very interesting professor. Thank you for that explanation. What do you think of the Vampire Defense raised by John Brooks on behalf of his client Hal Boyd?"

A sly smile eased across the face of Professor Bishop. "You get right to the point. So will I. I think it is outlandish grandstanding by the attorney. There is absolutely no chance that defense can succeed. I believe that from a psychological standpoint the announcement of the defense tells us more about the attorney than it does about his client."

"You have really unloaded on the attorney!"

"On the contrary, I believe that I have shown incredible restraint. For now, I think that I should keep the rest of my assessment of the lawyer to myself."

"Why does the defense have no chance of success?"

Professor Bishop laughed, then looked at Sandy Storm and said, "Forgive me for my outburst. I realize that you are just doing your job, and you have to ask certain questions for the sake of the public even if the answer is as obvious to any normal thinking person as is your beauty."

"Well, professor, thank you, but would you go ahead and tell our viewers the obvious, please?"

"Of course. Please forgive my momentary lapse. You see I have to deal with unusual stories that are invented for the purpose of claiming an insanity defense. Some are really very clever. This one is infantile. McNaughten insane is not a recognized psychological disorder. It is a mere legal fiction. The basis of the defense is that Boyd was so crazy that he did not know what he was doing; or, that he did not know that what he was doing was wrong. The basic facts known to the general public prove that the McNaughten legal fiction is not applicable to Mr. Boyd."

"How?"

"Clearly, Mr. Boyd knew what he was doing. He prepared himself in

52

advance to take the life of another human being. He raced his car through the neighborhood, fought with and killed one victim in the yard, then entered the house carrying weapons he had selected in advance for the purpose of taking a life. After he accomplished his murderous purpose, he left the house and confessed his crime to the first policeman he saw. All these actions demonstrate that this was a planned, premeditated murder. Clearly he knew what he was doing and knew the consequences of his actions. He even turned himself over to a policeman afterwards and confessed his wrongdoings. All these things disprove the McNaughten defense and we haven't even gotten to the biggest problem that the defense will encounter."

"And what is that biggest problem?"

"There is no such thing as a vampire. It is preposterous beyond belief that anyone this day in time would believe someone was a vampire. Even if Boyd did believe his victim was a vampire, that belief does not justify the murder of the supposed vampire. This is clearly a contrived last minute defense, invented without much forethought."

"Thank you, Dr. Bishop."

"My pleasure. Speaking of pleasure, I would very much like to show you around our little town one evening while you are here."

"You get right to the point, don't you Doctor?"

"Indeed."

"I will think about it. Thank you."

"Until next time then."

12

The office became a hub of activity. Karen dissected the police reports while Jackson glued himself to the computer research program. When Jackson applied himself he was an excellent researcher. In no time he was keyed into the law on the insanity defense and on pre-trial publicity. Skip went to the Eudora Welty Library, located downtown in the old Sears department store building. To Skip, the place was eerily quiet. After spending a few minutes wandering around wondering where to begin, he approached one of the librarians.

"Excuse me, Miss . . . ah, I wonder if you could help me find newspaper articles from around the country about a particular subject?"

"I will be glad to help you if I can. What subject?"

"Well, I am working on a really big legal case," explained Skip, "and I want to look at stories about similar crimes around the country."

"You're not working on that vampire case are you?"

"What, you've heard about that already?"

"Oh yes! Everybody has been talking about it. We were all glued to the TV during our break, watching that beautiful reporter, Ms Storm, talking about the case of the century in Jackson, Mississippi. Once we realized that she was talking about our town, we have been taking turns watching the news non-stop and telling each other about the latest developments. Imagine that someone is claiming to have killed a vampire right here in Jackson. That will make a great novel one-day. Of course, right now, it seems that the news media is making fun of our local lawyer, Mr. Brooks, for coming up with what they say is a ridiculous defense. Not only that, they are making fun of 'Mississippi lawyers' and 'Mississippi justice' and 'back woods Mississippians' in general. The newscasters and anchors sort of smirk and laugh and act like anything having to do with Mississippi is a joke. I sure hope Mr. Brooks doesn't embarrass us. We Mississippians have been embarrassed too many times. The good stories are never told and the bad stories are never forgotten."

Skip leaned over the counter, looked around in a conspiratorial fashion, and said, "I am working for Mr. Brooks. I can tell you from firsthand knowledge that he is a great lawyer, one of the best in the country."

"You are working for Mr. Brooks?" asked the librarian skeptically as she placed both hands over her heart.

"Indeed I am. And besides being a great lawyer, he is the most honest person I know. He has an unimpeccable reputation."

The librarian looked at Skip with puzzlement, then smiled. "Unimpeachable. You mean Unimpeachable."

"Yeah, right. I can't believe they would say such things about our John Brooks. And they say the defense is ridiculous. I will have you know that I have it on inside information that the victim really was a vampire."

"No way!"

"Way. At least he thought he was. If I'm not telling the truth, then my name's not Skip."

"Oh, my, the girls will be really excited to hear this. How can I help you Mr. Skip?"

"Great! Now, what is your name?"

"Clare."

"What is that short for?"

"Clarion."

"Well, Ms. Clarion, the librarian, I need to find articles about crimes like this one. I have a list of cities where similar crimes occurred."

"Do you have dates?"

"Is my name Skip?" he asked with a wink.

Clarion giggled.

"You bet I do," said Skip as he slid his list across the counter.

"Oh, this is so exciting! Would you mind if the girls and I help you with your research project?"

Skip could not believe his luck. "Well I hate to impose, but that would be a tremendous help. This is, after all, the case of the century. And we don't want the media making fun of our people, now, do we? It really is an issue of us versus them, you know."

"Oh, we certainly would not want them to continue making fun of us. It will be no trouble at all for us to tackle this research project. We could do a lot of it while we work, and with something as interesting as this, most of us would be willing to stay after hours."

"Wow, that is awesome! You and your co-workers will officially become part of the best legal defense team ever assembled."

"Wow, what an honor! Let me introduce you to your new research team."

Clarion led Skip behind the counter and introduced him to three ladies, all of whom were experienced researchers. In no time they bought into the project. Skip settled into a desk and was soon inundated with stories about similar murders in cities across America. After a few hours Skip's head was swimming from reading so many stories and the facts started blending together. He checked his watch and remembered that he had arranged a meeting tonight at Bobby's Trading Post for Jackson and John. He thought that he could use that as an excuse to get away from reading so much until tomorrow when maybe his head would clear and he could pay better attention to the details. So, he began excusing himself.

"Ms. Clarion, I have to go to a meeting with the defense team. I wonder if we could continue this tomorrow?"

"Why certainly. But, I thought you might be interested in this. We have observed that a mysterious person was mentioned in two of the articles so far. His name is Michael McCarty, formerly known as Father McCarty, who was defrocked by the Catholic Church. He was seen near the scene of similar crimes on at least two occasions. Would you like for us to find out more about him?"

"Indeed! Please do."

"All right. If I find anything interesting, I'll give you a call."

"Thanks!"

13

As if there wasn't enough to do already, John had an appointment to see a new client who wanted to meet at the little town of Goshen Springs, located on the Pearl River Reservoir about 20 miles northeast of Jackson. At least the appointment was after hours, so John wouldn't be missing too many calls and work opportunities. Getting a new big case, which might be a career case, was all well and good, but the bills still had to be paid. If he and Jackson were going to keep the office doors open, then they had to find paying cases. As John was leaving the office, Jackson said, "Wait up! If you're going to Goshen Springs, I'm coming with you."

"Sure, come on. How is the research going?"

"Good. I already had a bunch of cites from research I did in school, so it was pretty easy to update. I'll have it all organized in a notebook, indexed and tabbed like you like it, before lunch tomorrow."

"Way to go Jackson."

As they reached John's vehicle, an aging Isuzu Trooper, Jackson pointed toward a trio of gothic clad youths, two guys and a girl with black and purple hair, in the corner of the parking lot.

"Have you noticed your new fans, John?"

"What do you mean?" asked John as he glanced at the youths pointed out by Jackson and watched them climb into an old black Honda.

"They are watching every move you make, John. I've seen them around ever since news began breaking about our new case. They aren't the only ones. There are others all around."

"Huh. I guess they don't have much to do."

Then John noticed a note under his windshield wiper.

"What's this?" he said as he opened the note and read it aloud: **"You are in danger. Forces that you cannot imagine are working against you. Save yourself. Drop the Boyd case."**

"That's pretty melodramatic," said Jackson.

"You're right. I think I need to have a talk with our friends in the Honda," said John as he started walking toward the black car. He saw the girl gesturing towards him and the car drove away. The car was too far away for John to read the license plate number.

"Not very talkative, are they?"

"I guess not. Well, we've got an appointment so let's get going.

Why are you so interested in Goshen Springs anyway?"

"I've always wanted to be there after dark so I could hear the Ghost of Goshen Springs calling, 'Penny! Penny! My precious Penny.'"

"I bet our tattooed friends would love to hear that voice, too. The fact is this is just another one of those occasions when you will come home disappointed. There is no such voice."

"This time, you're wrong, John. This is for real. I know lots of people who have heard Goren Goshen calling in the night."

"They are either lying to you, or they have a vivid imagination and construed ordinary night sounds to be something supernatural."

"A non-believer now, but what will you believe when you hear the haunting sounds of Goren calling his beloved?"

* * *

Ted Lively wanted to meet at Bobby's Trading Post, an old country store near the lakeshore. The store was filled with fishing supplies and to the right of the cash register was a small restaurant with a few tables. Hamburgers were the specialty of the house. Ted was waiting at one of the tables with a cooler sitting at his feet. After the usual handshakes and greetings, John and Jackson settled into seats at the table and looked at the menu on the wall.

"The catfish po-boy is good, and so are the burgers," said Ted.

"I bet," said Jackson. "We might as well order."

"Ok, I'll try the catfish po-boy. But, I suspect that you didn't ask us here for supper. What's in the cooler?"

"Good call, John," said Ted as he reached into the cooler and pulled out three do-it-yourself beer bottles, with old-fashioned clamp down corks. "Bobby knows I'm bringing my own beer. It's okay. Bobby wants to be the first to sell it."

Just then, Skip the Middleman walked through the door. As soon as his eyes found John, Jackson and Ted, he hurried over.

"What are you doing here, Skip?" asked Jackson. "Aren't you supposed to be at the library?"

"Yeah. I found some great stuff that you will want to see, but I heard about Ted's new brew and I told him he should give you guys a call before he tries to sell it. Besides, I am waiting on a phone call to follow up with a great lead."

"Sell it?" said Jackson. "I had no idea you were brewing your own beer."

"Yeah, I will tell you more about that later. First, just try it. See what you think."

Ted handed another bottle to Skip. The corks popped almost like champagne and generous golden brown foam refused to stay in the

58

bottle. Instantly, a sweet, nutty aroma filled the room.

"Wow, smells good—let's give it the true test," said Jackson as he lifted the bottle to his lips.

After a first sip, he took a deep draw. "Man, that's good! I've never tasted a beer as rich and flavorful as this. No bitter taste, smooth, delicious. Of course, some people want their beer to be bitter, but this is really smooth and tasty."

John tasted the beer and agreed. "I think this is the best beer I've ever tasted. Good job Ted!"

"Thanks. Do you think it will sell?"

"If you can repeat this flavor on a consistent basis, I think you've got a winner."

"That's what I thought. I want your help protecting the recipe and marketing the beer."

"Ted, we don't know anything about marketing. I don't know much about copyrighting or patenting a recipe, but we can figure that out and help you."

Ted looked at Skip, then back at John.

"I think you can help me with marketing, too. I will let you in on the ground floor if you will help me now."

John and Jackson looked at each other and shrugged. "Let's talk about it. What do you have in mind?"

"No, before we get to that, tell us about your brewing experience," said John. "How did you create this recipe?"

"I didn't create it, I discovered it."

"Are we playing semantics?" asked Jackson.

"No, that's the best word for it."

"What do you mean?"

"I love this part of the story," said Skip.

"I found it."

"Found it? Now, that could be a problem. We probably won't be able to help you get legal protection for someone else's recipe."

"Even if they've been dead for two hundred years?"

John and Jackson looked at each other, first in puzzlement; then a realization struck them both at the same time. "Naw, no way. You're not claiming that you found Goren Goshen's beer recipe," exclaimed Jackson.

"Exactly!" said Ted.

"Wait. I'm not falling for this. You guys are trying to set me up for some elaborate joke. Jackson was talking some nonsense about the Ghost of Goshen Springs on the way up here. Now you claim to have found a beer recipe made by a ghost! I'm not biting. At least I'm not biting anything except this catfish po-boy."

Bobby, the owner of the store, took a seat at the table. "You've got to listen to this one, John," said Bobby. "It's a whopper."

"I love this story," said Skip.

"Well, you've got my attention at least while I eat this sandwich," said John.

"And drink your beer," said Jackson.

"Okay—I actually found the recipe to the most famous beer on the old Natchez Trace," said Ted breathlessly. "People used to come from Tennessee and New Orleans to buy barrels of this beer. Back then it was believed to be the best beer in America! Maybe the best beer ever made!"

"Ted, you've got to be kidding," said Jackson.

"No, I'm not! You tasted the beer. Don't you agree it's the best beer you ever tasted?"

John and Jackson looked at each other, and then back at Ted. They each took another swill of the rich, dark beer. John swirled the beer around his mouth and slowly swallowed, reluctant to let the nutty, not quite sweet taste leave his mouth.

"Ted, you're right about the taste of this beer. It's really good. Okay, I'm going to fall for your trick. Tell me the story."

"John, it's not a trick," injected Skip. "This is the real deal."

"Well, then I'm convinced," said Jackson sarcastically.

"That's right," laughed Bobby, exuding as much enthusiasm as Ted and Skip. "This is the real deal."

"I love this story," said Skip.

"For years I had heard the tale of the Ghost of Goshen Springs," said Ted. "You've heard it, too, haven't you?"

"Yeah, Jackson was telling me on the way up here about Goren Goshen calling his beloved Penny. He claims that lots of locals have been spooked by strange noises at night that sound to them like Goren calling Penny's name."

"Yeah, that's part of the legend. What you probably didn't realize is that Goren Goshen was a real person. Back in the early 19th century, Goren was a young man of limited means in Ireland, madly in love with Penny, a beautiful redhead from a well-to-do family. Her father would not permit her to have anything to do with Goren because he doubted Goren's ability to provide for his daughter. Still, they found opportunities to be together.

"Back then, lots of young Irishmen were seeking their fortune in America; so Goren decided to come to America, earn his fortune and after he was rich, return home to Penny. It was a hard decision and both of them hated the thought of being apart for so long. Goren and Penny met near the docks and said their tearful goodbyes. They promised to write each other, and Goren promised to return and marry her.

"He worked on the boat to pay for part of his passage and took a number of jobs as he worked his way across this big, young country. It is said that he had many adventures, including encounters with bandits and Indians, and that he hunted with Davy Crockett, before Crockett died at the Alamo."

"Wait a minute," interrupted John. "The organic fertilizer is getting a little too deep for me. I'm not so sure the timing could be right for all of that. Next you'll be telling me he had a bar fight with Jim Bowie."

"Actually, it was a knife throwing contest, but just hold on, I'm just giving you the background. Goren's grandfather had been a brew-master in Ireland. As a youth, Goren worked in the brewery and learned the trade from his grandfather; but the old man died and there was no place at the brewery for Goren.

"Later, as he was traveling through the Mississippi Territory along the Natchez Trace, which followed the course of the Pearl River, he came upon a cotton ferry that crossed the river. In a beautiful meadow in the forest, he found a clear brook fed by a natural spring. Nearby was good land, suitable for growing grain. The land could be had for a song. The river and the Natchez Trace provided easy transportation. Mississippi was a new state and the new state capitol was being built a few miles to the south along the Trace and next to the Pearl River. A plan began to hatch in Goren's mind. He knew there were lots of thirsty travelers on the Trace and soon there would be lots of thirsty state legislators needing a fine brew to wet their palates and loosen their tongues. As far as he knew there were no breweries around.

"So, Goren went to work. Early on, he decided that if he was going to do this, he would do it right, because he was doing it for Penny. And, Penny deserved the best. It wasn't long before he was brewing a pretty good beer. He grew his own grain at first. He opened a tavern on the Trace and started a wagon company, hauling his beer to Natchez and Nashville. When he delivered his beer, he filled the empty wagon with goods and hauled for hire. Before long he was operating a virtual trucking company. All the while he wrote to Penny about his love for her. It was said that he wrote a mountain of letters.

"He brewed different beers, depending on the season and the available grain. His business grew and he needed more grain, so the local farmers began growing grains at his request. A little community developed around the brewery, the tavern and the wagon company, and the area became known as Goshen Springs. He constantly experimented with his recipe, looking for the perfect beer. Then he hit upon this recipe. The recipe for the beer you are drinking now, the world famous Goshen Springs Beer."

"Come on, how do you know this is it?" asked Jackson.

"The pay-off for your patience will be great. Just hold on my friend. Now, where was I? Oh, yeah. He was already successful, but once people tasted this beer they didn't want any other. This became the most popular beer in the pre-Texas west. It was in demand everywhere from Nashville to Natchez to New Orleans. From New Orleans, it was shipped to ports in the Caribbean and the East Coast. It is said that some even made it back to Ireland.

"He demanded top dollar for his beer. He honed and refined the recipe and really began making money. He knew it was finally time to return to Penny.

"Up until then, he had been putting his money into his business trying to make it grow. Now, he was making real money. He had been gone only five years, but it seemed like forever to him. He didn't know how it was possible, but he felt that his love for Penny was even greater than when he had left Ireland. Five years is a long time to wait for a woman."

"I'll say," said Jackson.

"You ain't kidding," added Bobby.

"And let me tell you, he was a dashing, handsome young fellow, and many a woman came calling, but he was always true to Penny. He had eyes only for her. He called her his soul mate. They were born for each other. A match made in heaven. So, he thought."

Skip interrupted and said, "Yeah, considering the ghost story, it may have been a match made in . . ."

"Don't get ahead of the story, Skip," said Ted.

"At first, he did not know if he would bring her here to this wild new land or return to live in Ireland. He knew that she loved her home and her family, and he knew he would enjoy returning as a wealthy man, especially since he had been looked down upon by her father and others. So, he put the word that he was willing to sell everything, including the wagon company, the farm, the tavern, the brewery and even the recipe. He would trade it all for the one treasure that mattered, Penny.

"Once the word got out that the recipe for Goshen Springs Beer was available, it was almost like a gold rush. Offers poured in from every corner of the country. He had many offers of partnership and offers to run the place while he returned to Ireland to get Penny, but Goren was looking for the right deal with the right person.

"The mail carrier brought many an offer in those days and the tavern was a regular stop for him. One day he arrived with a special delivery addressed to Goren Goshen. As was his usual practice, he went straight to the bar to quench his thirst with the best beer in the land, compliments of the house, before he made his delivery. On this day, events transpired that caused him to momentarily forget his mission.

"Right behind him a small party on fine mounts with expensive saddles and quality traveling clothes arrived. There were five of them. One was a tall Indian with dark hair and an inscrutable expression. Two burly men with military bearing, well armed and watchful and two distinguished looking men, one with long graying hair, made up the rest of the group. They entered the tavern with an air of authority and command. The tavern grew quiet. All that could be heard was the clumping of their boots and the rustle of their riding clothes as they approached the bar.

"'We would like to see Mr. Goren Goshen,' said one of the men in a commanding voice to the bartender. The mention of Goren's name caused the postman to remember his delivery. He looked down at his mail pouch, fingering the cover.

"'Who should I say is asking?'"

"'Andrew Jackson, and my friend Andrew Fabber.'"

"Hold it! This is too much. Ted, we didn't come out here to hear fairy tales," John said, exasperated. "President Jackson and the brewer of New Orleans' own famous beer have worked their way into our story. This is just too much."

"I'm not kidding. This is real. Have another beer and just hear me out. I promise it will be worth your while."

"Yeah, let's hear him out," exclaimed Jackson with a rising voice.

Bobby sat on the edge of his seat and Skip said, "Yeah, I love this part of the story."

Ted resumed his story telling. "You can imagine the stir it caused when the people in the tavern learned that the famous general who saved New Orleans was present. All the tables were taken, but everyone got up and offered their table to the general. He selected a table against the wall, halfway between the front and back doors.

"As the two Andrews settled at the table, the Indian slipped out the back door and jumped up on the roof to be a lookout. The two big burly men positioned themselves to watch the doors and the patrons of the tavern. Soon, Goren Goshen entered the room, and the General introduced himself and his companions.

"'Who's on my roof?' asked Goren.

"'That would be my Choctaw companion, Kewaah. Best man I've ever known, and best friend anyone could have. He is just making sure that everyone who enters this establishment is friendly, if you know what

63

I mean.'

"'Maybe I do," replied Goren in his Irish brogue. 'We've never had any trouble here, but then again, we've never had anyone as distinguished as yourself here either. What can I do for you?'

"'My good friend here, Mr. Fabber, is a brewer in New Orleans. He has many years of experience in the business and quite a significant investment. But his business has taken a bit of a hit lately because of some upstart in the hinterlands who fancies himself a master brewer. The rumor is that some young Irishman named Goren Goshen has hit upon the recipe for the best beer in America. Now, that seems a bit of a stretch. What are the odds that the best beer in America would be found in the back woods of this frontier territory? Being lovers of great beer, we decided we would go to the source and see for ourselves if this beer can be half as good as its reputation.'

"'Billy!" yelled Goren to the bartender. 'Tap a fresh barrel and bring a frothing round to this table. Then give the house a round on me. We're about to be tested. I wager we won't be found lacking.'

"A great shout went up throughout the tavern. The buoyant party mood persisted until Kewaah burst through the door, Bowie knife in one hand and rifle in the other. Everyone froze until the General laughed and said, 'It's a-okay, Kewaah. Everyone is just having a good time.'

" Kewaah grunted, looked around to satisfy himself that everything was indeed all right, and backed out of the door. He leaped like a cat onto the roof again. Everyone except Jackson let out a sigh of relief, and beer began to flow again. Jackson just chuckled and shook his head.

"The General took a deep, long draw from his frothy mug. Fabber did the same. They simultaneously wiped away their foam mustaches and exhaled with a loud, 'aahh.' Jackson turned to his companions at the table, and said, 'A-okay is a Choctaw word meaning everything is as good as it can be. It's a great word. I predict everyone will be using it someday.'

"He took another long draw from the mug. Then the future President of the United States stood and held out his arms to quiet the crowd. The tavern was full when he arrived, but the crowd had tripled since then.

"'Gentlemen, let me have your attention. I have something to say about this Goshen Springs Beer brewed by your good man, Goren Goshen. I must say I have been misled about the quality of this beer, and I am sorely disappointed in those who gave me false intelligence. And, as any Englishman who has ever been to New Orleans would tell you, it is not good to disappoint the General.'

"There was hearty laughter from all who were present, except Goren, who was feeling quite anxious.

64

"'I was told this is the best beer in America. That, my friends, is a vast...' he paused for several breaths, then continued, 'understatement. This is the best beer in the world! This must be the best beer ever brewed!'

"The standing room crowd erupted with great cheers and applause.

"'Be still my friends, or my good Indian friend and protector may misapprehend your honest joviality.' Again the crowd laughed. Jackson motioned for Goren to stand and announced to the crowd, 'A toast, to Goren Goshen, the greatest brew-master of all time and to his beer, which must be nectar from heaven! It is A-okay, indeed.'

"'Here, here!' shouted everyone as they downed their beer.

"Fabber then threw a pouch of coins on the bar and said, 'The next round is on me. Everyone drink up!'

"The postman was happy to get yet another free beer. His delivery seemed less and less important as he joined in the festivities.

"Jackson motioned for Goren and Fabber to sit. They pulled their chairs up close to one another so they could hear over the raucous crowd.

"'We hear that you want to sell your recipe,' said Fabber.

"'I want to sell everything. I'm bound for Ireland to marry the love of my life. I must go home a wealthy man to be accepted by her family. That's why I came here. That's my mission. You understand missions, General. Maybe mine isn't as impressive as saving a country. But, as for me, I would trade the whole world for my Penny.'

"'Who can say what is more valuable, a country, or a woman's heart,' said Jackson.

"'It depends upon the woman,' said Goren.

"'Indeed it does my friend. Before we get down to serious business, I have a powerful hunger after this long ride and this fine beer. Do you have any food to offer?'

"'Billy, set the table for a feast!' shouted Goren. In a flash a roasted turkey was placed on the table, steam still rising from the platter. The air filed with the aroma of dressing, fresh vegetables cooked with spices and salt pork, gravy and dressing.

"'Dig in, friends,' shouted Goren. 'When we are finished eating the turkey, then we can talk turkey!'

"'Talk turkey! Ha, I'll have to remember that one,' chortled the General. 'We will get down to business after we've had this fine meal.'

"'My stars!" said Fabber. ' What is in this dressing? It is fantastic'.

"'We used our beer instead of water. Makes a fine dressing doesn't it?'

"The postman, not wishing to interrupt Goren Goshen on such an auspicious occasion, decided to wait until after supper to deliver the mail. So, he ordered a meal and another beer and ate at the bar.

"Andrew Jackson, Andrew Fabber and Goren Goshen told extravagant tales of their adventures as they ate. By the time apple cobbler was served, the three men were best of friends. It was then that Fabber said, 'Tell you what. Instead of negotiating, I will offer you three times more than I thought would be my highest and best offer. And, I will sweeten it even more. You see, I think this business will be much better with you as a partner than without you. So, here it is. I'll pay your fare, first class, to Ireland. And, I'll pay for the biggest and best Irish wedding that green island has ever seen. If you return, I'll pay for both you and Penny to return first class, and we will be partners in the brewing business. If you stay in Ireland, I'll help finance a brewery there, and we will take both the American market and the European market by storm. But, I tell you the truth, I would rather have you close by.'

"'That's all very generous, Andy.'

"'Oh, wait. I'm not through. For the privilege of being your equal partner, I am prepared to pay a king's ransom. Seventy-five thousand dollars!'

"Silence fell upon the tavern. No one spoke. Goren's heart seemed to stop.

"'Is there so much money in the whole world?'

"'For you and Penny, there is that much and more my friend.'

"'I am flabbergasted!'

"Jackson let out another hearty laugh and slapped Goren on the back. 'Where do you come up with such words my friend? I don't know what it means, but it surely sounds appropriate for the circumstances. I guess I need to learn to speak Irish.'

"'This is everything I dreamed of. You just got yourself a partner! Billy, another round for everyone!'

"Everyone let out a shout for joy! The postman was so excited and inebriated that he tumbled off of his stool. His pouch slid across the wooden floor and stopped at Goren's feet, the contents spilling out. Goren immediately recognized the handwriting on one envelope, addressed to Goren Goshen."

14

"Don't you just love law practice?" said Jackson. "Just think of the unusual stories we have heard today. It's never boring."

"True, but I'm not sure how to make use of this story," said John. "Nevertheless, you've got my interest. Let's hear the rest."

"I love this part of the story," said Skip.

Ted took a deep breath and continued.

"'A letter from Penny!' exclaimed Goren with great joy. 'What a great way to top off the day! Excuse me for just a moment. I can hardly wait to see what she has to say.' He hastily tore open the envelope, a look of pure joy and excitement on his face. His hands shook with anticipation as he unfolded the letter. 'Please forgive my rudeness, but I just cannot wait to read her words. I'll just take a quick look. I'll read it again more slowly later. Please excuse me,' he said as he began reading. His face changed from joy to confusion and then to shock. His legs seemed to grow weak, and he steadied himself by grabbing a chair. His eyes began darting about the room like a man gone mad. He crumpled the letter and bolted through the back door, dropping the letter on the ground as he ran.

"'What's happened?' asked Jackson.

"'Should we follow him?' said Fabber, 'She must have given him the worst possible news.'

"'I don't know,' said Jackson. 'He may need space. But, let's just step outside for a moment.'

"The two Andrews stepped through the back door, just in time to see Kewaah picking up the crumpled note. The guests crowded around the doorframe and peered into the growing darkness. There was still enough light that they could see Goren running into the brewery, crying 'Penny! No, no Penny!'

"Kewaah handed the crumpled letter to Fabber, who straightened it out. In the faint yellow light passing through the doorway, he began to read:

> **My Dearest Goren:**
> **You mean so much to me, and I love you so. By the time you read this I will be married. I never wished to hurt you, but five years is such a long**

67

time. My father has put much pressure on me to marry and he selected a fine man. You may know him . . .

"'FIRE!' cried a voice, soon joined by a dozen others as men poured out of the tavern. The brewery was burning and the fire was spreading fast. In the harsh yellow and orange light, Fabber could see the General taking command, ordering people to grab buckets and make a chain between the river and the brewery. In moments a bucket brigade was arranged and a steady stream of water was being thrown on the fire, but the blaze only grew hotter. A great cry was heard from the loft of the brewery. Everyone looked up and there stood Goren, flames all about him. He cried in a loud voice, over and over 'Penny! Penny! Penny!'

"So, I suppose that is why the ghost calls Penny at night?" asked Jackson.

"No, not at all. It was then that the most memorable and remarkable part of the whole event occurred."

"I love this part of the story," said Skip, as his eyes seemed to glaze over.

"This part of the story was related later by Andrew Fabber in a book he wrote about the event. Quite a commotion occurred in the tavern. All the men scurried about and hollered at one another as they tried to put out the fire. You can imagine that they created a great racket. Yet, somehow, above all that den of noise, a lady's voice suddenly was heard in the tavern.

"'Where is Goren Goshen? I've got to find him. Where is he?'

"'I am afraid he's in the brewery, ma'am,' someone said.

"A stunningly beautiful red-headed woman burst through the back door and ran straight into the postman. 'You didn't deliver that horrid forged letter did you? Tell me you didn't. I will never forgive my father for that forgery. Tell me you didn't. I came as fast as I could when I realized what my father had done.'

"The postman was so stunned it almost sobered him. His mouth opened, but he couldn't say a word. Fabber stepped up and handed the letter to her.

"'Is this the letter you are speaking of miss?'

"'Oh, no! He hasn't seen it, has he?'

"'I'm afraid he has, miss.'

"'Where is he? I've got to let him know it was all a lie!'

"'In response, Fabber looked towards the blazing brewery.

"With a scream that could wake the dead, she ran like the wind

68

towards the brewery. To a man, everyone stopped what they were doing, buckets in hand. All eyes were riveted on this red-haired beauty. Later, every man present said she was the most beautiful vision they had ever seen. She flew across the yard, her skirt hiked above her knees, hair streaming behind her, eyes and face reflecting the intense fire and heat. She ran like she was demon possessed, straight towards the fire.

"'Goren Goshen! Stop! Come out! Goren!' she screamed as she ran.

"The whole line of men in the bucket brigade was frozen, under the spell of the vision of her beauty and the power of the moment. Only one young man, the last in the line, was able to overcome the effects of the magic of the moment. He dropped his bucket, stepped in front of her and spread his arms to stop her. But, she would not be stopped. She ran so hard and fast that she ran right over him without slowing down. In an instant she was in the blazing brewery. That broke the spell that the men were suffering under, and they all charged as one towards the brewery to save the beautiful woman. But, alas, the heat was too intense. No one could get near the brewery. Then, everyone heard the sound that would haunt them for the rest of their lives: 'Penny, no, Penny, no . . . it can't be. No, Penny! Penny! Penny! Penny! Penny!'

"The flames burned all night. The brewery burned to the ground. The fire grew so hot, that men had to stand back a hundred feet or more, yet still they could hear him holler, 'Penny! Penny!' Some said that they heard him hollering until dawn. By first light, the brewery was all gone. They searched the ashes, but never found any trace of either body. Apparently, they were completely consumed in the fire.

"The men present were hard men, frontier men. They were warriors. Every one of them cried as they sifted through the ashes. Never had they seen such a love between two people. Every man felt that it was such a waste. Every man felt a little envious, that Goren and Penny loved each other so. They searched the ashes until the next night. But then several of the men claimed they heard Goren calling Penny's name. They were so spooked, that almost all of them left the ruins, never to return."

"I bet the guy who didn't stop Penny felt pretty bad," said Jackson.

"Yeah. He could not be consoled. Some of the guys began making fun of him because a woman ran over him. Because his name was Fulton, they started calling his failed effort to stop Penny 'Fulton's Folly.' He turned to the bottle for a few weeks, then, he became determined to do something significant to make up for his shame."

"You're not saying that this was the same Fulton who made the paddle-wheel steamboat are you?" asked Jackson.

"No, that was his father. This Fulton met a guy named Colt and helped him make the first revolver. But, until then, the moniker,

'Fulton's Folly,' followed him with everything he did until the revolver was a proven success."

John just sat and shook his head.

Skip said, "I love this part of the story. It gets better every time I hear it."

"Yeah, I bet it does," observed John.

"Now, as for the beer recipe, Fabber, who was already a brewer, really wanted that recipe. Fabber was told that Goren kept his recipe in a lock box in a safe in the loft. Others said the lock box was buried somewhere under the brewery. Fabber searched the ashes and found the safe, but it was empty. He brought men in to dig everywhere under and around the brewery. He was there every moment, watching every move to make certain that no one would steal the box. He kept the site under guard until they had looked everywhere, but they never found the lock box."

"I thought everyone stayed away because of the ghost," said John.

"Everyone except Fabber. Almost everyone he brought in left after just one day on the job. They would get spooked during their first night and leave the next day. To be sure, a few hardy men stayed behind, saying they never heard a thing and they didn't believe in ghosts.

"Fabber finally returned to New Orleans without the recipe and continued brewing. His beer continued to be successful well into the twentieth century. But the secret to Goshen Springs beer was lost, until now."

"So, I suppose you found the lock box," said Jackson.

Ted smiled and slid his chair back. He reached into a canvas bag sitting on the next table. Its contents were obviously heavy and dirty. With both hands he carefully pulled out a large, dented, rusty box.

15

After he visited with John Brooks, Travis T was returned to his cell. As the cell door slammed behind him, he sat on his bunk and thought, *here I am again. Is this all that life holds for me?* He stepped up to the cage door, put his hands on the bar and leaned his forehead against the cold metal, this time speaking to no one in particular: "Is this all that I am, just a common thief? Everybody is right about me. Even my momma was right when she named me. My whole life is nothing but a waste—a travesty."

Travis had not shed a tear since he was a child, so he was astounded when he discovered that his face was wet. He quickly wiped away the tears and looked around to make sure no one saw that moment of weakness. Then he remembered the New Testament in his pocket.

"What did that lawyer say? What was that foolishness?"

He pulled the Book out of his pocket, and said out loud to himself, "Now, where was that? I never can find anything in this book."

He noticed that a few pages were dog-eared. He flipped to the first turned down page, and exclaimed, "This is it!" He began to read. Time flew, and he kept reading. He read that God decided to bring Travis into the world even before He created the world. He learned that God knew beforehand that Travis would stray, but God created a way to bring him back. He read the story of the prodigal son, and he realized that he was that son.

He read that God has a purpose for him and that God had already set aside good deeds that only Travis could do. For the first time he understood that all sin is punished, but that Jesus took the punishment for his sins so that he would be free to have a relationship with God.

He took my place! Jesus really loves me that much? Nobody has ever loved me. There is nothing about me to love. But, He loves me anyway. God, I don't know what to say!

Travis found himself on his knees, weeping.

The lights went out, but Travis could not sleep. He found himself back on his knees again. "Thank you God for letting me know that I matter to You. I am so sorry that I have done nothing with the life You gave me. Nothing but bad."

Then he prayed: "God, I know that I am supposed to say something. I have always heard that it is by my mouth that I am saved. I want to be saved. I know that Jesus Christ is your only Son. I accept Him as my Lord and Savior. I don't deserve it, but, please forgive my sins, and let me be part of your family. I've never been part of a family before, so, I don't know how I am supposed to act. Please show me the way."

With that truth in his heart, Travis fell into a peaceful sleep that even the noises of the jail did not disturb. Down the hall, a guard stopped at the cell door of John Smith. He stared at Smith in the semi-darkness. Smith rose from his bunk and approached the cell door. The guard handed something to him through the bars, and said, "A present from the Bishop. He said that you were born for this. Now, go fulfill your purpose."

As the guard walked away, John Smith looked at the dirk in his hands, and he laughed out loud. He looked at the sharp point and the double-edged blade. He saw the shape and knew instinctively that it was designed for easy penetration and maximum wound size. Even though it looked homemade, it was a simple but effective killing tool.

"Tomorrow I will kill Hal Boyd. Tomorrow, I will fulfill my purpose."

With that lie in his heart, John Smith fell into a fitful sleep, interrupted by disturbing dreams.

* * *

Karen worked late, organizing the material from the prosecutor's file. She began compiling material on each potential witness and on each person whose name was mentioned in the documents. As the story started coming together she realized how much she loved her work. Karen loved solving puzzles and searching for the truth. Her sense of justice was strong and she had an intense desire to see wrongs made right. She thought that she might like to go to law school sometime, but for now she knew she was where she wanted to be.

She loved working for her little firm. In fact she felt it belonged to her just as much as it belonged to Jackson and John. She loved working with them. She laughed to herself as she thought about Jackson. *He is smart and funny and a good lawyer, although he doesn't always pay attention to details. Sometimes that causes us problems.*

She realized that the real reason she loved working here was John. She felt a special bond with him. There were no romantic feelings, but she knew deep inside that he was destined to do great things and she wanted to be a part of that. Nevertheless, she felt strong territorial sensations when that reporter entered the picture. Everything seemed perfect in her work and her life. Karen didn't want any change. She liked being the most important woman in the lives of Jackson and John. But when that Sandy Storm blew in, she seemed to be a threat to the way things have always been. Karen didn't know why for sure; but she knew that she felt threatened by Sandy Storm.

In John, Karen saw a man of character who always tried to do the right thing, no matter what it might cost him. His personality made her want to work for him. In her heart she knew that John was a man who could go far with the right breaks and the right people working with him. She knew that he could not afford a top-notch fully trained professional assistant. He couldn't afford to pay a decent wage to an ordinary secretary. So she had decided to become that top-notch assistant that he needed right now. Later, he could afford to actually pay someone to do what she did. For now, she would work any hours and perform any task to help him get over the hump.

This is the case that will get him over the top, she said to herself. Once he was over the top, it will be time to move on. This thought brought a moment of sadness to her, but she knew that she could not indefinitely work these hours at this pay. Besides, there were things she wanted to accomplish for herself.

Maybe after law school, I'll come back and work with him. Maybe we could be partners. She smiled at the thought, and noticed that it was getting late.

She decided to take everything to KanKo's and get copies made for everyone. As she gathered her files, she intentionally placed one file on top. It contained a few stories that mentioned one person of interest and included a single photograph, taken from a distance, of a man wearing a long dark coat and a wide brimmed hat.

"Father Michael McCarty, I want to know more about you," she muttered.

One report called him a "Christian terrorist." She chuckled to herself when she read that description. What a self-contradictory term. How can anyone be a Christian and a terrorist? She shut off the office lights, scooped up all of the papers, locked the door and headed for her car.

* * *

"I don't know if these masks you got us are going to work, man. I mean, what if they draw attention to us?"

"Shut-up Danny," said Gayle. "Listen to Erick. He knows what we're supposed to do."

She took a long draw from the marijuana cigarette they were passing around. The car was so full of smoke that it was getting difficult to see through the windows.

"I don't know. This just doesn't seem right."

"Do you want to be a part of this or not," said Erick. "'Cause we can drop you, just like that."

73

Erick snapped his finger on the second try.

"Quiet!" whispered Gayle with an urgent tone. "Here she comes."

"Okay, we're going to do this," said Erick as he waved a cloud of smoke away with his hand. "Danny, take the Taser and slip up behind her while she is getting in the car. When you zap her, put this hydrogen firalda noxide, or whatever it is, just put this stuff over her face. It's supposed to keep her knocked out for a long time."

"Why me? Why don't you do it? You're the one who is always talking so bold, saying how you've done this and that, and there's nothing you wouldn't do for the cause."

"You need to prove yourself. Here, take the Taser."

"I'm not touching it, man."

Gayle said: "Oh, you cowards! Give it to me, I'll do it!"

"No, I want Danny to do it."

"Hurry up. She's going to get away!" urged Gayle.

"I can't approach her now. The way she is turned, she'll see me coming. We won't have the element of surprise, and anything might happen."

As they watched, Karen opened the trunk of her car, put the files inside and closed the lid.

"Oh, I'll just do it myself," said Erick as he reached for the door handle. Before he opened the door, he paused for a moment.

"What are you waiting for?" asked Gayle. "Just do it!"

"No, the time is not right. She will be in the car before I can get there."

"That's what I was talking about," agreed Danny as he nodded affirmatively. "See, she's already in the car."

"Oh, I can't believe you two. Block her in before she gets away."

"No, we're going to follow her," said Erick. "This is going to all work out for the better, you'll see."

As Karen pulled out of the parking lot, Danny let the car roll slowly in place behind her, easing into the street and then staying a good distance behind her.

After two blocks Gayle noticed that Karen was no longer in front of them.

"Where is she? She's lost you in just two blocks."

"Oh, man, she must have turned back there. What do we do?"

"Make a u-turn, and hit it. We can still catch her."

"U-turns are illegal man. What if I get a ticket?"

"Kidnapping is illegal, stupid. Now, turn around quick."

Danny managed the u-turn and sped around the corner they had just passed. Within a minute, they were behind Karen again.

"Are you sure that's her?" asked Gayle. "I don't want to be following the wrong person. I sure don't want to kidnap the wrong person. For some reason, the Bishop wants this redhead. I asked if any redhead would do, but he said that she was perfect for his needs."

"That's her. I see that stupid 'Choose Life' tag. Gag me with a spoon!"

"Well, that settles it. She deserves to be kidnapped. Where are we going to do it?"

"We will take her at her home. That will be better."

"How will that be better?" asked Gayle.

"Because then they will know that they are not safe at work or at home. That plays right into our hands."

"Yeah, right. She is playing right into the mastermind's plans."

Gayle laughed until she snorted. Danny apparently thought it was funny too, because he started laughing with her and laughed until he cried.

"Stop laughing and drive. She's getting away again!"

"I can't help it. This is too funny," laughed Danny as he wiped tears from his face.

"Look—she's turning into 'KanKo's!" said Gayle as she laughed so hard she fell off the back seat onto the floorboard.

"Just pull up behind her and 'poop' the trunk," urged Erick.

The marijuana was making normal speech slightly more difficult.

All of a sudden, Erick seemed to be the best comedian in the world. To Danny and Gayle, 'Poop the trunk' seemed like the funniest combination of words ever uttered. They laughed so hard that Danny had to stop the car. Unfortunately, this turned out to be good for their "plan."

The car stopped behind Karen, who had just pulled into a parking space at KanKo's. As soon as they stopped, Erick jumped out, Taser in hand, just as Karen climbed out of her car and walked to her trunk.

Karen was full of self-confidence, secure in her world. It never occurred to her that she could be in danger, or that someone would be out to hurt her. She knew the night manager at KanKo's, where the motto was "Yes You Kan Get It Done 24/7!" From time to time she dropped work off when she left the office and picked up the finished product on her way to work in the morning. It saved time and effort and made her look even more efficient. She loved the compliments that Jackson and John gave her when she gave them professional looking products overnight. To them it seemed as though she had accomplished a miracle. She smiled as she thought about the compliments she would receive the next morning.

75

Suddenly, she was aware that someone was too close behind her. Before she could react, there was pain, a blinding white light, a noxious smell and she fell to the pavement, unconscious.

16

John and Jackson sat in stunned silence for a moment as they looked at the old rusty box. Finally, Jackson said, "Wait, you want us to believe that a recipe survived two hundred years in that?"

"Nope. In this."

He opened the box, and inside was a ceramic jar, with a cap, covered with broken wax. "It was in this jar, sealed in wax. I broke the seal when I opened the jar."

"Why didn't the fire melt the wax?"

"The box wasn't in the brewery. It was near the brewery, or far enough under the brewery that it was protected from the heat. At least that is my best guess."

"How did you find it?" asked John.

Ted looked around the room, leaned forward and said, "Actually, that is the most incredible part of the whole story. I'm not sure anyone will believe me."

"Well then, you really have nothing to lose by telling us the rest of the story," said John.

"Hmm. Have I been insulted?"

"I love this part of the story," said Skip.

"Okay. Here goes! The truth is, I followed Goren's voice."

"You what?" Jackson and John said at the same time. Bobby just smiled.

"I love this part of the story," said Skip.

"I know, it sounds crazy, but, that's what I did. I heard the stories about Goren calling Penny's name at night ever since I bought land near the original Goshen Springs."

"Where is the original Goshen Springs?"

"Under the reservoir. It's covered with water."

"Then how did you get the box, and how did it survive?"

"It was on one of the reservoir islands. I call it Goren Island, just south of where the Highway 43 Bridge crosses the reservoir."

Jackson and John just looked at Ted, without speaking and without expression.

"One night I thought I heard his voice. It was a windy night and I thought it was just the wind, but, still, it was real enough to give me the willies. The sound seemed to be coming from the lake. I heard strange noises on other occasions and I went outside to try to hear it better and to see where it was coming from. Finally, I decided that it seemed to come from one of the islands near the east shore of the lake. No one lives nearby. Some of the islands are little more than swamp, but this one rises several feet above the lake, and it's covered with trees. No one goes there, except birds. The place is covered with droppings.

"After I heard the voice and thought it came from the island, I went there many times. I found remnants of what could have been beer barrels, round rusty deposits that looked like they might be the hoops that go around barrels. There are lots of them out there. The dirt is black in places, like it's full of old charcoal. I saw lots of animal bones, too. I don't know what that has to do with a brewery, but there are lots of bones. I saw evidence that someone had camped there or something. Part of the shore of the island was eroding away, and I saw this rusty box poking out of the bank."

Bobby popped the top off of another beer and said, "And this is the result."

"I love this part of the story," said Skip as he squirmed closer to the edge of his chair.

"Is there any part of this story you don't love?" asked Jackson.

"Just the parts I don't know yet."

"Anyway," continued Ted, as he lifted the box with both hands and then set it down reverently, "The thing that was sticking out of the bank was the edge of this box." After a pause, he said, "Who knows, another rain and the bank might have sloughed off into the lake, and the box would have been lost forever."

"Yeah, it was meant to be," said Skip. "You were meant to find that box, Ted. I love this part of the story."

"I dug it up, opened it, and like Bobby said, you are tasting the result." Ted became excited as he described how the recipe not only gave the ingredients, but specific instructions on how to brew the beer. "I followed the instructions to the letter, and voila. Goshen Springs Beer."

"Wow! That's quite a story," said Jackson. "I am puzzled, though, why are you sharing this story with us?"

"I need a lawyer. I need help making this beer in quantity. I need help distributing this beer. I need help marketing this beer. Frankly, I don't know where to start, so, I'm calling my lawyer first."

"Yeah, I've been telling him that he needs to talk to you, John. Yep, I've been saying John Brooks will know what to do. Haven't I, Ted?"

"Yep. That's true."

Jackson sighed, and sat back. He looked at John, then said, "Ted, we don't have any experience marketing or distributing anything, let alone beer."

"Yeah, but, you're smart, and you know people, and . . ."

After a long pause, Jackson said ". . . and what?"

"Well, with all the notoriety that you and John have gotten lately with this vampire case thing and the ghost connection with the beer, Skip and I thought it sort of made marketing sense to get you involved."

"Oh man, this is unbelievable," said Jackson with exasperation as he slid back from the table. "You are not going to make a fool of my partner. John, let's go."

John didn't move.

Ted grabbed John's arm. "Wait, John. I trust you. I know you can help me with this. I don't have the money or the connections or the smarts to get off the ground. Help me."

"Yeah, help him, John," added Bobby and Skip with pleading expressions on their faces.

"I don't have money either."

"You will, as famous as you have become. Besides, you can figure out how to get investors interested in this. I need your help. If you can help me pay off the debt I've incurred making these first few batches, I'll make you an equal partner. What do you say?"

John squinted and said, "Debt? What are we talking about? How much?"

"I knew there was a catch," added Jackson.

"It's gotten out of hand for me. I've sunk about $5,000 into this. When my girlfriend found out how much I had spent, she left me."

"You know how it is with women," said Jackson. "Easy go, easy go."

"I thought it was easy come, easy go," said Skip.

"I never found the first part to be so easy, but the second part sure is."

"Yeah, I guess you're right," said Skip dejectedly.

"Hold on," said John with his hands raised. "The way to market this is with the story you just told."

"Are we still talking about women leaving?" asked Skip.

"You're not considering this beer deal are you, John?"

"I knew it!" shouted Skip. "We're gonna be rich!"

"Imagine this, Jackson. You write the story, and break it into numerous parts. Then, we print part of the story on the back of every label on every bottle of beer. As someone drinks the beer, they can see part of the story of Goren Goshen. Then, some people will want to keep buying the beer to get to the end of the story. If the beer is good, they will keep buying the beer for the taste."

"That's why you're my partner!" exclaimed Ted.

"No, that's why he's my partner," said Jackson. "This is great! This beer could become the next great fad. That is, at least until the story becomes old. Once we've told the whole story on labels, what then?"

"The beer needs to be good enough to stand on its own without the story. It is right now. The question is, can it be made this good in quantity? Anyway, there is no reason for the story to ever end."

"This is the part I love," said Bobby. Everyone laughed and took another swig of beer, except Skip, who said, "You stole my line."

"When we get to the end of the Penny and Goren story, we'll tell more stories about the adventures of Goren Goshen. He hunted with Davy Crocket. Probably kilt hisself a bar. He must have traveled across the country and down the mighty Mississip'. He added words and phrases to the English language, like flabbergasted, and talking turkey. Why, there may be no end to the stories that could be told about his exploits."

"Yeah, he could impart little words of wisdom, or jokes, or funny stories," said Ted. "We could keep it fresh and new. People would buy another six-pack because they want the next label just to see what Goren was up to."

"Yeah, that and because the beer is really good," said Jackson. "How do we start?"

John observed that excitement had gripped the men like a fever and that Jackson, though resistant at first, was now infected.

"Yeah, how do we start," said Bobby. Everyone looked at Bobby for a moment. "I've got the 5k."

In unison, Ted, Skip, John and Jackson said, "You're in!"

Not wanting to be left out, Skip said, "I'll match him."

Everyone looked at Skip for a moment. Then John said, "Jackson, we can't let this interfere with our case, but the case won't last forever. The case will be our priority until we're done. Later, I think we should visit a few small breweries. We should read whatever we can find about beer. We need to look for suppliers and equipment. We should look for any data on Goren Goshen. Was he a real person? Can we find out anything about him? We will visit Goren Island to see if there is anything there that can be used to add to the story. Maybe, we can get one of the state universities to do an archeological dig at the site and get it covered in the media. We could dig up relics, and put them on display as a way to affirm the story, or add intrigue and interest. We need to know what it will take to make a small, expandable brewery. How much money, staff and equipment will we need? We need to know what it takes to distribute beer."

"I know the local distributor of Bud, and the distributor of Coors," said Bobby. "Maybe they could help."

"I know the local Pepsi bottler," said Ted. "Maybe he could also bottle beer."

"We need to inform ourselves as much as we can before we go to anyone local," said John. "Ted, see if you can find some small breweries that we could visit, maybe on the West Coast, or in New England. Somewhere far enough away that they won't feel like we are competitors."

"Sure, I could start that in the morning," said Ted, with evident excitement. John's enthusiasm was contagious. Everyone was excited. Everyone wanted to have some part in the brewery project. Everyone immediately accepted John's leadership role.

"Jackson, why don't you see if you can find out anything about beer distribution networks and contracts. How is it done? Ted, I would like for you to arrange a little trip for us to Goren Island."

17

"I can't believe you just did that," exclaimed Danny.

"Awesome!" shouted Gayle.

"Quiet! Open the trunk."

Erick dragged Karen's body to the back of the car. He was not used to a lot of physical exertion, so he was already winded. "Danny, get back here and help me."

When he looked in the trunk he said, "Man, what is all this junk? How am I supposed to get her in the trunk when it's full of all this . . ."

"How was I supposed to know we were going to put her in the trunk? Nobody told me."

By then, Gayle was standing beside them, laughing.

"Shut-up, Gayle. Quick, help me get her in the back seat."

The gravity of the situation began to cause Danny and Gayle to sober up, but their coordination was still a little off from all the dope. It took several clumsy tries, but eventually they were able to lift Karen and place her across the back seat.

"Where am I supposed to sit?" asked Gayle.

"Just get in. I can't believe that nobody has seen us yet. We've got to get out of here."

By now, adrenaline had taken over, and the three of them were feeling a new kind of rush that they weren't sure how to handle.

"Oh, man—I am burning up," said Danny. "How about you?"

"Yeah, me too," said Erick. "It is hot in this car. Turn up the air!"

"I'm about to die of starvation," said Gayle. "Can we go through the drive through?"

"We've got a body in the car," grimaced Erick.

"They won't be able to see her. If they do, they'll just think she's even more stoned then we are. We'll order something for her so they won't be suspicious. Then we'll eat her share, and there will be more to go around."

"Yeah, you're right Gayle. That's really smart. If we don't get something to eat soon, I think I'm gonna pass out."

"You two are such amateurs. We can't go get food with our kidnap victim in the car with us."

"Nobody knows she's been kidnapped. She doesn't even know. She is out of it. I mean, way out."

"Really!" said Erick, with a leer on his face.

"Don't get any ideas, lover boy," said Gayle. "We have to take good care of her, according to the Bishop."

"Oh, I'll take good care of her," Erick said with a smirk.

"There's Wendy's—the drive through is open," said Danny. "Come on Erick, it will only take a minute.

"You morons. All right, make it quick."

It took a few tries, but eventually they placed a massive order, only to discover that they didn't have enough money to purchase all of the food. Danny collected the food from the attendant as he handed over a handful of bills and change. As the attendant said, "Hey, this is not enough!" Danny drove off.

"That was smooth Danny," said Gayle. "I'm proud of you."

"Good grief, they put mayo on my burger. I told them no mayo. Turn around, I want to give them a piece of my mind."

"I don't think that's such a good idea, Erick."

"Yeah, just kidding. But I'll remember her, and I'll be back later to get my revenge."

"I hope that I never do anything as bad as put mayo on your sandwich," said Gayle, who began giggling again. Soon, all three of them were laughing.

"Danny, turn onto the Trace. Let's drive up to Cyprus Swamp and eat our food. The Bishop will meet us there and I think they might take her to the island. From now on we don't use our real names. We use our code names."

He fished around in a bag and pulled out one of the masks they had acquired so that Karen would not recognize them.

"I almost forgot. Here, put these masks on."

"This is cool, I've got Marilyn Monroe," said Danny. "She will never recognize me with this mask. What's my code name?"

"Marilyn."

"Cool."

"Why can't I be Marilyn Monroe? Why do I have to be Freddy Krueger?" whined Gayle.

"Okay, swap."

"Will my code name still be Marilyn?" asked Danny.

"No, you're Freddy."

"I hope I don't forget. Oh, I get it. You are whoever your mask is."

"You're a genius."

"Thanks Erick."

"It's Einstein."

"Well, you're pretty smart, but I don't know about calling you Einstein."

"It's the mask, dummy."

"Oh, I thought that was like the Wicked Witch of the East from the Wizard of Oz."

"I thought so, too," said Gayle.

"No, don't you two know Einstein when you see him?"

"I guess not," they both said at the same time.

"Stay on the road!"

"I can't see very well with this mask on. It's really dark out here. Can I take it off, Erick? Please?"

"It's Einstein."

"Oh, yeah."

"Just sort of slip it down your face enough so you can see over the top. That way most of your face is still covered."

"That's smart. No wonder you picked the Einstein mask."

They raced up the Natchez Trace, encountering no traffic along the way.

"Wow, the water is beautiful at night," observed Gayle as they drove along the Pearl River Reservoir. Soon, they passed Highway 43, which crossed the reservoir between the Trace and Goshen Springs, and the lake disappeared from view. Trees closed in around them and the night grew darker. They continued driving north on the Trace for several miles through a tunnel of trees.

"This is kind of spooky, isn't it?"

"No Freddy, we are the spooks," said Erick "We don't get spooked. We do the spooking."

"Oh yeah, that's right—I forgot," said Danny as everyone began laughing.

Gayle snorted.

Everyone laughed at Gayle's snort.

They pulled off the Trace at Cypress Swamp and began a feeding frenzy.

"Man, it sure is hot in here," said Danny as he rolled down the windows.

Soon, they were slapping themselves.

"Good grief, where did all these mosquitoes come from?" asked Erick.

"Well, it is a swamp, Einstein."

"Get the windows up, quick."

"Get a load of this story about the swamp on the sign," said Erick. "Cypress Swamp. You are entering a realm of trees, water and reflections. Its subtle beauty and peaceful setting can soothe a tired soul.' Don't you feel soothed?"

"I feel itchy, from all the mosquito bites," said Danny.

"It looks eerie and kind of creepy," said Gayle.

"Listen to the rest of this, … 'a relaxed pace improves the likelihood of seeing wildlife. Along the way, you may experience the wonderment of discovery. Allow enough time for the magic to work.'"

Erick laughed and said, "I bet our little 'Miss Penny' here is going to feel like a million dollars when the Bishop finishes performing his magic on her."

Everyone laughed.

18

It was getting late, so John and Jackson stood up to leave Bobby's Trading Post. Ted asked them to wait saying, "Actually, the boat is ready. I can take you now. I knew you would want to see the island."

"It's dark and it's getting late," observed Jackson.

"Yeah, that will sort of add to the spookiness of the event," said Ted. "Maybe it will inspire you to write with more passion about the ghost."

A look of great worry was etched on Skip's face. "You aren't thinking about going to that haunted island after dark are you?"

"I'm game, what about you, John?" said Jackson.

"I'm not," said Bobby with a shiver. "You ain't getting me out there at night. Besides, I've got a business to run. I'm staying here."

"Well, we're here," said John. "What could be the harm in taking a little outing?"

Ted led them to the pier, where he had a ski boat ready to go. "I've got mosquito spray in the bag, and flashlights for everyone."

As they clambered aboard, a cloud covered the moon, and the water grew eerily dark. Ted turned the key, and the engine whined but did not crank. "That's funny. It has never done that before. It always cranks right up."

"Maybe the ghost is sabotaging our trip," laughed Jackson.

Just then, the engine turned over with a reassuring rumble.

"I don't like the feeling of this," said Skip, while Ted and Jackson untied the lines and shoved the boat away from the pier. Ted slowly guided the boat along Highway 43, which stretched like a long finger across the lake, until he reached the bridge, where boats could pass from the "up-river" part of the lake, to the lower lake where Goren Island awaited.

When he reached the bridge, Ted turned south into a stiff breeze.

"Wow, where did that come from?" asked Ted.

"I guess it just blew in," said Jackson. "Maybe the raised highway was protecting us from the wind."

The lake surface had already changed from smooth as glass to one-foot waves.

"I don't like this," repeated Skip.

"Maybe this is not the best night to visit the island. We could come back another time."

"Nonsense. This is nothing. I've been in much worse than this. We'll be fine."

"What's the weather supposed to be tonight?" asked Jackson as he hunkered down and turned his collar up to protect his neck from the cool wind. "Conditions can change fast on this lake, and the waves can be mean."

"Nothing tonight. I checked before I got the boat ready. There's a chance of thundershowers tomorrow when a front passes through. It is supposed to be fine tonight, with hardly any wind at all, and an almost full moon."

"A full moon?" repeated Skip. "Now, I know we should go back."

"Humph," said John.

By now, they were in the lower lake. Still, they had to stay in the marked channel for the first few miles. The channel wound back and forth, following the course of the old Pearl River now covered by the lake. Ted gave Jackson a powerful spotlight and asked him to identify the markers.

"Keep the red markers on the left, and the green markers on the right."

"Yeah, I got it. Red right returning."

"I get it, when we return, the red markers will be on the right," observed Skip.

"That's true, this time," said Ted.

Skip looked confused, so Jackson said, "What if we had gone the other direction, say towards Flag Island, Skip? Red would be on our right, and when we return to the starting point, where will the markers be?"

"On the left," said Skip. "Good grief, the saying is useless."

"No, it was meant for use on the coast, like when you are returning to the harbor you keep the red marker on your right," explained Ted. "It still works on streams. When you go upstream, away from the ocean, we keep red on the right. For now, as we go downstream, towards the ocean, we keep red on our left."

"Ocean, there's no ocean anywhere around here!" exclaimed Skip.

The temperature seemed to have dropped ten degrees, and the waves had doubled in size

"How far is the island?" asked John.

"At the next marker, we turn due east."

"Won't the water be shallow?" asked Skip.

"Yes, but I've been there many times. We can make it in this boat."

"Here's the next marker," called Jackson.

Ted used his compass to turn east. As he left the channel, he reduced the power and moved slowly into the dark, choppy water. The boat began rolling significantly as waves slapped the side. The windward side of the boat rose quickly as it was hit by a wave, then the gunnels dipped as the boat slid down the back of the wave into the narrow trough before the next wave. Before the boat could level, the next wave hit, while the gunnels on the windward side were still low. Water splashed up over the side of the boat and, driven by the growing wind, blew across the boat, spraying and chilling the occupants.

"This is getting rough, Ted," said John. "I'm not comfortable doing this tonight in the dark. Let's do this another time."

"What's that noise?" shouted Skip. "Did you hear that?"

"I heard it!" said Ted.

The wind had picked up considerably. The waves were now three feet high with white caps.

"Yeah, I hear wind howling through the trees on the island," said Jackson.

"No—don't you hear him calling her?" said Ted in a loud whisper.

At that moment a lightning bolt streaked from the cloud to the water nearby, followed almost immediately by explosive thunder that made everyone jump.

"Good grief, let's get back—now!" shouted John.

Then the rain started. It was driven by the wind so hard that it stung their exposed skin. They were immediately soaked to the bone. As Ted turned the boat to return to the channel, there was a sudden loud bang that jolted the boat. The engine began to whine and rev.

"Uh oh! The prop is gone. We've hit a stump or something!"

"It was the ghost!" yelled Skip.

Driven by the wind, the boat was quickly swept north. Another jolt shook the boat and was followed quickly by yet another.

"What was that?"

"Stumps, logs, I don't know," said Jackson.

"Man, oh, man, we are in one of those stump fields. This could be bad."

Near Highway 43, outside the river channel, there are the remains of trees that were not removed after the dam was built. As the water level rose, the trees died, leaving behind trunks that still rose above the water, like a forest of ghost trees. Many of the trunks had broken off at or below the water line. The boat was drifting sideways through the old, flooded forest. The bow hit an old trunk, then the stern hit another and the boat wedged between them. Waves splashed over the side of the boat and rain continued to pour down on them.

"We're in for a long night boys," said John. "I suggest you find something to bail with. Ted, does this boat have a cover?"

"Yeah, but not on board."

Back at the Trading Post, Bobby became concerned when the sudden storm blew in and the guys didn't return. He called the Reservoir Patrol. A dispatcher answered the phone. When Bobby explained the problem the dispatcher asked, "What in the world were they doing out there at night anyway, especially in a storm like this?"

Without giving it a second thought, Bobby answered, "They were ghost hunting, but it wasn't storming when they left."

"Must have a bad reception. Thought you said 'ghost hunting.'"

"Well, yeah, I guess I did. But what difference does it make? They are in trouble now and need your help."

"I'm not risking my people on a night like this for a bunch of nuts. We'll look for them in the morning."

The dispatcher had already set the rescue in motion, but was venting a little frustration by pretending that he would do nothing.

"These people are not nuts. They are well known lawyers and a prominent business man."

"Yeah, well who are they?"

"John Brooks, Jackson Bradley, Ted Lively and Skip Shafer."

"Brooks. Isn't that the vampire lawyer?"

"That's the one."

"Great, vampire lawyer goes out in a small boat on a stormy night, looking for a ghost, and I've got to risk the lives of my men to save him. Somebody's gonna pay for this."

He dispatched a rescue team and settled back in his chair, thinking about how unfair it was to be sending his friends into a storm to save the vampire lawyer, all because he was ghost hunting. Frivolous was the word that came to him. Then he remembered his comment that someone was going to pay for this. A smile crossed his face as he remembered a buddy who worked at one of the local television stations. He reached for the phone as thunder shook the windows.

19

Karen heard laughter and some voices. The odor of marijuana was almost overpowering. Something dripped on her face. It was cold and wet. It ran down her nose and along the edge of her lip. She tasted it with her tongue and realized it was Coca Cola. Memory started to return to her and she cracked open her eyes enough to see that there were a few French fries on her neck, a tomato on her chest, and lettuce and onions all over.

She saw that she was in the back seat of a small car. Her head was on the lap of Marilyn Monroe. Freddy Krueger and the Wicked Witch of the East were in the front seat. They were all voraciously consuming mass quantities of food from Wendy's and slapping themselves silly. She heard them talking about "the Bishop".

Suddenly, Marilyn Monroe's arm was around her neck, and she was screaming, "She's awake! Help me back here!"

Karen began struggling and realized that she might be able to overpower Marilyn. Miss Monroe realized the same thing and screamed all the louder for help. Karen heard Freddy Krueger, who was in the driver's seat, say, "Please, calm down lady. We won't hurt you. And besides, there is no way for you to escape. Resistance is fertile."

"It's futile, you nimrod," said the Wicked Witch, speaking with a male voice. The Wicked Witch, (Erick) reached over the back seat with both hands. With one hand, he tried to grasp Karen. In the other hand was a device that Karen instantly realized must be a Taser. Reacting without thinking, Karen struck out with all her strength at the hand holding the Taser. The force of the blow knocked the Taser hand into Erick's other arm, and the Taser discharged, sending a full blast of electricity surging through his outstretched arm. The Wicked Witch's body was thrown into convulsions in the confined space of the car and he began flailing about.

Freddy Krueger screamed and jumped out of the car. Marilyn Monroe was so distracted that she momentarily lost her grip on Karen, who sat up quickly, balled her fist and let fly a roundhouse that landed solidly on Marilyn's nose. The force of the blow knocked Marilyn's head back against the doorpost, and she was momentarily dazed by the pain.

Karen recognized her chance and jumped out of the car only to find herself face to face with Freddy Krueger. She screamed. Freddy screamed, and jumped back into the car and floored the accelerator. Karen stood for a moment in disbelief at her good fortune while she watched the car containing her captors peel off, leaving her behind.

Karen felt relieved, even exhilarated, until the car screeched to a stop. She could hear a female voice screaming, "Danny, are you crazy? Go back! You can't leave her after all that we went through to get her!"

"No way! Did you see what she did to Erick? I told you we should never have done this."

"Turn this car around and go get her. Now!"

Karen looked for a place to hide, and saw the entrance to the swamp trail. She ran down the trail and across a wooden bridge. A flash of lightning illuminated the path for a moment. She glanced over her shoulder in time to see the car return to the parking lot, followed by a second car, and then a third. She remembered her captors talking about "the Bishop," and her heart raced even more than it had before. She stumbled as she looked over her shoulder and fell into thick undergrowth along the side of the trail. A strong wind whipped the tree branches above her, and a sudden cold rain penetrated the forest canopy.

Karen realized that the rain and wind were both a curse and a blessing. While she would be miserable, the noise might mask her movements and the swaying branches and rain might conceal her. She moved deeper into undergrowth farther away from the trail. Angry voices from the parking lot reached her. She could not make out all the words, but she could tell that the newcomers were angry that her captors had allowed her to escape.

In the parking lot, eight men piled out of the two cars that had just arrived. They approached Danny's car. Gayle was already out of the car, her mask off, trying to stem the flow of blood from her nose with Wendy's napkins.

"Gregory, I'm glad it's you!" shouted Gayle. "She got away, and ran up the trail!"

She pointed at the entrance to the swamp trail.

Gregory was tall and muscular. He sported a tattoo on his triceps of a coiled viper and seemed to have a permanent sneer on his face. He moved boldly and carried an air of authority. He was clearly the man in charge and the men with him knew that he expected his commands to be obeyed without the slightest deviation or hesitation.

Gregory motioned for three of his men to pursue Karen up the trail, and then took in the scene at Danny's car. Gayle was disheveled and bleeding profusely from her nose. Danny still had on his Freddy Krueger mask, but was breathing heavily. Erick was unconscious and crumpled up on the front passenger side floorboard of the car. His mask was smashed and covered the side of his head instead of his face.

"I see that she was too much for the three of you to handle. You better hope that we find her. The Bishop doesn't tolerate failure. As for Erick, he was in charge of your little group. I expect that he will have to personally explain to the Bishop what happened here."

He motioned for everyone to come together.

"She is scared and hiding in the woods or bushes near the swamp," he said. "I sent three men down the path. They might see her, but more than likely they will spook her into hiding if she is not already hiding. The trail circles back to the parking lot, so they will be in position if she returns to the lot. I don't think that she will go into the swamp. Instead, I think that she will leave the trail, on the side away from the parking lot, and hide among the trees or bushes and hope we give up searching for her. Our flashlights will scare her, which is what I want. The person who finds a clue will turn off his light and will either follow the trail as best he can in the dark or set up in an appropriate position to catch her when she runs. The rest of us will move down the trail a distance and move into the woods for the purpose of flanking her and flushing her out. She won't run deeper into the woods because of the swamp, so she will be forced back towards the parking lot. Gayle and Danny, you will catch her if she breaks into the open. If you don't catch her then, believe me, you will live to regret your failure."

"Don't worry, we will catch her," said Gayle. "I knew you would know what to do—unlike that dolt."

She gestured at Erick's unconscious body.

Karen crawled into a bush that had an opening large enough to peer through. She saw that several men were slowly walking abreast to each side of the trail searching the ground with flashlights as three men ran up the trail ahead of the others. A shiver ran up her spine as she realized that the newcomers were not imbeciles like her captors. They were searching for clues on the trail and on both sides of the trail at the same time, while the others raced ahead to see if she was still on the trail.

She did not know if she had left any clues behind. Did she leave footprints or marks where she fell? Did she drop anything? Did she tear her clothes on the limb of a bush, or did she break limbs of bushes? Would they see any clues she left behind on this dark, rainy, windy night if she did? She prayed for more rain. Her prayer was answered by an enormous clap of thunder followed by a deluge so great that she was instantly drenched. She wrapped her arms around herself, shivered, and resisted an almost overwhelming urge to cry.

The searchers passed the point where she exited the trail without pausing and continued moving forward. Karen realized that she had not been breathing, and allowed herself to take a breath. *What was that?* she thought as she was startled by a sound nearby. Was it the wind, or was it someone moving through the forest? She held her breath again and froze. She cut her eyes left and then right, trying to concentrate on the night sounds. She looked at the searchers moving along the path, and saw four flashlights. *Wait, weren't there five lights?* she asked herself. She wasn't sure. Did one turn his light off and leave the path so he could move undetected? Then she noticed that two of the lights were moving back toward her, and two were moving away from the path on a course that would put them parallel to her. All four lights went out simultaneously, and Karen realized that they somehow knew where she was.

Suddenly, without warning, a hand grabbed her on the shoulder and spun her around. She was nose to nose with the ugliest man she had ever seen. She screamed in spite of herself as he laughed. He had leering eyes and an angular face. His expression was gleeful, yet evil. What she noticed most was the teeth, white and glistening in the faint light.

"How did you find me?"

"A pickle."

"A pickle," she repeated.

"Yes, a pickle of all things attracted my attention to the place where you fell beside the trail," he said as he spun her around again and pressed her face into the ground. "Then I found your muddy tracks. We're going on a little boat ride, my dear. And I may have myself some fun."

Stalling for time so that she could think of a way to escape, she repeated, "A pickle?"

"Yeah, go figure."

She could hear the others running through the woods towards them. A loud thump startled her, and Mr. Ugly collapsed. A man holding a thick limb and wearing a wide brimmed hat stood over him. A flash of lightning illuminated his bearded face.

"You!"

He held his hand out to her. "I hate to quote a movie line, but," he said with an Irish accent, offering a pregnant pause for her to finish his thought.

"I should come with you if I want to live?"

"You've got it."

She grabbed his arm and in a quick motion he had her on her feet and running, straight into the swamp. Mucky swamp mud sucked the shoes off her feet. The smell of death and decay rose to her nostrils with each step. Dark, dank, putrid water surged around her waist and sent chills up her spine. Vines or slimy sticks or maybe living things grabbed at her legs. Her companion placed his hand on her shoulder and pressed down hard until the two of them sank into the black waters.

20

At first light John and his friends were towed back to the pier sopping wet and cold. Jackson was shivering and had a distinct blue cast to his face and lips. Ted was a little wide eyed because he and Skip had convinced themselves that the Ghost of Goshen Springs had shipwrecked them.

When they arrived at the trading post the parking lot was full of television trucks and crews. Bright lights illuminated the pier and surrounding area in the pre-dawn light. Reporters bearing microphones eagerly waited to pounce on their prey.

"What the?" said Jackson. "I cannot believe what I am seeing. Why in the world would so many reporters be here?"

Questions came from the reporters in rapid-fire succession before anyone had time to answer. The first one to stick a microphone in John's face was Sandy Storm.

"Are you stalking me?" asked John. "You end up everywhere I go."

"Mr. Skip Shafer of your legal team has been quoted as saying that the victim really was a vampire. Is that now your defense?"

John stopped and looked at Skip, who shrugged like he had no idea what she was talking about. "No, Ms. Storm, I explained to you yesterday that Mr. Boyd believed that the deceased was a vampire, and this belief caused him to lose touch with reality in such a way that he was no longer legally sane."

"Mr. Brooks, is it true that you were ghost hunting in last night's storm?"

John was so surprised by the question that he didn't respond. He simply stood there for a moment with his mouth open.

"Is it safe to say that the lawyer for Mr. Boyd has lost touch with reality in such a way that he is legally insane?"

"What happened last night?" asked another reporter. "What were you doing out there?"

"Was it worth risking the lives of all these people to go on this wild ghost hunt?" asked another.

"Is the ghost going to be a witness in your vampire case?" asked Ms. Storm.

Everyone started laughing, including John.

This girl is good, thought John. He looked Sandy Storm in the eyes. "You've discovered our surprise witness. I can't hide anything from

95

professionals like you."

Everyone laughed except Miss Storm.

"No, the Ghost of Goshen Springs will not be one of our witnesses."

"Not cooperative huh?" asked Storm. "Does that mean it will be a witness for the prosecution?"

Again, everyone laughed.

May as well make the best of this opportunity, thought John. "Okay, you've got me. Actually, this has nothing to do with the Vampire Defense case. We were about to visit some of Mr. Ted Lively's property where he recently made an amazing discovery. He has found the recipe to Goren Goshen's world famous beer at the sight of the old Goshen Springs Brewery, where the finest beer ever made was brewed. The storm came upon us suddenly. We lost our prop and were blown into a stump field, where we rode out the storm until these fine men braved the storm, found us and brought us back. I can't tell you how grateful I am to officers Harry Milner and Sam Todd with the Reservoir Patrol."

Harry and Sam smiled and waved, appreciating the mention of their names. The cameras panned to Todd and Milner who both shuffled their feet and gave aw-shucks looks to the camera.

"Somehow, they found us in the dark and rescued us. I don't know how they did it in the teeth of that terrible storm. They are two real heroes. That's who you ought to be interviewing. Now, if you don't mind, we are wet, cold and tired, and we need to get into some dry clothes. Thank you for your interest."

Motioning for his cohorts to follow him to Bobby's Trading Post, John walked quickly through the cordon of reporters.

Not a bad recovery, this guy thinks quickly on his feet, Sandy Storm said to herself. *There is more to him than I thought.* She rushed ahead to get back into his path, elbowing her way past other reporters. She positioned herself in front of John again. John was approaching her fast, but she wouldn't move. The press was pressing in from all sides, so he had to squeeze past her brushing against her body. In order to keep the microphone near his face in the crowd of reporters, she thrust her chest into his shoulder. Both she and John were startled by a feeling, like electricity, that seemed to flow between them during the contact. He paused for a moment, looked into her eyes, and had to shake off a feeling that he wanted to gaze into her eyes for just a little while longer. After a slight pause that lasted maybe a second, but seemed much longer, John moved on. Sandy moved with him, prolonging the contact.

"Who is Goren Goshen? What was the Goshen Springs Brewery? Why do you say the beer is world famous? I've never heard of it. Wouldn't I have heard of the most famous beer in the world?"

"Well, Miss Storm, I really don't know your drinking habits."

"Maybe you should."

"Are you asking me for a date on national TV?"

"That's not what I meant," she said, blushing.

"Are you getting this?" Brooks asked the cameraman, motioning to Miss Storm. Bret was happy to comply, and panned over to Storm.

"No! Stop! I'm not the story, he is," she said. She motioned for him to turn the camera back toward Brooks and tried to smile and straighten her hair for the camera. The cameraman zoomed in on her face, which was blotchy and red from embarrassment.

"Oh!" she reached up and covered the camera with her hand. The camera turned back to Brooks in time to see the door to Bobby's Trading Post closing behind Ted, who was the last to step inside.

Storm caught him by the arm and turned him into the camera. "What happened to your boat, Mr. Lively?"

With wild, darting eyes, Ted exclaimed, "The Ghost of Goshen Springs broke our prop and pushed the boat into a stump field. He could have killed us, but he didn't. John stopped him somehow. I heard the ghost screaming 'Penny! Penny!'"

Jackson jerked the door open and pulled Ted into the Trading Post.

Skip yelled, "It's true! I saw it too!"

Jackson slammed and locked the door.

"Gotcha!" said Storm under her breath as she turned triumphantly back to the camera. "There you have it. Tonight, the Vampire Defense lawyer risked the lives of three companions and two deputies in a futile search for a mythical ghost. Obviously, he is playing the public for a fool. The real question is how long will this attorney continue to use pranks to draw attention to himself and to his case? This is Sandy Storm, CTN news."

"That was harsh," said Bret as he turned the camera off. "I would hate to see what you would do to someone you weren't attracted too."

"What! I am not attracted to that shyster. Keep your opinion to yourself and point your camera where I tell you. This is our story! We were the first to break this news, and we are going to ride it as far as we can."

"It doesn't pay to get you mad. Brooks had better watch out. Maybe I had better watch out too."

"Just do your job and we will get along just fine," said Sandy as she stormed back to the news van.

Inside the Trading Post, Bobby looked at both John and Jackson as Skip and Ted wrapped towels around their shoulders.

"What are they talking about? What is this ghost business? I think

I'm gonna love this part of the story."

"John and I didn't hear anything except the wind and the thunder," said Jackson.

"Well, let me get you dry. Then, you guys can head on out. I need to open soon for the fisherman. You can bet those reporters will still be outside when you leave."

"Yeah, this attention is already getting a little old and hard to deal with," said Jackson.

John popped him with his towel, and said, "Jackson, this is just the second day, and it's already old? You know you love all the attention."

"I would, but I don't get any. You get all the attention."

Everyone laughed, relieved to be out of the boat and in a warm place, away from the reporters.

"And what is it between you and that reporter? Do you hate each other, or are you hot for each other? Or, is it both?"

"Not my type, Jackson. She is way too confrontational. Too . . . I don't know, but too much of something."

"Too much woman. Afraid you can't handle her?"

"Jackson, I don't even think about her. She is just not for me. Besides, I am way too busy for a woman in my life. This is definitely not the time. And, she does nothing for me. No attraction at all. Nada. She's just not that . . ."

"Denial is not a river in China," said Skip.

Ted and Bobby crinkled their foreheads as Jackson and John looked at each other, shrugged and nodded their heads in agreement.

"Can't deny that," said Jackson. "It is definitely not a river in China. John, you've always told me the truth before, but if you claim that girl is not absolutely the most beautiful, hottest girl who you have ever seen, then you have told me a lie for the first time."

"Okay. She looks good, but, I haven't really . . ."

"Haven't what?"

"Never mind."

"That's what I thought."

After a brief pause, Ted said, "I'm glad y'all worked that out."

"Yeah, I love this part of the story," said you-know-who.

21

Shortly after the sun came up, Travis was allowed into the shower. The shower room had tile walls with showerheads every few feet. The floor was covered with the same beige tile as the walls, with several drains strategically placed to gather the runoff. There was one other person in the shower when Travis arrived.

"Do I know you?" asked Travis. "You look familiar."

The other man looked at Travis, but did not reply. He turned his back and faced the showerhead. At that moment, another man entered the room, dressed in only a towel.

Oh, that's Evil Eye Smith, thought Travis, and he moved to a showerhead farthest from Smith. When he realized that the other man in the room was the Butcher of Belhaven, his knees gave way for a moment.

"I've got to get out of here," he said under his breath. As he turned towards the door, he saw a knife in Smith's hand. Smith was staring at Boyd's back, and Travis knew that a killing was about to take place. He was frozen with fear for a moment, then 'flight control' took over, and he had an almost irresistible urge to run, but his feet betrayed him. They would not move. His mind shouted, *run feet!* But, they would not move. He looked at his feet with disbelief, wondering why they seemed glued to the floor. Then he looked back at the drama unfolding in front of him.

Smith closed the distance between him and Boyd's back.

Boyd had no idea that death was moments away.

Travis Thomas' whole life had been one selfish act after another. He always looked out for number one. He never got involved in someone else's fight. He wanted to run. *Oh God, why do I have to be here for this?* Travis pled in silent prayer. Then, he knew. Realization came to him suddenly, with a certainty he had never before felt.

I am here to stop this!

With a shout, he charged Smith, tackling him high. Smith, quick as a cat, turned and slashed Travis across the chest, then across the neck. Travis could see his own bright red blood spurting into the air as he struggled to get control of the knife, but Smith fought like a man possessed.

"You crazy idiot!" shouted Smith. "This is not your fight. Now, you're going to die. Your whole life has been nothing but a travesty."

99

Boyd heard the shout and turned to see the life and death struggle on the tile floor behind him. The young man with the knife was overpowering Travis and seemed certain to kill him. When Boyd heard Smith's exclamation, "this is not your fight," Boyd knew that his enemies had already found him in the jail.

The last thing Travis saw before everything went black was Boyd pulling Smith off of him.

Boyd grabbed the arm that wielded the knife with one hand and threw his other arm around Smith's neck. He could not believe the strength of the skinny young man. Smith slipped out of his hold and spun around to face Boyd who was still holding Smith's knife arm.

"You will die for what you have done, and I am here to send you to hell where you belong."

Boyd knew what he was up against. He knew that he had to end the fight fast. Without a moment of hesitation he lunged forward while holding the knife arm out as far as possible. He used his greater weight to slam Smith to the floor. They each put both hands on the knife, betting everything on arm strength. Slowly, Boyd was able to turn the knife on Smith.

Smith spit at him and cursed him. Animal sounds came from his mouth and his eyes burned as though they were on fire. As the blade reached Smith's chest, Smith found new strength and growled, "You will never escape us. We are the hounds of hell!"

"God forgive you, and God forgive me," cried Boyd, and with a final burst of strength, he forced the blade through Smith's chest and into his heart. Smith made a gurgling sound and the fire left his eyes.

Three prison guards ran into the shower room and found the Butcher of Belhaven, knife in hand, naked and covered with blood from head to foot, standing over two new victims, as their fresh blood swirled down the drain. Two of the guards, overcome with fear and dread, ran the other way. The remaining guard commanded Boyd to drop the knife. He did. Emboldened, the guard commanded that Boyd lay on the floor and put his hands behind his back.

Boyd did as he was told.

22

As John drove into town, he saw a ring of satellite trucks around the jail and the police station. Jackson called him on his cell and told him that reporters were stationed at the front door of the office, so John slipped into the back door of the building unnoticed. Arriving at the office, he found an indignant librarian impatiently waiting on him. She was dressed in a rather plain dress that reached almost to her ankles. Her lips were thin and sitting upon a rather small nose was a pair of large, round, horn-rimmed glasses that made her brown eyes appear large. She examined John from head to foot, with a semi-scowl.

"So this is the infamous John Brooks, ghost hunter, huckster and defender of vampire slayers," said the librarian. "When we agreed to be a part of this defense team, we didn't realize that you would be working so hard to make us the laughing stock of the nation. Indeed, laughing stock of the world for that matter. I have never been so embarrassed in all my life. I cannot believe that you and your friends took us in. Your episode of midnight ghost hunting while my team was spending the entire night doing serious research is beyond the pale."

John stood, frozen in his tracks, mouth agape.

"So, you have nothing to say for yourself, do you? I thought not."

"Miss . . . you have me at a disadvantage. Your name would be . . .?"

"Clarion Cartier, as if you didn't know."

She handed him an envelope.

"This is the official resignation of my entire team from your defense effort," she announced in an imperious fashion. "To demonstrate our good will, I have left our extensive research on your desk, though you surely don't deserve it. We found it to be a stimulating project. It is just too bad that we were working with someone who lacks professional judgment. Good day, sir."

"Wait a moment, please. I would like to ask you . . ."

"Don't even try to stop me. Our decision is irrevocable."

And with that, she was gone.

As Clarion left, Jackson stepped into the office from the hallway.

"Who was that?" he asked. "I just stepped down the hall for a minute and it looks like you have stirred up a hornet nest while I was gone."

"Beats me. She said she and her team were part of our defense team,

101

until this morning, when she submitted this resignation." He opened the envelope and scanned the letter. "Ms. Clarion Cartier and a team of three librarians from Eudora Welty Library having been retained by Mr. Skip Shafer on a research project, have formally resigned."

"Retained? Skip?"

"That's what it says. Oh, she also said she left some research on my desk. Let's take a look."

Jackson and John stepped into John's office and found three neatly arranged, six-inch stacks containing copies of newspaper, Internet and magazine articles concerning mysterious deaths around the United States.

"Wow! What a treasure trove."

"Yes, but it may be too much of a good thing. There is so much data here that it will take days to work through it. Besides, we don't know how these crimes are related to ours, or even if they are related."

"Karen is really good at organizing this sort of thing."

"Well, that is true, but she already has so much to do. Besides, it's sort of a self serving cop-out for us to pass the hard work off on Karen by saying she's good at it, don't you think?"

Jackson laughed. "Maybe you're right. Where is Karen anyway?"

"You were here before me, didn't you see her?"

"No, I had to open up this morning, which is weird, since she is always the first one here, and I am usually the last."

"No messages from her?"

"No."

"That is just a little too strange," said John as he reached for the phone and dialed Karen's home number.

"No answer." He dialed her cell. "No answer."

"We're ba-aack," sounded a familiar voice.

John and Jackson looked up in time to see Bret adjusting his camera on his shoulder.

"Again! What are you doing here?"

"My on-air personality just can't stay away from you."

"Hush Bret! That was unprofessional," came a huffy retort as Sandy Storm stepped around the corner. "This was easy access to both lawyers. Where is your little red-headed guard dog?"

"Speaking of unprofessional. You are going way too far."

"Touchy, touchy, I must have hit a nerve. That confirms what I thought."

"And what did you think?"

"That there is something going on between you two."

"You're wrong."

"Am I?"

"She is just missing today. And I am a little concerned, that's all."

"Really, that's interesting. Maybe she couldn't take the heat."

Bret cleared his throat noisily. Jackson raised an eyebrow.

"Pardon?" asked John.

Storm blushed, but recovered quickly with, "Maybe she doesn't like all the publicity swirling around this case and all the attention that is being generated about you, your office, this town. With so much journalistic firepower present in this little town, everybody's little secrets are bound to come out. Do you have any little secrets you want to share with my viewers now, or do you just want to hear about them on the evening news?"

"Sorry, I never see the evening news. I don't have time for that sort of thing. Now, if you will excuse us, we have work to do."

"We will get right out of your way, but first I want to get your reaction to the latest charges against your client."

"What do you mean?"

"Don't tell me the great all knowing John Brooks hasn't heard. Your client has just been charged with the murder of one John Smith, and aggravated assault on one Travis Thomas, who I believe is, or was another client of yours."

"What!"

"Yes, and the aggravated assault charge may be upgraded to murder any time now. It seems that Travis T, as he is known, is not expected to live."

"I am stunned. Where is Travis?"

"University of Mississippi Medical Center I believe. Are we rolling Bret?"

"You're hot."

"Thank you. But are we on the air."

"That's what I meant."

"Mr. Brooks, were these latest victims also vampires?"

"I am just this moment learning about the latest charges."

"So, are you suggesting that they may be vampires? Are we having a rash of vampire slayings in Jackson, Mississippi, or is it normal to find this many vampires here?"

"Miss Storm, I am not suggesting any such thing. Furthermore, we have never accused anyone of being a vampire. Mr. Boyd believed that one man who died in the house in Belhaven was a vampire. As for any new charges, I have nothing to say at this time. I need to learn more about the charges."

"Do you agree that these new charges are devastating to your unique

103

defense?"

"You and I don't seem to have anything that we can agree upon. Now, if you will please leave my office, we have work to do."

John turned and stepped through the doorway into his separate office. As he was closing the door, he turned to Jackson and said, "Please escort Ms. Storm and her cameraman out of the building."

"Oh, that won't be necessary. We have rented the space across the hall until our story is complete. Headquarters decided that this was a big enough story to keep a staff busy locally."

She motioned to an open door across the hall where two people sat at a folding table. "Meet Glen and Marty. They will be manning the office, following up on leads and editing some of our stories while Bret and I are in the field."

"Great. Nice to meet you," said John unconvincingly.

"We will be seeing you often until the public loses interest in this story, and then we will be gone. Good day." With that announcement, Sandy and Bret stepped across the hall.

"Good grief," said Jackson.

"You can say that again."

"Good grief."

"Jackson, would you please look for Karen and see what is up with her? It's not like her to not show up and not call. I'm going to try to find out what's up with these new charges."

"Sure. Be glad to."

"Oh, and if you don't mind, please see if you can rein in Skip. While you're at it, find out what is up with our librarian friends."

"I can't wait to hear Skip's explanation. Let me know what you hear about the new charges."

John hurried over to the University Medical Center. If Travis was about to die, he wanted to at least try to see him before it was too late. UMC is a sprawling facility with a myriad of buildings, parking garages and lots. It took a while to find a parking spot and learn how to find Travis.

John found his way to ICU and explained that he was Travis Thomas' lawyer and would like to see him if it was possible. Just then, two uniformed policemen approached. One said to the nurse, "This is Mr. Thomas' ex-lawyer."

"What do you mean?"

"Court says you've got a conflict, what with one client trying to kill another. Travis T is under 24-hour protective security and surveillance. He is going to be a key witness against your Butcher of Belhaven."

"Has Travis fired me?"

"He will when he wakes up. If he wakes up."

"Well, he's still my client until he fires me or until I withdraw. I don't know what has happened, so I don't know if I need to withdraw."

"You're going to have to withdraw. Three guards saw your client murder that poor kid, Smith, and cut Travis T to pieces. Your client was apparently performing some kind of ritual killing. He was stark naked and he had painted himself head to foot with the blood of his victims."

"If the guards saw this, why didn't they stop him? How could he have had time to do all that with three witnesses watching?"

"You never stop lawyering, do you? Here comes Mr. Travis T's new lawyer now."

John looked down the hall and saw retired Judge Bell walking towards them. Bell had recently returned to law practice. What was left of his hair almost matched his dark gray suit.

"Lawyer Brooks. Sorry to see you like this. I don't know what to think about our situation, but I got a call from the Court Administrator saying that you were being replaced as Travis T's lawyer, and I am now his new lawyer. You might think this is a travesty and it might be."

"I just don't know enough about anything right now. Do you know what happened?"

"No more than what these officers just told you. That, and I got a call from the high and mighty D.A. himself right after I was appointed. He offered me a sweetheart deal. Travis T walks on all pending charges and on his parole violation if he cooperates and testifies against Boyd. I never received such an offer so soon after being appointed. It's mighty peculiar. They really want your man Boyd."

"I guess they do. What's Travis going to do?"

"What do you think? It's a get out of jail free card. He will jump at it. Then he'll be back in jail next month on a new charge. The D.A. wins all around. He gets Boyd, and he gets Travis T later on some other charge."

"Are you sure Travis will take the deal?"

"In over 30 years of doing this I have never had a criminal defendant who didn't take a deal to swap testimony for a dismissal; but I haven't been able to talk to him yet. He is still unconscious."

John's cell phone rang. He looked at the caller ID and saw that Jackson was calling. "Excuse me Judge Bell, I think I need to take this. Hey Jackson, what's up."

"They found Karen's car at KanKo's," said Jackson. "Karen is missing."

John felt Judge Bell's hand grip his shoulder. "What is it son, all the color left you face. You turned white as a sheet!"

John could hear Jackson on the phone saying, "John, are you there?"

John leaned against the wall, shook his head and said, "Yes, Jackson, just a minute. Judge Bell, I've just gotten some really bad news. Can we talk later? I've got to go."

"Sure, John. Take it easy. You might need to sit down and gather your thoughts before you run off. Do you need a ride somewhere? I'll take you."

"Thanks, I'll be all right. It's just such a shock. Excuse me."

John hurried down the hall to get to his car. He didn't know where he was going or what he was going to do; he just knew he had to do something.

"Jackson, tell me everything you know while I get to my car."

As soon as he got off the phone with Jackson, he drove to KanKo's. A tow-truck was about to drive away with Karen's car when he arrived.

"It's being taken in for evidence," explained the driver.

"Evidence of what?" asked John, afraid to hear the answer.

"There's a policeman inside. He can tell you everything."

John rushed into the store and identified himself to the policeman.

"Where is Karen?"

"We don't know. It seems that the night manager was expecting her to drop some material off last night for him to copy and organize by this morning. She never showed. When he was leaving this morning, he saw her car in the lot. Her purse was under the back bumper. She was nowhere in sight."

John could not believe his ears.

"It can't be. No way. Not Karen. Oh, God! No! Lord, please protect her." He shook his head clear, then asked, "Did anyone see anything?"

"Not a thing."

"Thanks officer."

John dialed Rico's number.

"Yellow, Rico here." Rico often answered with "yellow" instead of "hello."

"This is John Brooks. I need your help."

"We're on different sides buddy."

"Not on this. Karen, my assistant, is missing. I think she may have been kidnapped. I received a warning note yesterday. I didn't think much about it. I didn't do anything about it. If I had, maybe this would not have happened. I need your help to find her."

"Slow down buddy. I've got some news for you."

John stopped and leaned against the wall. "Yeah, go ahead. Let's hear it."

23

District Attorney Buddy Tellers was a tough prosecutor, well known for his withering cross-examinations. He was also a master manipulator and an ambitious politician who was always looking toward the next election. He constantly gauged his chances to achieve higher office. Winning was everything to Tellers and it was believed that he would go to any extreme to win. There were rumors of corruption but nothing could be proven. He knew the rules of evidence and he knew how far he could stretch them without getting a mistrial.

He was not above committing reversible error in order to get a conviction. If the appellate court reversed him, he would just blame the "liberal judges" for letting the dangerous guilty criminal go free. It did not matter to him if the judges he railed against fit the public perception of liberal or conservative. As far as Tellers was concerned, any judge that ruled against him was a liberal. It was a double win for him. He would get positive press for getting the conviction; then he would be back in the press two years later railing against the courts when the conviction was reversed. He felt that the positive press he obtained guaranteed his re-election.

Recently a young lawyer was interfering with the tried and true political formula. He kept getting defense verdicts. That meant bad press for Buddy and a lost opportunity to fume at the dastardly appellate courts that tried in vain to keep him in check. He instinctively knew not to blame the jurors. They were, after all, selected from the registered voters. He wanted to find a way to get rid of this kid. Sometimes he thought he might try to use his connections to get him a good government job somewhere out of sight. Or, better yet, just beat him badly in court. Buddy was looking for just the right opportunity to put this young lawyer in his place.

Now, the kid had given him that opportunity. The world press was watching and Brooks had come up with a nutty defense. Buddy knew that if he played his cards right, this new case would become his career case. When he was done with Brooks, he could stick a fork in the kid's career. Brooks would be done.

Buddy had demanded that every local law enforcement entity give him prompt updates on any development having anything to do with the Vampire Defense case. He and his staff had already had their fill of laughs over the Ghost of Goshen Springs episode when he received another update, this one about the supposed kidnapping of John Brooks' secretary.

It seems that right after rescuing Brooks and company, the Reservoir Patrolmen Milner and Todd were returning upstream to Ratliff's Ferry and were flagged down by Karen Wilkes, who had this wild story about being kidnapped by three people who were wearing masks. This was just too good to be true. It was an unbelievable coincidence that Brooks' secretary would be kidnapped and taken to the same area where Brooks was last night. Then the same guys rescue them both? There was no way that anyone was going to believe this. Buddy saw an opportunity to permanently put Brooks away.

"Brooks will have no credibility left when I am through with him, Marsha!" he called to his secretary. "Arrange a press conference as soon as you can. I want to be the first to comment on this latest development."

Since every major network had a satellite truck at the courthouse around the clock, it did not take long to arrange a press conference. Buddy, wearing his best trial suit, adjusted his tie and approached a podium crowded with microphones. The gathered reporters waited expectantly. The click and flash of cameras filled the air. Tellers felt a moment of apprehension when he saw the number of cameras focused on him. His flirtation with doubt lasted only a second and was replaced by exhilaration when he realized that untold millions would be listening to his comments. As he looked out into the sea of reporters, he thought to himself that before this case was over Buddy Tellers would be a household name across America.

"Thank you for coming together on short notice. I want to announce a major development in the case that has come to be known as the Vampire Defense. You have already heard about the episode last night when John Brooks, the lawyer who invented the Vampire Defense, went wild ghost hunting on the reservoir. We were speculating that he might be looking for a supernatural witness to help him with his case, because he is going to need supernatural help to win."

Buddy waited for the laughter among the press corps to die down.

"We now have a report that Mr. Brooks' secretary was supposedly kidnapped last night," he continued. "She was found this morning unharmed in the same vicinity where Mr. Brooks was also found this morning. Because of the extreme coincidence surrounding the rescue of Mr. Brooks, coupled with the rescue of his secretary the same morning, in the same body of water, by the same rescuers, within a short distance of the supposed ghost hunt and the supposed kidnapping, I have instituted an investigation into the possible false reporting of a kidnapping."

There were several gasps in the crowd.

"One of the many features of Ms. Wilkes' story that alerted authorities to the need for an investigation was her claim that she was kidnapped by, get this, Marilyn Monroe, Freddy Krueger and the Wicked Witch of the East."

There was general laughter and shaking of heads among the press.

"This preposterous story, when coupled with Mr. Brooks' outlandish story about ghost hunting, re-coupled with the unusual circumstances that the kidnappers, Marilyn Monroe, Freddy Krueger and the Wicked Witch of the East would take Ms. Wilkes to virtually the same place that Mr. Brooks was ghost hunting indicates that this entire episode is some sort of attention grabbing gimmick, just like the rest of the supposed Vampire Defense."

Tellers paused for effect, and then he continued, "Ms. Wilkes is not the only member of the defense team being investigated. An investigator for the defense, Mr. Skip "the Middleman" Schafer, has been prosecuted for false pretense and is currently being investigated for false advertisement. Clearly, the entire defense team has a problem distinguishing truth from fantasy."

After a few groans from the reporters, Buddy continued, "I will not allow the public or the justice system to be taken advantage of by charlatans. Justice will be done. That concludes this press conference."

Tellers turned and walked away from the podium, ignoring the many shouted questions from reporters. When he returned to his office, he was greeted with applause from his staff. Assistant prosecutors, staff and friends rushed to him to shake his hand, pat him on the back and congratulate him.

"That was awesome!"

"Great presentation."

"That's the end of the Vampire Defense team."

They ushered him to a chair in the lobby, where three televisions were set up tuned to channels covering the breaking news about the Tellers press conference.

*   *   *

"Looks like you were right about that lawyer all along," said Bret as he took down his camera. "He sure had me fooled. I thought he was different."

"I don't know," said Sandy Storm as she continued looking at the empty podium. "Something just doesn't seem right about this."

"What are you talking about? You have been suspicious of this guy from the beginning. Now that your suspicions are confirmed you have doubts! I can't believe this. You haven't fallen for this guy, have you?"

"Bret! You know me better than that. I chase the story wherever it leads. Right now my gut is telling me that something is fishy about this announcement. I'm not ready to buy it. At least not yet."

"I can tell you this, after today's developments, I suspect a lot of networks will be reassigning assets. They are not going to want to waste so much effort on some Podunk lawyer making a fool of himself."

*   *   *

Moments later, several reporters caught up with Skip on the street near the law office. Soon the broadcast of their interview with "a prominent member of the Vampire Defense Team," was on every network.

"What do you think of the District Attorney's charge that Karen Wilkes falsely reported she was kidnapped?"

"He is making a mistake of epidemic proportions."

The press corps laughed.

"You are Skip Schafer, the member of the Vampire Defense Team that was charged with false pretense, right?"

"Those charges were dismissed, thanks to the efforts of John Brooks."

"Do you admit that you don't have any qualifications to work on a legal team?"

"I think you misunderestimate me."

More reporters chuckled and shook their heads.

"Don't you think that the criminal charges against you affect the credibility of your team?"

"I hadn't thought of that."

"Don't you think that it shows poor judgment on the part of Mr. Brooks to add you to the Vampire Defense Team, considering your reputation?"

"Well, I don't know. Hindsight is 50-50."

Again, the press corps laughed out loud.

Skip continued answering questions for several minutes, but he finally realized that the reporters were not interested in the truth; they were only interested in one sensational angle or another. Skip managed to escape and return to the office.

Skip's interview was replayed over and over on all the major networks for several days. At first, almost every commentator expressed the opinion that Skip was an idiot. However, a few contrarian commentators thought that his comments might be clever innuendos. They noted that he might have said exactly what he meant and speculated that a mistake of epidemic proportions might be one that leads to a rash of other mistakes, and hindsight is not always as clear as one may think.

Several in the media began to think that Skip might actually be a genius with a knack for describing complex ideas with a quick turn of a phrase. Everyone agreed that the term misunderestimate was perfect, because either they had not underestimated him enough, or they had totally underestimated him. Both definitions could be true, leading a few pundits to believe that Skip was a genius with an unusual mastery of the English language.

In any event, Buddy's announcement had the hoped for effect. The talking heads and "experts" on each of the national and cable networks were in general agreement that the Ghost of Goshen Springs episode coupled with the kidnapping charge exploded any credibility the Vampire Defense lawyer might have had. Now, he was seen simply as someone using outlandish claims to seek the spotlight.

By that evening, Professor Bishop had appeared on every network explaining how the day's events had proven his initial assessment correct. One network ran a poll on the likelihood of the success of the Vampire Defense. Less than 5 percent believed that the defense would succeed. Another famous network personality sponsored a "Pinhead vs. Patriot" poll on John Brooks. 92 percent voted "Pinhead."

24

John received the news about Karen from Rico. He was relieved that she was safe, but alarmed and angry that she had been kidnapped. When he returned to his office, he was not surprised to find an email from Karen explaining that she was so frightened by her experience that she simply could not stay in Jackson any longer.

"John," wrote Karen, "I am so sorry to leave when you really need help, but I am so afraid after what happened to me last night. If Father Michael McCarty had not rescued me, I just don't know what would have happened to me. I need to get away and recover at a place where I can feel safe. I am going home to stay with my parents for a while. I will call you when I am able to deal with the world again. I can't talk to you right now because I can't face you. I know you are disappointed in me for leaving you now when you need me most. Please forgive me. Karen."

John felt overwhelmed. The fear that she was harmed, followed by the relief that she was safe, followed by the realization that she was gone set him upon an unexpected emotional rollercoaster. He had asked for a career case. Now, it seemed that this was a career ending case. He sat behind his desk lost in thought, wondering what life would be like now that Karen was gone. She had been a part of his practice from the beginning; indeed, she had been a part of his life for five years. He had always relied on her. Now, she was gone. He was not sure what he felt, but he didn't like it. He stared out the window at the cordon of satellite trucks. He looked at the statue of Moses, the lawgiver, on top of the courthouse. He cast his eyes to Heaven, and said simply, "God, please help. Please help me help Hal. Please help Travis and Karen."

John heard Jackson's voice behind him saying, "He's not going to help you. I don't know why you believe in this God of yours. If there was a God, bad things wouldn't happen and we wouldn't have days like today."

John turned and found Jackson standing in the doorway.

"If there was a God, He wouldn't let so many bad things happen to good people like you."

At that moment, they both heard something in the lobby. Jackson turned his head and with a perturbed look on his face, said, "When it rains it 'Storms.' John, you can't catch a break today."

"Good grief. Tell her I don't have time for an interview."

"I'm not here for an interview, Mr. Brooks," said Sandy Storm as she and Bret stepped into the doorway beside Jackson. "I want to give you some information."

Both Jackson and John raised their eyebrows at that remark.

"Did I hear you right?"

"I just left a press conference by the District Attorney. He is accusing your assistant Karen of making a false report of being kidnapped."

"What!"

"He is treating it as a criminal investigation."

"You've got to be kidding! Are you here to get my reaction?"

"No. Not this time. It did not make sense to me. I can't ignore this new angle, but I plan to examine the claims made by the prosecutor, because they just don't ring true to me."

John almost collapsed into his chair and placed his head in his hands.

"Give me just a minute. Let me absorb all of this."

At that moment, Skip ran into the office, hollering, "John! John! You won't believe what they are saying about you and Karen!"

He ran into the office and saw Storm and Bret. "Oh, it's you! Don't talk to them John. They can't be trusted. They are trying to hurt you. All of them are. You won't believe what those reporters are doing. They are spreading the D.A.'s lies and trying to hurt you. I am sorry I brought them to you."

"It's okay, Skip," said John.

"No, it's not okay. They are accusing you and Karen of some sort of fraud, making up a kidnapping and other things."

Then Skip looked sheepishly at John and Jackson and said, "And they are using me against you. They know about my past, and they are trying to make you look like a fool or worse for letting me be part of your team."

"I knew it!" said Jackson with indignation. "That's why I didn't want you to let him have anything to do with us. But he begged you and you gave in. It's because of that soft heart of yours. All you let him do was go to the public library to look something up and look what happened."

"John, I am so sorry. I never meant for this to happen. I told you that I had never done anything worthwhile in my life, and you were good enough to trust me and give me a chance to be part of something big; now, I have let you down. I have to quit so they won't keep using my past against you."

Sandy and Bret had been looking at Skip and Jackson. Now all eyes turned to John. Before he could say anything, Ted Lively bounded into the office. "John, I am so sorry. I never imagined that when I asked you

113

to help me with the Goshen Springs Beer project, all of this would happen. I feel like this is my fault. Is there anything I can do to help?"

"Ted, Skip, don't blame yourselves. It's not your fault. The timing of all of this is just so improbable."

"No, it is my fault," said Ted. "I took you out at night on that trip to the island. You wanted to wait, but I insisted. Now, they are claiming that our trip was somehow related to Karen's kidnapping and it was all made up! It is just not right. I want to do something to help straighten this out."

Bret and Sandy looked at each other and Bret shrugged and raised his eyebrows, signifying that he found this interesting. Then, a tall young woman appeared at the door to John's office.

"Jennifer, what brings you back so soon?" asked Jackson.

"I heard on the radio that they were accusing my favorite customer of some kind of fraud, or false reporting of a crime or something. I knew that had to be a lie so I came here to see if there was anything I could do to help."

John rose from his desk and gave Jennifer a hug.

"Thank you, Jen. Sandy, Bret, Skip and Ted, this is Jennifer Wolfe, our computer programmer and de-bugger."

Jennifer said her hellos and then John said, "Thank you for being here, but I don't know what you can do to help."

"I am here to donate my time to help prove that you and Karen are innocent of any wrong doing and to help with your Vampire Defense. If you have a lot of data to organize, or Internet searches to conduct, or computers to hack, legally of course, then I'm your girl."

Jackson finally answered a ringing phone.

"Karen! Glad to hear your voice. Are you all right? Sure, just a second. We have a meeting going on that you would be interested in. Do you want me to turn on the speaker phone?"

Jackson pushed the speakerphone button and said, "Do you hear me?"

"Yes, I don't care who hears this," she said in a determined voice. "John, I just heard what they are saying about me and about you. I am so sorry I brought this on you. It is so unfair."

"It is not your fault Karen. I am so glad you are all right."

"Please forgive me for leaving when you need me most."

"Don't give it another thought. I understand completely. If you hadn't left, I would have sent you away for your own protection; there is nothing to forgive."

"Well, I am coming back."

"No way, Karen! I want you safe."

"I am coming back unless you are firing me. And if you dare even think of such a dastardly thing, I'll come back anyway and I will be in a really bad mood. Do you understand me?"

"Yes. But Karen."

"No buts. I am coming back."

"I can't stand the thought of something happening to you because of me."

Before Karen could say anything else, three athletic men stepped into John's office. The first one through the door said, "I guess you all are wondering why I called this meeting."

Everyone laughed, and Bret noted that the room was getting really crowded.

"Mitch, Max, Bubba!" exclaimed John. "What brings my rugby buddies here?"

"We heard the lies about you on the news. Some of the guys have been talking and decided that the team needed to stand by you. You know we don't believe the lies the D.A. is telling, but we felt like we might be able to help."

"Thanks Mitch, but what do you mean?"

"There are enough of us that we can arrange for someone to be around your office any time you or Karen or anyone else is here. Maybe having a few of us around will discourage the kidnappers and help keep them away."

"Problem solved!" said Karen over the speakerphone.

"Thank you, but that's too much, guys. Y'all can't afford to spend that kind of time here, and besides, you are not professional bodyguards."

"Don't you dare refuse their help! Don't you want me to be safe?"

"It's true that we are not bodyguards, but we can handle ourselves pretty well," said Max. "A few of the guys are looking for jobs, and they have time on their hands."

"Max, I don't have the money to pay them."

"John—I can't believe what you're saying," said Karen, with a lilting, hurt tone in her voice. "You mean I am not worth a few dollars to you?"

"No, Karen. I mean yes. That's not what I am talking about. I don't want a false feeling of security. If I can't pay them and if they get a job appointment or go on an interview, then who could blame them? But if we started to rely on them, then I might get you exposed to danger again."

"Don't worry, it's taken care of," said Bubba in a deep baritone voice. "The team is chipping in. Besides, you might want us to help prepare your defense. You could send us to look for witnesses. We can be pretty good amateur investigators, as you know. Some of us have done it for you before."

"That's true, and a fine job you did, too."

Sandy and Bret were both amazed at the group that had spontaneously appeared pledging help. Then Sandy asked, "Why are you all so willing to give your time and money to help?"

"If you knew John, you would know why," said Jennifer.

"He has helped us and never asked for anything in return," added Bubba.

"John is a good and honest man," said Ted. "If he tells you something, you can take it to the bank."

"He is in trouble, and we are going to help," said Mitch. "We will not let this man down."

"Wow!" said Bret.

"What can we do?" said several voices at once.

Sandy noticed Bret was looking at her and smiling. She was about to ask him why he was smiling when she suddenly realized that she had joined the chorus of voices asking, "What can we do?" She leaned over and whispered to Bret, "I can't believe I said that."

"Don't worry. It's contagious. I was thinking it when you said it."

"I am overwhelmed," said John. "All right. Jackson, we have an unbeatable team, especially with our rugby buddies, because they don't know how to lose. I've got a few ideas about where to start, but first I need to say thanks."

"Why am I not surprised?" said Jennifer as she rolled her eyes and looked at Jackson, who shrugged his shoulders in resignation.

"Sorry Jen. Jennifer is one of my non-believing friends. She can't stand it when people pray. She thinks it is superstitious mumbo jumbo. But, she tolerates me when I pray, right Jen?"

"Yeah, but you are the only religious wacko that I tolerate."

John took a knee and bowed his head and the room became silent.

"Wow! God, Jackson and I are overwhelmed. Thank you for answering that simple prayer so quickly and so decisively."

Jennifer looked at Jackson, who mouthed, "I'll tell you later."

John continued: "We know that when two or more are present in Your name, You are present with us. We welcome You here in our midst. Now that You have given us a wealth of help, please grant to us the wisdom to use it. Thank You for delivering Karen from the hands of the kidnappers. We ask that You place a hedge of protection around Karen, around everyone here, and around everyone on our team. Give us eyes to see the truth and access to witnesses and evidence that will help us know the truth.

"And finally, Lord, I ask that for those who do not yet know You, for

116

those who still doubt You, I pray that out of Your glorious riches You would strengthen us with power through your Spirit in our inner being so that Christ may dwell in our hearts through faith. And I pray that we, being rooted and established in Your love, may have power, together with all the saints, to grasp how wide and long and high and deep the love of Christ is for us and to know this love that surpasses knowledge. I pray that each of us will be filled to the measure of all the fullness of God. And now to Him who is able to do immeasurably more than all we ask or imagine, just as He has demonstrated in the last few minutes, to Him be the glory, in Jesus' name we pray."

The room was silent for several seconds. A few wiped their eyes. Jennifer and Jackson glanced at each other and held each other's gaze. They silently acknowledged to each other that they were both moved by the prayer.

"Thank you, John," said Karen over the speakerphone.

With a look of amazement on her face, Sandy observed everyone.

"Skip, I don't know how the librarians became part of our 'team', but they quit a little while ago over embarrassment related to the Ghost of Goshen Springs. They did some great research. I would like to get them back on our team. Ted, can you and Skip visit them and tell them about last night and about your discovery? See if you can get them back on our side. We will need all the help we can get. Later, they may be helpful to us when we need research on your project concerning Goren Goshen."

"Sure, John," said Skip excitedly.

"Yeah, I can do that," said Ted.

"Jennifer, we are going to need to organize information in such a way that we can absorb it and access it quickly. Is there something you can do to help?"

"There is some software that can help. I can scan documents and upload them into the cloud so that you can access them wherever you are, including the courtroom. I can add some data about each document to create a sort of index so that the documents can be categorized and searched more easily. And, with projectors, documents could be projected on a screen and you can add highlighting and text boxes. They could become very effective exhibits to show a jury."

"Great! Karen, when you get back could you work with Jennifer on that project?"

"Of course!"

"Mitch, could you arrange for someone to look around Cypress Swamp for any clues? Rico told me that Karen escaped from her captors at the swamp. I want you to take cameras. Video would be good. Still shots if you don't have video. Take both if you can.

117

"Jackson, we need you to finish your project on the insanity defense. Also, I want you to try to get in touch with this former priest, Father Michael McCarty. He could be a key. We need to canvas the Belhaven neighborhood and talk with every witness who knows anything about the event and about the occupants of the house."

"We've got that covered," said Mitch.

"I will be with Hal to determine everything he did leading up to the moment he arrived at the house. We will carry that back as far as we need to, which I suppose includes his relationship with his fiancée right up to the day of the killings. Jackson, please join me as soon as you are through with the research we need. Two heads are always better than one."

"Does the Vampire Defense case really matter now that there are two new charges?" asked Sandy. "Is it worth all this effort if he gets convicted anyway on the new charges? How do you feel about representing someone who committed a ritualistic murder of one or two people in the jail while he was incarcerated for multiple murders?"

The questions put an immediate damper on the buoyant mood in the room.

"Yes, it matters. Every case that we handle matters to our client. If we win the Vampire Defense and lose the other cases, so be it; but we don't know the facts of the jail cases yet. I will be seeing Hal about that shortly. I believe there is much more to that story than we know."

John looked around the room until his eyes fell on Sandy and Bret. The room became silent once again as all eyes fell on Sandy. Her eyes met John's and she heard herself say: "I am sorry for those questions. I can't help it. It's in my blood. But, to tell you the truth, being here and seeing all of you wanting to help makes me want to help too. I can't promise to be on your side. All I can do is tell you that we will fairly report what we find. In addition, we can take an interest in parts of the story that you might find helpful, if you understand what I mean."

"Thank you Sandy. I understand. You can get Karen's story out. You could talk with the officers who found her. You can let the public know that Karen did not make a fanciful claim that she had been kidnapped by Freddy Krueger, the Wicked Witch and Marilyn Monroe, as suggested by the D.A. Instead, she said that her kidnappers were wearing masks. Speaking of masks, do you think you could check with every place in the area that sells masks and see if you can find out who bought masks of Krueger, the Wicked Witch and Monroe in the past few days?"

"That would be vital to your case. Are you sure you want to trust that task to me and Bret?"

118

"I wouldn't trust anyone else to that job. I pity the poor prevaricating prosecutor who pits himself against you."

"Me too," said Bret.

Sandy's face broke into a huge smile, her eyes flashed with excitement, and she said with enthusiasm, "We're on it!"

As the group began to break up, Sandy caught up with Jennifer.

"Pardon my asking, but is John for real? That prayer was over the top, but he doesn't seem like one of those holier than thou types."

"He is the real deal. That is a good man, who tries to live out his faith; however misguided that faith may be. He believes it, and he tries to live it."

"How did you two become friends?"

"He dated a friend of mine for a while. We met and he found out that I do computer programming and consulting. He needed help, so he became one of my clients. We have become great friends. I call him from time to time with an ethical question related to business and he always gives me good advice. Even though our values are quite different, it seems that we often come to the same conclusions. We just get there from opposite directions."

"So, he is not dating your friend anymore?"

"No, that didn't last. Too bad for her, I say."

"What about you two? You really seem to admire him. Are you two, you know, a couple?"

Jennifer considered the question for a moment and decided to play with Sandy a bit. "We love each other."

Sandy's features dropped for a moment as she said, "Oh. Congratulations I guess."

"It's not like that. We don't date, and we never will. We love each other as friends only. You see, he goes to church all the time, his friends are predominantly Christians, he prays all the time, he doesn't believe in, well, doing some things until marriage."

"Really?"

"Really."

"I couldn't put up with all of that stuff. It would never work out between us. And then there is that 'unequally yoked' stuff that Christian men seemed concerned about when they are not trying to get you in bed."

"I know what you mean."

"Well, John was different. We actually had a discussion about whether we should take things to another level. He said that, because of our faith difference, the best way for us to love each other would be as friends, and not as lovers. Imagine a guy saying that."

119

"Is he seeing anyone now?"

"No. I tried to fix him up a couple of times, but most of my friends are the wrong kind of friends."

"What about his secretary, Karen?"

"No, they don't see each other."

"Do you know where he lives?"

25

It was an hour before sunset when John left the office with the notes his team had compiled. The story he heard from Hal was chilling. The kidnapping of Karen was proof to John that Hal was telling the truth about the attack in the jail. Hal had enemies who were able to reach him in the jail and arrange for the kidnapping of his lawyer's secretary. No one was safe while this case was pending. The day had been emotionally intense and he was looking forward to an evening to reflect on all that had happened. He imagined settling into a comfortable chair on the roof of his houseboat in the middle of the lake just in time to watch the sun go down. Later, he would study the pile of notes and memos his team had produced that afternoon.

As he headed for his Isuzu Trooper, he was far more wary than usual, trying his best to notice anything unusual. He watched his rearview mirror as he drove north on I-55, past Water-Works, St. Dominic, and Highland Village. He took the County Line Road exit, made his way to Lake Harbor Road and proceeded to Main Harbor on the reservoir. His usual parking space close to the stairway that led to the top of the dike was empty, so he pulled in and gathered his notes. When he topped the dike, he saw a giant of a man standing just inside the gate that controlled access to the pier. He knew only one person who consumed so much space.

"Crush! If you are my guard, I have absolutely nothing to worry about!"

Pleased to hear the compliment, Crush Ulysses Barnes broke into a broad grin. "You got that right little buddy," said Crush as he swung the gate open. "I got your back."

"Yeah, and my front and both sides."

"Nobody's getting past me," bragged Crush as they walked down the pier.

John noticed that the wide pier seemed too narrow when he shared it with Crush. When they arrived at John's Drifter, John was startled to see Sandy lounging on the forward deck sipping wine.

"How did you find me, and how did you get past Crush?"

"She told me she was your friend, and I let her in," explained Crush.

John noticed that Crush, who had been beaming, suddenly seemed crushed. John quickly patted Crush on the back and said, "She's fine,

Crush, I'm just teasing her."

"Crush and I are good friends now. He told me lots of stories about you. I learned about your rugby escapades. Some might make good human interest stories as fillers between reports on the vampire case." She looked at Crush and continued, "With Crush as your personal bodyguard, you will never have to worry."

Crush was beaming again.

"You're right about that. Now, how did you find my place? I don't have an address you can look up."

"We have our ways."

"Why are you here? Looking for another story angle perhaps?"

"Perhaps." She looked at Crush and winked.

Crush smiled and then said, "John, I'm going to be at the gate or in my car until Ryan gets here. Just call if you need anything."

"No, Crush, stay here. Let me get you something to drink, or how about something to eat. You're always hungry."

"Sandy fixed me up with a cooler with everything I could want. I'll be fine."

Crush slapped John on the back with a big paw and moved quickly and quietly down the pier in a manner that both belied his size and evidenced his innate athletic ability.

As John stepped on the deck, Sandy rose from her chair. He saw that she was in a short, white dress, gathered at the waist and cut revealingly low. Her dark tan was enhanced by the color of the dress. She handed him a glass of wine as she stepped forward to greet him. She observed that he was enjoying looking at her and she smiled, revealing a deep dimple on her left cheek. She stood close to him. He could detect the light flowery aroma of her perfume.

Their eyes met and she held his gaze. John could not remember seeing anything so beautiful as her eyes. His eyes were drawn to her full, moist lips as she sipped her wine. As she savored the wine, her lips parted for a moment and he watched as her tongue barely touched her lower lip seeking the last droplet of wine. She seemed to know that John was mesmerized. With a sly smile, she moved away, swaying her hips, and said, "You are full of surprises. Why did you decide to live on a houseboat?"

Pausing for a moment to recover from the spell she had cast upon him, John responded, "When I was looking for a place to live, an apartment did not appeal to me. I wanted to live on the water at the reservoir, but everything available was way too expensive. Then, it occurred to me that I could buy a houseboat and literally live on the water. Now, I can tell everyone that I live in an exclusive gated waterfront community," replied John with a laugh. "So, are you disappointed that I don't have a more suitable residence?"

"I think it's interesting, like you. Speaking of interesting, why don't you turn on your TV. I think that there will be something on in a few minutes that you will like."

"Actually, I don't own a TV."

"What? Are you living in the dark ages?"

"Yes, I guess I am. To tell you the truth, I am too busy to spend time watching TV. I haven't had one for years and I find that I just don't miss it."

"That is unreal. If you had a TV, you could see my interview of the reservoir patrolmen who picked up Karen miles from Goren Island. The D.A. implied the two spots were close together, but they are not. We asked the D.A. to explain that discrepancy, but he changed the subject."

"That's good. I wish I could see that."

"That's not all. We confronted him with his representation of Karen's claim that the Wicked Witch, Freddy Krueger and Marilyn Monroe kidnapped her, when in fact her story was that the people who kidnapped her were wearing those masks. We asked him if he misled the public by implying that she was deranged when she claimed that Freddy Krueger and others had kidnapped her. He just got angry and claimed we were nitpicking. He said the public knew exactly what he meant."

"Awesome. Some publicity finally goes our way. Thank you."

"That's not all. We got a lead on someone purchasing the masks. A fellow bought masks fitting those descriptions at a place called Jaki's International in Jackson. Except that he bought an Einstein mask instead of a Wicked Witch mask. He paid cash and did not have to use his name."

"Description?"

"Working on it."

"You're good. You are really good at what you do. I need to buy a TV, just so that I can watch you work."

Sandy was pleased by his comment. "Thank you, and yes you do need to buy a TV. How will you keep up with world events without having one? How will you keep up with my career without one? Now, why don't you show me around?"

"Sure, but that won't take long. In fact, I was just about to take her out, and do one of my favorite things."

"What's your boat's name?"

"Always Somethin'."

Sandy laughed. "Sounds like a typical boat and a typical female. What is this favorite thing of yours you were about to do?"

"I love to go to the middle of the lake, eat supper on the roof and watch the sunset. The colors on the water are spectacular at dusk."

"Sounds nice. Would you like some company?"

"Sure, let me show you around while I get the keys to the engine."

John ushered her into the small den.

"This is an older boat that I bought used. It has a new roof and a new hull, new carpet and a fresh coat of paint inside and out."

"It looks nice inside," said Sandy as she looked around. "I love the wooden shades. It's cozy."

"You mean it's small."

Sandy and John laughed. "It's a lot bigger on the outside than it is on the inside. But, it works for me. It's perfect for a single guy because there's not much to clean up. Besides, I spend most of my time outside on one of the decks or on the roof. Let me give you the nickel tour. This is the den, dining room and kitchen. The bathroom is right across from the kitchen, and just behind the bathroom is my tiny bedroom."

"Tiny is a good description. You don't have a lot of closet space do you?"

"I have about six feet, but there is room for storage in the bottom. I have a limited wardrobe, so it works for me."

"I probably take more than this on an overnight trip," joked Sandy as she opened the closet doors.

John became aware that his heart was racing as they stood alone in his bedroom. "Excuse me while I crank the engine before we cast off. I like to make sure that my old engine will crank before I set us adrift."

"Sounds like you are setting me up for an old trick. Are you going to get me out in the middle of the lake and claim that the engine won't crank?"

"I can't make any promises about the engine."

"Hmm," said Sandy as she raised her eyebrows.

The 1979 Drifter had a choke on the dashboard that had to be set just right, and John had to hold his jaw just so for the engine to turn over. John had learned most of the engine's persnickety traits. It coughed to life and after a moment settled into a smooth rumbling rhythm. John slowly disengaged the choke and listened to the engine for a moment.

"Way to go girl, you sound beautiful."

John felt Sandy pressing against his side as she peered over his shoulder. "Maybe if you talked to your girlfriends that way, they wouldn't leave you."

"Ouch! You have opened a sore subject."

John turned to face Sandy and found his arm around her waist, her arm around his. She was soft and warm. Again, his heart was racing. He cleared his throat and said, "Life jackets are tucked into the cubbyholes at the top of the walls."

"You are not inspiring much confidence in your beautiful boat."

"Well, it's *'Always Somethin'.* She might sink us out of jealousy."

"So, you think she should be jealous of me?" said Sandy as she stroked John's chest with her free hand.

"I'm not sure I remember how to think. When we get to the middle of the lake and watch the sun go down, sometimes it's refreshing to go for a swim. I might be able to find something you can use for a bathing suit."

"Who needs bathing suits?"

Sandy slipped her hand around the back of John's head; her fingers ran through his hair. She rose to her toes and tilted her head slightly to the side. He wrapped his arms around her and pulled her slowly toward him. He wanted to prolong the moment and let anticipation work its magic. As they drew close, he could feel her moist breath on his lips. Just as they were about to kiss, something happened.

"John! You've got a visitor!" called out Crush.

The boat swayed as someone stepped aboard. As they turned toward the door, they heard the hollow thumping sound of someone walking across the metal deck. There was another sound, like something rolling across the deck. John and Sandy were still holding each other when the door swung open and Karen stepped inside dragging a suitcase behind her.

Sandy pushed John away, scrunched up her face and said, "You!"

"John! What's going on here? Are you two seeing each other? Why didn't you tell me? Am I interrupting something?"

Karen's questions came out so fast and so furious that John could not keep up.

"I was . . . we were . . . , ah."

Crush, still standing on the pier, said repeatedly, "I'm sorry man. I couldn't stop her."

"I knew there was something going on between you two! Why didn't you tell me?" Sandy paused, letting her eyes say a thing or two. "I thought you were different, you two-timing hypocrite!"

Turning to Karen, he said, "Up until this very moment, there has not been anything between Sandy and me, although it is true that I did think that something was about to happen."

Then turning to Sandy he said, "Karen and I are not seeing each other. We are not an item. Up to this moment we have kept our work and our personal lives apart."

"Liar! Do you take me for a fool? She is moving in! Women don't move in if there's nothing going on. And as for anything happening

125

between us, you must be out of your mind! There is no chance of that ever happening."

John looked at Karen's suitcase and then at Karen, with a puzzled look on his face.

"So, I did interrupt something!" exclaimed Karen, with a mischievous smile. "Actually, Sandy, John is telling the truth about us. We work together, nothing more."

"So what's with the suitcase?" Sandy asked.

"I just got back in town and I'm afraid to go home. I don't have any place else to go."

She turned toward John with a pleading and hurt expression and said, "I thought if I came here, you would protect me and I would have a safe place to stay. I was going to ask if I could crash on the couch."

John stood with his mouth open, unable to speak.

"This is a little bit awkward isn't it, big boy," laughed Sandy. "Two beautiful women board your boat uninvited on the same afternoon. What's a fellow to do?"

John smiled and said, "Cast off!"

Then he stepped through the door onto the front deck.

Crush was standing on the pier with his neck scrunched down into his shoulders. "I'm sorry!" he mouthed.

"It's okay, Crush." John turned to the girls and said, "I'll unhook the water and electricity. If you ladies don't mind helping. Karen, please undo the forward lines and toss them on the pier. Sandy, please do the same with the aft lines."

Karen and Sandy looked at each other, shrugged, and went to work casting off the lines. Soon, the houseboat was motoring out of the harbor. Sandy and Karen settled into chairs on the forward deck. The forward motion of the boat made a cool breeze that ameliorated the late afternoon heat. The rumble of the motor and the sound of the waves on the bow soothed their souls.

John was inside the boat behind the wheel. Karen realized that John would not be able to overhear her conversation with Sandy. She slid her chair next to Sandy, leaned over, and asked, "What are your intentions with John?"

Sandy was perplexed. "Pardon me?"

"You know what I'm talking about. You will only be here while the case is going on. I don't want to see John's heart broken if he falls for you, which he will, if you are just interested in having a little fun with the local boy until it is time for you to leave town."

"I cannot believe that I am hearing this. You sound like a father grilling a boy before his daughter's first date. John's a big boy. He can

126

make his own decisions. What John and I do is our business. If I have a little fun with John, John will be having the same fun with me. No harm will be done. Besides, with the length of time cases last these days, it looks like I will be around for a long time. I want something to do while I'm here. A girl has to have a little entertainment. I'm not thinking about the future right now, but, who knows. If things work out, maybe we can keep seeing each other when the case is over. I don't know why I'm telling you all of this. It is really none of your business."

Karen just looked at Sandy for a few moments, soaking in all that she had said.

"You love him, don't you," observed Sandy.

"Yes, but not the way you think. I love him as a friend. I respect him as a really good man. There is something unique and special about John. He treats everyone with fairness and respect. He is honest to a fault. He will make someone a great husband. I want him to find a great wife. If he gets tied up with someone who is just looking for a good time, he won't be available if the right girl comes along."

"Do you think you are the right girl?"

"I'm not saying that. I'm just saying that he is different from other guys, refreshingly different. He won't use a girl just to have a good time and then drop her. That hurts so much. When it happens, it changes people. I don't want that to happen to him."

This time it was Sandy who just sat and looked at Karen for several moments, soaking in what Karen had just said. "You're right about him being different. I love that about him. I'll think about what you said, but I won't make any promises."

When the boat was about two miles from the closest shore, John shut off the motor and dropped the anchor. "Ladies, if you will meet me on the roof, I'll start grilling while we watch the sunset."

"You better hurry, it won't be long now," said Karen.

They were treated to a breath-taking view. High clouds reflected the sun's light long after it dipped below the horizon. The sky exploded in red, salmon, pink and orange. Every object took on a peach-colored hue. Even the air seemed to shimmer with soft colors and the water reflected it all. Sandy and Karen repeatedly commented how beautiful it was.

"I could get used to this," said Sandy. "This is so peaceful and relaxing. So different from the hectic fast-paced life I've been living."

Karen studied Sandy's face and smiled.

"You two seem to be getting along well."

Sandy and Karen laughed, and Karen said, "Yeah, I guess we are bonding."

"Yeah, I guess so," said Sandy.

127

Just then a flight of geese swooped over the deck, close enough that the wind could be heard whistling though their feathers.

"Wow!" said Sandy. "This is spectacular!"

"This is why I live on the water," said John. "Where else can you get this kind of beauty and this kind of peace and have such lovely company as you two ladies?"

"So, you bring women here often?" asked Karen.

"Every chance I get."

"Oh, you spoiled the effect," said Sandy. "We want to be the first."

Karen leaned over and whispered to Sandy, "That's right, the first and the only," prompting both to laugh.

"What's so funny?" asked John.

"Just girl talk," answered Sandy. "By the way, Karen says she has a couple of bathing suits in her suitcase if we decide to go swimming."

She looked at John for a moment and said, "You're not disappointed are you?"

John laughed.

"What's so funny?" asked Karen.

The high clouds provided plenty of light long after sundown. John grilled steaks and vegetables while Sandy and Karen made a salad, set the table, opened a bottle of wine and lit hurricane lanterns. The steaks were ready when John noticed a boat headed straight for them. Suspicious, he went below, unlocked a small, hidden gun safe, and pulled out a nine millimeter automatic. He chambered a round, checked the safety, put the pistol in his pocket and climbed the steps to the deck.

26

Erick was thinking back on what went wrong. He realized that somehow the girl had shocked him with his own Taser. He could not believe that things had gone so wrong. He knew he should not have relied on those two goofballs, Danny and Gayle. When he regained consciousness, he was bound and stuffed in the trunk of a car.

He could hear Gayle going on and on about how inept he had been.

Me! Inept! Compared to Gayle and Danny! Just wait until I get a chance to tell the Bishop what really happened. He didn't get the chance. He didn't realize that the next time he saw the Bishop would be his last.

Hours went by. He was hot, dirty and thirsty.

Finally, he was taken out of the trunk and allowed to clean up and eat. Gregory told him he was going on a boat ride. As the sun was going down, he was taken to a ski-boat and blindfolded. The boat began gaining speed as it cut through the reservoir water. A sting surprised him when a needle punctured his arm and he quickly felt drowsy.

When he came to, he was lying on his back. He could see stars in the sky and flickering firelight illuminated the tops of trees swaying in a light breeze. People were chanting something familiar in unison. It sounded to Erick like the black mass he had recently attended.

He cut his eyes to the side and saw black candles and the instruments of the coming mass. Then he saw the Bishop, clothed in flowing black robes emblazoned with dragons and symbols and topped with a black hood, reciting something in a language he could not understand. The congregation responded and sounded louder, more intense, more passionate than before. He tried to turn to look at them, but he was restrained and could not move his head.

"We thank our lord for providing to us this offering. And we wish to congratulate Erick, as he is about to become in a very real sense of the word, immortal."

Erick was amazed. Something great was about to happen to him. He was being honored for his efforts in the kidnapping. He knew that the truth would come out. The Bishop was not the kind of man who would be fooled by the sort of rumor spread by the likes of Gayle.

"After tonight, Erick will forever be a part of us when we renew our oaths as we drink of this blood and eat of this body."

Realization swept over Erick like a wave. At the same time, the gathered people trilled with anticipation. The excited chants of the congregation almost drowned out Erick's cries.

When they were finished, the Bishop sent his acolytes into the night, and added one more simple command to the other commands he had given, "Bring me the head of the Priest."

*   *   *

The strange sound carried across the sparkling water and mingled with the sounds of the night. An elderly couple was sitting on their screened porch enjoying the priceless view of stars reflecting off of the lake when they heard the undulating sound coming from the islands. The sound began low, rose in pitch and volume, and continued for several moments, then faded away. It had an almost human quality, or was it an inhuman quality. They were never sure.

"The Ghost of Goshen Springs is looking for his bride again tonight," said the man.

"Would you look for me as long as he has looked for Penny?" asked his wife.

"I would never stop looking for the love of my life," he said and kissed her on the cheek. She smiled and squeezed his hand.

27

As John watched the boat approach his Drifter, he was relieved to see Crush and Ryan. "What's up guys?"

Ryan called back: "It's our job to be with you. Something could happen out here and we wouldn't be able to do anything about it. So we decided we should be on your boat."

John looked at the girls, at the table they had set, and at the food he was grilling.

"Guys, you really don't have to do this."

"Don't even try to stop us. We agreed to take this job, so you just need to get used to us until all of this blows over."

John sighed and asked, "Have you eaten?"

"Yeah," said Crush, "but I'm still hungry."

"Now that you mention it, I haven't had anything," said Ryan. "Crush ate all the food before I arrived."

The girls looked at John and smiled. Sandy rose from her chair and sashayed over to John's side, where she whispered to him, "Remind me never to go, ah, swimming with you at dusk, at least not while you have bodyguards."

John broke into a wide grin, shook his head and called down to Crush and Ryan, "Tie up and come aboard."

"Yahoo!" shouted Crush. "That sure smells good!"

John looked at the girls and said, "I'll go below and see what else I can cook. Let's set some extra places."

The guys began helping themselves to snacks. Ryan said, "It just didn't seem right that you should be here all by yourself with all this food and with these two beautiful women, so we thought we should come help you out."

"I really appreciate that," said John. "I don't know what I would have done without you."

Crush noticed that a boat seemed to be headed straight for them.

Suddenly, tension was the common bond. Ryan and Crush were in fight mode. As the boat neared, they could see that Ted Lively, Skip and a female were on board and the tension evaporated. In the fading light, John could see that the lady was none other than Clarion, the librarian.

"Ahoy there—permission to come aboard?" called Ted in a nautical manner intended to impress his female companion.

John could hear Clarion giggling and saying, "This is so exciting!"

131

Karen joined Sandy and John at the rail and said, "It looks like Ted has found himself a new girlfriend."

"Yes, and she comes with a library and a research staff," said John. "Crush, will you help Ted tie-up and assist our new guests?"

"Sure."

Skip began sniffing the air and called out to John, "What smells so good?"

"We were just about to eat."

"Don't let us interrupt you. But if you have any leftovers, I'm starving."

"Oh, Skip—that's not polite," observed Clarion as Ted helped her aboard. She teetered for a moment as she stepped onto the deck, and Ted pulled her close to him. She giggled again, batted her eyes and thanked Ted profusely for saving her from falling into the drink. Ted was flattered beyond measure. His chest puffed out and he said, "Aw, it was nothing."

"It's okay, Clarion," said John. "You are all welcome to join us."

"Oh, please call me Clare."

"Okay, Clare." John turned to Sandy and Karen and said, "Would you ladies like to come with me to see what we can find to feed this horde?"

"Does this happen often?" Sandy asked.

"I wouldn't say it happens often, but it happens."

"Do you still think its peaceful here?" Karen asked Sandy.

"No, but it is fun."

"I'm glad to hear you say that," said John. "Now, let's get to work."

"You sure know how to show a girl a good time," joked Karen.

Karen and Sandy worked well together and somehow managed to create delicious dishes out of the odd assortment of available food. An hour and a half later, even Crush was satiated, at least for the moment. Ted brought a small quantity of his Goshen Springs Beer, which did not last long. Sandy had a taste of Goshen Springs Beer for the first time and announced that it was indeed the best beer in the world. John asked whether she had tried all of the beers in the world, and she assured everyone that she had indeed tried every single one, not counting the ones that she hadn't yet tried. Skip and Ted were excited to report some of their findings during the day and to report that the librarians were once again part of the defense team.

The sky was filled with stars. John began pointing out constellations, and Karen named some of the stars. Everyone gasped with amazement when a bright shooting star streaked across the heavens. When John went below to find something for his guests to drink, Sandy followed

132

him. When they were alone, she put an arm around his waist and said: "Thank you for letting me share this tonight. This has been special. Of course, it might have been even more special if we didn't have so much company."

"You are right about that. But, it's probably best that things turned out this way."

"What do you mean? Is there someone else?"

"No, there is no one with whom I would rather go skinny dipping. It's just that I would prefer to go slow and give us time to get to know each other. Once we take that plunge, we are involved. It would be a shame to find out later that we aren't right for each other."

"I wasn't proposing marriage," said Sandy.

"I know."

"Are you for real?" Sandy asked.

John smiled and did not answer, so Sandy continued. "Are you telling me that if I had taken the dive, you would have just stood there and watched?"

"No way. The truth is you are irresistible."

"That's more like it," said Sandy as she leaned into him and reached up to kiss him.

At that moment, Karen burst into the room with John's cell phone. "It's Jackson! He says it's urgent!"

"I can't believe your timing," said Sandy. "Are you always going to interrupt us at the wrong moment?"

Karen shrugged and said, "It depends."

"Depends on what?"

As John took the phone, Sandy's cell began ringing.

When John ended the call, he swung into action. "We've got to head back to the pier. Jackson has found Father Michael McCarty. He wants to meet us at midnight."

"That sounds a bit melodramatic, doesn't it?" Karen asked.

"You're right. I don't want to miss him."

John stepped on the deck and announced that they had to return to the pier. Crush lifted the anchor while John cranked the engine. Ted, Ryan and Skip secured their boats to the back of the houseboat and John was quickly underway. He did not notice that Sandy was sitting quietly by herself on the front deck, but Karen noticed and sat beside her.

"What's bothering you?" Karen asked.

"You were right. I can't get involved with John, or anyone else. I'm being called away to another story."

"What! Why? What about the office you opened across the hall? I thought this was your big story?"

133

"The District Attorney did such a good job discrediting the defense team today that the public is losing interest in the story. They think John is a crackpot. The ratings plummeted. All of the networks are pulling their assets and reassigning their crews. I've been reassigned. I leave first thing in the morning."

Karen could see that Sandy's eyes were filled with tears and her lips were quivering. Karen held her and felt Sandy's tears on her shoulder.

"I cannot believe that I am acting this way. I've been reassigned before. But this story has become so much a part of me. And now, I don't know. I was warned that I should never get too close to the people I cover. He and I weren't even, you know, intimately close."

"It's okay Sandy. This is not over yet."

"Yeah, well, we'll see."

28

Jackson was waiting for them at the pier.

"Sorry I missed the party," he said as he helped tie the boat to the cleats. "We've got to hurry to get to the meeting place on time."

"Ladies, I've got to go. Sandy, I'll talk to you tomorrow. Crush, can you guard the boat for Karen tonight?"

"That's okay, I will be staying with Sandy tonight," said Karen. "I think she has something to tell you."

"It will have to wait until tomorrow. We've literally got to run. Crush, and Ryan, can you follow the girls wherever they are going, and stay as long as necessary to make sure they are okay?"

John trotted to his Trooper with Jackson.

Sandy and Karen stared after him in disbelief. "Can you believe the nerve of him, to just run off like that?" Karen said.

"Typical man," Sandy said as she wiped away a tear.

As they climbed into John's Trooper, Jackson said, "What's the story with the girls at your boat? Is there anything you want to tell me?"

"Nothing to tell, Jackson. At least not yet."

"Hmm. Sure looked like something was going on. I couldn't tell if I was at a party or a funeral."

"What? What are you talking about?"

"I don't know, but I bet you will find out soon enough. Take a look at this note that the good Father sent us.

The cryptic message that Jackson had received directed them to meet the mysterious Father Michael McCarty " at midnight by the campfire, Lot 19, Mayes Lake, 3484."

"What do you make of this, 3484?" Jackson asked.

"I don't know. Just part of the mystery surrounding the right reverend McCarty."

"Not so reverend, it seems to me. Wanted as a person of interest regarding a number of murders, break-ins and kidnappings. He has been excommunicated from the Catholic Church."

"True, but he saved Karen, and for that I will be forever grateful," responded John. "As for the excommunication, that is not surprising if some of those allegations are true. The church can't have a rouge priest running around whacking people and breaking into houses and businesses."

"Considering that everyone is looking for him, I guess he wants to meet at Mayes Lake in order to be in a secluded place."

"Yeah, he picked a secluded place and time all right," said Jackson. "Did you know that Mayes Lake, together with Lefluer's Bluff, is one of the largest urban parks in the country?"

"I heard that, too. They're connected by a long nature trail along the Pearl River."

"I haven't been out there in years, but it is a beautiful place."

"Yeah, no one seems to know it's there."

"Here's the ballpark now!" said John as he turned off of Lakeland Drive and drove alongside the little league ballparks. They came to a small guardhouse.

"Looks like no one's home," said Jackson.

"You're right, and the gate is closed," observed John as he rolled to a stop.

"I'll check it," said Jackson as he swung open his door and climbed out of the aging Trooper. "It's locked."

Jackson looked closer at the lock and returned to the Trooper. He looked at the message, noted the code, and returned to the gate. "I know the meaning of the mystery numbers on the message. It's a combination lock."

In a moment, he opened the gate, waited for John to pass through, and closed and locked it. After Jackson climbed back into the SUV, John drove slowly into the woods. The paved road ended almost immediately, replaced by a gravel road. The truck tires crunched noisily on the gravel, and a dust cloud swirled behind the Trooper even though John was traveling only about 10 miles per hour.

"Look at that!" whispered Jackson in an excited voice as the SUV's lights illuminated three deer along the side of the gravel road. John stopped the truck, and they watched as the deer grazed their way into the woods.

"That was cool," said Jackson as the truck continued down the road. The first lake came into view on the right. Across the lake, Jackson and John could see that a couple of RV's still had lights on inside. The glow of a campfire was visible around a bend in the lake.

The gravel road wound around the lakeshore and crossed a narrow peninsula between two of the five lakes that comprised Mayes Lake. They rounded a turn, with a lake on each side and confronted a raccoon in the middle of the road. The coon stood on its back legs and seemed to consider whether fight or flight was the proper response when confronted by a truck. Eventually, he chose flight and scurried off of the road.

Tree limbs hung over the road and swayed with each puff of the night breeze. They reached a fork in the road. The Pearl River boat ramp was straight ahead and a sign on the right hand road said "Campers Only Beyond This Point."

"I guess that's our invitation," said John, as he turned right.

The road looped to the right along the lakeshore, then curved back to the left and returned to the entrance to the campground. In the center of the loop was a bathhouse. Campsites lined both sides of the road, with the best sites along the lake. They followed the road past the numbered sites to the apex of the circle, where the number "19" appeared on a roadside post. It was a large campsite, with plenty of lakefront. A thick hardwood forest began along the southwest side of the lot, which was to their left as Jackson and John climbed out of the SUV. In the center of the lot was an unattended campfire. Several sitting stumps were arranged near the fire. Jackson and John walked past the fire and peered into the dark in every direction. So much light reflected off of the lake that even in the dark, they could see a Great Blue Heron flying low across the water.

Jackson turned back to the campfire and gasped, "Whoa!"

John whirled about and saw the figure of a man sitting on the stump next to the fire. His hands were extended towards the fire, placing a pot on the coals. Jackson and John looked at each other. John shrugged and Jackson said, "That was spooky."

As they returned to the fire, John kept his eye on the mysterious visitor, while Jackson peered into the darkness to see if there were any more surprises.

"Father Michael McCarty I presume," said John as he slid one of the stumps up to the fire, a few feet from McCarty. Jackson purposely moved to McCarty's other side, so that he could watch John's back while John watched his back. Jackson was taking no chances.

McCarty was dressed in dark pants, a plain shirt and jacket with a long overcoat slung over his shoulder. A brimmed hat, with one side turned up at a jaunty angle, sat firmly on his head. Reddish gray hair protruded around the edges of the hat, and a full gray beard framed a face dominated by a long narrow nose. A pipe hung from his lips. He was a big man, with large, powerful looking hands. He looked Brooks and Bradley over as he removed a fagot from the fire and applied it to his pipe.

After a few puffs, he threw the flaming stick back into the fire and said with an Irish brogue, "It's just Michael McCarty. I no longer bear the title 'Father.' Pull your stumps a little closer to the fire. There's an unseasonable chill in the air tonight."

Jackson shivered, but not from the cool breeze.

"Thank you for what you did for Karen," said John.

137

"Don't mention it. Just another day at the office."

"Some office," said John as he took in the surroundings. "How did you happen to be present at just the right time to save Karen?"

"I didn't see the kidnapping, but I saw her escape. I was tracking one of her captors."

"Then you know that Karen told the authorities the truth. You could help her again by telling your story."

"I'm telling my story now."

"Why were you following her captor?"

"I hoped he would lead me to his coven."

"Oh, come on," said Jackson. "You are telling me there is a group of witches in Jackson?"

"Not necessarily witches, my friend. You are right that a coven is a group of witches, but it is also defined as a group of vampires, or a group led by a vampire. Something is here. There is a reason the vampire Hal was chasing chose to come here."

"What do you mean?"

"His name was Vlal Drumon. He thought of himself as a god. He needed worshipers. My experience is that he goes to communities where someone will welcome him. You have a serious problem with occult activities in your community and I wanted to get to the bottom of it."

"What was the urgency about meeting tonight? Why couldn't it wait until tomorrow?"

"Something big is going on tonight. I can't be certain where, but I am sure that it will be bad for someone, maybe you, maybe me. In my experience, the enemy has never felt stronger than it feels tonight."

"The enemy?"

"You and everyone that you love are in great danger. There are things that you must know in order to protect yourself and others."

"Why did they want Karen?"

"I am not sure, yet, but I have my suspicions. If I am right, then my services will be needed very soon."

"Why meet here?"

"I am a wanted man. I have to move and meet in ways that help ensure the longevity and success of my mission."

"They say you are a Christian terrorist," said John. "I had never heard the term before. I didn't know there was such a thing."

"Of course there are," said Jackson, "like Timothy McVeigh, Jared Loughner and the Norwegian who killed all of those children."

"Behring Breivik," said Michael McCarty.

"Yes, him. Christian extremists can be just as bad as other extremists, whether they be Muslim extremists or any other."

"Is it me you want to talk about, or do you want to talk about alleged Christians or would you rather talk about your client and the creature he had to slay?"

Michael McCarty reached into his coat pocket.

Jackson stiffened and reached for his pants pocket.

"Easy now," said McCarty as he slowly withdrew his hand from his pocket and produced two cigars. "I find that important discussions among men are more enjoyable and sometimes more productive when accompanied by good tobacco." He offered the cigars

Jackson pulled the same stick from the fire and, after a few puffs, had the end of the big stogie burning a bright red. The cool breeze blew through the trees, shaking branches and making the sound of a thousand rattles. Leaves fell in the dark all around them. A few leaves fell into the fire and were consumed in sudden bright bursts of flame. Nearby, an owl hooted three times.

John's eyes narrowed for a moment and said, "I definitely want to hear about my client and the people who kidnapped Karen, but I notice that you did not deny Jackson's accusation."

"Does that matter to you?"

"Perhaps. I am not sure. I am sure that I owe you for what you did for Karen."

"Fair enough. First of all, none of the men you mentioned were Christian, they were simply mentally disturbed people who committed heinous crimes."

"They were reported as dangerous Christian fundamentalists," insisted Jackson.

"That is an oxymoron. A Christian fundamentalist is one who takes the teachings of the New Testament literally. There is nothing in the New Testament that could reasonably be used to justify the killing of innocent people."

"Oh, come on, what about Pogroms, crusades, and burning witches," said Jackson with a sarcastic laugh.

"Which of Jesus' teachings would you say justifies the taking of innocent life?" asked Father Michael.

After a pause, Jackson replied, "I can't think of one."

"The most recent killer, the Norwegian, used the term Christianity loosely, to mean cultural Christians. He spoke in his manifesto of Christian atheists, another oxymoron, needing to band together with other cultural Christians, Buddhists and Hindus to repel what he believed was a threat to European Culture from Muslim immigrants. Because he called for a struggle against Muslims, the media called him a Christian terrorist. I doubt that you would have found his name in the Book of

Life."

"Are you saying he was a mentally disturbed cultural Christian, not a religious Christian?" asked Jackson.

"I am not sure he was even a cultural Christian, but I see that you understand what I am saying. It is like the old joke about the wars between the IRA and the Protestants in Northern Ireland. A man explained to a gunman that he should not be shot because he was an atheist. The gunman replied, 'Are you a Catholic atheist or a Protestant atheist?' Often the excuse for violence is cultural, or political, or simple human greed or a quest for power. Sometimes religion is one of the excuses men use to commit terrible sins; but, there is nothing in the Christian religion that justifies taking innocent life."

"As for Loughner," continued McCarty, "he shocked his classmates by laughing about aborting babies, which is not your typical Christian response to abortion. And McVeigh claimed that science was his religion. So did the murderers in the French revolution as they cut the heads off of priests and drug a statue of the goddess of reason into Notre Dame."

"How do you know so much about these murderers?" asked Jackson.

"Professional curiosity. Often my services are needed either to avoid such events or I am needed immediately following such events. In any event, not one of your examples fits your term 'Christian terrorist.'"

"Do you fit that term?" asked Jackson.

"Yes, I am a Christian terrorist."

Jackson and John said nothing for a while. The fire crackled in the silence.

"That is, if you ask the demons and their minions. I strike terror into their black hearts."

McCarty blew a large smoke ring into the air above his head and then blew a second smoke ring through the first.

Impressed with the smoke ring trick, Jackson said, "Well done," and proceeded to blow his own smoke ring.

"Don't you think that it is just a little too convenient? It's an old trick that we play on our minds to justify what we are doing to others. We dehumanize our enemies. We categorize them as non-humans."

"One of the oldest tendencies of humanity," said Jackson. "It makes it easier to be inhuman to your foes if you consider them to be inhuman."

McCarty briefly laughed, but his chortles lacked humor. "My friend," he said to Jackson, "you are suffering from at least two misconceptions."

"Pray tell."

"First, that cruelty towards humans is an inhuman activity. It may be the most human of activities. Even men who profess to be God fearing

140

can be inhuman to others. But, once you remove the influence of God from the affairs of men, anything goes. Cruelties that you cannot even imagine occur."

"Like burning at the stake?" asked Jackson.

"Child's play compared to the cruelties godless men have invented."

"I'm not convinced about your first point," observed Jackson.

"If you had seen what I have seen, you would be convinced."

Jackson looked at John, who raised his eyebrows. "There is a certain chill in the air isn't there?" said John as he tossed another piece of wood on the fire. "Odd for this time of year."

"So, what was my second error?" asked Jackson.

"Your assumption that I was trying to de-humanize people when I spoke of demons. I wasn't. When I say demons, I mean demons."

"Don't tell me you're one of those religious fanatics that believes in demons!" exclaimed Jackson, as he leaned back, laughed and shook his head.

"The Church believes it. I was an exorcist for the Catholic Church. Jesus believed it. He cast out demons. Your lack of belief does not change the truth that demons interact in our world, influencing the behavior of men." McCarthy leaned forward, lowered his voice for emphasis and said, "Sometimes, far more often than you can imagine, demons possess the bodies of poor souls."

A sudden wind swept into the fire, sending sparks swirling in the air and causing the coals to glow bright and hot.

"Good timing," said John.

"I suppose a demon did that," said Jackson.

"No, that was a coincidence; but coincidences happen often around me."

"Are you saying that the men we just spoke about were possessed by demons?"

"I really don't know their spiritual condition, at least not now. You have caught me in an error. I should not have presumed whether or not that young man's name was in the Book of Life. That was wrong of me. Nevertheless, those who are either influenced by demons or possessed by demons tend to do awful, even unthinkable things."

"Why aren't you with the church now?" asked John.

"We had a disagreement about my methods. I discovered that supernatural evil took many forms. The Church-approved method of combating evil did not seem to me to be effective against certain incarnations of evil. So, I became a maverick, then an embarrassment to the church. Now, I am a renegade. A sort of lone wolf, fighting the good fight with methods that some would not consider to be good."

141

"Such as?" asked John.

"Which brings me to your client. I hate to undermine your legal strategy, but Mr. Boyd was not crazy. He did what he had to do. Once he realized what he was dealing with, he believed that he had no choice but to destroy it."

"What was he dealing with and how do you know?" asked Jackson.

John skipped the obvious preliminary questions and asked, "How did Hal come to realize what you are about to say?"

"Right you are, Mr. Brooks. Your suspicion is correct. I told Hal that he was dealing with a vampire. I told him about the monster that had destroyed his fiancée. I told him that I had been tracking it for years. I told him that it had left a trail of death and destruction everywhere it went. I warned him to stay away, but he was determined to stop it before it took another life."

"Did you tell Hal how to stop it?"

"Yes. He needed to know, lest he become another victim. Even knowing how to kill it, it is a rare man indeed who can carry it off. It takes mercy, luck, skill, courage, and more luck."

Jackson interrupted with, "Are you saying you taught Hal to be a vampire slayer?"

"I could not stop him from hunting the creature. That was a decision he freely made."

"That free will issue that I keep hearing Christians talk about," observed Jackson.

"Right you are. Hal needed instruction on the skills and tools necessary to combat the creature, and he needed training. I felt that it would be irresponsible of me not to give him that instruction and training."

"What sort of training?"

"First and foremost, prayer."

"Yeah, right," said Jackson. "This is so medieval. No one will believe this, John."

"Without the power available to us through Jesus Christ, we would be no match for Vlal and his ilk. I told Hal he must put on the full armor of God, and I taught him how to do that. I told him that the assault would come before he sees Drumon."

"How would he be assaulted?" asked Jackson.

"Overwhelming, uncontrollable dread. The enemy assaults our minds. The mind is where the spiritual battle is fought. The enemy will fill your mind with fear, lies and confusion. Fear and confusion will overwhelm you if you have not bathed yourself with prayer. Even so, you will feel the fear and you will experience doubt, but you are less

142

likely to succumb if you truly turn the spiritual part of the fight over to prayer. Then, there is the physical part of the fight. To kill a vampire demon, one must cut off its head, drive a large object through its heart, or destroy it in a fire. All of these methods are fraught with danger because the vampire demon imbues enormous strength to its host. Fire seems easiest, but it only works if it is otherwise incapacitated. It will easily escape a fire long after any other creature would have been consumed."

Jackson and John could not believe their ears. "Why didn't you do the job yourself?" asked Jackson.

"It seemed to sense my presence. I could not get close to it. Additionally, its helpers never seem to be far away from me. They hound me."

"Helpers?" said Jackson.

The tobacco in Michael McCarty's pipe glowed bright red as he took a long draw. Prodigious amounts of smoke erupted from his nose and mouth as a canine howled in the woods nearby. Jackson and John turned to look across the lake as they heard the sound of a fast-moving vehicle crunching through the gravel, rocks clattering inside the wheel-wells. A streetlight illuminated a portion of the gravel drive that could be seen in a break in the trees. A pickup truck with a camper shell flashed by, followed by a dust storm.

"He really seems to be in a hurry," noted Jackson.

They turned back towards the fire to continue their conversation with McCarty, but he was gone.

"I don't believe this. He has to be somewhere nearby."

Both Jackson and John left the fire and moved into the gloom searching for any sign of Father McCarty. They both called for him, but there was no reply.

"I can't believe this. We were just getting into information that could prove how and why Hal went crazy. This character drove him crazy. If I stayed around him very long, he would drive me crazy."

After a few minutes, the pickup drove slowly around the loop. It was too dark to see into the cab, but two large dogs were visible in the camper window. The truck stopped for a moment at the beginning of the loop then rolled slowly to the fork in the road and turned towards the river.

John and Jackson waited at the fire for twenty minutes before deciding that the interview must be over. They had not seen any sign of Father McCarty, or the pickup, or the dogs. They climbed into the Trooper and returned to the gate. It was open.

"I guess the people in that truck were in too big of a hurry to lock the gate," said John.

"Yeah, and they were in too big of a hurry to mess with a combination lock," said Jackson. "The chain has been cut."

"Hmmm," said John.

"You can say that again."

"Hum."

"What are you thinking?"

"I think maybe we should go back and see what is going on."

"I don't know about that. We may be biting off more than we can chew. I'm not sure we want to tangle with Father Mike's enemies."

"We can't just leave him to the dogs either. Besides, he may be a critical witness for our case. I don't want him to disappear, or worse."

"Yeah, it's the worse that I am worried about. I don't want us to end up worse, if you know what I mean."

"Yeah. This may be stupid, but I am turning around. If you want to wait here that's okay with me."

"Are you kidding? I wouldn't miss this for the world. I just want to be able to say 'I told you so,' when things go wrong."

John turned the SUV around and quickly drove back to the fork in the road. This time he continued straight toward the river instead of turning into the camping area. They passed the entrance to the nature trail and after a few hundred yards came to a circular gravel parking lot. A boat ramp led down to the river. The only vehicle in the lot was the empty pickup.

They climbed out of the Trooper. John opened the back gate and pulled a flashlight out of a box. Jackson saw a tire tool and grabbed it just as John was closing the gate.

"I'll feel better if I have something in my hand," explained Jackson. "Where do we start?"

Just then, the dogs sounded in the forest, indicating they were on a scent.

"I guess that answers the question. They're headed toward either the lake or the nature trail. Jump in the truck! We'll try to get ahead of them."

They raced back to the entrance to the trail. Wooden posts placed about two feet apart across the entrance served as a vehicle barrier. John punched the 4-wheel drive button and swung the SUV around the barrier. The trail was barely wide enough to accommodate the truck. Leafy branches swished by, slapping through the open window. They raced a hundred yards up the trail when the headlights illuminated the figure of a man wearing a long coat with a brimmed hat. Two vicious dogs, teeth bared, were charging towards the figure. John honked the horn and punched the accelerator. He was too late. The first dog leaped into the center of mass, its jaws reaching just below the hat. The cloak and hat collapsed around the animal as the dog tumbled to the ground. John stopped the truck, grabbed Jackson's tire tool and jumped out of the vehicle just as the first dog yelped and staggered backwards with a thick stick protruding through its throat.

Undaunted the second dog entered the fray, grabbed the cloak with its jaws and shook back and forth viciously. Before John could react, McCarty, sans hat and coat, rushed out of the woods and struck the second dog a smashing blow on the neck with a sturdy limb. The dog fell instantly and didn't move.

"Thanks for coming back, but you don't know what you are getting into—leave now!" he said, as he rushed into the bushes on the side of the trail.

By then, Jackson had joined John. They looked at the second dog lying motionless on top of the cloak, and the first dog, lying on its side whimpering. A large pointed stick passed all the way through its neck.

"Wow, he set a trap for the dogs!" exclaimed Jackson. "How did he do that so fast?"

They heard huffing, puffing and the sound of men running up the trail. Two men armed with shotguns ran into the area illuminated by the headlight beams. They were tall, thin and dressed in dark clothing. They stopped and looked at the dogs. One of them said, "What have you done to our dogs?" The other said, "What are you doing here?"

"The dogs were attacking what we thought was a man," said Jackson. "Turned out to be just a coat and hat."

As he slowly brought the shotgun around so that it was pointing in the general direction of John and Jackson, the second man smiled and said, "You didn't take these dogs down with a tire tool, did you?"

"You're right, I didn't," said Jackson. "A man jumped out of the bushes and did them both in, then jumped back into the bushes. I never saw anything like it."

"Huh. I never heard anything like that before. Danny, have you ever heard anything like that?" said the second man as he pointed his shotgun at John. "Drop the tire tool."

Before John could respond to the demand, a 'whump' sound followed by a grunt came from Danny, who fell in a heap. A large rock bounced across the trail. The second thug whirled to his right, firing his shotgun once as he turned 90 degrees and a second time as his turn reached 180 degrees. Instinctively, John rushed the gunman, with the tire tool raised high above his head. John swung just as the gunman whirled back towards him. The tire tool caught the gunman just above the ear as the shotgun fired a third time, with the barrel just under John's left arm. The

145

blast sent pellets into the trees beside the Trooper. John wrapped his arm around the shotgun and wrenched it away as the second gunman fell at his feet. John jumped back and turned towards the first gunman in time to see Jackson scoop Danny's shotgun off of the ground. Both gunmen were motionless.

"Wow! John, what got into you? I never saw anyone move so fast. How did you have the guts to take those guys out?"

John felt as though the energy was draining from his body as the adrenaline rush suddenly ended. His knees felt weak, and he knelt on the trail.

"I didn't get Danny boy, I got the other one. How? I don't know, I didn't even think. I just reacted. If I had thought about it, I probably wouldn't have done anything." He looked around the dark and then yelled out, "Father Michael—where are you?"

"Well done, Esquire. I didn't know you had it in you," said Father Michael as he stepped out of the woods.

"Who are these thugs?" asked Jackson.

"Danny is new to me, but the other one, Gregory, is an almost constant companion of mine. He and his friends never seem to be far away from me. I suspect that they are friends of Karen's kidnappers. You two should leave now. I will take care of the mess they have made."

"That's a tempting offer," said Jackson. "I can think of a lot of reasons to leave quickly."

"What will you do with them?" asked John.

"That's not your concern."

"I disagree. If you intend to harm them, then I can't leave them."

"Then we have a standoff. I can't have them on my trail. They will be on your trail, too. You and everyone and everything you love is in grave danger. Leave now and let me help you."

John and Father Michael stared at one another for several seconds. Neither of them blinked. Neither took their eyes off of the other.

"Jackson," said John without looking away from Father Michael. "Find something to tie them up with, please. Then call the police. Meet the police at the gate and lead them here."

"You are making a big mistake," said McCarty.

"You are probably right. But I can't leave them to you. I will take responsibility for them."

"How are we going to explain all this?" asked Jackson.

"We will report what happened, and press charges against them for aggravated assault."

"They may press charges against us for the same thing. It's our word

146

against theirs."

"Right you are, Jackson. We let the chips fall where they may."

"John! We could lose our license to practice law! I don't want to take that chance."

"I don't either, Jackson. But I don't want to live my life wondering if I could have saved these two men. They may be ruffians, but nevertheless, they are men. I will not leave them."

Father Michael smiled. "I like what I see in you, Brooks," he said. "I had your principles once, before I knew what I know now. I'll help you tie them up and I'll help you watch them until the police are almost here. Then, I am afraid I will have to leave you."

"Well, that won't be long, actually, because here comes a park ranger," said Jackson as he pointed toward a pickup driving quickly up the trail.

"Well, gentlemen, it has been quite entertaining. We will have to do this again sometime. Farewell."

Father Michael grabbed his hat and coat and stepped into the woods, out of the line of sight of whoever was approaching in the pick-up.

"I need you at the trial," called John into the woods.

"That will not be possible. I am a wanted man. I am needed out here to continue the fight. I can't waste time in prison."

"Hal is depending on you. An injustice will be done if you don't testify."

"What could I say that would help Hal?"

"That you and he were tracking a vampire and you taught him how to kill it."

"No one will believe me."

"Trust me."

"I'll think about it. I'd like to help Hal, and I would like to trust you; but I don't see how it will be possible. Goodbye."

With that, he disappeared into the woods.

29

Ranger Bill was close to retirement. He loved his career as a park ranger. The job had its hard times, but he really enjoyed the quiet and solitude that usually ruled when he handled the night shift at Mayes Lake. As a law enforcement officer he was often required to carry a gun, but he had never had occasion to draw it or use it. His nightly rounds included a slow ride around the camping areas and a drive to the boat ramp at the river.

Tonight, he left the park and drove up to the curb food store on the corner. When he returned the gate was open. The chain was cut. "Kids," he said to himself as he reached for his radio and called for backup. Then he drove through the park looking for the culprit. He had made it to the intersection of the camper road and the boat ramp road when he heard three shotgun blasts. He stopped for a moment and considered his options.

"It will be just my luck to be shot by a poacher three weeks before retirement," grumbled Ranger Bill. He reported on the radio what he heard and slowly drove towards the sound. Every nerve in his body told him to stop, to turn back, to wait for backup, but a sense of duty drove him forward.

It was as though the pickup had a mind of its own. He placed his pistol on the seat beside him. Then he saw the lights of a vehicle stopped on the nature trail. He swallowed hard and quickly drove his truck around the barrier. In a few moments, he saw two men holding shotguns and two other men on the ground at their feet.

Why did I have to see this? he thought to himself. He sat in the truck for a moment, his hand resting on his pistol. The two men with shotguns were looking at him, shielding their eyes from his headlights. One raised his hand and gestured for Ranger Bill to join them.

"Lay down the shotguns!" he yelled.

Both men did as they were told.

Ranger Bill climbed out of the pickup, pistol pointed at the men he had caught red-handed, assaulting, or murdering others. His hand was shaking so much that he could not hold the front sight of his pistol on target. He laid his pistol arm across the hood to steady his aim and commanded the two men to lay on the ground with their hands behind their backs. They complied. *What a way to end a career*, he thought. *I sure hope back-up arrives soon.*

McCarty, concealed in the woods, watched events unfold. Soon, police cars, state troopers and wildlife officers began arriving, along with two ambulances. Flashing blue lights from the police cars, together with flashing red and white lights from the ambulances made eerie reflections in the woods. Police and ambulance personnel were moving about, some purposefully, some seemingly without purpose. A fire truck and a fire rescue truck arrived, adding to the confusion and chaos.

If only they knew what they were dealing with, they would not be so casual, McCarty said to himself.

Just as Jackson feared, the police handcuffed Jackson and John and put them in separate squad cars. McCarthy could hear Jackson say to John, "I told you so."

Gregory and Danny were placed on stretchers. IVs were started on both. Danny groaned and moved about some, especially when an IV was administered. Gregory remained perfectly still.

Too still, thought McCarthy. He suspected that Gregory was pretending to be unconscious and was looking for an opportunity to escape. When he did, McCarty planned to follow him back to his lair. This was an opportunity that McCarty could not pass up.

Gregory was loaded on the ambulance first. The attendants then loaded Danny in a separate ambulance. They were momentarily distracted by questions from a policeman and did not notice the passenger door to one of the ambulances open. Unknown to them, Gregory slipped into the woods. This was the moment McCarty had waited for. As McCarty made his move, he looked back at the squad car holding Brooks. He shook his head and stopped. He looked back in the direction Gregory had taken and made a decision. This Brooks fellow was an annoyance, but he was worth the effort. McCarty abandoned the hunt and looked for an opportunity to enter Danny's ambulance. He didn't wait long. He boldly walked out of the woods straight to the ambulance. He climbed inside and pulled the door closed. He didn't know how much time he had, so he moved quickly.

"Danny boy, do you know who I am?" he asked as he placed his hand over Danny's mouth and pressed hard. He made sure that Danny could see him fiddling with his IV, as though he were making some change to it. Danny's eyes suddenly widened with panic, as Danny uttered the muffled word 'Priest'. McCarty saw a needle and without hesitation slammed into Danny's neck without pressing the plunger, while suppressing Danny's scream with his strong hand.

"Listen, little cretin, I know how to find you. If you think your Bishop is someone to fear, you have no idea what fear is. I will call all the forces of the Creator of the universe to drive you into a living hell. I

149

will make your flesh rot off of your very bones. You will know agony you cannot imagine, unless you tell these policemen exactly what happened here. You must also tell them about kidnapping the lawyer's secretary. Do you believe me?"

He twisted the needle in Danny's neck.

Danny nodded his head vigorously.

"There's a good lad. Confession is good for the soul. Now, don't start your singing till I leave. But, you better be loud enough for everyone to hear you, including me. Do you understand me?"

Eyes wide, Danny nodded his head again.

"If you do as I say, I will leave you alone. There now, that wasn't so bad was it?"

McCarty withdrew the needle.

"Now, I am telling you the truth. You need to find yourself some new friends. Stay away from those servants of the devil. I am going to move my hand now. Don't start your yelling for five seconds after I close the door. Do we understand each other?"

Danny nodded again.

"All right, I am leaving. Now, go and sin no more."

With that, Father McCarty quickly lifted his hand and slipped through the passenger door, just as Gregory had done. The cover of the woods was only a step away. Without hesitation he began moving towards the boat ramp where he believed he would find Gregory's truck. He had gone only a few steps when he heard Danny screaming.

McCarty prayed out loud, "Forgive me Father, for I have sinned. I am truly sorry about the lie I told Danny about what I could have You do to him."

When he arrived at the ramp, the truck was gone. *There is only one way out, and it is risky for him to go that way. There will be plenty of police and emergency personnel to encounter.* McCarty considered following the road to see if the authorities had stopped Gregory. Then, it occurred to him to check the ramp. As he approached the ramp under the light of the moon, he could see sparkling wavelets on the lazy river. A short distance from the ramp, bubbles were rising in the dark river water. Then the water erupted as a large volume of air broke the surface.

He drove the truck into the river! He could be swimming across the river. If so, he would still be visible. McCarty approached the riverbank to search, when an intense realization struck him. He was being hunted. *This one is smart and dangerous.*

McCarty knew that he was exposed in the moonlight. Gregory wanted him to think that he was crossing the river so that Father Mike would be an easy target as he stood on the river bank peering into the

150

dark waters. Gregory knew McCarty would be coming for him and McCarty's only clue was the truck, so he set a trap for him. McCarty crouched and took two quick steps to the side hoping to spoil Gregory's aim. He sprinted to the water and dove. Even though he was expecting it, the gunshots startled him. The gunman was so near that the sound was deafening. Hot lead burned inside him. As the warm dark water engulfed him he wondered what unseen creatures would be attracted to his blood. That thought quickly passed as he realized it was the least of his worries.

30

District Attorney Tellers was conducting a morning staff meeting with six attorneys and three investigators. One of the investigators was delighted to give an update on the Vampire Defense.

"It seems that both Brooks and Bradley were detained last night regarding an aggravated assault investigation at Mayes Lake."

"You have got to be kidding me. These guys are renegades. Who did they assault?"

"I don't have any details yet, just this sketchy report. The officers and investigators involved are off duty now. They are all home asleep."

"Wake them up. I want to know what happened. If we can put these clowns away for good, let's do it. The sooner the better."

Marsha pushed a note in front of Tellers.

"What! They can't do that!" He shouted as he rose from his chair. "What is it?"

"The media is pulling out. It seems that I did too good a job discrediting Brooks yesterday. Everybody knows now that he is a joke, and the media doesn't want to waste its time with him and his ridiculous case."

"That's great—you destroyed him yesterday," one of the attorneys said.

Everyone chimed in agreement.

"No, don't you see, it's bad. This was a golden opportunity to get invaluable free press and worldwide exposure. There is no way to put a value on that, politically or otherwise."

"Yes, you're right. That's bad. But what can you do about it? Yesterday's big story is always replaced by today's big story, and today's big story is soon forgotten. It looks like our case is becoming yesterday's story."

That comment caused Tellers' face to turn beet red. "No, this was the case that was going to get me into the limelight. There must be a way to bring them back."

He paced back and forth for a moment and snapped his fingers. "Marsha, arrange for a press conference this morning with any national media still in town. If they are all gone, then arrange the conference with the local stations. Invite the locals regardless. Tell them a major announcement will be made on the courthouse steps in one hour. We are going to stir things up and add a little interest to the case."

152

"I'm on it."

*   *   *

It was almost 9:30 when Brooks arrived at his office exhausted from a very late night. Dark circles were under his eyes and he did not bother to put on a tie. He looked forward to a cup of coffee and a chance to catch his breath. He also looked forward to sharing the news about Danny with Karen. As he reached his office door, he noticed that the CTN office across the hall was closed.

When he stepped into the office, instead of being greeted by the usual bright smile from Karen, he was met by a scowl.

"Good morning," he said.

"Good for you, I guess."

John stopped and looked at Karen. "Is something wrong?"

"As if you didn't know."

"Just tell me."

Karen just looked at him.

"What's with the CTN office? Why aren't they open?"

"She's gone. They are gone."

"Who? What are you talking about?"

"Sandy was called away to another story. She left first thing this morning. She was trying to tell you last night, but you wouldn't listen."

"What are you talking about? We talked last night."

"When you rushed off with Jackson, she had just gotten a call. Her boss reassigned her and closed the office."

"She's gone!"

John felt as though the blood was rushing from his head. He needed to sit, but he knew that he was not welcome in Karen's lobby.

"Yeah. You just dropped her. You ran off and left her after she poured her heart out to you. That was despicable."

"What are you talking about? I had no idea. I was trying to do my job."

"You finally said the truth. You have no idea. And if you don't know what I am talking about, then we don't have anything left to talk about."

The phone rang. Karen swiped the receiver off the cradle.

"Hello," she shouted. "No, he's not in."

She slammed the receiver back in its cradle. She looked at John, then at the phone. She grabbed the receiver and pointed it at John and said, "If you don't want me to do this to you too, then you better stop staring at me and get in your own office."

With that, she slammed the receiver down again.

John tiptoed into his office and gently closed the door. He sat at his

153

desk and thought for a moment, then took out a notepad and wrote eleven words on the page. He tore the page loose and slid it under the door so that Karen would see it.

* * *

Buddy Tellers began his press conference before a greatly reduced press corps. Only one national media team was still present, but all of the local press was present, including newspaper, television and radio. Tellers loved the feeling that if he said jump, the media responded with "how high."

"There have been additional developments in the Vampire Defense case, and I have some announcements to make concerning scheduling. As you know, Mr. Hal Boyd has been charged with an additional murder and aggravated assault that occurred in the jail. The investigation of those cases is complete and the State's case is rock solid. In fact, we will be able to move forward on those cases immediately. Therefore, we will be conducting a preliminary hearing on the jail murder and assault charges Monday, April 16, the first date that the court is available. Also, on that day we will conduct a preliminary hearing on the obstruction of justice charges against Ms. Wilkes, the secretary of Mr. Brooks, the Vampire lawyer.

In addition to that, both of the attorneys involved in the supposed Vampire Defense case, Mr. John Brooks and Mr. Jackson Bradley, are under investigation themselves for possible aggravated assault charges arising out of an incident last night. We will have further announcements on those charges in the immediate future when the investigation is complete."

Several reporters raised their hands.

* * *

The paper on the floor made Karen mad.

"That's a childish and cowardly way to try to communicate," she said to herself. She ignored the page for a while, but eventually found an excuse to walk past the page. The first words generated nothing but anger. "By the way. Smart-aleck."

She swept the note up angrily and read out loud, "By the way, we... What!"

She swung John's door open and rushed inside.

* * *

"Mr. Tellers, will it still be necessary to proceed with the charges against Ms. Wilkes in light of the capture of one of her kidnappers last night?"

"Excuse me?"

"Yes, it is reported that one Danny Morton confessed to kidnapping

154

Ms. Wilkes, and a Freddy Krueger mask was found in his apartment."

Tellers looked over his shoulder for assistance. None was there.

"Is the aggravated assault charge against Brooks and Bradley related to their involvement in the capture of Danny Morton?"

"I am not able to comment on that right now. That is the subject of an ongoing investigation."

"Shouldn't Brooks and Bradley be treated as heroes instead of subjects of a criminal investigation?"

"Things are not always as they seem. Now, if you will excuse me, I must attend to other matters."

Tellers walked away from the podium as more questions were shouted at him.

*   *   *

"You caught one of the kidnappers!" shouted Karen as she rushed into the office. She ran behind John's desk, charged into his chair, and wrapped her arms around his neck. The chair rolled across the room until it collided with the wall.

"That is awesome!" she exuded.

Then she realized that she was sitting on him with her arms around his neck.

"Sorry," she said as she stood, and sat on the corner of the desk. "Tell me all about it."

"Well, we really can't take credit for it," said John. "It was your friend Father Michael."

After describing everything that occurred up until the park ranger made them lie on the ground, he added, "Soon after Ranger Bill nabbed us, several police cars, state troopers and ambulances arrived. Apparently, Father Michael found a way to get into the ambulance with this Danny fellow while no one was looking. He seems to be good at moving about unnoticed. Danny felt so threatened by McCarty that he shouted to the police for help and said he would confess to the kidnapping if they would protect him from 'the Priest.'"

"So, where is Father Michael?"

"He slipped back into the night, before Danny started screaming. He said enough to Danny to scare him into telling the truth. The other guy, the one that Father Mike called Gregory, slipped away while no one was looking. I don't understand how that happened. There were so many officers present. Anyway, I suspect McCarty went after him."

"Wow!"

"Yeah. Wow. We heard several gunshots. The police rushed toward the sound, but they found nothing."

"So you hit my kidnapper with a crowbar while he was shooting a shotgun? You're my hero," she said with a teasing smile.

"No, I hit Gregory, the other guy. Father Mike nailed Danny, your kidnapper, and got Danny to confess. He is the real hero."

"Danny was the reluctant kidnapper, the one with the Freddy mask. I don't think he would have done it on his own."

"Well, he was pointing a shotgun our way last night."

"Wow, this is just too much. What could happen next?"

31

The flight to Chicago seemed longer than usual. Sandy struggled with emotions, mentally kicking herself for getting too close to the story. She told herself that she had become enamored with the idea of the story. The Vampire Defense catapulted her from obscurity and created her first real opportunity to reach the big time. Her unprofessional conduct, she said to herself, had almost cost her that opportunity. And all she had to show for it was a hurting heart and a feeling that she had made a fool of herself over some bumpkin from Mississippi. She told herself that she had transferred some of the excitement and intrigue that she was feeling for the story to the lawyer and confused those feelings for attraction.

"How could I have ever been attracted to him?" she said under her breath. "That will never happen again."

The person seated next to her said, "Pardon?"

Sandy turned to the little lady who looked to be approaching seventy and said, "Oh, I'm sorry, I was just talking to myself."

"Say, aren't you that famous reporter on CTN?"

"Well, I don't know about famous. I'm not sure anyone knows who I am."

"Everybody knows 'Sandy Storm, reporting from the muddy banks of the Barnett Reservoir,'" said the silver-haired maiden, doing her best Sandy Storm imitation.

Sandy and Martha struck up a conversation about Sandy's career and the Vampire Defense. By the time the plane was preparing to land, Martha had chased away all of the gloom and doom Sandy was feeling about her future. Her cup was full again, and she felt ready to take on the world. Then, Martha said, "Everyone in my bridge club is wondering whether or not there is anything going on between you and that really cute lawyer in the Vampire Defense case. Is there anything I can tell them?"

"Why would they wonder about that?" Sandy said, as blood rushed to her face.

"Oh, everyone can see the attraction between you two. You are both working on this exciting case. Think about it. Of all the reporters trying to get his attention, he always talks to you. You pick at him and ask him embarrassing questions, yet he still lets you get to him first. He must really be attracted to you."

"He doesn't let me get to him, I have to fight my way through burly aggressive male reporters and cameramen, then I ask him the best questions."

Sandy was getting worked up and she was speaking faster and faster.

"Oh, I know skill has a lot to do with it, don't get me wrong, but your looks certainly don't hurt. You are a beautiful young lady with an exciting job and he is a handsome and available young man at the top of his game. How could the two of you not be attracted to each other? We think that you would make a handsome couple with an exciting future."

"Oh, you do. Well, you can tell your bridge club that there is no way in . . .," Sandy paused, caught her breath, and said, "Martha, I am sorry. You have been a delight to talk to, but I just don't want our conversation to end on this note. I don't want to talk about this subject."

"Oh, something happened," said Martha, putting her hand on Sandy's arm. "He has hurt you. I am so sorry."

Despite herself, Sandy could not prevent tears from rolling down her cheek. Martha kept trying to comfort her and Sandy kept saying, "No, no, I'm all right. No, there was nothing between us."

"It's okay, I understand, just let it out."

The plane landed and Sandy and Martha parted. Sandy made her way to baggage claim, while Martha called her best bridge friend to tell her about the break-up of the "affair" between Sandy Storm and the Vampire Defense lawyer John Brooks.

Sandy was once again feeling like a fool. As she wiped tears from her face she asked herself, "What am I crying over?"

"You are ruining your make-up," said a familiar voice. She turned to see Bret, already holding her bag. "We've got an interview in two hours with one of the state legislators that ran for the border in order to prevent a quorum from being present in Wisconsin. Do you want to freshen up before we leave?"

"Sure. Thanks Bret. I am just. Never mind. I'll be right back."

"I know. You made that Vampire Defense case. I can't believe that they pulled us off, just as things were getting even more interesting, if that was even possible."

"What do you mean?"

"You haven't kept up with the news?"

"No, I overslept and rushed to the airport."

"Wow, then you don't know. Your boy is a hero."

"What do you mean, 'my boy?' He's not my boy. He means nothing to me."

"At least I know we're talking about the same boy. Anyway, he caught the people who kidnapped his secretary last night, or at least one of them. Another one escaped from an ambulance."

158

"Caught! Kidnappers? Escaped from an ambulance!"

"Spoken just like a news man. Person. People. Person. Whatever. Anyway there is a preliminary hearing set a week from Monday on the new murder charge and aggravated assault charge, the ones from the jail."

"What? They set those without me!"

"Really. I agree. The nerve of the court system to operate without first checking with The Storm."

"You want to see a storm—I'll show you a storm!" Sandy said as she stepped closer, trembling with anger.

"Before you blow me away, I think you should know that I have your plane ticket for your return trip to Jackson in the morning."

Sandy's mouth was agape as she slowly took the ticket from Bret. "We've been reassigned?"

"Yep. Since we are already here, the boss wants us to get something out of the trip, so we are reassigned right after the interview."

"What are you waiting for? Let's get in the car."

"Ms. Storm, the car is this way," said Bret, indicating another direction and off they went.

32

The Bishop's features were inscrutable.

After Gregory described the events at Mayes Lake, the Bishop simply sat behind the table with his hands clasped in front of him. He observed Gregory for several seconds, rose from the table and began pacing. It was not always easy to tell if the Bishop was angry.

As he watched the Bishop, Gregory thought about Erick. Last night the Bishop didn't seem to be angry with Erick, but everyone knew what had happened to the fool for his failure. No one talked about it, except Gayle, who seemed to relish in describing Erick's fate.

"I want you to know that I have been very proud of your accomplishments. You have been most effective since you joined us. You are without a doubt the most intelligent and most valuable member of our congregation. Besides me of course."

"Of course."

"You, of all people, must set a good example."

"Yes, Bishop."

"I do not fault you for failing to kill the Priest. Many have tried. He is, how should I say this? Skilled. But, his day will come."

"I don't know that we didn't get him. I feel certain that I shot him, but it was like he had a sixth sense. He realized I was there a moment before I shot, then he moved faster than I ever imagined he could. He dove into the river, and I never saw him come out of the water. His body might have floated down stream, or he might have gotten hung up on the truck or some other underwater obstacle."

"Or, he might have eluded you, which is what I believe happened."

"I have men searching both banks of the river looking for his body or for him. If he is still alive, I believe he is injured. We found all of his possessions near the campground. He will be at a great disadvantage if he is still alive."

"Oh, he is still alive. Don't underestimate him. He is a powerful force to be reckoned with, and once he gets to a phone, he will call for help."

"Who will he call? I thought he was ostracized."

"He has many friends who quietly and privately support his otherwise lone crusade. After he licks his wounds, I predict he will be back. Now, let's talk about the example that you are setting for other members of our

160

group. We must learn from our mistakes. We cannot make many mistakes, because we are vastly outnumbered. We operate on the fringe of society for now. The general public, the unwashed masses, must not know of us, at least not yet. I think that your mistake was thinking that just two of you could capture the Priest."

"Yes, sir, you are right. We were one of several groups looking for him. He cleverly laid a trap for us, but we could have taken him if those lawyers hadn't shown up when they did."

"Humph," said the Bishop. "Your second mistake was taking only Danny with you. I know that you were trying to disciple him, trying to help him learn. We have many newcomers that need that kind of help. I suspect he would have been a handicap in an engagement with so formidable a foe as the Priest."

"You are right again, sir. I wanted to see if he was redeemable after what happened with the kidnapping. He performed reasonable well. He didn't run when the fight started, but the Priest knocked him unconscious."

"I could live with that. The Priest has put better men than Danny out of action. After all, the Priest killed Stewart the night of the kidnapping. Crushed his skull. Failing to get the Priest is not what has me so worried. It's what Danny did later that worries me. He started talking. Talk like that can threaten our very existence. He must be silenced before he talks about us. Do you understand me?"

"Understood. Indeed, the process of sealing his lips has already been set in motion."

"That is just one more reason that I have so much faith in you, my dear Gregory."

*   *   *

Ted and Skip rushed into Jackson's office with the exciting news that Ted had received a call from a possible investor in Goshen Springs Beer. The investor had seen the news report of John's endorsement of the "best beer in the world." The interview was being broadcast repeatedly now that John was suddenly considered to be a hero.

"He said he would put enough money in the project to make our beer available to millions of customers!" Ted excitedly explained. "I told him he needed to talk with our lawyers."

John was in his office studying reams of information produced by the librarians and organized by Jennifer when Karen announced that he had a call.

"It's a Mr. Anderson, from New Orleans."

"That's him!" shouted Ted.

Everyone ran into John's office with anticipation on each face.

161

"Have him hold for a moment please."

"Mr. Anderson, Mr. Brooks will be with you in about one minute."

"Don't make the man with the money wait!" exclaimed Ted.

"No, make him linger," said Skip. "This is good."

"Has everyone put in their money?" asked John.

"Yep, all five of us," said Jackson.

"What about me?" asked Karen. "Are you leaving me out of the action?"

There was a little grumbling, and John said, "She can have half my share if you guys won't cut her in."

"No, no, she can be in but can she pay the $5,000 that everyone else paid?" asked Ted.

"She will pay, or I will cover it for her," said John.

"I'll put up half of her share," said Jackson.

"Me, too," said Skip. "I'll put up the third half."

"Thanks guys. I've got my share covered. I can come up with five."

"Okay, you're in," said Ted.

"How much do we need to get off the ground?"

"Well, to get proper kettles, and to . . ."

"Not meaning to interrupt, just give me the bottom line."

"We can brew small scale now. But on a commercial scale, we need anywhere from $500,000 to $2 million."

"All right," said John as he picked up the phone. "Mr. Anderson, this is John Brooks. Yes, thank you."

Everyone in the room glued their eyes on John, hanging on every word.

"We haven't decided yet whether taking on another partner is advisable."

Skip and Ted were nodding their heads up and down, mouthing, "it's advisable."

"We would need to meet and do some due diligence on one another to determine if you would be a good fit for us and you need to see if we would be a good fit for you. That's right. You're thinking of an initial investment of $400,000."

Everyone sucked air.

"You would want how much interest? You think 80 percent would be fair, but you could not have less than 60 percent for that kind of investment. I see. Well, we are not thinking in the same terms. We are not interested in selling more than a 10 percent interest right now. $40,000, for 10 percent!"

Everyone's heads nodded up and down.

"I'm sorry, that is just not even in the ball park. We were thinking of

$2 million for a 10 percent interest."

Everyone's mouth dropped open.

"I understand that is a lot of money. Have you ever tasted the beer? Well, let's talk again after you've tasted it. Karen, my assistant will get your contact information and arrange a tasting for you. Thank you, Mr. Anderson."

John hung up.

"Karen."

"I'm on it."

"I can't believe that you turned down the chance to get 40 grand for 10 percent," said Jackson. " Do you know what kind of return on investment that would be for us?"

"I didn't turn down anything. I just set our goals high. We need $2 million, so that was our number."

"Why 10 percent?" asked Ted.

"Well, I had to offer him something. Would you begrudge him 10 percent?"

"I guess not."

"Okay then. Ted, why don't you have the librarians find out what they can about our Mr. Anderson? Now, let's get back to work. Enough dreaming."

*   *   *

Danny was released from the hospital into the custody of police officers. He was booked and placed in a cell by late morning. He had never been in jail before and the experience was frightening to him. He was second-guessing the choices that landed him in his cell when a guard called him to the door. He didn't pay attention to the long sleeved plastic gloves on the guard's hands.

"Danny, come over here. I've got something for you."

The voice seemed familiar. As Danny approached the door, he realized where he had seen the guard before.

"Oh, I am so relieved it is you. You remember me, don't you? I've been at the meetings with you."

"Yeah, sure, Danny. I'm here to look after you. Jail can be a dangerous place for someone who isn't careful."

Danny stepped up to the door, and said, "You've got to get me out of here. I've always been told that the Kroth has friends everywhere and that it will take care of us. Now, I see that is true. I was beginning to have my doubts."

"Don't worry, Danny, you will never doubt anything again," said the guard as he sank a shaft deep into Danny's abdomen and shoved the blade down with all of his weight.

Danny staggered, and looked down in astonishment as his insides spilled out. The guard reached through the bars and grabbed Danny's collar, pulling him close. He inserted the knife into Danny's heart. Danny collapsed onto the messy floor, a stunned look on his face. The guard walked quickly down the hall, stripping off the plastic gloves. He went straight to the cell occupied by Hal Boyd and tossed the gloves and blade through the bars. Boyd heard something hit the floor of his cell with a liquidious plump followed by a clattering sound. He looked down to see the bloody gloves and knife. Blood spatter was everywhere. By the time he looked towards the door, whoever had thrown the gruesome items was gone.

33

McCarty felt hands searching him. He remembered pulling himself on shore during the night. He didn't have the strength to move away from the river, so he pulled mud and grass over him as best he could before passing out. Now, he knew someone had found him. He cracked open his eyes and saw an old woman. Dirt was smeared on her face. She wore a cloth hat and ragged clothes. She was patting him down, searching his pockets. McCarty groaned and the woman jumped back.

"You're alive! I thought you was dead. Sammy! I've got a live one here!"

She hollered at her companion, and laughed at her joke.

"Yeah, a live one; but I don't know for how long."

Sammy, sporting an unkempt beard and clothes that looked as though they had never been cleaned, arrived at her side and said, "Well Mert, what you got here?"

"I figure it's another victim of them vampires, that's what I got."

"Vampires. That's silly. You've been convinced that we have vampires ever since that Belhaven murder happened."

"Before that I tell you. That's what happened to Evan and Whittles. Vampires got 'em."

"Naw, it was just time for them to move on, that's all."

"Well, here's proof of vampires. Just look at him."

"Mert, it's just a washed up old bum like me, that's all."

"Well, let's get him away from the river," said Mert, and she and Sammy grabbed McCarty under his arms and helped him into a thick stand of black oaks. The gnarly black trunk trees love to grow in low-lying sandy ground. As they laid him down in the soft, dry sand Father Michael feebly uttered, "Thank you."

"You're welcome," said Sammy. "We would do it for anybody who's down and out, and you're pretty down and out."

"I'll get him some good water and something to eat," said Mert.

"You ain't got much. The little bit you got won't make no difference, I reckon."

"Well, I reckon it won't hurt none either."

Mert ambled off to her home under a bush. She and a few other homeless people lived in the woods near the old Water Works station. She returned a few minutes later with a gallon jug of water and a package of stale crackers. "I've been saving these for a special occasion," she said and she and Sammy laughed at her joke.

McCarty drank the cool water, and felt a little better. He gratefully took the crackers that Mert offered.

Suddenly, Mert, said, "Shush. I see them vampires. They're coming for us."

"What do you mean girl. That's nothing but a bunch of kids walking along the river."

"Look how they are dressed."

"All kids wear black clothes these days. That don't mean nothin'."

"You've got to go now," said McCarty. "If they find you with me they will kill you." Sammy and Mert were shocked. They looked at each other and saw fear bordering on panic in each other's eyes.

"Dad gum, Mert, you might be sort of right this time."

Sammy considered the predicament for a moment while he watched the men search the riverbank. "Naw, Mister. We ain't leaving you to them, whatever they are. Come on, Mert, let's slip a little further into the bush with this fellow."

Mert and Sammy watched as five young men scoured the riverside.

"It looks like they are looking for something," said Sammy.

"Naw, they are looking for someone. They are looking for you," Mert said to McCarty. "Are they vampires?"

"They are looking for me, but they are not vampires. They are worse than vampires."

"How can they be worse than vampires?"

"They are humans who help vampires by betraying other humans. This group calls themselves the Kroth."

"The Kroth!" Mert said as she punched Sammy's shoulder. "I told you there was vampires."

"Just cause he says it don't make it so," Sammy responded. Suddenly, a look of shocked realization erupted on his face. "They gonna see our track marks!" exclaimed Sammy as he eased his way back into the black oaks and tried to obliterate their marks in the sand.

"Sammy, they gonna see you. Come back here."

"Hush little woman. I gotta do this. Don't make no noise."

Sammy rubbed the track marks and blended the sand as best he could, then eased slowly back into the bush with Mert and the stranger. One of the young men seemed to see their tracks along the river and followed their trail into the black oaks. The ground was heavily shaded and it was difficult to make anything out.

"You see anything?" someone nearby asked.

The man hesitated and then said, "No. Nothing here."

Mert and Sammy watched the five men troop off along the river until

166

they were out of sight.

"They're gone," said Mert.

"They will be back," said McCarty. "We can't stay here."

McCarty found an inner well of reserve strength and with the help of Mert and Sammy, moved deeper into the woods. He convinced them not to start a fire, as it would attract the hunters.

"You've been shot," said Sammy when he saw the bullet hole through his leg. "We have got to get you to a hospital. The bullet went clean through from one side to another. You have lost a lot of blood."

"I can't go to the hospital. They will find me there and kill me. If they kill me, they will kill others. I can't go."

Sammy and Mert looked at each other for a few moments.

"Well, we can't make him go," said Mert. "I wouldn't go. You know what they will do if I were to have one of my spells."

"What are we going to do? He's going to die from infection, or blood loss or something."

"We're all going to die from something."

"We can't just let him die. We've got to do something. His leg is already getting hot from infection."

"We are going to pack his wound with tobacco to pull the infection out, just like pulling poison out. Then, we are going to nurse him back to health."

"All right Mert. I think that's crazy cause we're gonna bring them vampire helper people on us, but let's give it a try."

"Thank you—God bless you," said McCarty.

Mert started shaking and mumbling.

"Not now Mert. Them Krothers are going to hear you. She's fixin' to have one of her spells!"

Mert fell to the ground and began thrashing about.

"I don't know what it is," said Sammy as he held her arms. "They say it's not epilepsy. She can't hold no job and nobody will put up with her cause she acts so crazy for a while after she has a fit. Help me hold her. She's gonna start hollering in a minute and them vampires will hear her and come back."

"I'm not sure, but I may be able to help," said Michael as he crawled over to Mert. "I have seen something like this before. I think she may be why I was sent here."

He placed his hand on her forehead and began to pray.

"What do you mean, sent here? You're as crazy as she is. You must have forgot that we pulled you out of the river, friend."

* * *

Karen fielded another of the endless daily phone calls.

"John, it's an attorney named Bell."

"That's Judge Bell. I want to talk to him."

John picked up the phone.

"Judge Bell, any word about Travis?"

"Yes, he is doing much better. He will make it and he is talking."

"I see."

"I understand that you have a preliminary hearing Monday on the charge of aggravated assault on Travis and murder of John Smith."

"Yes, that's right."

"Do you ever use preliminary hearings as an opportunity to do some discovery?"

"Sure do. Sometimes I get the State's witnesses there so that I can do the equivalent of a deposition."

"I thought so. Do you ever try to put on evidence yourself?"

"To try to prove innocence?"

"Yes."

"It's hardly worth it," said John. "It will just give the prosecution early discovery about my case, and I won't get the case dismissed because the State's burden is so low at the preliminary."

"That's right. All the State has to do is meet probable cause."

"And most judges believe that almost any evidence that the defendant might have committed the crime is probable cause."

"True, but what would a judge do if you convinced him that your client was innocent?" asked Bell.

"Well, I guess if the judge were convinced of innocence, it would be hard for him to rule that there was probable cause of guilt."

"I guess you're right."

"What are you suggesting?"

"I'm not suggesting anything you would not have thought of yourself," said Bell, "I'm just saying, without violating any attorney client privilege, that it might behoove you to subpoena your former client to the hearing."

"That's interesting."

"I thought you would say that. Goodbye."

"Karen, we need to issue a subpoena for Travis Thomas for Monday's hearing. We need to get it served as fast as we can. Who is available for that?"

"Crush just walked in," said Karen.

"I'll do it. I'm glad to do anything to help."

"Thanks, Crush. If anybody can get the job done, you can," said Karen.

Crush broke into a wide grin and said, "I promise I won't let you down."

*   *   *

Again, the phone rang.

"Excuse me Crush," said Karen. "Brooks and Bradley! Yes. Oh no. Just one minute. John, you better pick up. Hal is being charged with another murder."

Jackson and John rushed to the jail to see Hal. This time, the jailers would not allow Boyd in the same room as John. He was placed in the visiting room, a panel of unbreakable glass between them. They had to speak through a telephone. Hal's legs were shackled and his right arm was chained to his waist. Only his left arm was free to use the telephone.

After they heard Hal's story, Jackson said "How do they think that you accomplished this murder when your cell door was locked? Why would they think that you would keep the glove and knife, but lock your door? Why would you even use a glove, and then keep it? If you could get in and out so easily, why are you still here?"

"They want to believe that I did it. It had to be a guard or a trusty."

"As Governor Barnett said, if you can't trust a trusty, who can you trust?" said Jackson.

"Hal, we're going to court Monday for a preliminary hearing. We will discover some of the evidence they believe that they have against you. Usually, the prosecutor puts on as little as he can get away with in order to meet his burden of proof, which is very low at the preliminary. He can even use hearsay, such as an investigator testifying about what he learned from witnesses and from the crime lab. It is nothing like a real trial. There is virtually no chance of winning anything at a preliminary hearing."

"I understand."

"In spite of that, I want to try something a little different."

John explained his strategy and his intention of calling Travis as a witness. He explained that Travis might testify against Hal in order to get a deal. "He has a get out of jail free card if he tells the prosecutor what he wants to hear."

"It's not supposed to work that way. People are supposed to tell the truth in court."

"People aren't supposed to kill, rob and steal either."

"Travis could hurt us bad, or he could help us."

"That's right. It's a gamble."

"You're my lawyer. I trust your judgment. Let's do this your way."

169

34

While she was still in Chicago, Sandy Storm filmed a segment summarizing the Vampire Defense case. The segment included film of the burned house and of the Belhaven neighborhood, clips of Boyd in handcuffs, clips of the courthouse and jail, clips of Brooks, Bradley and Karen and of their office, and images of some of the victims. In the background of every shot was the title 'The Vampire Defense,' complete with blood dripping from the letters:

> Breaking news in the sensational Vampire Defense case in Jackson, Mississippi. Hal Boyd, who has been called the Butcher of Belhaven and a purported vampire slayer, has been charged with yet another murder in the jail, this time while he was locked down under maximum security. Authorities allege that Boyd somehow escaped from his maximum-security cell and committed the gruesome bloody murder of Daniel Morton, who was locked in another cell.
>
> According to authorities, after killing Morton, Boyd returned to his locked cell. A bloody knife believed used in the slaying was found in Boyd's cell along with other evidence, according to District Attorney Buddy Tellers. Authorities do not explain how Boyd managed to escape from his cell and enter the victim's locked cell, or why he returned to his own cell after escaping.
>
> You might remember that Morton was arrested last night on charges of kidnapping Karen Wilkes, the secretary of Boyd's lawyer. Adding more intrigue to this bizarre development is that Boyd's attorney captured Morton and turned him over to authorities.
>
> To recap the events of just this week, a mansion in a fashionable neighborhood in Jackson, Mississippi, was burned to the ground. Hal Boyd was captured leaving the burning house and confessed on the scene to killing one of the occupants. Numerous witnesses said that they saw him shoot another person to death in the front yard of the house. A total of three charred bodies were found in the house. Boyd was charged with arson, three counts of capital murder and a separate count of murder. It was later revealed that he is a person of interest in the investigation of a string of murders

170

across the country.

Later that day, Boyd's lawyer, John Brooks, shocked the world by claiming that Boyd killed because he believed that one of his victims was a vampire. That resulted in this case being known across the world as the Vampire Defense.

The next day, Boyd was involved in a bloody knife fight with two inmates in the shower of the jail. One inmate was killed and another severely wounded. Boyd was then charged with another count of murder and with aggravated assault as a result of that fight. Coincidentally, the person injured was at that time represented by John Brooks, the same lawyer that represents Boyd.

In the meantime, Karen Wilkes, Brooks' secretary, reported that three people wearing masks resembling Freddy Krueger, Marilyn Monroe and the Wicked Witch kidnapped her. To add more intrigue, the District Attorney announced that he doubted the kidnapping report and suggested that he would be bringing charges of obstruction of justice against Wilkes for making a false report of crime.

That unusual development was topped by the report last night that lawyer Brooks had captured two of the kidnappers. Morton reportedly confessed to his part in the kidnapping after his capture by Brooks. It was reported Brooks and his partner Jackson Bradley, Morton and another suspect had been involved in a struggle. The authorities did not know at first whether to arrest Brooks and Bradley or Morton and his companion until Morton confessed. During the confusion that ensued while the police were trying to decide whom to arrest, one of the kidnappers escaped. Brooks was hailed as a hero for capturing one of the kidnappers and preventing the prosecution of his own secretary.

Sandy's voice-over paused and there was a brief film clip of a jailer saying, "I don't know how he did it. It gives me the willies."

The jailer visibly shivered.

Sandy returned to the screen and continued: "Authorities say they now have Boyd under 24-hour surveillance. This is Sandy Storm."

171

35

Racked with fever, Father Michael lost track of time. He lay on a makeshift bed under a tarp extended between trees. Mert patted his forehead with a cloth. Throbbing, burning pain seared his leg. Mercifully, he passed out again.

"I don't know how he did it, Mert, but you started calming down. After an hour or so you woke back up and you didn't have that crazy time you usually have after you have a fit."

"The voices in my head are gone, Sammy. He did something. I feel like me again."

"The scuttlebutt is that the Kroth will pay big money to anyone who finds the Priest for them," said Sammy. "Do you think he is a priest?"

"He don't look like one. But he sure prays a lot. Where did you hear that?"

"Wilson said that those kids we saw on the river roughed him up and threatened to kill one of us a day, starting tomorrow, until somebody brings them the Priest, dead or alive."

"What's everybody gonna do?"

"Everybody has moved out of the woods and away from the river. They are getting as far away from here as they can."

"I could never do that. The river is my home. I love these woods."

"Wilson said they told him whoever brings them the Priest would get a big reward."

"Does anybody know we got him?"

"Don't know for sure."

"What are we gonna do?"

"We don't have no choice, Mert."

*   *   *

Jackson, Mitch and Rob organized volunteers from the rugby team into groups of three to canvas the Belhaven neighborhood. They went door-to-door telling neighbors they were investigating the murders. At first, people were reluctant to talk, but the players were so gregarious that soon people started opening up to them. Indeed, it seemed that everywhere they went, someone knew someone who was somehow connected to the team. Within a few days they learned everything that anyone in the neighborhood had ever said or thought about Vlal Drumon, Godfry Plova, Hal Boyd, the old house, the fire and each of the witnesses, with one exception.

Jackson, Rob and Larry stood on the front porch of the Robins' house. They had knocked and rung the bell. Someone seemed to be home, but no one came to the door. After a few minutes, Jackson said, "I guess we should go."

The door opened, and a brunette stuck her head out of the door. "I don't know why you people keep coming to our house. I want you to stay away, or I will call the police."

"Yes ma'am," said Jackson. "We meant no harm. We are investigating the fire and the homicides and we understand that your son is a witness."

"My son Jack is not talking to anyone. This has been a terrible trauma and we just want to forget about it. Now, just leave us in peace."

"Yes ma'am. Here is my card. Please call me if you change your mind."

Mrs. Robins took the card, but said, "We won't be changing our mind. Goodbye."

She closed and locked the door.

"Icy reception," said Rob as they walked away. "Maybe we could get to him through Patrick."

"Great idea," said Jackson. "Why don't you two try that avenue? I need to go to the jail and see if I can find out who was working when Danny Morton was killed and when John Smith was in jail."

"You're going to try to cross-reference and see who worked both times?"

"You got it. Knives got into the jail somehow. An employee would be one possible source."

173

36

Preliminary hearings usually take place in one of the Municipal Courtrooms inside the City of Jackson Police Department. Because of the extreme interest in the case, the District Attorney arranged for the hearing to take place in the spacious Courtroom One in the Hinds County Courthouse. The courtroom features massive mahogany doors, somber mahogany paneling, and an impressive wooden bench with "Justice" emblazoned on its face.

National and state flags are positioned behind the bench, announcing to the world that the judge speaks with the full authority of law. Above the bench are elaborate carvings of symbols of justice. To the right of the bench is the mahogany witness box, flanked by the jury box. Attorney tables and chairs face the bench, and additional mahogany desks are strategically placed for use by the court reporter, the stenographer whose difficult job is to preserve every utterance during the trial, a court clerk and the bailiffs, who are charged with keeping the courtroom secure and enforcing order in the court if necessary.

A carved mahogany bar bisects the room, separating the public area of the courtroom from the portion that only members of the bar and participants in a case may enter. Inside the bar is where drama is played out, where lives and fortunes are at risk, and where, it is fervently hoped, justice is dispensed. Humans crave justice, but because of human limitations, even the best justice system will sometimes fail to deliver.

Two-thirds of the room lies beyond the bar and is filled with row upon row of pews capable of holding 300 to 400 people. If that was inadequate, a mahogany-lined balcony hung over a third of the courtroom, providing a bird's-eye view of the proceedings for more spectators.

Courtroom One is a beautiful, impressive, somber place. It is well designed to convey to those who enter that serious business takes place within these walls. Simply entering the room tends to cause the average person to become quiet and respectful. There have been many times when a notorious criminal would fight against his jailers every step of the way from his cell to the courtroom door, only to become quiet and respectful upon entering the ornate courtroom.

Preliminary hearings are routine affairs that in ordinary practice have very little impact upon the outcome of a case, although occasionally it becomes apparent that a defendant is being held without any real evidence. In those cases the defendant is released. But, generally the prosecutor is able to put forward some evidence that the defendant committed a crime. The prosecutor does not ordinarily put forward all of the evidence available to him, because his only burden is to show that the defendant probably committed a crime. The judge will permit hearsay at a preliminary hearing, so there is no need to ask witnesses to leave their jobs to come wait outside the courtroom for his or her turn to testify. The prosecutor also prefers not to give the defense lawyer an opportunity to examine the State's witnesses under oath before the case is actually tried.

Since preliminary hearings are routine and seldom critical to the outcome of any given case, the District Attorney assigns assistants to cover the hearing. Sometimes, the separately elected County Attorney handles the hearings. Since there was tremendous local interest in the Butcher of Belhaven case, a moniker that seemed even more appropriate after the brutally bloody jail slayings, the District Attorney intended to handle this hearing himself. He knew that many voters would be watching. Indeed, his reason for setting the hearing was to obtain as much publicity for himself as he could. He pulled a few strings and managed to obtain the most desirable courtroom as a venue to showcase his talents to the watching world.

Tellers picked his easiest cases, the slaying in the jail of John Smith and the stabbing of Travis Thomas. To keep the defense busy, he threw in the second jailhouse murder as well. All of his immediate goals would be met if the judge found sufficient evidence that the crimes of murder and aggravated assault were committed. The positive publicity would enhance the prosecutor's reputation, and the negative publicity for Boyd would make conviction in the underlying Vampire Defense case even more likely.

The beauty of this strategy was that there was no real risk to the prosecutor. Even in the event that the judge found against the State, a result that Tellers did not consider to be possible, Boyd would remain in jail because of the underlying murder charges. The only flaw in the plan was Tellers' eagerness to keep the attention of the international media. Because he loved the limelight, he sped up the process and set the preliminary hearing before the charges were fully investigated in order to keep the international media from leaving town. This meant more news specials on the case and more coverage for the District Attorney, who boasted to the world that he won over 99 percent of his cases.

Because of the lowly status of preliminary hearings, the court generally does not provide a court reporter, saving them for use in hearings of more significance. As soon as the preliminary was scheduled, Karen called Candace, the private court reporter Brooks and Bradley always used. Jackson was relieved to see Candace present when he and John arrived early for the hearing. Candace is a professional who performs her duties and is not bullied by lawyers. Jackson worried that the prosecutor might try to make a stink over the presence of a private court reporter and he was confident that Candace would know how to assert herself and gain a seat at the reporter's desk. Candace had finished setting up and she smiled and nodded to John and Jackson when they entered the courtroom

The courtroom was three-quarters full when the defense lawyers entered. Cameras were only recently allowed in the courtroom and John and Jackson could hear the click of shutters as they entered the room, crossed the bar and took their places at one of the attorney tables.

A few minutes later, Assistant District Attorney Robert Thornton entered the courtroom from a door to the left of the bench. Camera shutters clicked. Thornton scanned the room and seemed somewhat uncomfortable by the presence of so many reporters. He placed his file on the opposite table and pulled a chair up next to Jackson. He leaned over to Jackson, and said in whisper, "I understand that you like to brag that your partner is unbeaten against us in criminal cases."

"That's right. 7 and 0, but who's counting besides me and you and the District Attorney. 8 and 0, if we count the way Mr. Tellers counts."

"How do you figure that?"

"Your boss threatened to charge our secretary with the crime of obstruction of justice following her kidnapping. Now that John and I caught one of the kidnappers, I presume you will not be proceeding with that bogus charge."

"Well, your best witness, the purported kidnapper, is dead."

"Are you still threatening Karen? After all, a search of his apartment turned up the Freddy Krueger mask that Buddy laughed about."

"No, we won't be prosecuting Karen."

"Okay then, 8 and 0, but who's counting."

"Well, you and Brooks are about to enter into a long losing streak."

As soon as he sat down at his new table, Thornton became aware of the court reporter. He realized that she was not one of the usual reporters and must be a private reporter. Thornton quickly crossed the distance between them and asked her name and why she was there.

"Ms. Avery, professional reporter, here to record the proceedings by authority granted by this and every other court in the State of Mississippi. May I have your name and the party you represent for the record, please?"

"Robert Thornton, Assistant District Attorney. We will want a copy

176

of your transcript."

"I will be glad to provide that to you upon satisfactory arrangements to pay the fee for transcription. And, since Mr. Brooks and Mr. Bradley are paying my appearance fee, if you want a copy of the transcript, I presume you will be paying half of the appearance fee?"

"Well, I . . . whatever the usual arrangements are is what we will do, of course."

"Of course, that is all that I expect. Thank you Mr. Thornton. Is it all right if I call you Robert, or do you go by Bob?"

"Bob."

"Thank you Bob. Do you want next day transcription, or is one week all right with you?"

"Next day sounds good."

"That comes at a premium of course."

"Oh, of course, yes."

As Thornton turned from the court reporter he observed that every seat was taken in the spectator area. The balcony, which was not generally used, remained closed. Thornton made his way back to his table and heard an audible trill go through the gallery as Hal Boyd entered the courtroom. He was shackled with both hands cuffed and chained to his waist and both ankles cuffed and attached to short chains that allowed him to do no more than shuffle along. Four guards watched his every move and kept an eye out for possible threats from onlookers. Boyd and his four guards made their way to the defense table. Another half-dozen deputies and policemen entered the courtroom through the main door and took up positions around the room. The display of force impressed the reporters, who took it all in and conveyed the tense atmosphere to a waiting world.

Buddy Tellers, with a natural flair for timing, entered the courtroom just as the tension and anticipation reached a peak. He was instantly recognized because of his commanding appearance and authoritative demeanor. Tall and lean with a shock of perfectly coiffed gray hair, he was wearing his best suit and power tie. Cameras clicked and the background murmuring raised a few decibels. Mr. Lee, the bailiff, used his booming voice to demand, "Order in the Court! Quiet please, or I will have to ask you to leave."

No one wanted to leave so the murmuring ceased for a few minutes.

Jackson leaned over and whispered in John's ear, "Looks like the high D.A. himself will be handling this little hearing today."

John raised his eyebrows and smiled at Jackson. He wrote on a legal pad, "Bring it on!"

There was a loud knock on the door directly behind the bench, and the bailiff called out in a loud voice, "All rise!" Everyone stood. "Hear ye, Hear ye, the County Court of the First Judicial District of Hinds County, Mississippi, is now in session, the Honorable Harmon Groom presiding."

37

Judge Groom took his seat behind the massive bench, looked out into the packed courtroom and said into the microphone, "Please be seated."

Everyone settled into pews and seats. Television programs across the world were interrupted to carry the proceedings live.

Judge Groom looked at the printed docket waiting for him on the bench and announced to no one's surprise, "The case on the docket is The State of Mississippi vs. Halbert Boyd, here on a preliminary hearing on two counts of murder and one of aggravated assault. Is the State of Mississippi ready?"

Buddy Tellers rose and stated in a voice that projected to every corner of the room, "The State of Mississippi is ready and will be represented today by me, District Attorney L. Buddy Tellers, and my Assistant District Attorney Robert Thornton."

"Yes, Mr. Tellers, I am sure you needed no introduction, but since you have been kind enough to introduce yourself to the gallery, I will ask the defense to first announce whether they are ready to proceed and then to identify themselves and their client for the record."

John nodded to Jackson, who smiled, stood and responded, "The defense is ready to proceed. I am Jackson Bradley, attorney for Halbert Boyd, who is seated here," gesturing towards Hal. "My partner, Mr. John Brooks, seated next to me, also represents Mr. Boyd. Mr. Brooks will be handling the examination of witnesses.

"All right, Mr. Tellers, call your first witness."

"The State of Mississippi calls Sony Winsted."

Winsted entered the courtroom dressed in slacks, a sport coat and tie. He had salt and pepper hair and appeared to be close to 60 years old. After he was sworn to tell the truth, the whole truth and nothing but the truth, he took his seat in the witness chair and explained that he was for many years an investigator with the County Sheriff's Department. After his retirement he took a job as an investigator with the Office of the District Attorney. He had examined the evidence in all three cases and talked with all of the witnesses, with the exception of one of the victims, Travis Thomas, who was in intensive care and unavailable when he went to the hospital to interview him.

"What did you learn from your investigation?" Tellers asked.

"Objection, hearsay and calls for a narrative answer," said Brooks as he rose from his chair.

Tellers chuckled and shook his head in apparent annoyance and frustration and said, "Judge, this is a preliminary hearing and any first-year law student would know that hearsay is admissible."

"Object to the comments," said Brooks.

"The objection to the comments is sustained. The hearsay and narrative objections are overruled since this is a preliminary hearing."

Not satisfied at having merely won the point, Tellers whirled towards the Judge, and said, "But, your Honor, I have to state my objections!"

"Mr. Tellers, I am in control of the courtroom, not you. Your comments are unnecessary, inappropriate and unappreciated. You will not use this courtroom as a platform for grandstanding to your audience."

"Judge, I am doing no such thing. The State has a right to a fair hearing and I have a right to state my objections. It was such a waste of time to make a hearsay objection at a preliminary hearing that I was surprised by the apparent lack of knowledge of my opponent."

Judge Groom turned toward Brooks and said, "He has a point about the objection. I am going to allow hearsay at this level of the proceedings."

"Of course, your Honor, I understand that hearsay is admissible at your discretion at a preliminary hearing. I just believe that at some point your Honor will see that the hearsay evidence that will be offered by the State is so tenuous that you may choose to exercise your discretion to refuse to rely upon it."

"What!" shouted Tellers, waving his arms in the air and turning toward his audience, "I have never heard of anything so ridiculous. The State can't afford to bring in every Tom, Dick and Harry who might have some inkling of knowledge about this case at a preliminary hearing. We do that for a jury trial, not at the probable cause stage. We can't be expected to try every case twice!"

"I see this hearing may be a bit more tiresome than the average preliminary hearing," said the Judge. "Mr. Tellers, defense counsel did not ask you to bring in every Tom, Dick and Harry, he simply pointed out that I have the discretion to accept hearsay evidence. Having the discretion to accept such evidence at least implies the discretion to reject such evidence."

"I can't believe what I am hearing. If the State has to worry about which evidence might be acceptable to any judge," said Tellers, infusing the words 'acceptable' and 'judge' with as much contempt as he could convey, "then the State could be forced into producing every shred of evidence it has at its disposal, causing every courtroom to be tied up for weeks at a time on probable cause hearings, at great expense to the State and considerable inconvenience and burden to the witnesses and to the courts."

Sandy Storm was seated on the front row with other reporters. She leaned over to the reporter seated next to her and whispered, "I bet the viewers are eating this up."

"Mr. Tellers, your reaction seems a bit extreme, especially considering the fact that I overruled the hearsay objection. Enough of this! Mr. Brooks, I don't want an interruption every few minutes. You have made your point."

"May I have a continuing objection your Honor?"

"Yes, you may. Mr. Winsted, please answer the question if you can remember it."

"Yes, Judge, I remember the question. Wednesday before last, I received an assignment to go to the scene of a stabbing in the shower of the City of Jackson Jail, located here in the First Judicial District of Hinds County, Mississippi. I was taken to the shower by Officer Joseph Colby, one of the witnesses of the crimes."

"What did you find there?"

"A gruesome sight. There was blood everywhere. I arranged to secure samples of the blood for testing. Another officer was present taking photographs and otherwise documenting the scene."

"Did you speak to any witnesses?"

"Yes, I identified three witnesses and spoke to all of them. Officers Colby, Whitaker and Spencer, all with the Jackson Police Department assigned to the jail."

"What did you learn from them?"

John cleared his throat, without looking up from his legal pad. Tellers looked at him with annoyance. The witness paused. The Judge instructed Winsted to continue.

"The Defendant, seated there at the defense table, stabbed one inmate, John Smith, through the heart, killing him, and grievously injured another inmate, Travis Thomas. He used a shank, a handmade knife, which was taken from Mr. Boyd after the guards confronted him."

"How did they describe Mr. Boyd?"

"He was naked and covered with blood from head to foot, swinging the blade about wildly and moving from foot to foot as though he was doing some strange ritual dance."

The audience gasped and reacted with disgust.

"Order in the Court!" commanded Judge Groom. "If you cannot control yourselves, then you will be removed from the courtroom. Does everyone understand what I am saying?"

Everyone nodded yes.

Tellers picked up an object and some documents from his table, and said, "May I approach the witness, your Honor?"

"Yes."

Tellers walked across the courtroom and handed Winsted a knife. "What is this?"

"This is the shank that was taken from Boyd. I can tell because I put my tag with my initials on it, along with the initials of other officers who were involved in collecting and preserving the evidence."

"We offer this as evidence, your Honor, and request that the witness be allowed to regain possession of the murder weapon at the end of the hearing and transport it back to the vault for safekeeping."

"Object to calling it a murder weapon, but no objection to the release of the exhibit to Officer Winsted after the hearing."

"So ruled."

"What is this document?"

"This is a coroner's report concerning one John Smith. There is very little of the usual identification information on this report because we could not discover the name of his parents or where he was born. Indeed, we don't know his name for sure. We only know that he used that name when he was arrested. I suppose that his parents are looking for him, not realizing what has happened."

The spectators murmured again, and looked at Boyd with disgust.

"What was the cause of death?"

"Stab wound to the heart."

"What is this document?"

"A medical record from the University Medical Center from that Wednesday, showing significant slashing and other stab wound injuries to Mr. Travis Thomas."

"Is UMC where Mr. Thomas was taken after he was assaulted by Mr. Boyd?"

"Objection to leading."

"Sustained."

"Where was Mr. Thomas taken after he was found bleeding and unconscious on the shower floor?"

"To UMC."

38

"Were you assigned another investigation at the jail last week?"

"Yes, sir. You assigned me to look into another death in the jail, this time inside one of the cells."

"What did you find?"

"An even more gruesome scene than the first. There was a foul smell throughout the wing and I found the late Mr. Danny Morton lying in a large puddle of intestines and blood. He had a look of sheer terror frozen on his face."

Again the audience gasped.

A reporter leaned over and whispered to Sandy, "Things are looking pretty grim for your boyfriend."

Sandy shot him an icy look.

"Did you collect any evidence?"

"Yes, another bloody shank and blood-smeared gloves were found in the cell of Mr. Halbert Boyd."

"Do you have those items with you?"

"No, they are at the crime lab for testing."

"Do you know the results of any of the tests?"

"Yes. I asked for a speedy comparison of the blood on the knife and glove to Mr. Morton's blood. The crime lab confirmed a match."

"Is the coroner's report ready for Mr. Morton?"

"No, but I confirmed the cause of death with the coroner."

"What was the cause of death?"

"Massive blood loss and stab wound to the heart caused by an instrument such as a knife or shank."

"When Mr. Boyd was confronted with this crime, did he make any statement?"

Hal Boyd turned his head toward his lawyers and shook his head, whispering that he knew nothing about this statement. Without waiting on his client's explanation, John rose to object.

"Objection, Judge, we are not aware of this. He was represented by counsel and had a right to have us present before any questioning took place. We further object that no foundation has been laid, such as Miranda warnings, and so forth."

"I can lay a foundation concerning the issues raised in the objection, your Honor," responded Tellers.

"All right, I will reserve ruling. Proceed."

"What were the circumstances of Mr. Boyd's statement?"

"Officers found the body of Mr. Morton at 15:15. He was last seen alive at 15:00. A search of the jail immediately ensued, and blood was seen on the floor of Mr. Boyd's cell. Upon inspection, the knife and glove were found in his cell. When officers entered the cell, Boyd spontaneously said, "It's not my knife," indicating that he knew of the presence of the knife. No one asked him anything he just volunteered that statement. We found it interesting that the only denial he made was of ownership of the knife. He didn't choose to deny that he had murdered Mr. Morton."

"Objection, your Honor. Mr. Boyd is not required to deny anything."

"Overruled. There is no jury present Mr. Brooks. Your client suffers no prejudice from the statement, and a future judge will consider the admissibility of the statement before a jury hears it."

"Thank you, your Honor," said Tellers. "The State rests."

Brooks rose from his seat and said, "Your Honor, I think that it may be premature for the State to rest, since the cross-examination of the first witness has not taken place."

"Yes, well, I will I take it that the prosecution has no further witnesses."

"That's right, your Honor and considering the burden of proof at this hearing, we feel we have met that burden of proof regardless of the examination that Mr. Brooks might attempt."

There were a few satisfied chuckles from the gallery.

"All right, Mr. Brooks, you may proceed with your cross-examination of the witness," said Judge Groom.

"Thank you, your Honor," said John as he took his place at the podium. "Mr. Winsted, did any of these three eyewitnesses to the stabbing death of Mr. Smith and the slashing of Mr. Thomas attempt to prevent the assault?"

"They did not have time to prevent the assault."

"In order to witness the assault, they would have to be inside the shower with the inmates, or they would have to be in the hallway just outside the shower, is that true?"

"I suppose."

"That means that they would have to be 40 feet or less from the assault, is that a fair estimate?"

"Yes."

John stepped outside the bar a distance into the audience, and said, "This is about 40 feet, wouldn't you agree?"

"That's about right."

"The assault didn't happen at the back of the shower did it?"

184

"I don't know where the assault happened."

"Where was the blood?"

"Near the middle of the shower."

John moved halfway to Winsted.

"Closer to the hall, or closer to the back wall?"

"Closer to the hall."

John took a couple of steps closer.

"How close to the hall?"

"Six or eight feet."

John moved about 8 feet from Winsted.

"Are you telling us that three trained officers were as close as you and I and just stood there and watched a life and death struggle between John Smith and Hal Boyd, saw him stab Smith in the chest and struggle with Travis Thomas, slash him to within an inch of his life, cover himself with blood and do a rain dance before they could travel from where I am to where you are?"

"Well, I wasn't there. I can't tell you what they did or didn't do."

"Exactly. In fact, none of the witnesses said that they actually saw the assault did they?"

"I was informed that they saw the assault."

"Excuse me, but I am not presently asking you if someone else told you what they said, I am asking you whether or not any of the officers told you that they actually saw Hal Boyd stab anyone."

"Not in so many words, but what else could have happened?"

"Isn't it true that the officers told you that they saw Boyd standing over Smith's body, and that he had a knife in his hands?"

"No, they saw him dancing over Smith's body."

"Exactly. When they arrived, they saw Mr. Boyd moving from foot to foot over Smith's body, holding the knife you have identified."

"Yes. They said that."

"Back to my earlier question, they did not say that they saw Boyd stab, cut, or assault Smith or Travis, did they?"

"No, they weren't the ones who told me that."

"Who told you that?"

"That would be Mr. Tellers."

"Objection," said Tellers. "He has confused the witness. We were just talking with him in our pre-hearing conference about the evidence, as we understood it. This is attorney work product and we object."

"Yes, that's right," said Winsted.

"Objection overruled," said Judge Groom.

"I believe that two of the officers told you that when they saw Boyd, they ran to get assistance, and Officer Colby stayed behind, alone, and ordered Boyd to drop the knife. Is that true?"

"I believe so."

"Hal dropped the knife, didn't he?"

"Yes."

"Colby then ordered Boyd to lay face down on the floor and Boyd complied, is that true?"

"That's what I was told."

"On the second incident, concerning the death of Mr. Morton, Danny Morton was locked in his cell at 15:00 when he was last seen, isn't that true?"

"Yes."

"When he was found at 15:15, he was still locked in his cell, wasn't' he?"

"Yes."

"At 15:00, Mr. Boyd was locked in his cell under what was considered to be maximum security, wasn't he?"

"As far as we know."

"And when he was found, after 15:15, he was still locked in his cell under maximum security, wasn't he?"

"Yes."

"Did he have a key to his cell, or to Mr. Morton's cell?

"No, the locks are operated remotely."

"Tell me what you mean by operated remotely."

"The cells can be unlocked from one of two places remote from the cells themselves. After the lock is disabled the door can be opened. Individual cells can be opened by a key."

"Boyd's cell was searched, and no key was found, isn't that true?"

"Yes, but he could have hidden that on the way from one cell to another."

"Keys aren't made available to the inmates, are they?"

"Not intentionally."

"Isn't it more probable that the cell doors were opened by someone who had access to either the keys or the remote lock switches?"

"Object to the speculation," said Tellers.

"Overruled."

"Whoever had access to the locks, would also have been able to throw the knife and glove into Boyd's cell wouldn't they?"

"Well, that's ridiculous. We would have to think that a guard killed Morton with a knife. We've already proven that Boyd has a propensity to kill inmates with shanks, and here he is with the murder weapon a second time. The odds against that coincidence are astronomical."

"That presumption assumes that the circumstance is a coincidence,

186

doesn't it?"

"What, I don't understand your question."

"Let me ask it this way, without a key, or access to the switch, or without help in the jail, you know of no way that Mr. Boyd could have committed this murder do you?"

Winsted hesitated. Then said, "No, sir."

"You do not have any evidence that he had a key, or access to the switches, or that he had any help, do you?"

"No."

"No other questions."

"No redirect, and the State rests again and we move that the Defendant be bound over for action by the grand jury on two counts of murder and one of aggravated assault," said Tellers.

Brooks rose and said, "With all due respect to Mr. Tellers, we would like to proceed with additional evidence, your Honor. We have some witnesses we would like to call."

"Objection, this is totally improper and a waste of time. He is just trying to get free discovery from our witnesses. This is a waste of the Court's time. We have met our burden of proof and the hearing should be over."

Judge Groom responded, "I understand that the burden on the State is light, but I believe that basic due process affords the Defendant the right to call at least some witnesses. I will state that my patience will be limited if I conclude that this is a mere fishing expedition, Mr. Brooks."

"Thank you, your Honor. We call Officer Wilson, of the Jackson Police Department."

Tellers dropped his pen on the table and Thornton tossed his note pad onto the table in evident exasperation.

39

The portly Officer Wilson, still in uniform, entered the courtroom, was sworn and took the stand. The first few questions elicited his name and position with the police department.

"Do you have access to the roster of officers who were on duty in the hours that Mr. John Smith was incarcerated and the hours that Mr. Daniel Morton was incarcerated."

"Yes, I do."

"Are these rosters kept in the ordinary course of the business of running the jail?"

"Yes, they are."

"Do you find these rosters to be reliable?"

"Yes, I rely on them every day."

"What did you find?"

Tellers rose quickly from his chair and said, "Objection, hearsay."

Judge Groom grinned and looked at Brooks for a response.

"Your Honor, I recently had the privilege of attending a lecture on the subject of the admissibility of hearsay evidence at preliminary hearings, given by a renowned prosecutor."

"I believe I attended the same lecture," said Judge Groom with a smile.

Laughter rang through the gallery.

John looked at Tellers, who was red-faced.

"In any event, I believe this evidence would fit under the business record exception to the hearsay rule."

"I agree. The objection is overruled. You can answer the question."

"Yes, your Honor. I observed that Mr. Smith's incarceration occurred entirely within one 12-hour shift and Mr. Morton's murder occurred in another 12-hour shift of personnel assigned to the jail cell areas. There is overlapping if I include civilian personnel, management, investigators and so forth, but if I look only at those who regularly work in the jail and have access to the cells, there would ordinarily be no overlap."

"You said ordinarily."

"That's right, one officer assigned to inmate security during the night shift asked for an extra shift and happened to be on duty during both events. His name is Roger Young."

"Would Mr. Young have access to keys to cells and to the remote

188

switches?"

"Yes."

"Does the jail have video surveillance of the cells?"

"Yes."

"Did you check to determine if there is any video of Mr. Morton's cell between 15:00 and 15:15?"

"I did, and there is no video during that hour. It appears to have been erased."

"Would Officer Young have access to the videos?"

"He could."

"No further questions."

Tellers charged the podium, pointed an accusatory finger at Officer Wilson and said, "Who gave you the authority to dig into these records and share them with Mr. Brooks?"

"Mr. Tellers, I have the authority to control and care for the inmates entrusted to me. I take that responsibility seriously. If someone is harming my inmates then I will do what I must to protect them. I take it as a personal insult that two inmates were murdered and another seriously hurt in my jail. If a jail employee broke our professional trust and responsibility to our inmates, then I want that employee prosecuted to the fullest extent of the law."

"Why haven't you pursued any charges against this officer?"

"I turned my findings over to internal investigations today. I just saw Officer Young in the witness room and told him that he was not to report for service today."

"I see. No further questions."

"Judge, we would call Officer Robert Young as the next witness," Brooks announced.

Anticipation filled the courtroom and a low buzz of whispered conversation swept the gallery. All eyes turned towards the massive doors. Everyone sat on the edge of their seats as the door opened and Karen Wilkes entered the room. Karen made her way to John's side and whispered to him. Again the door opened and a court bailiff announced, "Officer Young is not in the witness room and does not respond to calls in the hallway."

Gasps could be heard from the audience.

John stood and said, "Your Honor, I've just been informed that Officer Young was seen leaving the courthouse."

Judge Groom motioned for Mr. Lee to approach the bench. After a whispered conversation, Mr. Lee huddled with the other officers in the courtroom. Half of the officers rushed out of the courtroom. The other half remained to continue to watch Boyd and provide security.

"We will be in recess for fifteen minutes," announced Judge Groom as he struck his gavel with a distinctive thwack on its resounding block.

As soon as Judge Groom left, the courtroom erupted in a sort of organized chaos, as reporters scrambled to inform viewers, readers and listeners of the events. Some reporters rushed to the bar to get comments from the lawyers. Introductory words like, "Stunning developments," and "Brilliant lawyering" and "Jailer implicated in murder flees the courthouse," were heard as cameras started rolling. When reporters approached Tellers, he quickly left the courtroom saying only, "This is ridiculous. No comment."

Thornton was about to follow Tellers out of the courtroom when Jackson caught up with him. "Bobby, you are going to drop charges against Boyd in the Morton murder, aren't you?"

"Why didn't you tell me what you had on the jailer? We never would have brought this charge. I think you two were just grandstanding, trying to get positive publicity for yourselves and your client."

"Do I hear some projection going on?"

"What?"

"I think it was your boss looking for the headlines. Besides, how much time did we have to get ready for this hearing? Our case is a work in progress and we don't have time to share our work product with you, Bobby. It's all we can do to keep up with the new charges your boss keeps throwing at us."

"If you can't work with us, we sure can't work with you. And after this little kangaroo show you just put on, I can guarantee you that your client isn't getting any deals. You, Brooks and your client are going down on these cases. If we don't get Boyd on one case—big deal. We will get him on the others."

"You and I don't need to be taking this personally. I just wanted to know if you would relent on this one case."

"That's up to the boss."

"Might be up to the judge."

"We can go around him if we have to."

"Really."

"This is only a probable cause hearing. If the judge doesn't think that there is probable cause, then so be it. We can still take the case to a grand jury and they can independently find probable cause. Buddy is so good with grand juries that he could get a ham sandwich indicted. No matter what happens with this charge, after today, your partner's little winning record that you are so proud of will be over."

Across the courtroom, reporters were asking John, "What made you suspicious of the jailer?"

190

John smiled and said, "No comment. We are in the middle of a hearing and this is not the time or the place to conduct interviews. The hearing is not over and I owe my full attention and allegiance to my client. Our defense team will continue in our efforts to prove Mr. Boyd innocent of all charges."

"Isn't it unusual for the defense lawyer to prove not only that his client did not commit the crime, but then provide convincing proof who did commit the crime?"

"Not after today. Excuse me, I have work to do."

Sandy asked, "Does that mean you will have more surprises today?"

John smiled and said, "Thank you, no comment."

Sandy passed him a note, then motioned for Bret to follow her outside. "Let's get some shots from the front of the courthouse and let's see if we can find someone who saw the jailer leave."

Bret gathered his gear and followed her out.

"The examination of those witnesses by John went out on the live feed. The world was watching. Your boy just became one of the most famous lawyers alive."

"Yeah, I just left him a note saying exactly that. I don't think he realizes how his life is about to change. His phone will be ringing off of the hook with prospective new clients."

"He's going to be too busy for you after this."

"He won't be the only one busy after this case."

Crush entered the courtroom, and the sound level was reduced slightly as people noticed his massive presence. He leaned over and whispered in Karen's ear. Karen's face reflected urgency as she turned towards John and motioned him over.

"Listen to what Crush has to say!"

"The jailer that everyone is talking about got in the car with a girl with black and purple hair and they left pretty fast in a beat-up old Honda."

"Do we have a tag number?"

"No, I couldn't get close enough in time. I saw a policeman leaving the courthouse at a fast pace. I didn't realize it was the jailer at first, until I saw him get into the passenger side of her car. She was driving, and they left pretty quickly. I was too far away to see the tag."

"Wow! Still, that's good work Crush."

John looked up from his huddle with Karen and Crush and spotted the Bailiff.

"Mr. Lee, this gentleman has some information that you need," said John as he motioned the Bailiff to join them. Soon there was another huddle of the remaining law enforcement officers in the room and half of

191

them ran from the room to act on the new information.

One young man sat in the back of the courtroom taking it all in. He was dressed uncomfortably in a white long-sleeve shirt that covered his tattoos. He thought that his red tie was going to choke him when he first put it on, but he was beginning to get used to it. He knew that his usual dark clothing might attract attention, but he still looked out of place. He watched the proceedings with interest, taking notes just like the reporters. He observed the number and position of the security personnel as they entered the courtroom. He paid attention to their coming and going. He observed the relative position of the officers to the defendant. He sketched the courtroom and noted the position of the participants. He smiled to himself as he realized that three-fourths of the security force left the courtroom to deal with the missing witness. He laid the notes down on the pew beside him and reached under his seat. He felt the duct tape. With a quick pull, the tape came loose and he had a knife in his hands.

I may never get a better chance than this, he thought.

There was considerable confusion in the courtroom, with people coming and going and reporters speaking into cameras. No one noticed the young man as he walked up the aisle, no one except Crush.

"That kid looks out of place," Crush said to no one in particular.

Crush watched the young man walk up the aisle. He never took his eyes off of Boyd. When he got to the end of the aisle, instead of turning toward the door, he went straight and opened the swinging gate in the bar.

"Hey!" shouted Crush.

The man glanced at Crush and sped towards Hal.

Everyone was startled by Crush's shout, and they were staring at Crush instead of the young man. Quicker than seemed possible, Crush moved toward Boyd. He knew he would not get there in time. A cameraman was standing next to Crush, camera on his shoulder. With a fluid motion, Crush swept the camera into his right hand and threw it like a football.

"Hey! You can't do that!" shouted the cameraman.

The camera whacked the young man on the forehead. He fell backwards in a heap, unconscious. The knife fell from his hand.

"Sorry about your camera. I'm afraid I might have messed it up."

192

40

The young man was carted off to the jail on a gurney. The courtroom was emptied and security details combed every square inch. Spectators were thoroughly searched before they were allowed back into the room. Two hours later court was ready to resume.

The Bailiff called out in a loud voice, "All rise!"

Judge Groom re-entered the courtroom.

"You may be seated."

Judge Groom waited a few moments for everyone to find places in the crowded courtroom. The sound of feet, seats, purses, gear, papers and people settling into their places slowly died down.

"What have you to say about Officer Young?" asked the Judge.

Mr. Lee responded, "He has not been found. However, Mr. Brooks gave us a lead. It seems that a member of the defense team saw Officer Young get into an automobile and skedaddle. He gave us a description of the car and we hope to have him soon."

"Well, Mr. Brooks. It seems that you and your team are competently filling several jobs at once, defense lawyer for your client, prosecutor of Mr. Young, apprehender of alleged kidnappers, detective and locator of missing persons, defender of the courtroom."

The audience broke into admiring laughter. Several officers smiled and shook their heads. Mr. Tellers was red-faced.

"Do you have any announcement concerning the Morton murder charge, Mr. prosecutor?"

"No, your Honor."

"I see. Well, I do. I don't see any reason to continue with the Morton hearing. There is no probable cause to believe that Mr. Boyd committed the crime of murder of Mr. Morton and that charge is dismissed."

There was a general murmur of approval in the Courtroom. Jackson reached from his seat toward Thornton with a note in his outstretched hand. Thornton took it, unfolded it and frowned at Jackson. He slid the note to Tellers who read, "That makes us 9-0."

Tellers shook his head and crumpled the note.

After a moment the Judge continued. "Now, as for the remaining charges, I believe that the State has . . ."

"Excuse me, your Honor," said John, "we do have another witness to offer regarding the remaining charges."

"Oh, excuse me, I am getting ahead of myself. That's right, you have

193

not rested. Who will your next witness be?"

"Travis Thomas."

Tellers and Thornton rocketed to their feet and Tellers shouted, "Objection!" Both had looks of shock on their faces.

"He can't call Thomas!" said Tellers. "Thomas is represented by counsel. He can't be asked questions without his counsel present. That would violate his constitutional rights because he is charged with a crime."

"Now I have the prosecutor taking the role of defending a person charged with a crime. Everyone keeps changing roles in this case," observed Judge Groom and the courtroom erupted in laughter.

A man on the first row stood and said, "If I may, your Honor, I represent Mr. Thomas."

"Yes, Judge Bell. The District Attorney was interposing an objection on behalf of your client. What say you?"

"Mr. Thomas has no objection to testifying in this matter."

"What!" said Tellers.

"He said that Thomas does not object to testifying," repeated Judge Groom.

"Could we have just a moment, your Honor," said Tellers.

"Yes, but don't take long. There have already been too many interruptions."

Tellers and Thornton rushed over to Bell.

"What are you up to?" Tellers demanded in a loud whisper that could easily be overheard in most of the courtroom.

"He wants to testify."

"To what?"

"The truth."

"What is he about to say?"

"I am sorry . . . but I am not at liberty to say."

"Why not?"

"Attorney client privilege."

"The privilege is waived when he takes the stand."

"He hasn't taken the stand yet."

"You are playing games."

"No, Buddy, I am just following the rules."

"The deal is off."

"You mean the deal in which you promised that you won't prosecute his parole violation if he testifies to the truth? He is about to testify to the truth. I plan to hold you to your promise."

Tellers glowered at Bell. The courtroom door was held open for Travis in a wheelchair. Thomas was wheeled by a bailiff to the witness stand and sworn to tell the truth.

Brooks asked him, "Travis, do you understand that because of the criminal charges against you, you do not have to answer any questions having to do with those charges?"

"Yes sir."

"In that regard, you have the right to remain silent. Anything you say could be used against you in a court of law. You have the right to the assistance of a lawyer during questioning. If you cannot afford a lawyer, the court will appoint one to represent you. You have a right to stop answering questions at any time. Do you understand those rights?"

"Yes, sir. My lawyer is here and he has told me about those rights."

"Please tell us your name."

"Travis Thomas. Everyone calls me Travis T."

After a moment, several people in the courtroom struggled to suppress a chuckle.

"Were you incarcerated in the city jail Wednesday morning two weeks ago?"

"Yes I was."

"What unusual thing happened that morning?"

"There was a knife fight in the shower. I was stabbed and hurt real bad and another fellow was killed."

"Tell us what happened."

The courtroom was suddenly completely quiet, except for the light clatter coming from the court reporter's stenographic machine. Then, even that stopped as she caught up.

"Well, I was in the shower by myself at first, when I saw Mr. Hal Boyd enter the shower."

"Could you point him out?"

"That's him all shackled up there at your table."

"How did you know it was him?"

"Everybody knows about the Butcher of Belhaven, the Vampire Slayer, and all of that. Besides, you used to represent me and him, so I knew who he was."

"What happened next?"

"I decided it was probably time for me to get out of the shower, cause I don't want to be in the shower with no butchers, if you know what I mean."

Tellers laughed, along with most of the audience. Sandy leaned over to Bret and whispered, "Looks like John has bitten off more than he can chew with this witness."

"Then what happened?"

"Well, before I could leave, Mr. Evil Eye came in."

195

"Mr. Evil Eye?"

"Yeah, he called himself John Smith. The way he looks at you gives you the heebie-jeebies, so I called him Mr. Evil Eye. Anyway, with both of them in the shower, I knew I didn't need to be there. So I really was about to leave, when I saw Mr. Evil, I mean Mr. Smith had a knife and he was slipping up behind Mr. Butcher, I mean Boyd. Then I knew I had to go. But, a funny thing happened."

"What's that?"

"My feet wouldn't go."

Everyone laughed.

"I know it may sound funny, but they wouldn't. There was like a fight going on in my mind. I wanted to run, but part of me wanted to keep a killing from happening. Next thing I knew, I jumped on Smith's back, grabbed his arm and I started hollering for help. Smith was a lot stronger than I expected. He sort of shrugged me off and was all over me with that knife. There was blood everywhere. It was like it wasn't even real. I saw him stabbing me and I saw blood everywhere and it took me a minute to realize it was my own blood that was going everywhere. Next thing I know I was on the floor and Smith was on me and I knew I was about to die."

"Let me ask you this, did Mr. Boyd cut you or harm you with a knife?"

"No, sir, he saved me. It was Smith who cut me."

Again there was murmuring from the audience.

"Order in the Court," said Judge Groom.

"Please continue."

"I told God that I was counting on Him to come through with that promise."

Everyone laughed again.

"Next thing, I saw Boyd's hand grab Smith's knife hand and they started to fighting. They went back and forth a while, and everything just faded out. I woke up in the hospital."

"Other than the knife that Smith had, did you see any other knife or weapon in the shower?"

"No, sir."

"Did Boyd attack Smith?"

"Not until he pulled Smith off of me. Before that, Smith was slipping up on Boyd and was about to cut him from behind."

"Objection to speculation," said Tellers.

"Overruled," ruled the Judge.

"Boyd saved me. And I thank him for that. If he hadn't protected me and his own self, we would both be dead."

196

"No further questions."

Brooks returned to his chair and dropped his note pad on the table. Judge Groom turned slowly towards Tellers and said, "Your witness."

Tellers and Thornton leaned into each other. It was obvious that they were in an animated yet whispered discussion. Several pregnant seconds passed.

"Mr. Tellers, we need to move along," said Judge Groom.

"One moment please, your Honor."

Tellers sighed and leaned back in his chair, staring at his notepad. Thornton doodled on his notepad. He rested his left elbow on the table and rested the side of his head in his left hand.

"Well?" asked Judge Groom.

"No questions," responded Tellers as he tossed his pen on his notepad.

Judge Groom turned towards Travis and said, "Thank you, Mr. Thomas. I hope you have a speedy recovery. Mr. Tellers, will you be offering any other evidence on either of the remaining charges at issue today?"

"No, your Honor."

"Very well." The Judge then looked directly at Boyd and said, "I was puzzled as to why the prosecution sought to set these matters for hearing. Mr. Boyd has three capital murder charges and will remain in jail without bond regardless of the outcome of today's hearing. As it turns out, this hearing has been helpful in narrowing the issues that the Court will have to address in the future. Therefore, today's hearing has proven valuable. I find that the State has failed to demonstrate probable cause to believe that Mr. Boyd committed the crime of aggravated assault against Mr. Thomas, and that charge is therefore dismissed."

Camera's clicked. Papers shuffled as members of the press scribbled notes. Jackson caught Thornton's eye and held up both hands, extending all ten fingers and then formed an O with one hand. Thornton rolled his eyes.

"As for the charge of the murder of one John Smith, I find that the State has failed to demonstrate that there is probable cause to believe that Mr. Boyd committed that crime. Therefore, that charge is also dismissed."

Jackson wrote 11- 0 with a dark marker in large characters across a blank page on his note pad. Judge Groom continued. "However, there are still three pending capital murder charges against Mr. Boyd and one charge of murder less than capital. Mr. Boyd will remain in custody without bond on those charges. Mr. Bailiff, will you please arrange to return Mr. Boyd to the jail. And please confirm that extraordinary measures are taken to protect Mr. Boyd. This hearing is adjourned."

Judge Groom whacked the sound block with his gavel, rose and retired through the door directly behind the bench.

Hal looked at John, nodded and simply said "Thank you," to both John and Jackson.

Tellers and Thornton quickly made egress through the door to the left of the bench. As Thornton was about to step out of the courtroom, he looked back at the defense table and caught Jackson's eyes. Jackson smiled and held up his new sign, "11 – 0." Thornton smiled, shook his head and mouthed, "Good job." He then stepped through the door and pulled it closed.

Reporters started surging forward to ask questions of John and Jackson until Mr. Lee's booming voice froze everyone in place.

"Everyone, be seated now, for security reasons! We will be removing the Defendant from the courtroom. Once he has been removed you will then be free to move about."

41

It took Jackson and John an hour and a half to work through the cordon of reporters and well-wishers and return to the office. John avoided talking about the case other than to say: "Hal Boyd is innocent, unless and until the State proves him guilty. We don't believe that the State can meet its burden of proof. In fact, we intend to prove that he is innocent."

Ted and Clarion Cartier were waiting for them at the office.

"Way to go guys, we heard about the outcome in court today," said Ted. "Everyone is talking about what good lawyers you are."

"The girls and I are thrilled to be part of your team. We are so proud of you. And we are so proud that you are proving to the world that we really can do great things here in Mississippi. They run us down so much, that we can't help but pull for one of our own that does well. And, John, you did well."

"Thanks—it's teamwork," said John. "All the credit goes to our team. By the way, is anything going on with Goshen Springs Beer?"

"How does he know why we are here?" asked Clare.

"That's John for you," said Ted. "Yes, I had a call about a half hour ago from Mr. Anderson who wants to come to terms with us on the investment. He was impressed with all of the good publicity that you are getting right now and thinks this opportunity is too good to pass up. He thinks we should begin producing and distributing as fast as possible to take advantage of the good will you are building."

"It will take time to set up a brewery and get started," Jackson pointed out.

"He has some solutions for that, he says. Before we talk about that, I wanted Clare to tell you what her team has learned."

"Yes, well, we found that there is some truth to the legend. There really was a Goren Goshen, and he really met with Andrew Jackson and a master brewer named Andrew Fabber. There was a fire that destroyed the brewery. I haven't confirmed the Penny story yet, but we aren't through with our research."

"Well, that is interesting, but I think that is not what you are excited about," said John. "You are holding something back. What is it?"

Clare and Ted looked at each other and smiled. Clare squeezed her shoulders together in excitement as she handed John and Jackson a research report

"Mr. Anderson is a direct descendant of Mr. Fabber. His family almost bought the rights to Goshen Springs Beer long ago. They searched for the recipe long after the fire, but never found it. Anderson is almost desperate to get the recipe. He is coming here from New Orleans and will be in town tomorrow night."

Clare was bouncing on her toes with excitement.

"Wow!" said Jackson. "Should we sell it to him, or remain partners with him in the production of the beer?"

"Good question. Karen, do you think that you could get in touch with James Roache' and see if he will open for dinner tomorrow night? He usually only opens on Thursday, Friday and Saturday nights, but he might open for us for a special occasion."

"I'm on it," said Karen. "I'll tell him that it will be dinner for fourteen."

"Fourteen!"

"Well, it needs to be worth his while."

"Who will be there?"

"All six partners, including me, Clare and her librarians, that makes ten, Mr. Anderson, and at least two or three of our rugby buddies."

"That was some quick math," said Jackson. "I am impressed."

*   *   *

For the rest of the afternoon, Jackson was brimming with admiration for his partner and did not miss an opportunity to sing his praises to the press. The press was inclined to receive and repeat that praise. Soon, words like, "brilliant, masterful, exceptional," were commonly used to describe John Brooks and Hal Boyd's defense team. Jackson was unselfish in his praise, giving John far more credit than he was due and taking none for himself.

On the other hand, when the press described the district attorney, words like, "outwitted, outmaneuvered, overmatched," became common. Tellers retreated to his office in a rage for two days. Every news report drove him into more fits of rage. His plans for higher office seemed out of reach, dashed by this upstart of an attorney. How the press could turn on him so abruptly and so completely was unfathomable to Tellers. The tension in the prosecutor's office was palpable.

Tellers was not the sort of man who would stay down. "I didn't get where I am without taking a few licks," he said to himself. "If it's war he wants, it's war he will get! This is far from over!"

On Wednesday, Tellers called a staff meeting. Six Assistant District Attorneys, two investigators, six clerical workers and two interns packed into the conference room. Everyone was quiet and the mood was tense

200

as they waited for their boss. They quietly shared horror stories about the past two days of rage. No one wanted to do anything that might aggravate the District Attorney, or cause his rage to be directed towards them.

Tellers burst into the room with an air of explosive energy. He stood at the head of the table and announced: "I want a report on my desk this afternoon listing every case in our office and every case coming to our office from any law enforcement agency, involving the Brooks and Bradley firm. I want every one of their cases set for trial as soon as possible. No plea deals on any case for any reason. Resist every motion and every request of any kind. There will be no cooperation with that firm in any respect. I want a scorch-the-earth policy with every case involving those lawyers. Make them work for everything. I am sick of the haughty attitude of that firm and the bragging about never losing a case. They are trying to make all of you look bad, trying to make you look like inept jokers. Well, I won't put up with it. We will put them in their place. We will not allow them to disrespect this office any longer. Does everyone understand?"

A chorus of yes sirs erupted around the room.

"Is everyone on board with me? If you are not, then there's the door. Don't come back."

"Yes sir!" was the harmonious reply. "We're with you!"

"Good. This meeting is adjourned. Go make life miserable for Brooks and Bradley."

*   *   *

The Bishop paced around his Madison office, eyes darting left and right. Gregory had never seen him so intense. To Gregory, the room seemed filled with energy and he felt the hairs on the back of his neck stand up.

"I underestimated this lawyer. He is a capable foe. I don't have faith in the court system. We will have to take care of this ourselves. I can't believe that Boyd has survived this long. Let's increase the pressure. I leave it to your discretion as to how to do it. I don't want the details. I just want success. And I want that woman!"

"I understand."

"What about the Priest?"

"If he survived, he might have drifted down river. We found a colony of homeless people in the woods down river from Mayes Lake. They should know if he survived. We made a few threats and promises. If he is there, they will bring him to us."

201

42

A late afternoon shower cooled the humid air. The Trooper splashed though the puddles as John drove down West Jackson Street in Old Town Ridgeland to the corner of North Wheatley, where Ro' Chez' occupied a coral colored single story old house. A weathered metal roof hung over a wooden porch that wrapped around two sides of the house.

Old Town Ridgeland has a single block of small wooden buildings that over the years housed gift shops, photo labs, antique shops, butcher shops and a restaurant. Recently, a number of new two-story brick buildings with balconies and covered sidewalks, built to look as though they're a hundred years old, had grown up around the original town. The new Old Town Ridgeland was filled with shops and restaurants.

John, Jackson and Karen climbed out of the Trooper and tromped through the puddles to the porch. The cozy waiting area was already filled with close to twenty people.

"Wow, our guest list has really grown!"

"Yep. When I let the word out that we were having a special seating at Ro' Chez', everyone wanted in on the act."

"How are we going to pay for this, Karen?"

"Already paid for by Mr. Anderson."

"Wow!"

Everyone exchanged greetings and hugs. James Roache´ was busy behind the tiny bar serving wine and beer, while the guests packed around the five small tables in the room. Burlap sacks hung from the ceiling and local art was displayed on the walls.

Kevin Anderson was with Sandy Storm at the bar. She was laughing at something he said as John approached.

"John, have you met Kevin Anderson?"

"Haven't had the pleasure until now."

"Pleased to meet you and your friends, John. Your rugby buddies have kept me entertained and Ms. Storm can be mesmerizing."

Sandy gave a demur smile as John agreed with Kevin.

"This is an interesting little place. Why don't you tell us about it?"

"Sure Sandy. Let me call Karen over. She is the expert on all things Ro' Chez."

John motioned to Karen, who worked her way through the crowd. "Why don't you tell us about this place?"

"James Roache´ is the chef. I don't remember how many years he has been at this, but he has never repeated his menu. We can expect a unique and delicious five-course meal. It will be memorable, I guarantee. James will call us into the dining room when dinner is ready."

At that moment, the background music changed to 'Rawhide,' with the refrain, "Head 'em up, move 'em out," as James guided his guests into the dining room.

A small fluffy pastry with duck and a savory sweet sauce awaited them. James called it "Lagniappe, a little something extra." Everyone enjoyed the duck while James described the five courses to come. Soon, crab and borsin cheese, folded in custard with a fine crust, topped with flash fried spinach and a drizzle of sauce tantalized everyone. Ted distributed Goshen Springs Beer and the room erupted in oohs and ahhs and laughter as the nutty beer blended with the food. Wood smoked bread, mushrooms, artichokes, salmon and filet followed at well-timed intervals. The meal was finished with cinnamon apple bread pudding.

"Brooks, I am ready to talk business. Where can we talk?"

"Why not here? Half the people here are partners in our venture and the rest are our close friends. Whatever you can say to me, you can say to them."

*   *   *

Outside the restaurant, Gregory waited in an SUV. Members of his team were in two other cars, one positioned on West Jackson, the other on Wheatley.

"When they start pouring out of the restaurant, look for the redhead. Take her in the confusion."

*   *   *

Anderson continued. "Very well, I am prepared to make an offer. As part of the offer, I want Ted to be my brew-master at a salary of $300,000 per year and I am prepared to accept your marketing proposal with your firm to handle marketing contracts and all legal issues on a $20,000 per month retainer. As for your offer, I will pay double your demand, but I must have 51 percent of the rights to the recipe and the resulting company."

Several people in the room gasped.

"I suppose that now you wish we were alone," said Anderson. "They may have given away your position on money. Perhaps I offered too much?"

"No, they were shocked that you would demand 51 percent. Give me a moment to regain my composure after hearing your demand. I suppose you will be providing the money and the equipment necessary to brew our beer. You won't be calling on us to spend our funds producing the beer, am I right about that?"

"Of course!"

"Make it 45 percent and you've got a deal."

"49."

"What's four percent among friends?"

John looked around the room for approval and saw astonished eager nods.

"All right, you've managed to acquire the world's finest beer for your family brewery."

"Fantastic! You've no idea how excited my family will be! This has been a two hundred year quest. I assure everyone in this room that the beer we brew will make you proud. My family has been searching for this recipe ever since the brewery fire."

Crash! A flaming bottle burst though a dining room window, followed by the sound of breaking glass in the front room. Flames were everywhere. Women screamed. Mitch scooped up the flaming bottle and threw it back though the broken window. The bottle burst on the pavement underneath a car stopped outside the restaurant. Fire enveloped the auto as it sped away. The driver lost control and crashed into a light pole. Sparks flew as the lamp flickered, then the pole fell across the front of the car.

Rugby players yanked the cloths from the tables, sending plates, glasses and flatware sailing. They quickly smothered the flames in both the dining room and the front room.

"Look at James!" Sandy screamed. She was pointing outside, and everyone turned to see James Roache´ sprint from the restaurant toward the burning car. Firelight glinted from the blade of a knife in his hand. Headlights from a black SUV racing up Wheatley illuminated James' face as he turned back to look at it.

The SUV swerved at James aiming to run him over. James dove to the edge of the street and rolled to his feet as the SUV raced past him and stopped at the burning vehicle. Two men jumped from the burning car into the SUV. James roared and hurled the knife. A man screamed as the knife buried itself to the hilt in his thigh. He was pulled into the truck and the SUV raced away. Everyone spilled out into the street to check on James, who was shaking his fists in the direction of the fleeing attackers and yelling, "Come back!"

"It's okay, James. It's good that they are gone."

"No, I want them to come back! The sucker got away with my favorite knife!"

*   *   *

Father Michael was aware of intense pain and discomfort as he was placed in the bottom of a small johnboat. The night seemed pitch black. After a few minutes he realized that he was on the river and that Sammy and Mert were quietly paddling, keeping the johnboat in the middle of the stream. The forest on both banks was black against the dark sky. The roaring sound of the nearby interstate highway masked any sound the paddles might make. Soon they could see the lights of downtown. Occasionally they could see the levee that usually contained the river.

It was a long night. Father Michael was alternately shivering and sweating. As dawn began to break, Sammy directed the johnboat to a pier near the old swinging bridge at Byram. He whispered to Mert he would be right back. Ten minutes later Sammy returned with another man.

"You did the right thing, Sammy," said the other man. "You will surely get your reward."

205

43

Mitch insisted that the entire defense team attend the rugby game Saturday because it would be much easier to provide security if everyone was in one place. The pitch was on a 30-acre patch of land purchased by team members at the corner of Interstate 220 and Highway 49. Two full sized pitches had been carved out of the hills and the grass had been lovingly tended on a shoestring budget. This gave the team a permanent place to practice and play. Since the team was formed in 1974, the Jackson Rugby team had moved from pillar to post in search of places to practice and play until it acquired its own field.

The team played its way into national championship tournaments three times over the years, each time making it to the final eight. Even though the level of play was often quite high, the team emphasis was always on giving every member playing time rather than putting the best players on the field. Rugby is a club sport and the members of the club want to play the game.

Since John had been too busy lately to practice with the team, he had no intention of playing. Everyone on the team felt that those who made it to practice should have priority when player selections were made. The match was against perennial rival Mobile. Mobile loved to beat Jackson and Jackson's favorite team to beat was Mobile. Jackson was usually pleased with the outcome of the game.

The atmosphere was festive. A few tent canopies provided shade along the sidelines where girlfriends, wives and spectators mingled with players. Iced beer, a rugby postgame tradition, and gumbo awaited the teams in a pavilion located at the head of the pitches where teams socialized after beating each other's brains out all afternoon.

Clarion Cartier and the librarians were with Ted and Skip. Jackson, Jennifer and Karen arrived together. John took them to the sidelines and introduced them to the players. He was pleased to see that the librarians and the players were getting along famously and that some of the players were glad to explain the game to them.

When the game started, John and Karen walked up and down the sideline, following the action, and John gave a play-by-play explanation of the events to Karen. He explained scrum downs, hookers, line-outs, penalty kicks, the twenty-two meter rule, offside, laterals, kicking, switches, reverses, skips, up and under and more. He explained that the players would run about three miles during the game and the players who were in the best shape would always manage to be in the right place at the right time to make a play.

"I am not in shape, so if I were playing, I would not be able to be in the right place at the right time. That would hurt the team, so, I would rather not play."

During halftime, a CTN news van lumbered up the dirt road to the pitch. Bret and Sandy climbed out, and Bret began filming the players and the pitch. John and Karen greeted Sandy with a hug.

John took her to the sidelines and began describing the game as the second half unfolded. Bret filmed several crushing tackles by one big man.

"Is that our bodyguard, Crush?" asked Sandy.

"That's him. He is a monster."

"Well, he's a gentle monster when he's not on the field," said Sandy.

As the second 40-minute half was winding down, Mobile surged ahead with a try to make the score 12-10.

Play continued until Eric made a face-first tackle. Blood covered his face. He assured the ref that he was okay and wanted to continue playing. He also insisted that the ref's two fingers were four.

"Brooks, we need a wing," shouted Mitch. "Get in the game!"

"Excuse me, ladies, but I've got to go score a try before this game is over," said John with a chuckle as he trotted into position. John played the wing position, the last player in the back line. Jackson was awarded the ball in a scrum down. The burly linemen from each team locked heads in a massive knot of sweating muscle and limbs. The ball was tossed into the middle of the scrum and the teams surged against one another, each trying to drive the other off of the ball. Crush and his teammates would not be driven back. They slowly pushed Mobile's pack backwards.

"Push!" yelled the scrum half.

The ball rolled free on Jackson's side of the scrum and the scrum half scooped it into his arms. His choice was to kick the ball to gain advantage, run with it, or pass the ball to the fly half, who had all of the same options as the scrum half and so on all the way to the last man in the back line.

John was the fourth and last back in the line. The ball seldom made its way all the way to the wing. If the ball ever reached the wing, the wing had better do something good with it. Bodies flew and collisions were heard on the sidelines. Tomasin, the scrum half, passed quickly to Bryan, the fly, who slipped one tackle but was swarmed and thrown to the ground just as he released the ball to Andy at inside half. Before Andy could use his great speed, Mobile's inside half slammed his shoulder into Andy's chest. Somehow Andy shuffled the ball to Stephen at outside center. Stephen had no time to make a play because Mobile's outside center was in his face. Instead of catching the ball, he slapped it hard towards John.

The ball sailed long and John turned to chase it, running shoulder to shoulder with Mobile's wing. John edged ahead, caught the ball on his fingertips and turned the corner. He slipped through an attempted arm tackle by Mobile's wing and ran free down the sideline, but trouble was in sight. Mobile's entire back line angled towards him at full sprint.

John had given up valuable turf by running sideways to catch the ball. This gave Mobile's back line the chance to recover and get into position to cut him off.

Come on legs, give me all you've got, John thought. He used mental tricks to try to eke out every bit of speed he could muster. He imagined himself being shot out of a cannon. He imagined springs on his feet. And he imagined being a cheetah. He dug deep to find more speed and was rewarded by a burst of acceleration. Even though Mobile's back line had the angle on him, he pulled away, first from the outside center, then the inside center, then the fly half, each in turn fell behind. But Mobile's fullback arrived at the goal line first, turned, set his shoulders and crouched in anticipation of the coming collision.

Now it was just John and the fullback. Everyone else was a step behind. John realized that any change in direction would mean getting caught from behind. The game could be over at the next stoppage of play. It was now or never. He locked eyes with the fullback, who crouched further and set his jaw in determination.

John leapt forward. The fullback expected a shoulder-to-shoulder collision and had to quickly adjust to the new line of attack. He sprung upward and slammed his shoulder into John's waist, wrapping his arms around John's upper legs. An instant later the entire Mobile back line flew into the ruck, creating a writhing and struggling mass of humanity. John stretched the ball in front of him with both hands. The mass of players pushed the pile toward the goal and the ball struck the ground on the line. A fine white cloud of lime popped into the air around the ball. The referee raised one arm above his head at an angle, signaling score, and blew his whistle in several short pulses, signaling game over.

The whistle was music to John's ears. Jackson players and fans were jumping up and down in celebration. The fullback looked John in the eyes, and said, "Good play. You beat me this time. But, it won't happen again."

The teams lined up at midfield and congratulated each other for a good game, then made their way to the pavilion for beer, fellowship and

208

song. John rejoined his friends along the way.

"So, do you always make the winning score?" asked Sandy.

John laughed and said, "No, I seldom score. I make a thousand mistakes for everything I do right."

"If you are so bad, then why do you play?"

"Because the one right thing feels so good!"

"Not everyone is willing to suffer the thousand errors."

"If they ever had a taste of success they would. Everyone should have a taste of success. What sport do you play?"

"Why do you think I play a sport?"

"Because of the way you work. I suspect those competitive juices you demonstrate were primed in some sport. Maybe tennis?"

"Good guess, but I don't have time to play anymore."

"Maybe we can play sometime," John was saying when Karen interrupted him.

"John, do you know that girl?" asked Karen as she pointed at a girl who had black and purple hair.

"No, why?" responded John as he looked in the direction Karen indicated.

"There is something about the way she is looking at me. It gives me the creeps."

John walked over to Crush. "Do you recognize that girl?"

"That's her! That's the girl that drove the policeman away!"

Gayle saw Crush and John looking her way.

"I knew I didn't need to be here alone," Gayle said to herself. "Where is everybody?"

Gayle jumped into the Honda and sped down the dirt and gravel drive towards Forest Avenue. It was a long run from the middle of the pitch to the parking area. Gayle was long gone by the time that Jackson, John and Crush climbed into their cars and pursued her.

Gregory and his team watched from the woods. "That's right brave boys, chase after Gayle and leave the woman behind!"

"Shall we get her now?"

"Not yet. There are still too many people around and one of them has a camera. Let's wait a little while and see if more people leave."

"What was she doing here?" John asked himself.

"What did you say?" asked Jackson.

"Why would she be here by herself?"

"Good question. I don't like this."

"Let's get back to the pitch. Something is not right."

Gregory watched Karen like a predator. He waited for her to walk close to where he waited, or for her to become isolated from the others

209

during the confusion caused by Gayle.

"They are coming back!"

"What! I thought more of this guy. I didn't think he would give up the search for Gayle so easily. Let's back off. A better opportunity to catch her will come."

44

As the summer heated up, so did the phone lines of Brooks and Bradley. The Goshen Springs Beer project was still in the works and they hoped to finalize the deal in July. Skip, Ted and others were already planning how they would spend their money even though John warned that plenty of things could still go wrong before the deal was done.

It became apparent by the middle of June that the firm's clients were being treated differently than others by the D.A.'s office.

"They are contesting absolutely everything," said John. "People with minor charges are being offered the maximum penalty. Every discovery motion is contested. Every subpoena is contested. Every case is set for trial right away. We don't have time to work on Goshen Springs or Hal's case. Something is up."

"Payback," said Karen.

"We can handle anything they throw at us," said Jackson. "If it's war they want, we can play that game, too."

"Yeah. I don't want to be pushed around, but what about our clients?"

"What do you mean?"

"If anyone else was representing them, they would be getting a better offer. Every issue would not be contested."

"We just have to work harder."

"But is that fair to our clients? They hire us because they want the best representation, and they want the best outcome they can expect."

"They are getting the best representation," said Karen.

"Absolutely," agreed Jackson.

"But if someone else represented them, they wouldn't have to fight so hard, and some of these cases that ought to be settled could be."

"What are you saying?"

"I think that we ought to let all of our criminal clients get other counsel."

"What! That lets Tellers win!"

"No, it lets our clients win. Maybe the heat would be off their cases if we were not in the picture. It may be the best thing we can do for our clients right now."

There was silence for several moments as Jackson and Karen pondered the suggestion.

"I know this beer deal might work out, but it might not," said Karen.

"How will we pay our bills if that doesn't come through? How will we pay the bills until it comes through?"

"I'm not sure. We just have to have faith that if we do the right thing, somehow things will work out for the best."

"Good grief. I hope your faith is big enough to pay my bills as well as yours," said Jackson. "Nevertheless. I am proud of you. We will be putting the interest of our clients ahead of our own interest. It is the right thing to do. I'll start drafting motions to withdraw."

"Thanks Jackson."

"I'll start calling some disappointed clients," said Karen. "They won't like it."

"Let me talk with them. Please set appointments with each one."

"Will do."

*   *   *

The trial was scheduled for October. The nonstop media coverage finally ended and reporters, including Sandy, scattered to the winds chasing other stories. Ted was excited over his new job as brew master and Skip was employed shipping the new product. Jackson's legend of the Ghost of Goshen Springs was printed on the back of the labels as planned, and the beer was a success as soon as it hit the market.

In September, Jackson, John and Karen shut down all other work and focused on the upcoming trial. Every day and night was devoted to trial preparation. Potential clients were asked to call back after the trial.

An elderly Choctaw man entered the office during the last week of September and asked to see John Brooks.

"Who shall I say is here to see him?"

"Frank Dalton."

"Oh, Mr. Dalton. We talked on the phone last week, didn't we?"

"Yes, we did."

"Well, as I told you last week, we really don't have time to handle another matter right now. We decided to focus on the trial, which starts next week; but I promise that he can see you right after the trial."

"When will the trial be over?"

"I don't know for sure. We think it will be over by either the end of next week or sometime the week after."

"I hope it's over next week, because I don't think I can wait any longer than that."

45

District Attorney Tellers makes his opening statement.

"Hal Boyd gunned down Godfrey Plova in front of seven witnesses in Belhaven. That was murder, for which he should receive life in prison. Then, he broke and entered the home of Vlal Drumon, with the intent to murder him. He stalked Drumon for three years before breaking into his home, armed for the purpose of murder. His motive? Jealousy! Revenge! Vlal stole the heart of Boyd's fiancée, Sally Renfroe. His murderous rage was so great that he would kill anyone who stood in the way. He murdered Godfrey Plova to get to Vlal. To kill Vlal, he set the house on fire. He didn't care that two other people were in the house. They both died in the fire, collateral damage to Boyd's hateful actions. One can only imagine the agony they felt as they burned to death.

"Murder ordinarily carries a maximum penalty of life in prison. But if there are aggravating circumstances that make the crime more heinous, then the death penalty can be appropriate. This is a death penalty case. To prove that Boyd deserves to die, we must prove that the murder of Vlal Drumon or either of the two victims was committed while Boyd was engaged in the crime of burglary of an occupied dwelling, or while he was engaged in the crime of arson. We will prove beyond a reasonable doubt that Hal Boyd broke and entered the occupied home of Vlal Drumon with the intent to commit the crime of murder of Vlal Drumon, and that he burned the house down, killing two persons who have yet to be identified.

"We will ask you to return three verdicts of guilty of murder with aggravating circumstances, and guilty of the murder of Godfrey Plova."

District Attorney Tellers looked each juror in the eyes, holding each person's gaze for a moment, then turned and glowered at Boyd as he returned to his table.

The gallery murmured its approval of the brief and effective opening statement. Judge Robert Richards pounded his gavel once and a hush came over the courtroom.

"Mr. Brooks, you may make your opening statement now, or you may reserve your opening until you begin your side of the case."

"We will open now, your Honor."

Brooks strode to the podium. At first, he was vaguely aware that hundreds of eyes were on him and cameras were projecting his statement to an anxiously waiting world. He pushed the thought out of his mind.

213

By the time he reached the podium, the only people he was aware of were the jurors. When he began to speak, it was as though he and the jurors were the only ones in the room.

"You are about to start a search for the truth. Your search for truth will cause you to explore the haunting realm of sanity and insanity.

"We are trying four cases at once. The first case involves the death of Godfrey Plova. You will learn that Mr. Plova attacked Hal Boyd and was attempting to kill him with a handgun. After a struggle, Hal Boyd shot Plova with Plova's own handgun, killing him in self-defense. The State cannot prove that Hal Boyd is guilty of murder of Mr. Plova beyond a reasonable doubt, because the evidence will show that Plova was the aggressor and you should find Hal not guilty on that charge.

"The State blames Hal for two deaths by arson. The State must prove beyond a reasonable doubt that Hal Boyd intentionally and unlawfully set fire to the house. It is insufficient to prove merely that he was present when the house burned. There will not be any proof that Hal set fire to the house, because he didn't. The State will not be able to meet its burden on the charge of murder by arson, and you should find Hal not guilty on both of those charges.

"That leaves only the charge of the murder of Vlal Drumon. The proof will show that Hal killed Drumon. The proof will also show that he did so while suffering from a delusion, a defect of mind that caused him to honestly believe that Drumon had to die in order to save the lives of others. Hal believed that others were in imminent danger of death or serious injury. We will prove that an extraordinary set of circumstances and misfortunes occurred which overwhelmed Hal's mind driving him into the depths of depression, obsession and insanity. He became convinced, in every fiber of his soul, that Vlal Drumon was a monster who murdered innocent people and then drank the blood of his victims."

"Objection! He is trying to demonize the victim! This is nonsense hocus pocus, argumentative and prejudicial."

"Sustained."

"We intend to show that Hal Boyd was so insane that he believed that Vlal Drumon was an actual vampire, the kind you have seen in the movies, with all of the dangers and horrors that implies. Because he believed that Drumon was a vampire, Hal did not know that killing Drumon was wrong. We will show that his mind was so overwhelmed with this obsession that he cannot be held criminally responsible for his actions. Instead, he should be institutionalized because of his illness. It is the burden of the State to prove beyond a reasonable doubt that Hal Boyd was sane at the time of the killing. The State will not be able to meet that burden; therefore, a verdict of not guilty by reason of insanity

214

will be the only lawful verdict."

As John returned to the defense table, jurors settled back into their chairs and glanced at one another. Some grinned at each other and raised their eyebrows in anticipation of the story that would unfold before them.

"That concludes the opening statements," said Judge Richards. "As I told you yesterday after you were selected to serve as the jurors of this case, you should not consider the statements of counsel to be evidence. The evidence comes from the witnesses and the exhibits that I allow to be placed into evidence." He looked towards the prosecutors' table and bellowed, "Call your first witness."

"Patrick Simmons," responded Robert Thornton.

A moment later, all eyes turned to the courtroom door as a twelve-year-old, sandy blond-haired boy entered. Patrick paused when he realized every eye was on him. A bailiff placed a hand on his shoulder and led him though the gate and inside the bar. When he settled into the witness chair, the Judge directed the bailiff to place the microphone close to Patrick's mouth. Then the Judge leaned over and with an effort to make his voice as soothing as possible, said, "Good morning, Patrick."

"Good morning, sir, your Honor, sir."

"These gentlemen will be asking you some questions shortly. When you answer the questions, I want you to speak loudly and into the microphone, okay?"

"Okay!" shouted Patrick.

"Not that loud," Richards said over courtroom laughter.

"Sorry."

"It's okay. Now, I have to ask you a few questions before we can begin. Before I do that you will be asked to take an oath to tell the truth."

"Cool."

"All right, raise your right hand. Do you swear to tell the truth, the whole truth and nothing but the truth, so help you God?"

"I do."

"Do you know what you just did?"

"Yes, sir. I've seen it on TV like a million times, but I never thought I would be doing it."

"What do you understand that an oath means?"

"That I better tell the whole truth or else."

"Or else what?"

"I will be in like big-time trouble."

"Thank you Patrick. All right, gentlemen, I am satisfied that this young man understands the nature of the oath and is qualified to be a witness. You may proceed."

215

Thornton glanced at his notes, then at the boy on the witness stand. "Please tell the jury your name."

"Patrick."

"What's your last name?"

"Simmons."

"Do you remember the day of the fire in your neighborhood?"

"Do I ever! I saw it all!"

"Tell the ladies and gentlemen of the jury what you saw."

"Me and Jack Robins, Jack's my best friend, we were daring each other to knock on 'Got Fried's' door, when we heard squealing tires."

"Who is 'Got Fried'?"

"He's the guy who lived in the house that burned. We saw him get shot dead that day."

"Would his name be Godfrey?"

"Object to leading."

"Sustained."

"Um. Anyway, we jumped out of the way and this car slid to a stop right in front of us. Then 'Got Fried's' car slid to a stop and wham, it knocked the door right off the first car." Patrick was animated, making motions with his hands and arms and squealing noises like tires.

"Who was driving the first car?"

"Don't know his name, but I see him."

"Would you point him out for us?"

"That's him at that table."

"May the record reflect that the witness has identified the Defendant, Hal Boyd?"

"So reflect."

"What happened next?"

"That butcher fellow right there jumped out of the car."

"Objection to the description, your Honor."

"Sustained. Patrick, please don't call Mr. Boyd names."

"Sure, yes sir, your Honor. Do you mean don't call him either the butcher, or the vampire slayer?"

"That's right."

"Okay, I won't. Sorry. Anyway, he jumped out of the car and was running toward the house when 'Got Fried' tackled him. They wrestled around on the ground, and then Bang! Bang! There were gunshots and Mr., ah . . . that ah . . . him right there, stood up over 'Got Fried.' Then he ran to the house and kicked in the door and ran inside."

"What did Godfrey do?"

"Nothing. He was dead."

"When did you next see Mr. Boyd?"

216

"When he came out of the burning house, a policeman arrested him and took him away."

"No further questions."

"Cool. Can I go?"

"Not yet, Patrick. Another lawyer wants to ask you questions."

"My momma told me never to talk to lawyers or strangers."

"Just this once it will be okay. Mr. Brooks, your witness."

"Patrick, where was Jack when all of this happened?"

"Most of the time he was with me, but when Mr. Boyd went into the house, Jack ran around the side of the house. I stayed in front where all the action was."

"When Godfrey tackled Mr. Boyd, was he carrying anything?"

"Yep. A gun."

"Is that the gun that you heard fire?"

"Must be. It's the only gun I saw."

"Why were you and Jack daring each other to knock on the door?"

"Objection, relevance."

"Overruled. You can answer the question Patrick."

"Cause the house is haunted."

"Objection."

"Sustained."

"Between the time Mr. Boyd went into the house and the time that he came out, did your hear anything unusual coming from the house?"

"Yeah, the scariest noises you ever heard. Screams and shrieks and groans and growls, the kind of noises you hear from a haunted house."

Thornton stood to object, but hesitated, shook his head, shrugged and returned to his seat.

"Did you hear Mr. Boyd say anything just before the shots were fired?"

"He hollered for God to help him."

"Did you remember if you saw anything in the window?"

"Yeah. I saw Mr. Drumon, at least that's who Mr. Coleman said it was."

"Was there anything unusual about him?"

"Just that he looked real scary."

"Objection."

"Sustained."

"Describe what this person looked like."

"Your honor, Mr. Drumon is not on trial, and this witness doesn't even know if that was Mr. Drumon."

Judge Richards looked toward John in anticipation of a response.

"His appearance contributed to my client's belief . . ."

217

"That's what I am talking about judge. This is inappropriate."

"I am going to sustain the objection."

"When you saw this person, were you startled?"

"I about jumped out of my skin."

"At that moment, while you were startled, did you say anything?"

"Yep. I said . . ."

"Objection, hearsay."

"We rely upon the excited utterance exception to the hearsay rule."

"Objection overruled."

"What did you say Patrick?"

"I kind of hollered at Jack that I saw something in the window."

"What did he do?"

"He moved around to the side of the house to get a better look."

"No further questions."

"Thank you Patrick. You are excused to return to school."

"I'd rather stay here. This is way more fun than school."

46

The prosecution called Mrs. Adams, Mr. and Mrs. Baker, and Mr. Coleman to the witness stand, one after the other. Their testimony was similar, but Mr. Baker said that he saw Vlal Drumon for a moment through a window of the house just before he realized that the house was on fire. Officer Ayers was next, ending his testimony with a description of Boyd stumbling out of the burning house, and his description of Mrs. Baker spontaneously shouting, "That's him! That's the murderer!"

Sandy leaned over to Karen. "Why didn't John object to that statement. Isn't that hearsay?"

"I heard him and Jackson talking about that. The rugby guys got her statement and they knew she was going to say that."

"Why didn't he object?"

"He said that was an excited utterance, and it would be allowed in evidence as an exception to the hearsay rule."

"Oh. I still think he should have objected."

"Did Boyd say anything to you when you approached him?"

"Yes."

"Was he under arrest?"

"No."

"Did you ask him anything?"

"Yes, I asked him if there was anyone else in the house."

"What did he say?"

"There's no one left alive."

"What did you do?"

"I asked him what he meant by that."

"What did he say next?"

"He said I killed him."

"No further questions."

"Mr. Brooks, your witness."

"Thank you, your Honor."

John took no notes to the podium. He paused for a moment and then looked at the jury while he asked the next question.

"Mr. Boyd said, 'I killed him,' that was a singular him, right?"

"That's what he said."

"Did you ask Mr. Boyd who he killed?"

"I did."

219

"What did he tell you?"

"He said that he killed the vampire." The courtroom was completely silent. It was as though no one took a breath.

"No further questions."

Max Myers from the State Crime Lab testified next. Thornton began questioning him about his impressive credentials when John stood and said, "Your Honor, we accept Mr. Myers as an expert in the field of forensic investigation, the identification of human remains, cause and origin of fire and cause of death."

"That is an interesting and sweeping offer of stipulation, Mr. Brooks."

"Just trying to save the Court and jury some time, your Honor."

"Hmm. What says the prosecution?"

"We accept the offer of stipulation. With your Honor's permission, we will go straight to the point."

"Please do."

"Did you find human remains in the home at 1299 Euclid Avenue?"

"Yes, we found three bodies in the rubble after the fire was extinguished."

"Were you able to identify those remains?"

"Somewhat. Clothing and soft tissue was consumed in the fire, but we were able to tell from skeletal remains that there were two females and one male."

"How can you tell sex from a skeleton?"

"There are several clues in both the structure of the skeleton and in the skull. The eye socket structure is one of several features that differ between men and women."

Myers proceeded to give the jury a crash course in the identification of the sex of skeletal remains, ending with, "It was obvious that two of the remains were female."

"Were you able to identify the females?"

"No, I'm afraid not. Somewhere there are loved ones who do not realize that they are dead."

"Was the fire sufficient to cause the death of both of these ladies?"

"Anyone remaining very long in that house at the time of the fire would be killed. Yes, the fire was hot enough to kill anyone."

"What did you learn about the other remains?"

"Male, 6 feet 3 inches tall, which fits the description of Vlal Drumon."

"Cause of death?"

"The fire did too much damage to determine a cause of death with any certainty, but we did note something unusual. We found him lying on top of a collapsed wall. Most of the studs were still present, but were badly charred. The wall board was mostly consumed in the fire, but some remained. In the center of the skeleton's chest was a piece of wood, like a thick stick or small board."

"Like a stake?"

"Yes, exactly like a stake. It is depicted in a photograph."

"Is this the photograph?"

"Yes, I took this photograph of the body the afternoon after the fire. We took numerous photos the day after the fire to document the search for remains and other evidence. When the male skeleton was located, we noted that there was no retrievable tissue or organs. The fire had even consumed some of the skeletal structure, but we found the charred remains of a piece of wood in the center of his chest. I thought that was remarkable since the fire was intense enough to burn the body so badly, but leave some wood. You can see that the charred wood is shaped like a stake and it passes through his chest, through the wallboard and into a wall stud."

"How much force would be required to drive a wooden stake through the wall board and into a stud."

"Tremendous force."

"Considering the position of the wall, the stake and the body after the fire, can you tell us to a reasonable degree of probability where they were prior to the collapse of the wall?"

"It appears that the body of the male was pinned to the wall with a wooden stake driven through his chest."

Gasps were heard in the jury box and the courtroom. Paper rustled, cameras clicked, whispered murmurs swept through the gallery.

Judge Richards banged the gavel on the resounder. "Order in the court!"

After a pregnant pause, Thornton continued, "Would that be sufficient injury to cause death?"

"Absolutely."

"No further questions."

John walked slowly to the podium, arranged his notes, looked at the jury and then asked the Judge, "May I proceed?"

"You may."

"Beginning with the female skeletons, you do not have enough information or evidence to determine either a cause of death or a time of death, do you?"

"I know the time of the fire, and the fire would be a time and cause of death."

"You know that there was a fire at a certain time, and that these bodies were found in the remains of the house, but you don't know

221

whether either of these ladies was alive at the time of the fire, do you?"

"I don't have any reason to believe that they were dead at the time of the fire, and the fire was more than sufficient to kill them."

"You do not know who caused the fire, do you?"

"No, I don't."

"No further questions."

"We call Ann Renfroe Bryant to the stand," announced Tellers.

A dark-haired beauty came to the witness stand. Everyone noticed that she glowered at Hal Boyd as she took the oath.

"Please tell us your name."

"Ann Bryant."

"Where do you live?"

"Just outside Seattle, Washington."

"Do you know the Defendant, Hal Boyd?"

"Unfortunately, I do."

"Tell the jury how you know him."

"He stalked my sister Sally Renfroe right up to the date of her death."

"How did he know your sister?"

"She and Hal dated for a year and they were engaged for several months. I knew Hal very well, I thought, until he and my sister broke up."

"When did they end their engagement?"

"In August of 2007. Hal called me to say that he thought something was wrong with Sally because she had broken up with him. I told him that just because she wants to move on with her life without him did not mean that something was wrong with her."

"Why did they break up?"

"Why does anyone break up? Only the individuals really know. My sister simply said it was not going to work out between them. Hal believed there was someone else. He was insanely jealous of another man that Sally met. It is true that she quickly became smitten with her new boyfriend. It's like I told Hal, these things happen. Just give it time and you will find someone else. I told him that Sally was moving on with her life and he needed to do the same."

"What was Hal's response?"

"He was inconsolable. He was obsessed with Sally's new lover and was convinced that something was wrong. He was determined to save Sally from her new fiancé."

"So, Sally became engaged to her new boyfriend?"

"Yes, he was handsome, wealthy, and charming and just swept her off her feet. She was madly in love with him."

"What was the name of this new lover?"

222

"Vlal Drumon. The man Hal murdered here in Jackson."

"Objection!"

"Sustained. The jury will disregard the last comment by the witness."

"Was Hal able to just let your sister go?"

"No, he followed her everywhere. Tried to talk with her. Contacted her at all hours of the day and night. She obtained a restraining order against him."

"Your Honor, I would like to offer as the next exhibit a certified copy of a restraining order from King County, Washington, ordering Hal Boyd to not contact Sally Renfroe and to stay at least 500 feet away from her."

"Any objection?"

"None."

"Let it be marked."

Sandy whispered to Bret, "What is John doing? He is just rolling over and letting Tellers walk all over him."

"What happened with your sister?"

Ann turned in the witness stand so that she could look directly at Hal while she answered. "She mysteriously died. Her health seemed to fail. She became sickly and she passed away four years ago. The cause of death was not determined, but I think that Hal knows exactly what happened to her."

"Objection," said John.

Ann raised her voice to be heard over John's objection. "You know exactly what you did to her, don't you!"

"Objection!"

Ann suddenly stood in the witness stand and shouted at Hal, "You killed her! Admit it!"

"Miss Bryant, control yourself!" shouted Judge Richards.

Pointing at Hal, Ann yelled, "Tell us how you did it! You poisoned her, didn't you!"

"Bailiff, remove this witness from the courtroom. Ladies and gentlemen of the jury, please disregard this outburst. I am instructing you not to allow anything that she said concerning her opinion as to how or why her sister died, or who she thinks is responsible for her sister's death, to affect your decision in any way. This trial will be governed by rules of law and evidence. Every citizen is entitled to a fair trial before a jury, and it would not be fair to judge Mr. Boyd on unsupported innuendo and opinion. Can each of you tell me with certainty that you will not allow anything that Ms. Bryant said just now to influence your decision in any way?"

Every juror nodded yes.

"Thank you. I ask you to step into the jury room. We will be in recess for ten minutes."

47

Jackson leaned over to John and said, "We are guaranteed a mistrial after that episode."

"You're right. The question is, do we want one?"

Jackson looked at John incredulously, "You've got to be kidding! There is no way Hal can get a fair trial after that outburst."

"You might be right. But there is so much in what she said that could be useful to us."

"Useful? Like what?"

Hal was listening to the exchange intently. Karen joined them and leaned over so she could hear the discussion.

"Hal, all of the testimony about stalking will come out anyway. Our position is that Sally's condition is one of the reasons you worried about her and became suspicious of Drumon. But the image of Ann shouting to the world that you murdered Sally will stay with the jury. They will be impressed by her conviction that you are guilty. The question is, will her conviction cause your conviction?"

"I loved Sally. There is no way that I would hurt her."

"The prosecutor will say that you loved her so much that you didn't want anyone else to have her. He will suggest that you killed her so that no one else could have her, and that you then stalked and murdered Drumon for revenge because he stole Sally from you."

"He is going to say that anyway. What is the effect of this mistrial that Jackson says we can get?"

"We will start over with another jury."

"No, I want this over with now. I expect to be convicted anyway, whether by this jury or the next. I just want the chance to say that I didn't hurt Sally. I would never hurt Sally. I just wanted to save her and others from that monster. Vlal won't hurt anyone anymore. If it means I have to die or spend the rest of my life in prison, it will be worth it. I am willing to pay that price. Just get this over with now."

"Order in the Court," demanded the bailiff as Judge Richards re-entered the Courtroom.

"Do you have a motion?"

John stood and looked briefly over the packed courtroom. He caught the eyes of several lawyers. He saw expectant looks on their faces. Friends and acquaintances were smiling in anticipation of the argument that they expected John to make. A mistrial with the whole world watching would seem like a victory. John realized that if he failed to ask for a mistrial, the lawyers watching the trial would view his decision as a grave error. There would be talk of malpractice and incompetence. If Hal was convicted, or worse, received the death penalty, then this would be the moment in the trial that everyone would point to and say, "This was where Brooks blew it."

"No, your Honor. We are satisfied with your admonition to the jury and we have faith that they will follow your instructions."

Tellers and Thornton had both risen, anxious to make their response to the expected motion for mistrial. They looked at each other in disbelief. They could not contain their relief, as they smiled and winked at one another. Murmurs swept the courtroom. Judge Richards looked on with a furrowed brow as he stroked his chin. John could see that the Judge was considering whether he should grant a mistrial even though none had been requested.

"Your Honor, I have discussed with Mr. Boyd the motions that might ordinarily be considered after an episode like the one we just experienced. It is my client's position that he wishes to complete this trial, with this jury."

"Very well. Will you have any questions of the last witness?"

"No, your Honor."

"Mr. Tellers, call your next witness."

"Doctor Curtis Bishop."

Professor Bishop strode confidently to the witness stand and raised his right hand.

"Do you swear to tell the truth, the whole truth and nothing but the truth, so help you God?"

"I affirm."

"Please have a seat in the witness chair and talk directly into the microphone."

Tellers stood at the podium and smiled at his witness. He scanned the jury then addressed Judge Richards. "May I proceed, your Honor?"

"Please do."

"Doctor Bishop, please tell us your name and profession."

"Curtis Grady Bishop, I am a doctor of psychology. I graduated with an M.S. from the Pacific University School of Professional Psychology in Hillsboro, Oregon, and after a stint as a professor of psychology at North Seattle Community College I enrolled in the Adler School of Professional Psychology in Vancouver to obtain my doctorate. It is one of the top psychology schools in the world. I was especially attracted to its holistic view of psychology and its emphasis on social justice. I thought that would be a perfect fit for my choice of a dissertation, which was titled Fundamental Religious Beliefs as a Cause of Certain Mental Illnesses. For economic reasons, I had to return briefly to work and then completed my doctorate in psychology at Walden University, where I earned degrees in both clinical psychology and, more to the point for today's hearing, forensic psychology. Then I worked for four years as the head of the Department of Psychology with the Navajo Indian Reservation in Arizona and New Mexico, working both as a clinician and as a forensic psychologist. I then returned to private practice briefly in Phoenix before obtaining another teaching job at the College of the Redwoods in Eureka, California, where I was also in private practice and assisted local law enforcement with unusual cases. Because of my experience with forensic psychology and assisting with the profiling of serial criminals, I developed a specialty and found myself in demand around the country; however, that much travel is difficult on anyone, so I was pleased to hear that a position opened in Madison, Mississippi, at the new branch of Tulane University. Tulane is, of course, a fine university, and I was very pleased when I was asked to accept a position on staff there. Because of my interest in forensic psychology, I still find myself assisting with unusual criminal cases, such as the case at hand."

"What is forensic psychology?"

"It is the point at which law and the science of psychology meet. It is particularly useful when the authorities or others need to understand the inner workings of the criminal mind. I focus on both the formation of the *mens rea*, that is, the formation in the mind of criminal intent. Also, I specialize in the development of profiles to help the authorities identify, locate and capture serial criminals. You see, all people have certain mental characteristics in common. But some people seem to have received extra doses of certain characteristics. Understanding those characteristics can lead to an understanding of what a person is likely to do next. For instance, I know that your next question is likely to be whether or not I have ever testified before in a court of law."

"Have you ever testified before in a court of law?"

Laughter spread through the jury box and the courtroom.

"More times and in more places than I can count."

"Has a court ever accepted you as an expert in the field of forensic psychology?"

"Every time."

"Your Honor, I offer Doctor Curtis Bishop as an expert in the field of Forensic Psychology."

"Any objection?"

"I would like to *voir dire* the witness, your Honor."

Tellers was visibly irritated. "I object to that delaying tactic, your

Honor. We covered his qualifications in detail. He has been accepted all over the country as an expert in forensic psychology. There cannot be any doubt about his qualifications."

"Nevertheless," said Judge Richards, "the defense is entitled to question the qualifications of a witness proffered as an expert prior to his offering an opinion. Your objection is overruled. Mr. Brooks, you may *voir dire* the witness."

Bishop turned slightly in his chair towards Brooks, a smug look was on his face. He was confident that he had more courtroom experience than the young lawyer who was about to question him. He knew that he had matched wits with better minds than Brooks and he always came out on top.

"You told us that you obtained your doctorate from Walden."

"That's right."

"Walden offers on-line doctorates in psychology. Was your doctorate obtained on-line?"

"Partially."

"Well, the part that was obtained on-line was the doctorate degree, right?"

"I received instruction and credit hours from some of the best in the world from Adler and from Pacific University."

"Both of those schools offer doctorates in psychology, don't they?"

"Of course."

"And for whatever reason you were unable to complete the course of study at either of those institutions."

Tellers shot out of his seat. "I object to that characterization. That is grossly unfair."

"Overruled. He is on cross-examination."

Bishop's voice remained calm, but his eyes revealed his annoyance. "Like many who later obtain doctorates from schools other than the first school they attend, I did not obtain my doctorate from either of those fine institutions. I believe that changing universities became an advantage to me because I was able to study under a variety of great professors at fine institutions and I learned to take the best from the best and apply that to the exercise of my profession."

"Ultimately, after failing to complete the course of study for a doctorate at either Pacific or Adler, you obtained a mail order doctorate?"

"Objection!" shouted Tellers.

"I object to that characterization as well. Walden is a fine institution that is accredited and has an extremely demanding course of study that is well respected in my field. My degree has been accepted everywhere I have gone."

"You said that Walden is accredited, but the doctorate program in psychology is not accredited, is it?"

"It soon will be."

"It is not accredited, is it?"

"No."

"You taught at both North Seattle Community College and at the College of the Redwoods, is that right?"

"Yes. If you had been paying attention you would have known that I already testified about that."

"You testified that your stint at those schools was short?"

"Yes."

"You did not complete a semester at either college, did you?"

"I don't know what that has to do with anything."

"Was there litigation involving your departure from either of those institutions?"

"Objection," said Tellers exhaling as though he was exasperated with such a ridiculous question. "That is not relevant to the issue of Doctor Bishop's qualifications."

"If the good doctor's employment at community colleges was not relevant to his qualifications, then I wonder why it was raised during the prosecution's examination of his qualifications?"

"The objection is overruled. You may continue."

Bishop hesitated.

"You may answer, Professor," said Brooks.

"I am not permitted to say. There is . . ." Bishop hesitated again.

"An agreement? A confidentiality agreement?"

"Objection, your Honor. That is unfair. If there was such an agreement, then Doctor Bishop could not comment. This is patently unfair."

"Overruled."

"Judge, I will move on to my next point," said John. "What are you paid for your opinions?"

"I am paid for my work, for my expertise and for my time, not for my opinions."

"Excuse me, I did not mean to imply that your opinion is for sale. What are you paid for your time?"

"One thousand dollars per hour."

"How many hours do you bill in a typical year for your forensic work?"

"There are no typical years."

"Is it true that you billed about 1,500 hours, or about one and one half

229

million dollars last year for your forensic work?"

"That sounds about right."

"How much have you billed for your work in this case so far."

"I have no idea."

"More than one hundred hours?"

"I told you, I have no idea."

"So, you may be paid by the taxpayers of Mississippi more than $100,000 for your opinion in this case?"

"Objection! That is speculation. He said he didn't know."

"Your Honor, I would like to end my *voir dire* of the good doctor on that note of uncertainty. We object to the professor testifying as an expert."

48

Red-faced with veins standing out on his neck, Bishop swiveled his head back and forth between Brooks, the Judge and Tellers. The knuckles on his hands were white as they clutched the arms of his chair. *I wasn't finished speaking about my qualifications. This is not fair!* He felt that the Judge needed to hear more. He knew that an adverse ruling on his qualifications would do incalculable damage to his practice. He opened his mouth to protest when the Judge responded to the objection.

"Objection overruled. He will be accepted as an expert in the field of forensic psychology."

"Thank you, your Honor," said Bishop with obvious relief.

"Did you have the opportunity to examine the Defendant, Halbert Boyd, regarding his plea of not guilty by reason of insanity?"

"I did. I was selected by the Court to review the opinion of his psychiatrist and to review his psychological profile and I had the opportunity to interview him regarding his sanity, or lack thereof."

"What standard were you requested to use to determine his state of mind at the time of the crime?"

"I was asked to use the McNaughten standard, which is used by Mississippi courts. That standard holds that a person charged with a crime, who calls into question his mental ability to form an intent to commit a crime, is presumed to be legally sane unless he can show that he was suffering from a mental defect or disease that rendered him unable to realize the nature of his act or rendered him unable to recognize whether his actions were right or wrong. If he knew what he was doing at the time of the crime, and if he knew that what he was doing was wrong, then he was legally sane and can be held responsible for his actions."

"Did you form an opinion as to whether Mr. Boyd met the McNaughten definition of legally insane?"

"I did."

"And what is that opinion?"

"He was most definitely legally sane at the time of the crime. He was not McNaughten insane. He knew what he was doing and he knew that what he was doing was wrong."

"Upon what do you base your opinion?"

"First of all, the standard requires a showing of a mental defect or disease. His psychological testing showed neither. He was essentially normal in thought processes, although he showed a tendency towards obsession concerning his former fiancée and her new lover and there was a tendency towards paranoia. None of these tendencies were severe enough to be called a mental defect or disease. There was no history of any brain injury or disease and no indication of any recognized mental disorder. His tendencies were just that, tendencies. We all have tendencies toward one area or another. That is normal. His tendencies did not reach the level of a disorder or disease. Secondly, his actions over the past three years and immediately before and after the crime show that he was not McNaughten insane."

"Explain to the jury what you mean by that."

"What we have is a revenge killing. Boyd was engaged to marry Sally Renfroe, until Vlal Drumon entered the picture. We don't know what really caused the failure of the relationship between Boyd and Sally. Usually a relationship fails for a number of reasons that sort of pile up over time. Sometimes a parting is mutual. Sometimes one party decides to leave before the other party is ready to let go. This is what happened between Boyd and Sally.

"When their relationship ended, Boyd was hurt deeply and needed to find something or someone to blame other that himself. He blamed Vlal Drumon. He stalked Sally and Vlal for a time, even to the point of having a no contact order entered against him concerning Sally. As far as we know, he stayed away from Sally after that order was entered, demonstrating that he knew that he had to abide by that order. He turned his anger on Vlal Drumon, and continued to stalk him, ultimately killing him here in Jackson, Mississippi.

"He clearly knew what he was doing. He prepared himself in advance. He brought a weapon, in this case a wooden stake, and fought his way into the house by killing a friend of Mr. Drumon. He clearly knew what he did, because when he left the house he said he killed him, meaning Drumon. He knew what he did was wrong, as demonstrated by the fact that he turned himself over to the police after killing Drumon.

"In short, his actions were those of a man intent on revenge. This was a mean spirited, pre-meditated, hunting and killing of another human being. Nothing more."

"Objection. Goes beyond the scope of his expertise."

"Sustained."

"What about all of this vampire nonsense?"

"Objection."

"Overruled."

"That is the perfect word for the defense. Nonsense. Boyd didn't want to admit to the world that he lost his loved one. He wanted to claim that no mere mortal could have separated him from his loved one. So, he fancied that Vlal was more than mortal, a super human. He liked this fanciful idea and acted out his fantasy by driving a stake through Mr. Drumon's heart. Nothing in Boyd's psychological testing or profile indicates that he could actually have believed that fantasy. His profile simply indicates he was using hyperbole, or exaggeration when referring to Drumon as a monster, or as a vampire. Based on his profile, it is my opinion that the use of the vampire moniker occurred to Boyd when he felt as though the life had been sucked out of him when he lost his fiancée. We have all suffered a broken heart. We hurt for a while and we get over it. Mr. Boyd felt that his life had been sucked out of him, and he blamed Vlal Drumon. Later, it occurred to him to claim that Vlal was like a vampire who sucked the life out of him, not out of his fiancée."

"Did Halbert Boyd know the nature of his actions?"

"Absolutely."

"Did he know that his actions were wrong?"

"Definitely."

"Was he legally sane at the time of the murder of Vlal Drumon and Godfrey Plova?"

"He certainly was."

"No further questions."

"That was brutal," Jackson whispered to John.

Judge Richards looked at Brooks and said, "Your witness."

"Thank you, your Honor. Professor Bishop."

"It's Doctor Bishop."

"Excuse me, Doctor. You are not a medical doctor, are you?"

"No, I have two PhDs, as I said earlier, both in Psychology."

"And you did a dissertation titled *Fundamental Religious Beliefs as a Cause of Certain Mental Illnesses*?"

"Yes, I testified to that."

"Indeed, you wrote that in your opinion, conservative evangelical Christians are mentally ill, deranged or deluded and are a danger to society, didn't you?"

"That was intended as hyperbole, but many other intellectuals believe that anti-scientific beliefs such as those espoused by evangelicals can and do create a drag upon the progression of society, preventing the natural evolution of society and of the human mind."

"Briefly tell the jury how a fundamental religious belief might cause or contribute to a mental illness."

"Some fundamentalists have claimed that they heard the voice of God, or otherwise received a message from God, which they use as an

233

excuse to perform horrible atrocities in the name of a God that they describe as all loving. It is a mark of insanity to simultaneously hold views that are so conflicting that they are antithetical. "

"Do these people sometimes think they must kill in order to do the will of God?"

"Yes. They have attempted to justify murder, mayhem, genocide, racial discrimination, slavery and all manner of social ills in the name of their all loving God."

"When you say genocide, you mean the killing of a person because of his race or nationality?"

"Yes."

"And such behavior is insanity?"

"What else could you call it?"

"So, in your opinion, to kill an Armenian simply because he is an Armenian is insanity?"

"Yes."

"Likewise, to kill a vampire simply because he is a vampire is insanity?"

"No. Everyone knows that there is no such thing as a vampire."

"One would have to be crazy to believe in vampires, right?"

"Objection!"

"Sustained."

"One last point, Doctor Bishop. I spoke with your dean about your qualifications and background, and he seemed surprised about your short work experience at the junior colleges."

"That was you!"

"Are you involved in a disciplinary action at Tulane?"

"Objection, relevance."

"Overruled."

"I don't know what that has to do with anything."

"Besides questions about your teaching experience, are there questions about your relationship with some of your students?"

"That is a lie!"

"Objection!"

The Judge leaned forward, considering the objection. Without waiting on a ruling, John pressed on.

"Have your teaching privileges been suspended pending investigation by the school?"

"That is nonsense! There is a minor misunderstanding and I took a short vacation from teaching to focus on research and on this case."

"No further questions."

Doctor Bishop turned to face the Judge, then turned towards Tellers.

234

He was desperate for an opportunity to tell his side of the story. He knew that he could repair any perceived injury to his testimony if he could just keep talking to the jury a little longer.

"No further questions," said Tellers. "State rests."

"Doctor, you are excused. You may step down."

Doctor Bishop hesitated, clinched his jaw, left the witness stand and walked quickly towards the gate in the bar. He paused when he was even with John. With a glowering expression, he leaned toward him and whispered in a gruff voice, "You will pay for spreading these lies! Mark my words."

49

When Doctor Bishop left, John made a motion to dismiss the charges, a typical motion made by the defense whenever the State closes its case. The judge overruled the motion and asked, "Will you be calling witnesses for the Defendant?"

"Yes, your Honor. We call Doctor Richard Webster."

A few moments later, Doctor Webster was sworn and settled into the witness chair. John asked him to tell the jury his name and profession.

"My name is Richard Webster. I am a Board Certified Psychiatrist and I maintain an office with my partners at the Institute for a Healthy Mind."

"Tell us about your background and your qualifications."

"I grew up here in Jackson and graduated from St. Andrews High School. I obtained my undergraduate degree at SMU, then went to medical school at UCLA for four years, then four years of residency in psychiatry at NYU."

"Does that cover the alphabet?"

"Pretty much. Then I found an opportunity to come home and I helped start the Institute for a Healthy Mind in Ridgeland, Mississippi, almost ten years ago."

"Have you ever testified as an expert in psychiatry in a criminal case?"

"Many times, on either the subject of the competence of a person to stand trial, or on the issue of legal sanity. I have also testified regarding the need to commit a person for treatment."

"What do you charge for your work regarding criminal cases?"

"$350 per hour."

"If I told you that Doctor Bishop charges $1,000 per hour, what would you say about that?"

"I don't charge enough I suppose."

Jurors snickered.

"You are a psychiatrist and Doctor Bishop is a psychologist. What is the difference?"

"Medical school. Both receive extensive training in the diagnosis and treatment of mental disorders. Psychiatrists are medical doctors who specialize in mental health. Psychologists are not medical doctors."

"Have you had the opportunity to examine Hal Boyd regarding the

236

legal standard for sanity?"

"Yes, I spent about 12 hours interviewing him, reviewing his test data and observing him for the purpose of determining whether he was legally sane, or legally insane at the time of the alleged crimes. As the jury has probably heard, the standard for legal sanity in Mississippi is called the McNaughten Rule. I believe that that standard has been adequately described to the jury already. Since it was clear that Mr. Boyd knew what he was doing, I focused solely on the issue of whether of not he realized that what he was doing was wrong."

"Were you able to reach a conclusion to a reasonable degree of psychiatric certainty concerning whether or not Hal Boyd knew that what he was doing was wrong at the time of the alleged crimes?"

"Yes. Mr. Boyd was legally insane at the time of the fire and the death of Mr. Drumon and Mr. Plova, because he did not know that what he was doing was wrong. Indeed he was utterly convinced that what he was doing was right and necessary."

"Please explain to the jury the basis of your opinion."

"It was clear that Mr. Boyd had a delusional yet earnest belief that Mr. Drumon was a vampire. This delusion began about three years before the deadly encounter between Mr. Boyd and Mr. Drumon. It became an all-consuming obsession that dominated Hal Boyd's life for those three years."

"Why do you say it was an obsession?"

"Hal dropped out of normal life. Most of us have a daily life of going to work, seeing family and friends, taking an occasional vacation. We have interests that we work into our lives, like going to ball games or fishing or golf. Once in a while we even spend too much time on endeavors outside of work and family. We soon realize that and return to a more balanced life. That is normal. Hal's focus on Drumon became the only thing in his life. He left his work, abandoned his home, lost contact with family and friends, and focused his entire life, his entire being, on tracking and ultimately killing Drumon. That is obsession."

"Is obsession a sign of mental illness?"

"Yes."

"Why was he obsessed with Drumon?"

"He blamed Drumon for the death of his former fiancée. This drove him past the edge of sanity and he came to believe that Mr. Drumon was a vampire and was a clear and present danger to other persons. We, as sane persons, will have a hard time understanding why Hal would believe that Drumon was a vampire. That is because insanity is illogical.

"Hal believed that Drumon had to be killed in order to save countless other people. Once his psyche accepted the absurd thought that Drumon

237

was a vampire, destroying the vampire seemed to him to be a reasonable and necessary act. Please understand that I am not saying that his belief made his actions right, I am simply saying that his actions were right in his mind. He had a fixed illogical thought or delusion that Drumon was a vampire. That is insanity. With that delusion and obsession as his starting point, killing Mr. Drumon seemed to Hal like a right thing to do. Again, that is insanity. To this day, he honestly believes that he has done something good. In interviewing him, he expressed regret over the death of Godfrey Plova, but claimed that Godfrey was trying to stop him from killing Drumon and that Godfrey would have killed him to keep him away from Drumon.

"His actions immediately after the killing demonstrated that he believed that he had done nothing wrong. The first thing he did as he left the burning house was to tell a policeman he had killed the vampire. He didn't have much time after the killing to concoct a crazy story. He didn't need to concoct a crazy story in that short time, because he had been living with this crazy delusion for three years. He did not try to run. He did not try to conceal what he had done. There was no reason to do so, because in his mind he had done the world a great favor.

"This delusion is not unlike one in which the mentally ill person believes he is a member of the CIA and has to stop a KGB plot before the world is destroyed, or someone who has a delusion that someone is the anti-Christ. That does not make the actions taken by the mentally ill person acceptable; it simply means that we treat the person who has these delusions in a mental institution instead of sending them to prison."

"Did Hal Boyd have a recognized mental disorder?"

"Yes, he did. We use a publication that we called the DSM IV, which stands for the Diagnostic and Statistical Manual of Mental Disorders. It is a useful tool that helps standardize diagnostic terminology in the mental health field. Using that tool, we can see that Mr. Boyd fits the criteria for Delusional Disorder. This diagnosis involves a delusion of more than one month duration, usually a non-bizarre type delusion, such as someone is following me, or my spouse is cheating on me, when such is not the case. It can include a belief that mafia hit men are out to get me, that sort of thing. The delusion that Mr. Drumon was a vampire might seem bizarre, but it is really no more bizarre than delusions of grandeur or delusions that mafia hit men are out to get someone. Here, the delusion lasted more than one month. Second, Delusional Disorder may or may not include hallucinations. Third, other than during times when the person is operating under the delusion, the person is not otherwise odd or dysfunctional. That means he can seem quite normal and function in society in an ordinary way, with the exception of matters related to the delusion. Fourth, the delusion is not due to a substance abuse or an apparent medical condition, which is the case with Mr. Boyd. A fifth criterion applies only if other mood disorders occur during the delusion. We don't know if this criterion applies, but three criteria are enough to meet the diagnosis and we have at least three; therefore, Mr. Boyd suffers from a known mental disorder or disease, Delusional Disorder."

"Doctor Webster, in your opinion as an expert in the field of psychiatry, was Hal Boyd McNaughten sane or insane at the time of the fire and deaths of Godfrey Plova and Vlal Drumon?"

"Hal Boyd was McNaughten insane and was therefore not guilty by reason of insanity."

"Objection. It is up to the jury to determine guilt or innocence."

"Sustained. Ladies and gentlemen, you will decide guilt or innocence. In doing so you may consider the opinions of the experts who have testified."

"No further questions."

"Any cross examination?"

"Indeed," said Tellers as he hurried to the podium with a gleeful look on his face.

"You agree that Boyd knew what he was doing?"

"That's right."

"In other words, but for this vampire delusion, you would say that he was McNaughten sane."

"True."

"Ordinarily, when someone suffers from a delusion, we can see a progression of the illness, with evidence of the illness for a prolonged period in a person's life."

"That is often true, but not necessarily. Sometimes disease, brain injury, or severe emotional trauma can cause or contribute to an onset of mental illness."

"Still, a person's history is important in making a diagnosis of a mental disorder, don't you agree?"

"Certainly."

"Prior to three years ago, there was nothing in Mr. Boyd's history that would indicate that he had a predisposition of any kind towards a mental illness, isn't that true?"

"Yes."

"His school records indicate average to above average performance. His childhood seemed normal. He had a steady job, with no disciplinary actions, until he abruptly quit his job four years ago. There is no apparent drug or alcohol abuse and no criminal record before he began stalking his girlfriend and then stalking Mr. Drumon. Do you agree that this is not the history that you usually find from someone suffering from severe delusions and mental illness?"

"Yes, I agree that his case is unusual."

"Concerning Mr. Boyd's mental history, he has no record of ever having any treatment from any psychologist, psychiatrist, counselor or any mental health professional, correct?"

"That's right."

"So, you would be the only mental health professional to ever diagnose Mr. Boyd as having any disorder or delusion."

"Yes, that logically follows."

"He has no record before that last four years of any psychotic thoughts, or obsessive or compulsive behavior, correct?"

"Yes, that is correct."

"He has no history of hallucinations, correct?"

"I am not sure about that. He told me he had met a vampire slayer who trained him in the lost art of killing vampires. He called him Father Michael and spoke of him with reverence as though he were the Arch-Angel Michael. I considered that to be another delusion, or hallucination."

"And when did he hallucinate this vampire slayer?"

"Around the time of the death of his fiancée."

"And this hallucination of Father Michael was one of the reasons that you believe that Boyd was insane?"

Jackson and John looked at each other, and then looked over their shoulder at Karen. As they made eye contact with Karen, her head sank low between her shoulders and she raised her eyebrows.

"Yes, that was one reason, but not the only reason."

"What impact would it have on your opinion if this Father Michael was a real person?"

"You mean he really is a vampire slayer?"

Laughter swept through the courtroom.

"No, I asked you what effect it would have on your opinion if you learned that he was a real person, not that he was a real vampire slayer."

"I don't know. I suppose it might change my opinion that he was suffering from a hallucination about his existence. As I consider the implication of your suggestion, a person who identified himself to Boyd as a vampire slayer would have reinforced his delusion and made the delusion that much more real to him. It could have been the last straw that pushed Boyd into insanity."

"Would you agree with me that if Boyd's motive for killing Drumon was revenge for stealing his girlfriend, then he does not qualify as

MaNaughten insane?"

"Do you mean that if I assume the reason he killed Drumon was not because he believed Drumon was a vampire; instead, if I assume the reason he killed Drumon was to get revenge for stealing his fiancée, would that change my opinion?"

"That's right."

"Yes, that changes everything. One who seeks revenge does not care whether the action is right or wrong. The avenger just wants personal justice as opposed to public justice, even if it requires a wrongful action to obtain that personal justice; however, that is not what I found to be the case regarding Mr. Boyd's motives."

"He was angry at Drumon for stealing his fiancée, wasn't he?"

"I am not sure it was anger, but he did obsess on that, yes."

"And he blamed Drumon for the death of his fiancée, didn't he?"

"He did blame Drumon for her death, yes."

"Well, he was angry enough to kill Godfry Plova to get to Drumon and then kill Drumon, right?"

"Again, I am not sure it was anger."

"You are *not* sure if Boyd was angry enough to murder, but you *are* sure that he was so insane when he murdered two people that these jurors should set him free?"

"Objection!"

"Sustained."

"No further questions."

"Judge, could we have a brief recess before we call our next witness?"

"Yes, Mr. Brooks. Ladies and Gentlemen of the jury, I ask you to step into the jury room for a few minutes. The Court will stand in recess for fifteen minutes."

50

Jackson, John, Karen, Skip and Crush huddled around Hal as people in the courtroom stirred with activity. People were coming and going. The courtroom doors were opening and closing and people were talking and milling about. The noise level rose and the defense team concentrated on the task at hand in order to shut out the hubbub. No one noticed a man purposefully enter the courtroom and pass though the gate in the bar. He took a seat near the defense table as though he belonged there.

"Any word about the boy, Jack Robins?" asked Jackson.

"Yeah, his parents say they might let him testify tomorrow afternoon," answered Skip. "But they might not. We did deliver the subpoenas the way you told us."

Jackson looked at Crush. "Any word about Father Mike?"

"Nothing. It's like he fell off of the face of the earth. And the sheriff's deputies are looking for him just as much as we are. They have the courthouse surrounded, hoping that he shows up since he is on our witness list. They want to arrest him on suspicion of multiple murders."

"That leaves you, Hal," said John. "If you are going to testify, now could be the time. We already have the issue of sanity in front of the jury. The jury might agree with us and find you not guilty by reason of insanity. There is a good chance they won't agree with us. If you testify, the prosecutor will eat you alive and we may blow our chances of winning. It is a gamble either way. Are you still certain you want to tell your story?"

"Yes, I am ready. I need to tell my story. I don't care about the consequences; if they convict me, so be it."

"All right, we will call you next, and there will be a significant gap of time before we can call the boy as the last witness, if we can get the boy. I hope the judge will allow us to have that much of a gap in our case."

"Order in the Court!" called the Bailiff, and everyone began returning to their seats. The jury began filing into the jury box. With so much movement in the courtroom, no one paid attention to the rather tall gentleman who walked purposefully from the defense table and took a seat in the witness stand. John and his defense team were still huddled together when Judge Richards called out, "Mr. Brooks, please identify your witness."

John swung around to address the judge and announced, "Your

Honor, the defense calls Mr . . .” John hesitated when he saw the man in the witness chair.

“Yes, Mr. Brooks, you were saying?”

“The defense calls Father Michael McCarty as its next witness.”

Jackson, Karen, Skip and Crush were still standing where they had been huddled together. They stared at the witness chair with their mouths open. There sat Michael McCarty dressed in slacks and a long sleeve white shirt and tie. Tellers and Thornton did not notice the man in the witness stand and instead looked toward the courtroom door when they heard McCarty’s name. They nodded to several deputies in the courtroom, giving them the pre-arranged signal to seize McCarty as soon as he appeared. Two deputies rushed out of the courtroom to intercept McCarty in the hallway.

Thornton leaned over to Tellers and whispered, “There is no way he will get past the front door of the courthouse, let alone get into the courtroom.” Thornton and Tellers were still fixated on the courtroom door when they were startled to hear the judge say, “Raise your right hand. Do you solemnly swear to tell the truth, the whole truth and nothing but the truth, so help you God?”

“I do.”

The prosecutors were stunned to see McCarty in the witness chair.

“Your Honor, I object,” exclaimed Tellers.

“What are the grounds for your objection?”

“I, um.” Tellers hesitated.

“Yes,”

“I withdraw the objection.”

“Very well. Mr. Brooks, will you ask your defense team to have a seat.”

“Certainly, your Honor.”

As they were having a seat, Jackson whispered to John, “How does he do that?”

John shrugged.

Jackson continued whispering, “Are you sure you want him to testify? Our expert thought that he was a hallucination. Our expert opinion is solid right now. This may hurt that.”

“So be it. The truth is, he is not a hallucination.” Then John raised his voice and said, “Please tell the jury your name.”

“Michael McCarty.”

“Are you known as Father Michael McCarty?”

“I was; however, I lost the privilege of carrying that title. I was formerly a priest in the Catholic Church, but I have been excommunicated. I suppose that means that the veracity of my testimony will naturally be called into question; nevertheless, I will tell only the truth, no matter how hard it is to hear, or how much it may challenge your perception of reality."

"Objection to that answer. It was not in response to any question."

"Sustained."

"Did you have any special ministry while you were with the Church?"

"Exorcism."

"Objection to relevance."

"The relevance will be made apparent shortly after my next question."

"I will reserve my ruling for a question or two."

"Do you know the Defendant, Mr. Hal Boyd?"

"Yes, I met him because we had a mutual interest."

"What was that interest?"

"We were both tracking a vampire by the name of Vlal Drumon. I taught Hal how to kill it."

The courtroom erupted in gasps. Tellers shot to his feet shouting, "Objection! Objection! This is outrageous! This man is wanted for murder and we object to this perversion of the justice system!"

"Objection, your Honor to the comments of the prosecutor. Those comments are entirely inappropriate and give rise to a possible mistrial."

"Yes, mistrial is appropriate your Honor," shouted Tellers, "you should grant a mistrial."

Judge Richards banged his gavel several times and shouted, "Order in the Court. Ladies and gentlemen of the jury, please step into the jury room. Mr. Tellers and Mr. Brooks, meet me in my chambers."

Judge Richards virtually charged though the door behind the bench. Tellers looked to the courtroom deputies and commanded, "Watch McCarty. Don't let him out of your sight." Six deputies quickly surrounded the witness stand while the attorneys followed the judge through the door into his chambers.

"Tellers, you know better than to shout those accusations in front of the jury. If I have to call a mistrial this late in the game, you will personally pay all of the jury costs and every other cost of another trial. This case has dominated my docket for months and we were almost through. Brooks, who the heck is this witness? Are you saying that he is crazy too? Do you expect me to allow the jury to listen to the ramblings of a lunatic? Are you fishing for a mistrial? I want to know what you are up to."

"I am going to show that Father McCarty . . . ."

"Ex-Father."

"Yes, your Honor, Ex-Father McCarty had a significant influence on the sanity of Hal Boyd. He has a powerful personality, and he told Boyd

244

things that reinforced Boyd's delusion. In other words, the things McCarty told Boyd helped to drive him crazy. McCarty was part of the reason that Boyd earnestly believed Drumon was a vampire."

"This is preposterous," shouted Tellers. "Brooks is showboating and is going to make our court system the laughing stock of the world."

"Don't be accusing anyone of showboating, Tellers," said Judge Richards.

Tellers was red-faced and took a moment to control himself. "Your Honor, this witness is apparently insane. He may not be competent to testify. I request that he be examined by a psychologist before he is allowed to testify."

"He makes our point. McCarty is insane, yet Boyd is sane?"

"Mr. Tellers, I am aware that you arranged an all points bulletin on McCarty. If you could have had him arrested before he arrived here in the courtroom, we may never have known of his availability as a witness."

"Judge, I resent that remark. You are accusing me of attempting to subvert justice."

"I am suggesting that you were more interested in capturing this witness and in winning this case than in allowing the jury to hear what he might have to say. Nevertheless, I am concerned about the competence of the witness to testify. This is an unusual circumstance, so I will take the unusual precaution of allowing the prosecutor a limited *voir dire* of the witness on the issue of competence and also on the issue of self-incrimination before I allow him to testify. I recognize that there has already been an implication of his possible guilt, because he said that he encouraged Boyd to kill Drumon."

"Yes, your Honor," said both lawyers at the same time.

Judge Richards pushed an intercom button. "Mr. Lee, please put the jury back in the box. There has been enough delay. I want to get this case back on track and I don't want the jury to see all of the extra security surrounding Mr. McCarty. They don't need to be so close. I fear that may affect the juries' view of his credibility. I don't want an unnecessary issue on appeal."

"Yes, sir."

The jury was already filing into the jury box as Tellers and Brooks re-entered the courtroom. The deputies moved away from the witness stand. The gallery was alive with knots of people in excited discussions. Several reporters were motioning for the lawyers to meet them at the bar rail to see if they could get a scoop on what was happening. The courtroom was in more disruption and confusion than at any other time during the trial. Then bedlam broke out.

The lights suddenly went out, and the room seemed to be in utter darkness. There was an ear-piercing scream followed by shouts and the sound of someone falling in the dark and more screams. Someone bumped into John, almost knocking him down.

After what seemed an eternity but was actually three minutes, the lights winked back on. Mert, dressed in her homeless finest, was standing near the courtroom door when the lights came on. She screamed, swooned and fell in the doorway, effectively blocking the door.

"Where is McCarty?" shouted Tellers. "I told you to watch him!"

All of the jurors and everyone else in the courtroom looked at the empty witness stand. No one said a thing or moved for a moment. Then a deputy shouted: "Everyone take a seat! No one is to leave the courtroom except my deputies."

The deputies were delayed getting out of the courtroom momentarily while Mert was given attention. They spread out and searched the courthouse. When some of the deputies began searching outside the courthouse, they saw a man dressed exactly like Father Michael running away from the courthouse.

"That's him!" one deputy shouted. They chased the man down, tackling him in front of City Hall. When they rolled him over, one deputy immediately recognized him. "That's Sammy, the homeless guy that lives by the river. Where did you get these clothes Sammy?"

"A really nice man gave them to me, and told me that if I didn't get away from the courthouse quick, the police might think that I stole them."

51

The court was in recess for over an hour while the deputies thoroughly searched for McCarty, but he was not to be found. Judge Richards ordered the lawyers to meet him in chambers again.

"What am I to do with you, Brooks? Your witness appears without explanation and then disappears. He had to have help and I want to know what role you played in getting him into and out of the courthouse."

"Judge, we were as surprised as anyone when we realized he was on the witness stand. I was just about to announce that my client would be the next witness. I have no idea how he arrived or how he left."

"What about you, Bradley, what do you know about this?"

"I am dumbfounded, Judge."

"Well, the deputies found that the lock on the electric closet door was broken. Someone switched the breaker off and turned it on again, creating a diversion that gave McCarty an opportunity to escape. Somebody had to help him."

"It had to be Brooks!" asserted Tellers indignantly.

John looked at Tellers for a moment and sighed. "Judge, I wanted his testimony. Now he's gone. It is the prosecution that didn't want him to testify, not me. In any event, I believe he must have planned his escape in advance, because he didn't want to leave the witness stand and go to jail."

"That is where he is headed as soon as I find him."

Judge Richards sighed and looked John in the eyes. "I believe you. You wanted his testimony. In any event, I must decide what to do next. A witness has started testifying. There is an objection to his testimony. There has not been any cross-examination, only direct examination."

"And our direct examination had not really started. I had a lot more information that I needed. I expected McCarty to testify about the things he told Boyd that convinced him that Drumon was a vampire."

"And I could not wait to get him on cross," grumbled Tellers.

"Well, it seems that both of you will be disappointed," said Judge Richards. "I intend to finish this trial before we all become McNaughten insane. I will recess until tomorrow to see if McCarty can be found. If he is not found, then I will instruct the jury to disregard his testimony, such as it was, because McCarty's testimony was incomplete and his story has not been tested by cross-examination. If the jury cannot convince me that they will ignore his testimony, then I will declare a mistrial and we will start over with another jury. I don't want to see any of you again until tomorrow morning at nine. Good day."

*   *   *

"Where are we going, Sammy? How did you find the money for a car?"

"It was part of the reward the church arranged for me when I told Father Andrews about Michael McCarty. He said that Father Michael had friends who would help us. And on top of that, Mert, I got a job!"

"No kidding! I don't know what to say, a car and a job! This is the best day of my life. Where are we anyway?"

Sammy turned down a dirt driveway and drove slowly through hardwood trees along the river. He stopped at a small house elevated high above the flood plain on pilings.

"What are we doing here?"

"This is your new house!"

Mert began crying. "No, don't tell me that. This is perfect. This is everything I ever wanted."

Sammy showed her around the place, which didn't take long. Mert believed it was the finest house in the world.

"This is the best day of my life. I love you so much, Sammy."

"Just one more thing," said Sammy as he took a knee. "Will you marry me?"

*   *   *

All of the members of the defense team, except John, met at the office.

"Where is John?" asked Jennifer.

"He is at the jail with Hal. He will probably be there for hours going over his testimony over and over," explained Karen.

"Any word on the Robins boy?" asked Jackson.

"Patrick talked with him, but his parents are against him testifying," said Crush.

"Can we force the issue?" asked Karen.

"We may have to, but if we get an uncooperative witness, there is no telling what we will hear," explained Jackson. "The truth might always be just one question and answer away, but every question is a high stakes gamble. Especially at this late date."

"How could we force the issue?" asked Jennifer.

"Since we have served a subpoena on his mom and on Jack Robins, we could ask the Judge to assist us in getting them to court. He would send deputies to pick them up. If you think Mrs. Robins is mad now, imagine how she will be after she and her son are picked up by deputies and forced to come to court."

"What choice do we have?"

"Maybe none. Still, I want to wait a little longer before we pull that trigger."

*   *   *

Hinds County Deputies and Jackson Policemen scoured the area for McCarty. He was not found.

52

The next morning the Judge instructed the jury to disregard the testimony of "Father" Michael McCarty. Every juror assured the Judge that McCarty's testimony would not be considered in any way during deliberations. Jackson leaned over and whispered to John, "Everyone just agreed that they would pay no attention to the skunk in the jury box."

John smiled and nodded, then announced to the court, "Your Honor, our next witness is the Defendant, Mr. Hal Boyd."

The sound of 300 people scooting to the edge of their seats filled the courtroom.

Hal was neatly dressed in a blue shirt, tie and khaki pants. He exhibited no signs of nervousness as he took the oath and settled into the witness chair.

"Please tell us your name, where you are from and what you do."

"Hal Boyd. I grew up in the Seattle Washington area. I received an Associates Degree from a Community College in computer science, and worked as a programmer until about three or four years ago."

"Who is Sally Renfroe?"

"She was my fiancée. She died, or rather she was killed, a little over three years ago."

"Describe your relationship with Sally."

"We met each other at school and found that we had everything in common. Soon, we were seeing each other every day. We became best friends and then we fell deeply in love with each other. The greatest day of my life was the day she agreed to marry me. We planned our future together. She was amazing. It seemed that every dream I had for the future, she had the same dream. We talked all the time about our plans and how we were going to help each other achieve our dreams."

"What were some of those dreams?"

"We both loved the outdoors, hiking, boating, camping, cooking out. We loved our work with computers. We decided we would combine our love of the outdoors and our love of computers into a third world ministry. We made a trip together to Mexico for a week through our church and we were able to use our computer and projectors to display a really great program that was well received."

"We talked multiple times every day. The first thing either of us did when we woke was to call the other. We were so close we even had the same thoughts at the same time all the time. My heart would leap in my chest every time I saw her, and she was the same way with me."

"Did that change?"

"Yes. It was like a switch was thrown. Literally, one night we were together talking about our special love for each other. We were excited about the wedding coming up in a few weeks. I kissed her good night and left her at her apartment. The next morning, she wanted nothing to do with me. Everything changed between us, and all of her interests changed. This beautiful healthy woman who loved the outdoors and physical activity suddenly started sleeping all day and staying up at all hours of the night. She wanted nothing to do with the outdoors; she just wanted a night-life."

"Did anything unusual happen that last 'normal' night between you?"

"Yes. We were at dinner. We tried a new place, a new steak house. It was nice, but unusual. The menu did not appeal to us because it was filled with raw items. We sent our steaks back twice because they were way undercooked."

"Did that ruin your evening? Did you quarrel?"

"No, we laughed about it. It never mattered where we were or what was going on around us. We were always so happy to be together that bad food was something to laugh about and good food was something to share, but something else happened."

"What was that?"

"An unusually tall, thin man, dressed in dark clothes walked by and stopped at our table. He made a comment about our steaks being overcooked. I chuckled at that since they were still red on the inside. Karen just stared at him with a strange far-away look on her face. He put his hand on her shoulder and touched the birthmark on her neck and said, 'You are so lovely.'

"I was becoming a little irritated and was about to say something when he stepped back and looked at me intently. It was very unsettling. I told him to keep his hands to himself. He grinned at me and walked away. She stared at him for a long moment, then shivered and said, 'He gives me the creeps.' I agreed with her. His eyes, when he looked at me, were so strange."

"Who was that man?"

"Vlal Drumon."

"What happened next?"

"The next morning, I called her as soon as I awoke. No answer. I didn't hear from her, so I called her again, later in the morning. No answer. By lunch time, I was worried, so I went to her apartment. Her car was there, which was odd. I knocked and rang the doorbell. I was just about to let myself in, when she opened the door and said, "Go away!" She said it in an urgent, loud voice. I was confused, so I asked her what was wrong. She said it was over between us. I wasn't sure I understood what she said, so I just stood there. Then she handed me the engagement ring and said the wedding was off. My knees buckled. My head spun. I found myself on the ground on my hands and knees."

Tears ran down Hal's checks. His voice broke and he took a moment to regain his composure.

"It was, to say the least, a difficult moment. I was literally dizzy. I don't think I knew which way was up or down. I couldn't speak. Then she said something that made no sense at all. She said, 'I've found someone else. We are to be married this weekend.' I sat back on my heels and said, 'Sally, this is not a funny joke. Don't say that.' She told me it was no joke and I should leave, or she would call the police. I told her to call them, because something was wrong. Anyway, things did not go well that day. Or any day since then."

"Did she get married?"

"She said she did. That very weekend."

"To whom?"

"Vlal Drumon."

"Did you talk to Sally again?"

"Yes. The whole thing was such a shock that I could not let go. I followed her for a while. I saw them together. Every night. I watched her change from a healthy, vibrant young lady to a shell of her former self. I watched her grow pale and weak. I knew something was wrong. I felt that I needed to save her, but I didn't know how. My efforts were complicated by the fact that she apparently didn't want to be saved. She called the police on me twice. A no contact order was entered against me to have me stay away from her. I would have except for something she said to me."

"What was that?"

"Objection, hearsay."

"We don't offer the statement for the proof of the matter asserted in the statement. We offer it to show the effect that the statement had upon Mr. Boyd's mental health; therefore, it is not hearsay."

"Overruled. You may answer."

"She said it was better for me that she marry Vlal. I laughed at her and said 'How is that better for me? I would be better off dead.' She said emphatically, 'No! Don't say that. Go away and forget me.'

"Those words haunted me. How could her marrying Vlal be better for me? So, I didn't stay away. The last time that I saw her was the night before she died. She was in the yard in front of his house in

252

Seattle, retching, throwing up. She was very ill and very pale. I shouldn't have been there, but when I saw her that way I went to her and asked if I could help. She looked at me, cried and said, "Oh Hal, I am so sorry. No, go away now, and never come back. If you love me, go now and never come back."

"What happened next?"

"Vlal hit me from behind so hard I was senseless for a moment. I didn't realize he was there. I was half conscious when he dragged me to the side of his house and worked me over. Every time I tried to get up he knocked me down. I never encountered such strength. I had dreamed of a chance to fight him, but I was no match for him. Finally, he grabbed me by the neck and lifted me off the ground. He grinned at me and said, 'You puny persistent little man. Run away before I take everything else away from you.'"

"'I've got nothing else to lose,' I told him. 'You've already taken everything.'

"'Not everything, not yet'"

"At that moment his sidekick, Godfrey Plova, appeared and urged Vlal to kill me. Vlal said, 'No, I made a promise, and it pleases me to leave him alive for now. Leave him something to remember us by.' He threw me against the house and left. Godfrey worked me over for a while. I was already so weak from Vlal's beating that I was unable to fight back. I have never been so helpless. He pulled a knife and said he was going to carve his initials in my face so that I would remember them. I felt the knife cut my face here," Hal pointed to a scar on his cheek. He continued, "Then Godfrey grunted and fell on me, knocked out. Father Michael was standing over him. The next thing I remember, I was in a motel room. Father Michael McCarty was taking care of me. He saved me."

"What happened to Sally?"

"She died that night or the next day. I was inconsolable for weeks. It was just as well, because it took me weeks to recover from the beating."

"How did Father Michael happen to be there?"

"Objection. He could only know that by hearsay."

"Once again, we offer this on the issue of mental state, not to prove the truth of the matter asserted."

"Overruled."

"Father Michael was watching Vlal, studying his habits, looking for an opportunity to slay him."

"Why?"

"He told me he had been on Vlal's trail for years, and that Vlal had killed dozens of people, mostly women, including Sally."

"Objection. Hearsay, relevance, prejudice outweighs any probative value."

"This goes to the mental state of my client. It develops the reason why my client believed that Vlal Drumon was a vampire."

"I have allowed you a lot of leeway, but I think you are going too far. I sustain the objection."

"Did you begin tracking Vlal Drumon?"

"Yes, I did. After I trained with Father Michael for about a year, I followed Drumon to the Southwest, San Antonio, Houston, and New Orleans. I was always just behind him. Everywhere Vlal went, there were mysterious deaths."

"Objection."

"Sustained. Ladies and gentlemen of the jury, please disregard that answer."

"Finally, I found him here in Jackson. Once I learned where he was, I knew I needed to get to his house before the sun went down."

"Why did you have to get to him that night?"

"I learned from his habits that he always feeds on a full moon, and a full moon was rising that night. I had to get there before the sun went down."

"Objection," said Tellers with exasperation.

"Sustained."

"How did you catch up with Dumon?"

"I learned that he had purchased a house in the Belhaven neighborhood in Jackson. I needed to enter the house shortly before the sun went down because that was the moment he would be weakest."

"Objection. This is preposterous."

"Where are you going with this, Mr. Brooks?"

"The events of that late afternoon and night."

"I will allow this, for now. Keep the testimony to the point."

"Yes, your Honor. What did you do?"

"I had already armed myself with a stake, a cross, a Bible, and Holy Water. It was my intent to drive a stake through his heart just as he awoke. I could not find my mallet, so I stopped at a hardware store. When I left the store, I opened the car door and slid in. I was still a little sideways in the car and I hadn't even closed the door when Godfrey popped up from the back seat and stuck a knife in the back of my neck. He sort of growled at me and whispered, 'I told you the next time I see you I kill you.' He had been following me and I didn't realize it.

"My heart jumped into my throat, but I remembered a move that Father Mike had taught me. If you put a pen against my neck, I will show you what I did."

"Objection. This is going way too far."

"Overruled."

John stepped up to the witness stand and placed his pen against the side of Hal's neck, making sure the view of the jury was not obstructed. "Like this?"

"Yes, just like that. He had the knife there on my neck and I did this move."

Hal twisted his head and neck quickly away from the pen while his hands and arms moved in a blur. He caught John's hand with both of his and rotated John's hand toward John's body, while he bent the wrist back. John grimaced and released the pen. John's body followed his wrist down towards the ground to avoid the pain.

"The pain momentarily disabled Godfrey and while he twisted his body the way John is doing now, I was able to strike him on the temple with my elbow," said Hal, as he demonstrated the elbow strike in slow motion.

John found himself on one knee. He rose slowly and brushed himself off. "How did Godfrey react to the elbow strike?"

"He was rendered unconscious. I drove to the back of the parking lot, pushed him out of the car and headed for Belhaven."

"Did Godfrey stay knocked out?"

"No. I was approaching Euclid, where Vlal's house was, when I saw Godfrey racing up behind me. Then the race to the house was on. I arrived a moment before he did. You heard what happened in the yard. The boy, Pat, told it pretty much the way I remember it. Godfrey tackled me. I was able to take his gun and shoot him. I hate that I had to do it, but I had no choice. The door to the house was locked, so I kicked it in. I rushed inside to confront Vlal. I needed to find his resting place at sundown. There would be a few moments when he was awakening that he would be truly vulnerable. I knew if I waited too long, he would be too powerful."

"Why not come sooner?"

"His spirit, such as it is, is not always in his body when he is asleep. Killing his body would do no good. He would just move to another body. He must be awake for me to truly kill him."

"Your Honor," said Tellers with a huff. "This is beyond ridiculous. I object to this bedtime story."

Judge Richards sighed. "We've come this far, I will let him finish if it won't take much longer."

255

53

The gallery was completely quiet. The jurors listened intently. Every eye was on Hal, watching his every word, his facial expressions, his hand and eye movement, noting his cadence and inflection.

"How did you know that he must be awake to truly kill him?"

"I was trained by Father Michael. It's what he taught me, and I believed it to be true."

"Object to the hearsay."

"Not offered for the truth, but to show that he believed the statement."

"Let me see counsel at the bench."

Brooks, Bradley, Tellers and Thornton approached the bench. John took the position in the center.

"This is crazy. You don't expect me to allow the jury to continue to hear this insane story, do you?"

"Judge, you have just made our point for us. Yes, we do expect you to allow the jury to hear the insane story of a mad man, whose defense is insanity."

"This is absurd," said Thornton indignantly. "This is a total waste of time. Brooks should be sanctioned for foisting this travesty on the court system."

"You both seem to have a point. Brooks, we've gone this far. I'm going to allow you to continue, but I don't know how long I can stand it." The Judge then looked at the jury and said, "Objection overruled. Mr. Brooks, you may continue."

"Once inside, what did you do?"

"I looked for his lair, a dark place in the house suitable for him to park his body during the day. He doesn't need to use a coffin like in the movies, but he could use one. The problem with a coffin is that it attracts too much attention, so I thought Vlal would use some other method of keeping light out of his room. As I moved from room to room, I stumbled into him. He was already awake. I was already too late, but I did not know that at the time. I rushed him to try to pin him to the wall or throw him down."

"Why did you need to pin him down?"

"So that I could drive a stake through his heart."

Jurors gasped.

"Were you able to pin him down?"

"No. As I rushed him, he stepped quickly aside and sort of flicked me as I passed by. It seemed almost effortless on his part, but I was completely off balance as I stumbled across the room and crashed into the wall. He said, 'You didn't expect me to be awake so soon, did you? You are a little early for the party. I am having guests tonight. They will be delighted to have you for dinner."

John noticed that three jurors on the front row stared at Hal so intently that their eyes seemed to be bulging out. "Tell the jurors what happened next."

Hal looked at the jurors. "I know you will think that it's corny, but I was armed with a cross, a vial of Holy Water, a mallet, a wooden stake, Godfrey's knife, and I still had Godfrey's pistol. When I crashed into the wall in a kitchen dining room area, I reached into my bag and pulled out the first thing my hand wrapped around, which was the cross. I held it in front of me. Vlal laughed, and said through his teeth, 'Oh, that is sooo scary. You think that stick of wood will stop me?'

"He started moving obliquely toward me in slow, measured steps. He was dressed all in black. His face seemed so pale and his eyes seemed so dark and empty. He suddenly took two quick steps towards me and hissed, then took one step back. I was so scared that I almost panicked. He laughed.

"'So much for your faith, little man. You are all alone now. No one will help you. Not even your supposed Savior. It's just a piece of wood."

"I felt I had to change the atmosphere he was creating, so I lurched at him, holding the cross in front of me. Quicker than a cat he stepped back, but for just a moment I saw a startled, even fearful look in his eyes. Then he hit me across the face. He moved so fast I barely saw his fist coming. I hit the ground and slid across the floor. The cross fell from my hand and bounced out of reach. My duffle bag was still in my other hand. I reached in and grabbed the first thing my hand found. It was the vial of Holy Water.

"Before I could move, he was kneeling on my chest. He pulled my face close to his and said, 'I remember you. I took your woman from you. I am surprised that you found me, but you have made the mistake of your life. You will know terror tonight.' He turned and called out, 'My darlings, I have a treat for you. Make him last long enough for our guests to have some entertainment tonight.'

While he was looking away I pulled the vial of Holy Water out of the bag. He looked back at me and I threw the water on him. He screamed and fell backwards. I jumped up and charged him, but he hit me again. I think that he knocked me out, because when I recovered, I was lying face down in the kitchen. There was blood on the floor. I heard a scream

257

across the room. I reached into my bag and took out the mallet and stake. When I looked up, he was against the wall looking down at the dismembered body of a woman. He had blood all over his face. Smoke was filling the room, and I could see flames.

"I knew this would be my only chance, so I sprang off of the floor and rushed him. I had the stake extended out in front of me. I held the mallet behind me like this. The moment the stake struck his chest, I gave it a blow with the mallet with every ounce of strength I could muster. The stake passed all the way through him, and pinned him to the wall. There was a look of surprise, shock, and terror in his eyes. He let out a long wail so loud that it seemed to shake the house. He clawed my chest and grabbed the stake, but I would not let go. Then he went limp. I stumbled away from him and saw the bodies of at least two women on the floor. Neither could have been alive. They had been decapitated. It was awful. I stumbled out of the house and into officer Ayers. I didn't even realize that I was still carrying the mallet. I told him what I had done."

"Did you expect him to believe you?"

"It didn't matter to me. This long quest was over. The monster was dead. My mission was accomplished. My purpose was fulfilled. Whatever happens now, it will have been worth it. I did what I had to do and the world is a better and safer place because of what I did."

"No further questions."

Tellers spent the next day and a half cross-examining Boyd, rehashing his background, his relationship with Sally, his stalking Drumon and the killings. He tested the story over and over, implying that revenge was one of Boyd's motives. Boyd was on the witness stand so long that he had plenty of opportunities to sound or act crazy, but he did not. Tellers made it clear to everyone that if Hal were hallucinating, his only hallucinations had to do with Drumon. He implied that it was odd Boyd could seem as ordinary as the next person on any subject other than Drumon. It was convenient, he said, that Boyd's only crazy thought had to do with Drumon. Boyd responded that he wasn't crazy. He said, over and over, that he was telling the truth that Drumon was a vampire. At last, Tellers ended his cross-examination. The consensus in the gallery was that no one would believe Boyd was insane, and the only remaining logical conclusion was that Boyd was an elaborate liar. The jury mumbled among themselves and looked at Boyd with disgust.

John, Jackson, Karen and Hal conferred in whispered tones at counsel table. "What do you think?" asked Hal.

"I think you did great," said Karen.

"I agree, but the jury isn't buying what we're selling," said Jackson.

258

"Well, I will understand if they don't believe me. I never expected to be believed."

"We gave it our best shot."

"Any word on the boy?"

"None."

"We may have to rest our case if we can't answer the Judge when he asks us for our next witness."

"Who is your next witness, Mr. Brooks?" boomed Judge Richards.

Crush rushed into the courtroom and to the defense table. "The boy is here! He's right outside the door. His story is a doozy!"

54

"Let's bring him in!"

"Your Honor, we have one more witness," said John.

"Who will it be?"

"Jack Robins."

"Objection—he is not on the witness list," said Tellers.

Thornton tapped him on the shoulder and handed him a document. "Excuse me, your Honor, he is on the list. We withdraw that objection."

A redheaded twelve-year-old entered the room and hesitated when he realized that hundreds of eyes were on him. A bailiff guided him through the gate in the bar and to the witness stand. Just as he had done with Patrick, Judge Richards questioned Jack concerning his competence to serve as a witness. The Judge made sure that Jack understood the oath and the importance of telling the truth. He tried to reassure Jack so that the boy would be a little more comfortable. Then he turned to John and said, "You may proceed with your witness."

"Thank you, your Honor. Jack, I want to call your attention to the day the house burned in your neighborhood. Do you remember that?"

"Do I ever! I mean, yes sir, I do."

"Patrick told us about the car wreck in the front yard and the shooting, do you remember all of that?"

"Yeah, it all happened right in front of us. We saw it all. We were hiding in the holly bush and we got all scratched up."

"Did you stay in the holly bush the whole time?"

"No. After the man kicked in the door to the haunted house, I moved to get a better look."

"What man?"

"You know, that man right there, sitting at your table."

"May the record reflect that the witness has identified the Defendant?" asked Tellers.

"The record will so reflect," responded Judge Richards.

"Where did you go, to get a better look?"

"There is a mimosa tree with lots of low branches on the side of the house. We would climb in it sometimes when the house was empty. You could see into the house pretty good from there."

"What part of the house could you see from there?"

"The kitchen."

Every juror perked up. Some scooted to the front of their seats.

Others leaned forward and seemed to study the boy intently. Nearly everyone in the courtroom reacted the same way as the jurors.

"There was this really tall guy, dressed all in black. He was pretty creepy looking. That was Mr. Drumon. Pat saw him in the window just before I ran to the tree. He was beating up the guy that broke into his house. What's his name?"

"This man?"

"Yeah."

"Hal."

"Okay, Hal. Well, when Mr. Drumon had worked Hal over pretty good, Hal quit moving. He was just laying there face down. Then, Mr. Drumon called some women into the room."

"How many?"

"Two."

"What happened?"

"It looked like one of them wanted to bite Mr. Hal, and the second woman pushed the first woman away. They started fighting and it was real bad."

Jack hesitated. His lower lip trembled.

"Do you want to take a minute?" asked John.

Jack nodded his head, took a breath, and said, "I'm okay. It's just that they fought really bad." It was as though a dam broke. Jack started crying. A woman in the audience rushed the bar, shouting, "Leave my boy alone!"

"Order in the court!" Judge Richards called out as he struck his bench with his gavel, further startling the boy.

"I'm sorry son, I didn't mean to startle you. Mrs. Robins, why don't you come up and see your son? Ladies and gentlemen of the jury, we will take a short break. Please step into the jury room."

Mrs. Robins rushed to her son's side and hugged him to her breast. She glowered at John. "I never should have let your people talk to him. He shouldn't have to relive that nightmare."

"I understand," John started.

"No you don't! If you understood, you wouldn't be doing this to him. Judge, Jack has been through enough. May we be excused?"

"We join in Mrs. Robins request and ask that the witness be excused. The Defendant has already confessed to us what happened in that room. The boy's testimony confirms that already. Any further evidence from this child is unnecessary on the sole issue at trial, which is the sanity of the Defendant at the time of the murders."

"Judge, my client is on trial for murder. This is an eyewitness to the event. Basic notions of fair play, of due process, and our right to a fair trial are at stake. I don't want to trouble this young man, but we must have his testimony in order for Hal Boyd to have a fair trial."

"Mrs. Robins, it seems as though your son was in position to see important events at issue in this case," said Judge Richards in as soothing voice as he could muster. "He is an eyewitness. I will certainly give him time to compose himself, but I believe that he should testify."

"You don't mean that he will have to continue with this torture, do you?"

"Mom! I'm okay! I just needed a minute. I want to do this. I need to tell what happened. It is the right thing to do. Let me finish, please!"

Mrs. Robins, looked at her son, wiped a tear from her face and smiled. "You're right, Jack. I'm proud of you. Just tell them the truth." She then whirled around and faced John, "And if you badger him, you will have me to answer to, do you understand me?"

"Yes, ma'am. I would never badger him."

Tellers and Thornton were snickering.

"And that goes for you too!" she said to Tellers and Thornton as she quick-stepped to her seat.

"Well, I suppose there are no further instructions needing to be given to the attorneys," observed Judge Richards. "Ask the jury to return to their seats."

Once the jurors were seated, Judge Richards said to Jack, "You were telling us that the women fought real bad. Do you think that you are able to finish telling us what you saw?"

"Yes, sir. I am ready."

"Okay. Take your time. If you need to take a break, just let me know and we will stop; is that a deal?"

"Yes, sir."

"Mr. Brooks, you may continue."

"Tell us what you saw, Jack."

"Well, two women came in the room. They circled Mr. Hal a couple of times, kind of holding their arms out really funny like. Then the first one stooped down and lifted his head so she could see his face. She started stroking his face and his neck. The other one stopped moving and sort of stared at Mr. Hal. Then the first woman bent down and acted like she was going to bite him, and all kind of craziness broke out."

"What do you mean?"

"The second woman, she was blonde haired, the first one had dark hair. Anyway, the second woman pushed her away from Mr. Hal, and seemed to be trying to protect him. They started fighting over him. They were clawing at each other and pushing and hitting and biting each other. They were tearing each other up pretty bad. They knocked over some black candles and a fire started. The blonde haired lady fell forward into the window."

"Did the window break?

"No, but her face was plastered against the glass for a moment, and her eyes looked straight into mine. She must have seen me, cause I could see her blue eyes. I could even see a little mark shaped like a heart, she had right below her ear on her neck."

Hal stood. Everyone was so focused on Jack that no one noticed Hal standing.

"She turned and went back into the fight. This time, though, she had a knife. I guess she picked it up off of the counter by the window. She stabbed the first woman over and over, until she fell to the ground. Then, she," Jack hesitated again.

"Then what?"

Jack whimpered. "She cut her head off."

Gasps were heard throughout the room.

"Do you need a moment?"

"No. I need to finish."

"What happened next?"

"Mr. Drumon seemed real mad. He started towards Mr. Hal, like he was real angry and the blonde lady, she jumped across the room and sort of stood over Mr. Hal, with the knife in her hand, like she was defending him."

"Sally!" All eyes turned in the direction of the sound of her name, and saw Hal standing at the defense table. Hal's voice rose as he repeated, "Sally, Sally, Sally!"

Shocked looks spread across the faces of the jurors.

"Mr. Brooks, tell your client to have a seat!" said Judge Richards.

"Yes, your Honor." Jackson popped out of his seat and placed his hands on Hal's waist and shoulder and gently directed him back into his seat.

"Please tell us what happened next."

"Well, Mr. Drumon and the woman that Mr. Hal says was Sally, they . . ."

"Objection!" shouted Tellers.

"Overruled. You may continue with your story son."

"Anyway, Mr. Drumon circled Hal, and the girl who might be Sally stood over him and turned so that she was always facing Mr. Drumon. Then, he jumped so fast I could hardly see what happened. He pushed her all the way across the room, and she hit the wall. Then Mr. Drumon, he, oh my, it was awful." Jack paused again, then continued. "He took the knife from her and cut her head right off, and threw her away so fast I could hardly see his hands move."

"Oh, God! No!" cried Hal. He dropped his head to the table and began weeping uncontrollably. Jackson and Karen put their hand on him, trying to see how to comfort him.

"Ladies and Gentlemen of the jury, we will take a ten minute recess. Please step into the jury room." No one moved. "Members of the jury," repeated the Judge. The spell holding the jurors attention seemed to be broken as several jurors looked up at the Judge with a startled look, as though they finally realized that he had been talking and they hadn't been listening.

"Please step into the jury room."

*   *   *

When the jurors left, Judge Richards said, "We will be in recess for ten minutes." As soon as he left the room, all of the reporters made a mad dash to the door. Sandy and Bret recorded a breaking news item, "Incredible story unfolds in the Vampire Defense. A twelve-year-old eyewitness to the killings described a macabre scene . . ."

*   *   *

After the recess, John continued questioning Jack. "You were telling us that Mr. Drumon threw the blonde-haired lady away after he hurt her."

"Yes, sir. He hurt her bad. I didn't know that bare hands could do that. Anyway, Mr. Drumon was still looking in the direction that he threw her when all of a sudden Mr. Hal rushed across the room and nailed him to the wall with a big hammer and a big stick. Drumon screamed like you wouldn't believe and scratched and clawed at Mr. Hal, but Mr. Hal didn't let him go and didn't stop nailing him to the wall. Up until then, I had been so scared that I couldn't move. But that was it for me. I jumped out of the tree, ran home and hid under my bed."

"Thank you, Jack. You are very brave. No further questions, your Honor."

Tellers stood at his table and looked first at Jack, then at his notes. He glanced at Thornton, who shrugged. He looked around the courtroom for a moment and saw all of the expectant faces, waiting for his next move.

"No questions," he said as he sat down.

55

"How long do you think the jury will be out?" asked Sandy, microphone in hand.

"It's hard to say," said John. "It took the judge an hour just to read the instructions of law to the jury. I think it will take several hours."

"As Yogi Berra said," interjected Jackson, "predictions are notoriously unreliable, especially if they involve the future."

"Is your client relieved that the charges concerning the death of the two women in the house were dismissed by the Judge?"

"Indeed—indeed he is very grateful," said John.

"The judge gave several possible forms of the verdict to the jury. Could you explain the forms of the verdict for our viewers if they find him guilty and if they find him not guilty?"

"Well, they could find Hal guilty of either murder or of manslaughter of Godfrey Plova. They could also separately find Hal guilty of murder or of capital murder of Vlal Drumon."

"What happens if they return a verdict of capital murder?'

"Then, the case will re-convene on the issue of whether Hal will get the death penalty or life without parole. Both sides will be allowed to put on evidence in that phase of the trial."

"What is the form of verdict if they find for the Defendant?"

"Our defense was insanity. If the jury finds that Hal was insane at the time of the crime, then they should return a verdict of not guilty by reason of insanity. That single verdict could cover all of the alleged crimes."

"Care to speculate as to the outcome?"

"We have always maintained that Hal Boyd was not guilty by reason of insanity."

There was a stir of excitement in the courtroom and the bailiff asked Sandy to postpone the rest of the interview.

"Certainly. What's up?"

"The jury is ready to return a verdict."

"Already! It's only been twenty-five minutes."

"Nevertheless, they are ready."

Judge Richards entered the courtroom.

"All rise!" announced the bailiff.

As the judge took his seat, he said to the assembly, "When the verdict is read, I want there to be no outburst of any kind. No expressions of

265

surprise, delight, disappointment, or any other emotions will be allowed. This jury has been through enough. We will have order in the courtroom during this process. After the verdict is read, I want everyone to remain seated until the jury is excused. They will be escorted from the courthouse before anyone can leave this room. If you cannot abide by that instruction, then I invite you to leave the courtroom now."

No one moved.

"Very well. Bring in the jury."

The jurors filed into the room. No discernable expression could be read on anyone's face. They took their seats without saying a word and without cracking a smile or a frown.

"Have you reached a verdict?" asked the judge.

"We have," said a gentleman on the front row.

"Please hand your verdict to the clerk."

The clerk handed the verdict to the Judge. He read it, and paused. He sighed, and scratched his chin. "Ladies and gentlemen, the verdict is not in the proper form. I need for you to review the instructions and select the form that describes your verdict. When you all agree on the verdict, then notify the bailiff that you are ready."

The foreman said, "Your Honor, if I may. We examined the forms of the verdict that you provided. None of those forms described our decision; therefore, we prepared the form that you have in your hand. It is our unanimous decision."

"I see." Judge Richards read the verdict again and stared at the page for almost a minute. The delay seemed like an eternity. He looked at the ceiling for a moment and then turned back to the jury. "Very well. I believe I will accept the form you have chosen. Madam Clerk, please read the verdict. Mr. Boyd, please rise and hear the verdict of the jury."

Hal and his defense team stood.

The clerk took the verdict from the judge and turned to face the Defendant. She glanced at the verdict and then at Hal. She looked at the Judge, who nodded at her. At last, she read: "We the jury find the Defendant not guilty of all charges."

Hal was so relieved his knees buckled slightly, but he quickly recovered. Karen and Jackson patted him on his back. Hal wiped tears from his face. Tellers and Thornton looked down and shook their heads. John had a puzzled look on his face. Then Tellers halfway raised his hand, and said, "Your Honor, I don't believe that the entire verdict was read. If they find for Boyd, they should find him not guilty by reason of insanity."

"That was their verdict: Not Guilty. Do you want me to poll the jury?"

266

"No, your Honor, this is an improper and impossible verdict. We object!"

"I will poll the jury."

The Judge asked each juror in turn, "Is this your verdict?" every juror nodded yes.

"Very well. Mr. Boyd, the jury has found you not guilty. You are free to go. Mr. Bailiff, please arrange to get Mr. Boyd's items from the jail and have them delivered to him promptly."

"Yes, your Honor."

"Judge, this verdict is impossible! He confessed to murder. He can't be released! Now anyone accused of murder will make up a story about vampires!"

"Mr. Boyd has been tried by a jury of his peers and has been found not guilty. This case is adjourned."

56

Jackson escorted Hal through the courthouse to the lobby of the jail where Hal was presented with his few possessions. Karen made her way back to the office to make arrangements for a celebration. John spent the next two hours answering questions from the media. At last, he made his way back to the office, where Jackson, Karen, Hal and the entire defense team awaited. Jennifer popped the first bottle of Champagne, and the celebration began.

"How does it feel to be a free man?" asked Skip.

"It is indescribable. I never expected to walk out of the courtroom a free man. I have all of you to thank. I don't know where to begin. I owe all of you, especially Karen, Jackson and John, for believing in me. Today I learned that I owe everything to Sally." Tears streamed down Hal's face. "But for this trial, I would never have known what she did for me. Now I know why she left me. I know why he didn't kill me that night at his house. She made some sort of bargain with him and made him promise not to harm me. I would rather have died than have her make that bargain."

"She felt the same way, Hal," said Karen. "She would rather die than have something terrible happen to you. She sacrificed herself for you."

Hal's knees felt weak. He found a seat and wiped the tears from his face. "You're right. I know you are; but, still, I should have been the one to die, not her."

Skip said, "I don't get it. If she died three years ago in Seattle, how could she be in Drumon's house the night you killed Drumon?"

"Exactly," said Jackson.

Karen and Sandy rolled their eyes at Jackson and hugged Hal. Sandy said, "She truly loved you. She never stopped loving you. Her love kept you alive."

"We could have fought him together."

"The two of you did fight him together. But it took you three years to get ready to fight him. If you had fought him too soon, he would have won."

"You are all talking crazy," said Jackson. "You are talking as though you really believe that a woman who had been dead for three years was fighting Vlal that night."

Karen, Sandy and Hal stared at Jackson with perplexed looks on their faces.

268

"It's okay," said John as he affectionately slapped Jackson on the shoulder. "Let Jackson have his reasonable, rational, logical fantasy. He is still not ready to believe in the reality of another world."

"Am I the only sane person in the room?" asked Jackson.

"Yes, and I love ya' brother," laughed John.

At that moment, a disheveled looking Indian, wearing patched pants appeared at the door. "I've got to see John Brooks as soon as I can. I was told I could see him when the trial was over."

"Oh, Mr. Dalton, we are in the middle of a celebration right now. We just won a big case," said Karen.

"But, I have to see him now!"

"John, this is Mr. Dalton," said Karen as she walked toward John and rose on her toes to whisper in his ear. "He came to see you last week, something about a foreclosure. He's a little crazy. He had a story about a buried treasure on his property."

John smiled and said, "Okay, this probably won't take long." He turned to the man and said, "Mr. Dalton, why don't you step into my office for a minute. Jackson, keep the party going, and I will be right back. Do you want to join us, Karen?"

"No, I've got to run down to my car. I baked some brownies last night because I felt like we would need them today. I'll be right back."

John led the elderly man into his office. He observed that Mr. Dalton was a bronze-skinned man, perhaps seventy years old. He looked tired and worried. His bright green eyes darted about the room, evidencing his agitation. Dalton grabbed John by the arm and looked into his face. "They are going to foreclose on my family farm next week. You've got to stop them. They are after the treasure."

"Slow down just a minute, Mr. Dalton. Take a seat and tell me where your farm is, what treasure and who is after it."

Without taking a seat, the old man said, "I'm Frank Dalton. My great-great-granddaddy was Frank James. He buried a treasure on my great-great-grandmaw's family farm way back in either 1865 or 1867. We've been looking for it ever since he left. Now, the white side of the family, from Texas, has somehow bought our mortgage. They are foreclosing next week unless you stop them."

"Wait a minute. Frank James in Mississippi?"

"Yeah, the James gang robbed a bank in Carthage and in Silver City. Frank was shot and hid out on my family farm at Neshoba County, where my great-great-grandmaw, Sankky, nursed him back to health. He had been there a couple of years before, too."

"What makes you think there is a treasure there?"

"We always knew he buried his treasure there. Some say that the first

269

time he came to the farm, he was carrying Mexican gold to be delivered to the Confederates. The war ended before he could deliver it and he hid it somewhere. I know for sure he was there the second time. That's when he was hurt. I think he might have been coming back for the Mexican gold and robbed a couple of banks on the way. After Sankky nursed him back to health, the posse nearly caught him. So, he left and said he was coming back for his gold and for Sankky. He never did. Sankky wouldn't let nobody look for the treasure while she was alive. Ever since she died, our family has been looking. Now, we are about to lose everything. And we're going to lose it to those Daltons in Texas. They already got everything else. Now, they want to take what little we got."

"Frank. Let me tell you the truth about how I feel. The treasure story seems like an old rumor, a legend. The gold probably doesn't exist. Nevertheless, I will do my best to help you keep your farm. I can't make any guarantees. As soon as Karen gets back, we will get the details. We need the mortgage information, payment history, the date and place of the sale and so forth."

"God bless you. Thank you. You don't know what this means to me and my family. Don't worry about your fee. We will pay you out of the treasure." He pulled from his pocket a small black velvet bag sealed with a draw string.

John couldn't prevent a chuckle from escaping his lips. His chuckle was cut short when Frank shook the bag over John's hand and a gold coin fell into his palm. "EMPERADOR MAXIMILIANO," read John out loud. He turned the coin over and read, "1865. Interesting. Where did this come from?"

At that moment the door to John's office burst open. Crush Barnes, breathless and almost in tears, shouted, "John! Come quick! I'm so sorry. I should have been with her! They got her! I don't know how she got out of my sight! I'm so sorry!"

"Who, what?" said John as he handed the coin back to Frank.

"Karen! They kidnapped her again!"

Without a moment of hesitation, John sprinted out the door and down the hall, hollering, "Jackson! Call the police! Crush! Show me where you last saw her! Everybody outside! Find her!"

57

Karen's car was parked behind the building. She hurried to get the brownies because she wanted to return to the party as soon as possible. Karen was brimming with pride for the work the team had done. She could not remember a time in her life when she felt more satisfied. She had helped John and Jackson win the biggest case ever. She said to herself, "I will have to share him with the world now." She laughed with joy as she opened the car door. A familiar creepy feeling swept over her and she spun around.

"You!" she said as she stared into Gayle's eyes.

*   *   *

"Shocking news update! A kidnap occurred just moments ago. While the Vampire Defense team was celebrating its historic victory in the Hal Boyd case, Karen Wilkes, the defense team paralegal, was kidnapped in broad daylight outside the offices of Brooks and Bradley. This is the second time that she has been kidnapped since the Vampire Defense began. She was also in a restaurant that was fire bombed in April of this year, again while the defense team was celebrating court victories in the Vampire Defense case. Authorities have the area cordoned off. I am about to question her employer, Mr. John Brooks. You may recall that Mr. Brooks actually captured one of the previous kidnappers. Even though the police were quick to arrive on the scene, he has been visibly frustrated by the time the investigation has taken. He has been urging the authorities to act quickly before the kidnappers get too far away."

Sandy turned to question John, but no one was there. "Mr. Brooks, what . . . Where is John?"

"He just left," someone shouted. "There he goes!"

John's Trooper raced by and was captured for a moment by the camera. The camera caught Sandy running down the street behind the Trooper, shouting, "Wait for me! Don't you leave me, John!"

Sandy turned and noticed that all of the rugby players except Crush had disappeared. Crush was walking away from an interview with a policeman. She ran in front of him and put her hand on his chest. "Where did they go?"

"I don't know what you mean ma'am."

"Don't you lie to me! Where are they?"

"John told us to go get every boat we could find and meet him at Bobby's Trading Post."

"Why?"

"Because they took her to Cypress Swamp the first time and said something about taking her somewhere by boat. He thought the police were moving too slow, so he said we had to start looking."

"Take me with you."

"Ma'am, I'm in enough trouble already."

"You won't believe how much trouble you will be in if you don't take me."

Crush hesitated only a moment before saying, "We've got to hurry."

"Well, what are you waiting for?" Sandy asked as she motioned for Bret to join them.

*   *   *

Two hours later Crush had his uncle's fishing boat in the water at Bobby's Trading Post. Two other boats were tied up next to it. Five rugby players, Sandy and Bret stood by with John and Hal.

"Everybody listen up," called John as he gathered everyone around him. "We already have four boats working the river upstream. The first boats were in the water an hour ago. We have a couple of jet skis working the area around here. The rest of us are going to search the area from Highway 43 south, into the main lake."

"Why did you start the search upstream?" asked Sandy.

"The first time Karen was kidnapped, she was taken to Cypress Swamp, which is upstream from here. They talked about putting her in a boat. The ruggers found a wooden staircase that descends into the river near Cypress Swamp. The kidnappers may have planned to use that to put her in a boat, but she escaped before they could do it."

"Why are we doing this instead of the police?"

"The police are searching for her their way. I am following a hunch. They don't want to waste time on a hunch. We can't waste time on police procedure. So, enough talk, let's get to work."

John directed one boat to search the western shore of the lake along the Natchez Trace, one boat to search the eastern shore, and said his boat would check the islands.

"The sun has already gone down. We still have some light but, it will be dark soon. Keep searching until we find her. When you have finished your area, join any other search still in progress. Any questions?"

No one had any questions, and boats began leaving.

John was climbing aboard the remaining boat with Hal, Jackson, Skip, Sandy and Bret when they heard a car racing up to the boat ramp. It skidded to a stop. The door swung open and Father Michael jumped

272

out.

"I know where they have taken her!"

Father Michael jumped in the boat and commanded Jackson to head south on the lake as fast as he could. Ignoring the "leave no wake" signs, they raced west along Highway 43 until they came to the bridge where they turned south. Night was coming fast. The sun had set to their right and a full golden moon hung above the tree line to the left.

"Where are we headed?"

"There is an island on the lake that legend says is haunted. They will be taking her there for a detestable ritual."

John and Jackson looked at each other knowingly.

"Coincidence?" asked Jackson.

"Remember the animal bones and charred remains?" asked John. "Who are they, and what is their ritual?"

"You have a den of devil worshippers here in your community. They call themselves the Kroth. They are planning the ritual sacrifice of an innocent woman at a black mass in hopes of creating a replacement for Vlal Drumon. "

John's mouth hung open, aghast. Words would not form in his mind.

"John, the ritual requires a terrified female victim and cannibalism."

"Oh God!" exclaimed Jackson.

"Why Karen?" asked Skip.

Hal answered. "They want someone who exhibits loyalty and true love. Traits the enemy hates, yet envies."

"They realize that Karen is the perfect victim," said Sandy.

"What do you mean?" asked John. "Why Karen? I get the loyalty, but the true love? She is not even seeing anyone."

Sandy shook her head, "You are so blind."

"They believe the person who eats of her flesh and drinks of her blood gains great power because of her traits of love and loyalty," said Father Michael. "It is a warped, twisted version of a true mass, where the congregation shares in the body and blood of Christ. Everything God does, the enemy mimics in a corrupted way."

"Jackson, hurry to Goren Island," urged John.

"You know the island?" asked Father Michael excitedly.

"Yes. It is supposedly haunted. Two lovers were killed in a fire at a brewery there two hundred years ago."

"Yes, I know the legend. It is part of my job to learn such things wherever I go. Most are nonsense. Some are not."

After a moment, Father Michael told Jackson to slow down. "We must not let them realize that we are on to them. If they know we are coming, they may kill her. As long as they think that they are unobserved, they will proceed with the ritual, which won't be completed until well after dark."

"How can we be sure that they will be on Goren Island?" asked Skip.

"You have to understand the way they think. They believe that all of the psychic and spiritual energy associated with the tragedy on the island will create a portal between our world and the spiritual world where an interchange is more likely to take place. They want a beautiful redheaded woman because they think she is likely to attract the attention of the ghost, who is looking for a beautiful redheaded woman. The spell claims that great power can be gained if the ritual is performed in the presence of a spirit, a ghost."

"This is crazy!" said Jackson.

"True, but it is happening nonetheless. I am not saying that the spell is true, my friend. I am simply saying that Karen's kidnappers believe that it is true. We must use their belief against them. Their belief is helping us find them and gives us the time to save her."

"What kind of interchange are you talking about?" asked Skip again.

"They think that a demon will physically enter the body of the person who performs the ritual and will give that person enormous power— power that must be fueled by the blood of human victims," answered Michael.

"Another vampire," said Hal.

"That's right. They are trying to create another vampire," agreed Michael.

"We need weapons," said Hal. "What do we have?"

"A couple of wooden paddles," John responded.

"Oh, God, help us!" exclaimed Jackson.

58

An hour later four boats with rugby players, including John, Jackson, Father Michael, Hal, Skip, Sandy and Bret gathered behind a swampy island just north of Goren Island. More vessels stood off to the south and west of Goren Island, waiting for a signal to approach. Mitch leaned over and whispered to John, "There are at least four boats concealed in a cove on the south side of the island. Something is definitely going on. There are at least two sentries posted on the island. Your job will be to take out the sentries and signal the other boats to come ashore. The full moon may allow the sentries to see your approach."

"Clouds are moving in, and it's getting a little windy," said John. "Maybe that will provide cover for us. How much time do we have?"

Michael answered, "The ritual takes about four hours, three after the moon rises. I think we have about an hour left. If we hear a steady drum beat, the end is about ten minutes away. In the last two minutes chanting will begin and the drum will beat faster and faster, reaching a crescendo, ending with a bloody . . ."

"Never mind," said Jackson. "Let's get this over with before the drum beats. Is everybody ready?"

"Everyone is in place," said Sandy. "Hal and Michael have created a couple of stakes from one of the paddles, and John made a club out of the other. What will you use, Jackson?"

Jackson held up his flashlight.

"What about you, Crush?"

Crush held up his fists.

"Guys, let's say a quick prayer," said John. Every head bowed. "Lord, we are going into battle. We ask that you go ahead of us and fight the battle for us. We ask for your protection over every one of our people and especially Karen. Please give us courage and strength. Help us save Karen. And God, please give Karen the courage she will need. In Jesus' name we pray."

Everyone said, "Amen."

Crush, Skip, Jackson, Father Michael, Hal and John gathered into one of the boats. John, Michael, Crush and Hal were to subdue the lookouts. Skip was to pilot the boat. Jackson was to signal the other boats to rush the island when the sentries were taken out. Towels, blankets and life jackets were packed around the motor to muffle the sound as much as possible. Still, a puttering sound emitted from the motor.

Silver moonlight reflected off the dark water as the boat eased slowly around the west side of the swampy island, taking advantage of the moon shadow. Wavelets sparkled in the moonlight as a freshening wind rose from the south. They could see the slight glow of a fire somewhere in the middle of Goren Island. Already, they could hear a monotonous drone of a single voice that seemed to be chanting some incantation.

"The hair is standing up on the back of my neck," whispered Skip.

"Mine too," whispered Jackson.

"There's one of the lookouts," whispered Crush, pointing at a spot on the dark island. At that moment, a cloud covered the moon and the whole world seemed to be cloaked in utter darkness. Skip maintained course, trusting his instincts. Soon their eyes adjusted and, except for the glow at its center, the island seemed to be blacker than the rest of the world.

The wind freshened and dampness was in the air.

"Rain is coming," whispered Jackson.

They were fifty yards from the island when Skip whispered, "The water is blacker than a witch's heart." Indeed, the water seemed blacker than anything John had ever seen. A flash of lightning illuminated the shore for a moment and everyone could see that the boat was headed towards a bank about two feet high.

*　*　*

Karen awoke to a flash of lightning. She was on her back, dressed in an elaborate red satin gown adorned with depictions of dragons and demons. The gown barely covered her breasts and exposed most of her bare legs. She was tied to an elevated platform so that she could not move. A man in a dark, hooded robe stood over her. His robe was similarly adorned. He wore a horned headdress over his hood. A thunderhead dominated the visible sky. A large fire burned in the center of the clearing where she lay. Hooded figures seemed to be everywhere.

"Welcome to our feast. We are so glad you could join us!"

The voice was familiar, but she could not see the face.

"I know that voice. Who are you?"

"It is a pity that we will know one another for such a short time. I would enjoy having you as my first wife upon my ascension to immortality."

"Doctor Bishop!"

"Right you are, my dear."

"Why?"

"Ah, the ultimate question. Tonight, your name is Penny. Remember your name and this whole affair will end much better for you."

276

"Penny? How exactly will it end better for me?"

"Much less pain my dear."

At a signal from Bishop, a drumbeat began. He opened a pouch and began spreading a foul smelling powder in a circle around the raised platform where Karen lay. With each movement of his hand he uttered, "Here lays Penny, betrothed of Goren, queen of the fire, possessor of his heart." Then he began uttering unspeakable sounds and unrepeatable phrases. The fire in the center of the clearing brightened and grew. Karen realized that an evil ritual was underway and terror began building in her heart.

*　　*　　*

At last they reached the island. The wind increased to fifteen knots and waves were two feet high, with froth on each crest. Everyone except Skip jumped ashore. The shore party divided into two groups and belly crawled toward the corners of the island where lookouts were last seen. John took the lead in one group, with Jackson and Hal following. Father Michael and Crush crawled toward the other sentry. The tall grass parted with a rustle as John moved towards the sentry, his only weapon the wooden club he fashioned from the paddle.

As they crawled, a steady drumbeat started. John looked back at Jackson and saw the worry on his face even in the faint light. They quickened their pace and startled a gaggle of geese sleeping in the weeds. As the geese honked, John paused for a moment. He saw the sentry walking towards them.

Maybe this is a good thing, John thought. *The sooner I get him, the sooner I can get to Karen. Keep coming.* The geese honked and hissed at the lookout. He laughed at them and turned back. John rushed him from behind, striking him on the back of the head with the club. The club broke. The sentry collapsed at John's feet.

"In thirty seconds, make the signal," John said to Jackson.

"What about the other sentry?"

"We have to trust that Father Michael and Crush have taken care of him."

John and Hal moved quickly toward the center of the island. A few seconds later, Jackson began flashing the signal.

*　　*　　*

"My disciples, you are truly blessed. Tonight you will see the evolution of man into a greater being. When blood is spilled upon this altar, you will witness the creation of a god!"

The frenzied chanting and the drumbeat reached a dramatic climax as the wicked priest brought his hands together over his head with the knife pointed at Karen's chest. Bishop waited for a look of terror to fill Karen's eyes. He waited for the scream he was certain would come. He wanted all of the emotional energy Karen could muster. As soon as she screamed he would complete the ceremony.

Terror rose from the pit of Karen's stomach. Panic began to overcome her. Then, a peace that surpassed understanding soothed her. "God, I know I belong to you," she said to herself. "If this is my time to meet you, I am ready."

Bishop watched Karen's mouth open wide as she sucked air into her lungs. He grinned in anticipation of her scream.

"I am Karen," she yelled. "I am not Penny!"

*   *   *

John and Hal halted at the edge of a clearing taking in the scene as the drum beat faster and faster. A fire burned in the center of the clearing. Bamboo screens with strange symbols surrounded the fire. At least twenty people cloaked in dark hooded robes stood in the clearing, chanting, with their arms raised and pointed towards the fire. A man sat at a large drum, striking it harder and harder at an ever-faster pace. Yellow lightning danced inside a thunderhead, followed seconds later by peals of thunder. The wind increased as the chant grew more intense.

John realized Karen was tied to a crude alter. A man in a horned headdress stood over her with both of his hands stretched towards the sky. Firelight glinted off a long curved knife clutched in his hands. Karen shouted out her name, and John rushed into the clearing, with Hal a step behind.

At that same moment, Father Michael and Crush rushed into the clearing from the other side. Bishop stepped away from the altar and yelled, "Seize them!"

Gregory, who was already on the move, made a diving tackle of Hal. Acolytes ran into the fray from every direction. Crush swung haymakers, knocking one acolyte after another to the ground. John ran straight to Karen, covered her body with his and began untying her.

Father Michael rushed directly at Doctor Bishop, the stake in his right hand, ready to strike. Bishop sidestepped Michael and slashed him across his chest with the long curved knife. Michael fell at Bishop's feet; his blood spattered onto the altar. The stake bounced and slid away.

"You fool, did you think you could stop me! The process has already begun!" Bishop threw his head back and called out into the sky, "I am invincible!"

278

59

Bret and Sandy were on the first boat to reach the island after Jackson's signal. Bret leaped out of the boat and ran with his camera on his shoulder to the island center, filming the drama. Boats were running aground all over the island. Ruggers were yelling at the top of their lungs and rushing headlong toward the center of the island, joining in the fight against the Kroth.

Devil worshipers were stunned by the sudden attack from all directions. Their brief resistance quickly turned into flight as the disciples of the Kroth scattered, only to run headlong into rushing ruggers coming from everywhere. Ruggers took them to the ground hard and cries of "Don't hurt me!" and "I surrender!" and "I give!" were mixed with the manly bellows, shouts and roars of victory all over the little island.

Oblivious to the disintegration of his congregation, Bishop stabbed Michael a second time, then turned towards Karen and John. His face was so distorted that he no longer looked human. His eyes seemed to be coals of fire. John stood to face Bishop, while Sandy rushed to Karen to finish untying her. Bishop struck John with such force that he was lifted off of the ground and hurled away. John rolled onto his feet and sprinted back to defend Karen.

"Goren, come see your unfaithful bride," cried out Bishop. "Penny is here. Come join me and bring your search to an end!"

A great gust of wind whipped the trees. Flames danced high above the screens. The screens burst into flame. Cinders swirled and seemed to come together in the form of a human, twisting above the flames. The strength of the wind redoubled. Trees groaned as they twisted in the wind and seemed to emit the sound of a human voice, shouting, "PENNY!"

"Penny waits for you in heaven!" yelled Karen.

Thunder peeled and the cloud burst. Blinding rain fell in wind-whipped torrents. A whirlwind swept up the burning screens and embers into a tornado of fire that swept over Bishop, igniting his robe. The Doctor screamed in agony as flames engulfed him.

John grabbed Karen and Sandy's hands and pulled them away from the altar.

"Run!" yelled John.

They turned to run away, but one disciple of the Kroth stood in the way, knife in hand.

"Not you again," said Karen to Gayle as she balled her fist and smacked Gayle in the nose. Gayle fell on her butt, splashing in a rain puddle.

Gayle cupped her nose and cried, "Why do you always have to hit me in the nose?"

Karen and Sandy ran past her.

As John faced Bishop again he remembered Bishop's last words in the courtroom, "You will pay . . ."

*   *   *

Hal and Gregory were engaged in deadly combat. At first they tumbled on the ground; then Gregory drew a knife. Hal carried only the eighteen-inch long wooden stake he had fashioned out of a paddle.

"What are you going to do with that little stick, you fool?"

Hal parried the first three knife thrusts, but Gregory slashed Hal's arm with the next attack. Screaming ruggers rushed into the clearing tackling acolytes. Gregory quickly assessed the situation, smiled at Hal, and said, "Perhaps we can finish this some other time." Gregory sprinted into the night and disappeared. Hal spun back towards the altar in time to see flames sweep over Doctor Bishop.

*   *   *

After signaling the ruggers to raid the island, Jackson moved along the shore toward the boat where Skip waited in case he needed to help load Karen and his friends. A figure sprinted out of the darkness straight to the boat. In the flickering firelight, Jackson recognized the profile of Gregory.

Skip, alone in the boat, waited impatiently for everyone to return.

What if these devil worshipers are armed? What if they capture John and Jackson? What if they need me? I can't just sit here and wait, thought Skip as he listened to the sound of battle on the island. Then he heard the sound of someone rushing through the high grass toward him. He looked around the boat for something to use as a weapon, just in case. The only thing he saw was the anchor.

Gregory reached the boat, pushed it away from shore, leaped aboard and shoved Skip aside. Jackson bounded onto the boat behind him and struck him across the back of his head with the flashlight. The flashlight shattered. Gregory spun and flattened Jackson with a vicious blow. Skip swung the anchor with all his might and struck Gregory on the temple.

280

Gregory fell in a heap.

"Way to go, Skip. Let's tie him up with the anchor line, quick, before he wakes up."

*　*　*

"Come back!" yelled Bishop as he ran after Karen, flames swirling behind him. A powerful roar as loud as a jungle cat rose from Bishop's throat as he pursued her. John raced to intercept Bishop and dove into his legs, making a clean tackle. Bishop tumbled to the ground and rolled onto his back. Before the doctor could rise, Hal jumped on top of his flaming body and drove the stake into his chest.

"In the Almighty Name of Jesus Christ I command you to return forever to the pit from which you came!" shouted Hal as he pounded on the stake, oblivious to the pain of the fire that scorched him.

"No! It can't be! I was promised immortality! Noooo!"

*　*　*

The storm stopped as suddenly as it started. The clouds broke and moonlight bathed the island. Professor Bishop's smoldering lifeless body lay at Hal's feet. As the fire at the center of the clearing flickered and died, embers swirled above the ashes rising high and finally disappearing into the night sky.

Karen ran to John and wrapped her arms around him. "Is it over?"

John stroked her wet hair and held her close. "Yes, baby, it's finally over. I was so afraid for you. I thought I had lost you."

Karen wept in his arms.

"Are you getting this?" asked Sandy.

"Are you kidding?"

"Did you get it?" she demanded with urgency.

"Every bit of it."

*　*　*

Dawn came with an explosion of color reflected from the retreating storm clouds. Lawmen covered the island, interviewing rugby players and handcuffing devil worshipers. News crews were on the island, in boats surrounding the island and in helicopters circling overhead. Someone had given Karen a coat, but she was still barefoot. She would not leave John's side.

Jackson showed Rico the charred bones they had found on the island earlier.

"I'm not sure that all of those are animal bones, Jackson."

Paramedics loaded Father Michael onto a stretcher while Hal, hands

281

wrapped in bandages, stood by his side.

John motioned for Jackson to join them and they walked over to Michael.

"How many people were hurt?" asked Jackson of the paramedics.

"Amazingly, only three casualties. Father Michael, but he will be alright. Doctor Bishop, who will not be all right, and a female devil worshiper who suffered a broken nose."

Sandy overheard the comment and called to Karen, "Way to go, girl!"

"Well, Jackson, it looks like your prayer was answered," said Father Michael.

"What are you talking about?"

"You know, when you said, 'God help us.' Clearly, he did."

Jackson smiled and shrugged.

"I have found my replacement, Lawyer Brooks," said Father Michael as he nodded towards Hal. "It's time for me to retire."

"We'll see. He is trying to convince me to travel to a certain monastery for more training."

"What about you, Michael?" John asked.

"I'll be needing a good Vampire Defense lawyer. Do you know any that might be available?"

"Father Michael, it will be my honor to represent you."

"You are so famous now, I fear I can't afford you."

"After what you have done for us, your tab is paid in full for life."

"I have so many charges against me in so many places that you will be a pauper," laughed Michael as the paramedics carried him away.

Skip sauntered up to Crush, looked up and said, "Did you hear that I bagged one of those devil worshipers?"

"Yeah, big guy, I heard—way to go!" said Crush as he looked down at Skip.

Skip beamed with pride as two deputies escorted Gregory past them. Even though he was chained and held by two large officers, Gregory muscled his way to Skip's side.

"I won't be in jail forever. When I get out, I'm coming for you first."

Skip's eyes bugged out as big as saucers as he involuntarily flinched and ducked behind Crush. He felt a big comforting hand on his shoulder and his bravado returned.

"Yeah, well, come on if you are man enough, you hear" said Skip from the safety of Crush's shadow. "And I'll do it again. Yes, I will."

"Easy now, big boy," said Crush as he patted his little friend on the shoulder with his big paw.

Gregory chuckled as they led him away.

Sandy finished her last update and sauntered up to John. "Well, you did it. You wanted a big case, and I don't think there has ever been a bigger case with more coverage than this one."

"I was blessed with great friends who, with the help of God, saved the day."

"I think you and I would have made quite a pair."

"What do you mean?"

"I mean it's time for you to move on to the next case and for me to move on to the next story. This story is a wrap."

"So, that's it?"

"Yep." Sandy slipped her hand behind John's head and pulled his lips down to meet hers. She held him for a moment in a deep passionate kiss. Karen looked on, frowning.

Sandy released him and said, "Goodbye, John. I'll be watching your career."

"I'll be watching yours," said John, as he touched his hand to his lips.

Sandy and Bret boarded a boat and headed back to the Trading Post.

"So, you chased him all this time and you're leaving him just like that? Why?"

"I can't handle the competition."

After watching Bret and Sandy leave, Karen took John's hand and led him to a waiting boat. "Come on John. Our clients need us, and we have a farm to save."

"Oh, yeah, you're right, and maybe Maximilian's Treasure to find."

"What . . .?"

20003150R00166

Made in the USA
Charleston, SC
22 June 2013